NEXUS
+ OTHER STORIES

GREAT FICTION FROM THE DARK IMPERIUM

NEXUS
+ OTHER STORIES

GREAT FICTION FROM THE DARK IMPERIUM

Thomas Parrott · Chris Wraight · Guy Haley
Rachel Harrison · Peter McLean · Dan Abnett
Danie Ware · Mike Brooks · Phil Kelly · J C Stearns
Josh Reynolds · Robert Rath · Steve Parker · Marc Collins

BLACK LIBRARY

A BLACK LIBRARY PUBLICATION

'Kraken' first published in 2012.
'Redeemer' first published in 2019.
'The Test of Faith' first published in 2019.
'The Darkling Hours' first published in 2018.
'Lightning Run' first published in 2018.
'Missing in Action' first published in 2011.
'The Crystal Cathedral' first published in 2019.
'To Speak as One' first published in 2019.
'Where Dere's Da Warp Dere's a Way' first published in 2020.
'Redemption on Dal'yth' first published in 2020.
'Void Crossed' first published in 2019.
'Light of a Crystal Sun' first published in 2018.
'War in the Museum' first published in 2020.
'Headhunted' first published in 2009.
This edition published in Great Britain in 2020 by
Black Library,
Games Workshop Ltd.,
Willow Road,
Nottingham, NG7 2WS, UK.
10 9 8 7 6 5 4 3 2 1

Produced by Games Workshop in Nottingham.
Cover illustration by Amir Zand.

A CIP record for this book is available from the British Library.

ISBN 13: 978 1 80026 033 7

See Black Library on the internet at

blacklibrary.com

Find out more about Games Workshop
and the world of Warhammer 40,000 at

games-workshop.com

Printed and bound by CPI Group (UK) Ltd, Croydon, CR0 4YY

Dear Reader,

Thank you for buying this book.

Welcome to the grimdark future of Warhammer 40,000. Before you lies a galaxy in flames. The Imperium of Man teeters on the very brink of destruction, beset on all sides by the heretic, the alien and the witch. As planet after planet falls to their vile predations, the defenders of mankind clash with these despoilers upon countless bloody battlefields, where the only respite is death.

Herein you will find a host of great stories that explore this distant, horrifying future. Witness as heroes fall, legends are made, and the fate of the galaxy is decided. These tales will guide your way to further adventures, recommending your next reads from the thrilling and extensive Black Library range.

Remember – there is no rest, no mercy. Prepare yourself for battle.

CONTENTS

NEXUS

THOMAS PARROTT

The Emperor's Finest, the **Adeptus Astartes**,
the Angels of Death.
Throughout the galaxy, these genetically engineered
super-soldiers are known by many names, but all
spell annihilation for the enemies of mankind. Of all
the Space Marine Chapters, the **Ultramarines** are the
exemplar – noble, honourable and utterly devoted to
the purge of the alien, the witch and the heretic.
In *Nexus*, Brother-Sergeant Allectius fights a brutal
war of attrition against a seemingly endless xenos
foe. But when a mysterious pall falls over him and
the people he protects, Allectius must take his fight
beyond the walls… for more than just victory, now
mere survival is at stake.

PROLOGUE

The ruins of a space station hung in the void. Before the battle, it had not been much to look at: a haphazard construction assembled by rogues. Now it was little more than a dead husk of metal. Its power-producing generatoria had been destroyed. Its bridge was assailed and scoured. The crew had been put to the sword. The vessels that had berthed here were just as broken. Some had tried to flee, but there was no escaping the judgment that had fallen upon them. The transhuman warriors known as the Space Marines were very thorough in their work.

A ship drifted amongst the debris, its thick fore armour blackened from shell impacts but its hull intact. It was nearly three miles long, a formidable war vessel bristling with mighty macrocannons. The front was surmounted by a gargantuan turret, a bombardment cannon. Below that was the opening of the launch bay, capable of unleashing whole squadrons of Thunderhawk transports and other small craft.

This deadly war machine was known as a strike cruiser, the mainstay of the fleets of any Space Marine Chapter.

Covered in baroque decorations, two markings stood out. One was the ultima symbol of the Ultramarines Chapter. Theirs was a storied lineage that stretched back ten thousand years to the Great Crusade that had founded the Imperium. Though battered in endless war, they had recently been revitalised by the return of their primarch, Roboute Guilliman. The other declared the name of the vessel: *In Nomine Imperator*. This example of the line was newly launched by the standards of the Imperial fleet, only a few decades from its commissioning at the forges of Mars.

One of the Thunderhawk transports was returning. It carried a cargo of deadly potency: thirty Space Marines, garbed for war. One of them was Sergeant Allectius. They were fresh from battle, though in the sergeant's opinion it scarcely justified the name. These renegades and pirates had grown fat intimidating the easily cowed locals. Confronted with the genhanced warriors of the Adeptus Astartes, as the Space Marines were formally known, they had proven no match.

Yet while the battle itself had borne no opportunities for glory, there had been honour. Allectius and his squad had been chosen to escort the senior lieutenant into battle. He was proud of his men. They had fought well in the past ten years of the crusade, and it was being recognised. Heretics, cultists and corrupted Traitor Astartes alike had fallen before their assaults. As long as Allectius stood with his brothers, he was confident there was no challenge they could not overcome.

The resounding *thunk* of the Thunderhawk landing in the launch bay pulled the sergeant from his musing. The hatch opened with a hiss, revealing the bustling labour of the deck. People in simple work greys hurried this way and that. These were Chapter-serfs, baseline humans in service to the Ultramarines. They provided crew for their ships and filled other menial, yet necessary, roles. A few of the red-robed priests of Mars, masters of the Imperium's technology and half machine themselves, stood amongst them. They tinkered amongst the machinery with strange tools and argued with each other in their strange language of static and chatter.

'You all fought well today,' came the resonant voice of Lieutenant Triarius. 'Thank the spirits of your wargear and see that it is returned with all due honour to the armouries. Lieutenant Falerius, Sergeant Allectius, you will attend me.'

'As you command, lieutenant,' replied Allectius. He switched to the private vox-link that connected him to his squad. 'Any walking wounded are to see the Apothecary immediately after rendering your war-plate to the armoury.'

The group of Space Marines strode from their transport and out into the ship. It was a proud sight that still stirred the sergeant's heart. Any Astartes warrior was a formidable sight unto themselves, towering above the height of a normal human and clad in the ceramite armour of their holy war-plate. The hiss of articulated joints and the steady hum of power packs, amidst the heavy tread of their boots, announced their movement.

The serfs hastily made way for them, offering the fanned fingers of the Imperial aquila in thanks for the presence of their masters. Even the proud scions of the tech-cult Adeptus Mechanicus stood aside. To be Adeptus Astartes was to be a symbol as much as a man. It was to be the will of the Emperor made manifest. The obligations thereof were a heavy weight, but the Ultramarines bore it with pride.

While most of their brethren left for the armoury,

13

Lieutenant Triarius led the two he had selected towards the ship's bridge.

'How do you feel about the mission, sergeant?' asked Triarius as they strode through dimly lit corridors, lined with thrumming conduits and hissing pipes.

His tone was easy, but Allectius knew their company commander was not given to idle chatter. Thus, he considered his response carefully before speaking. 'The men comported themselves in a manner that did credit to the Chapter. I have never seen them do otherwise.'

Lieutenant Falerius glanced back to the sergeant. 'A cautious answer, if a true one. We serve amongst the best. I cannot speak for Triarius, of course, but I would be interested to hear your thoughts on a grander scale.'

'Indeed,' responded the commander. 'I would hear you speak your mind freely.'

'Very well,' agreed Allectius. 'It did feel a waste for this task to fall to us. Surely hunting pirates, even to their havens, is a task the Imperial Navy could see to.'

The two officers exchanged a glance and Falerius chuckled. 'There it is. Nor are you completely wrong, sergeant.'

'Indeed,' agreed the commander. 'Under ordinary circumstances, we would have done just as you suggest and left this to the Navy.'

'Then why did we intervene this time, if I may ask?' said Allectius.

Lieutenant Triarius seemed to consider his own words carefully this time. 'There is more to a crusade, especially one of this scale, than merely the fighting. You would do well to remember that, sergeant. Sometimes we must act to make a statement. Other times, the only way to see something done quickly is to see to it yourself.'

The sergeant took a moment to absorb this. 'I am glad it is not my place to worry about such things. My squad is battle ready. That is what I can guarantee you.'

'Your efficacy as a squad leader has not gone unnoticed,' said the lieutenant. 'We approach the bridge. We can finish this conversation at a later time.'

The hatch ahead led onto the bridge, just as the lieutenant had said. Control consoles filled the great space, their operators wired into their stations with varying levels of permanence. Tech-acolytes walked amongst the controls, swinging censers in which burned sacred incense as they sang binharic chants exhorting the machine-spirits. The locus of all this activity was the ship's captain, Caepasia Damasippa. Though 'merely' a serf, she had risen far in the estimation of the Chapter and taken on a position of great authority.

A writhing mass of cables extended from the base and back of her skull, connecting her to her command throne. Her eyes and ears were gone, replaced by bionics that facilitated her connection to her beloved ship. A veritable flock of hovering servo-skulls and mechanical cherubim served as her senses now. Further connections encompassed her lower body, seeing to her physical needs.

One of the fluttering, infantile machines lingered by the entrance and must have reported their arrival. Her amplified voice echoed throughout the chamber only half a second later. 'Give thanks to the Emperor, for we are in the presence of His Holy Angels. Blessings upon you, Lord Triarius, and be welcome in this place.'

It was a ritual greeting as old as the ship. The lieutenant took up his part. 'May the Emperor watch over you and yours, ship-captain, for we do His work together.' It was a stentorian declaration. He lowered his voice as he approached the throne, his words losing the air of rehearsal. 'I hope you are well today, Caepasia, and that the *In Nomine Imperator* suffered no undue damage in the battle.'

'I am alive and pleased to be of service, my lord,' she replied graciously. 'It will take more than such pirate filth to see the *Nomine* laid low.'

'I have no doubt,' replied the Astartes company commander. 'If you would be so kind, please open a vox-channel to the planetary governor. I must converse with him.'

'Of course, my lord,' she replied.

A servo-skull hovered up. The skull and spine of a human, it travelled via its own anti-gravity and was fused with a variety of arcane technological devices. One of them, a green lens, powered up once it was nearby. The shimmering monocoloured image of Lord Governor Quinton's face formed mid-air before them. He was a narrow-faced man with a goatee and thin lips.

'My lord, it is good to hear from you. I hope you bring glad tidings.'

'I do, governor. The pirate haven in your system has been cleansed. The recidivists have paid for their crimes with their lives, and their flotilla lies ruined.' The commander crossed his arms with a creak of armour plates. 'How proceeds the fortification of Cassothea?'

'Everything is on schedule, my lord.' The governor hesitated. *'Some of the populace have expressed displeasure at the changes to their world. They are, perhaps, unhappy to see their world made a redoubt for the crusade.'*

'Then I can bring you further good news, governor – the Emperor does not demand their happiness, only their fealty.' The words were sharp, but his tone eased immediately.

'Tens of thousands of worlds suffer yet in the grip of darkness, just as Cassothea suffered. The fleets will need places to refuel, the armies stocks of ammunition, if we are to save them all. We must all make sacrifices to see that done.'

The governor bowed his head. *'As you say, my lord. His will be–'*

'Forgive me, my lords,' interjected Ship-Captain Damasippa. 'I have detected a distress signal coming from Cassothea.'

Lord Quinton looked surprised and turned to the side, speaking sotto voce with someone outside the scope of the projection. He looked back quickly. *'This is news to us. We're just now receiving it as well.'*

'Patch it through, ship-captain,' said the commander.

'It is badly scrambled, my lord. Something is causing interference,' she replied. 'There is little intelligible. I have, however, managed to refine a pict-feed from the location.'

Another servo-skull approached. This image was projected in red light. It showed the courtyard of a half-built military facility. Human figures fled across it. Sizzling arcs of energy cut them down as they ran, stripping the flesh from them in the blink of an eye. Sergeant Allectius tensed as he watched, hands tightening into fists.

The first of the enemy stepped into view. It resembled nothing so much as a skeleton on the march, decorated with strange symbology and heavy plates. It bore a great weapon which unleashed the arcs of energy as it walked on, a mechanical stride. Scattered return fire struck it as it walked, las-blasts glancing harmlessly from its body. Seeming to sense the presence of the pict-capture, it turned and fired. The view dissolved into static with a flash.

'Necrons,' said Triarius grimly.

'Here, my lord?' asked Allectius.

'What is a necron?' asked the ship-captain.

'A nightmare of this forty-first millennium. Some strange horror crawled forth from the abyssal depths of time before the Imperium claimed the galaxy. They were not present when Archmagos Cawl chose us for the Primaris project.' The commander shook his head. 'I have not faced them, but I have read reports from those who did.'

'*What do we do, my lord?*' The governor seemed understandably shaken.

Triarius looked to the ship-captain. 'Put us on a course for the planet.' He turned to the lieutenant and Allectius. 'Muster the troops for immediate drop-pod assault.' At last, he addressed the governor. 'Gather the defence forces and prepare for battle, governor. We did not secure this system just to abandon it to xenos. Cassothea must stand, and the Ultramarines stand with her.'

Allectius pressed his fist to his chest and strode from the bridge to bring the word to his troops. These 'necrons' seemed more formidable than the pirates. Glory enough for everyone in sweeping the aliens from this world.

Another triumph for the Indomitus Crusade awaited.

CHAPTER 1

EIGHT MONTHS LATER

Sergeant Allectius sprinted through the trees towards the sounds of battle. Trunks blurred around him as he wove amongst the foliage with superhuman precision. A Space Marine standing by was a terrifying sight unto himself. It was seeing them move, however, that most often sparked 'transhuman dread' in mortals. It seemed impossible for something of such size and power to move so swiftly.

A pity, then, that the foe they faced seemed beyond fear.

The forest was filled with cacophony. The thunder of bolt weapons, the howl of chainswords and the odd sizzling whine of the xenos weaponry. The latter made his teeth ache every time he heard it, seeming to vibrate up and down his bones on some odd continuum. The former, however, was a comfort: his men were still alive, still fighting. For now.

Allectius saw the first knot of battle up ahead. Two of his brothers were duelling fiercely with a xenos horror. A skeletal torso surmounted a tripod of legs, skull face leering in its fixed grin. The forearms had been replaced; it had no more use for hands. Great blades ran down the sides instead, crackling with strange energies. Destroyers, they called them. Mindless abominations, whose only urge was to dismember and destroy. Even the necrons treated them like beasts, herding them into the foe. The sun-dappled beauty of their natural surroundings only made the stark horror stand out more.

The sergeant absorbed all of this in a beat of his dual hearts and angled towards the creature's back. Thoughtless the creature might be, but it did not diminish its deadliness. Even as he approached, one of its hyperphase swords slashed straight through the chainsword of the Astartes on its left. The blade carved on and through his torso, spraying blood across the greenery. His partner seized this opening and lunged forward, chainsword gouging a sparking hole in the monster's side.

The moment the Space Marine withdrew his weapon and stepped back from a counter swipe, the necron's wound began to close. Metal flowed together like liquid, sealing the opening as inner workings grew back together.

Allectius was there. It sensed his charge at the last second, turning its head. Too late. He aimed his plasma pistol, powered up to maximal mode, and fired. An incandescent blue-white beam of fury erupted from the sidearm. His war-plate's systems reported a heat spike just from holding the weapon. The coruscating blast struck the necron in the back and punched clean through the other side of it in an eruption of liquid metal and sizzling fragments. It continued on, scything through several trees before it had spent its ravening energy.

With a distorted, machine-like groan the xenos collapsed.

Before it struck the ground, it was already shimmering with viridian light. The sergeant lunged forward, the chainsword in his other hand raised high. He brought it down with all of his might, but it passed through empty air with a *whoosh* and crunched into the ground. The severely damaged mechanoid had been teleported away. That was the way with the necrons. Only the utterly annihilated were not spirited off, presumably to be repaired and fight again.

Allectius' own men could not be saved so easily. He strode on to kneel beside the fallen Space Marine. The other man's in-built armour biodiagnosticator could be accessed via their squad noosphere. Brother Volusius was his name. The wound was serious, even for a Space Marine. A mortal man would have been struck dead instantly. Only the synthetic cells his genetically engineered Larraman's organ produced were keeping him from bleeding out, clotting faster than natural platelets ever could.

The sergeant activated the locator beacon built into the wounded warrior's plate, then stood. If the Apothecary reached him in time, he might be saved. If he did not, at least the fallen warrior's gene-seed could be salvaged.

'With me, Numonis,' he said.

'Until the end, brother-sergeant,' replied the other Assault Intercessor and fell in on his flank.

They hastened onward. It was not far before they erupted into a clearing that was the site of a raging battle. Two more of the Destroyers were locked in furious battle with the other four members of Allectius' squad. A third lumbered towards them, its blade-arms outstretched with mindless longing to rend. An insectile figure lurked in the wood line behind it. It had a solid body mounted on long legs, a strange mechanical proboscis waving in the air before it.

'Join the others, I will deal with the plasmacyte,' barked Allectius.

Numonis charged into the fray and the sergeant put his brothers from his mind. All were warriors of the Chapter, the finest mankind had to offer. He trusted them absolutely. For now, he had to focus all of his attention on his foe. His plasma pistol hummed in his left hand as his chainsword revved in the right. Distance-devouring strides carried him towards where the xenos machine lurked.

It skittered back into the shadows. Unlike their mindlessly destructive charges, the plasmacytes were often evasive. Their strength lay in the power they could infuse the Destroyers with, not in confrontation. Allectius' eyes narrowed, he had no intention of allowing it to escape so easily. He raised his plasma pistol and squeezed off a shot, counting on the power of the blast to carve through any intervening cover.

Instead, the weapon gave what could be described as a wheezing cough and powered down. The hydrogen flask was spent. A growing problem as the war for Cassothea dragged out. Allectius holstered the weapon and suppressed a growl of frustration. He would simply have to dismantle–

His thoughts were interrupted by the sudden lunge of the canoptek machine. It must have sensed weakness and acti-vated new programming. There was no time to ponder. It was fast now that it was on the attack, lashing at him with the proboscis. The bladed tip was designed to punch through the living metal hide of a necron, and was more than capable of piercing his power armour if it connected right.

It struck at his face, aiming for his optic lenses. He ducked aside as fast as he could, diverting the strike to scrape a glancing hit along the side of his helmet instead. There was no chance to try to seize that machine tendril. It was striking now with its bladed legs. He caught the sweep of one on the edge of his chainsword, whirling teeth meeting the limb in a spray of sparks.

That monomolecular tip was stabbing at his face once more. Allectius was ready for it this time. With superhuman reflexes his hand flashed out and caught the proboscis, then with the other, he brought his chainsword around in a howling arc. It cleaved away in a flare of emerald fire. The machine staggered backwards, a strange mechanical warbling erupting from it.

The sergeant gave it no time to recover. He pushed forward as it retreated, hacking at the body now with the snarling blade. Each blow tore new rents in its mechanical hide, exposing the arcane workings of its innards. The Space Marine did his best to not commit any of that bizarreness to memory. He was no Techmarine, but even he understood that xenos machines were a corruption of technology. They were fit only to be destroyed.

He hacked away one of its legs and it toppled to the ground. The sergeant stomped on it with all his might, staving it in with a last eruption of viridian sparks that sizzled and flared into the underbrush. With a final strangled bleat it went still. He turned and charged back out into the clearing to find the combat there had entered its final moments.

Two of the Destroyers were gone, vanished back to whatever foul tomb birthed them. Haloed with green energies they shimmered into translucence and then were gone. It was not without cost: one of his brothers lay in the grass, dead, his head and arm hacked from his body by necron blades. The last of the twisted abominations found itself under the concentrated assault of all the remaining Space Marines at once.

They attacked in perfect concert, the product of years of elite training. Individually, they might not have been a match for the terrible mechanoid strength of a Destroyer. Yet their foe was a mindless butcher, while they were expert warriors. They carved it apart en masse. Then it was gone just as the others, little more than a green shimmer fading into nothing.

The sounds of battle died away, echoing off among the trees into silence. Allectius rested a hand against a nearby trunk for a moment. Adeptus Astartes did not tire as quickly and easily as mortals did, but the past months had been draining. Endless battle with little opportunity for recuperation. Skirmishes like this might have appeared to be victories to an outsider, but he knew better. The xenos defeated today would be repaired or replaced; their onslaught would not even slow. The Imperials had no such reinforcements on the way. The last allied warship to arrive in-system had been so badly damaged from some unknown catastrophe it had crashed behind enemy lines.

The sergeant let his arm fall back to his side. It would not do to let the men see any weakness on his part. He activated the vox-link to central command.

'Redoubt Primus, this is Squad Allectius. Our patrol encountered resistance in the Sanral Wood. Destroyers accompanied by plasmacyte. They've been neutralised. One of our brothers has fallen and one needs medicae retrieval.'

'*Acknowledged, Squad Allectius.*' Allectius recognised the voice as Dacien, one of the serfs who worked the comms. There was a curious reticence in his voice. '*Return to base immediately.*'

Allectius frowned. 'Our strength is not depleted, Redoubt Primus. We can continue the patrol.'

There was an extended pause. *'Negative, Squad Allectius. Come back with all speed.'* There was a note of real distress in that voice.

The sergeant narrowed his eyes. It was possible the serf was exceeding his authority in this matter. It was not an argument to have on the vox, however. 'Acknowledged. Squad Allectius on the move. We will bring our casualties with us.' He gave a single sigh and switched his vox-channel back to the squad network. 'We are to return to the redoubt, brothers. Collect Volusius and Landrian. We shall see them home ourselves.'

Allectius scanned the treeline one last time to make sure there were no further enemies lurking about. In the back of his mind, however, that hitch in the serf's voice lingered. Misguided the mortal might be, but something had shaken him. With any luck, he would have answers soon.

Squad Allectius walked amongst the skeletons of burned out buildings. Autocarriage wrecks were piled up in the streets, many showing the tell-tale 'peeling' of necron gauss weaponry. A stillness pervaded the devastation. It made the heavy tread of the Space Marines seem even louder than normal, echoing from broken glass and crumpled metal. The sound came back strange, set him on edge. He was relieved when he saw the great slab of rockcrete up ahead.

Redoubt Primus was what remained of Cassothea's capital city. Allectius had been told the name once. Macuth. It did not matter now. It was ruins. They had tried to defend it against the necron onslaught during the first month, but it had been a lost cause from the beginning. The defence efforts contracted with each assault, a shrinking ring that left a growing number of civilians on the outside.

Some rioted. The smart ones fled into the countryside. It was a poor hope, but still a more likely chance out in the wilderness. There, at least, they might go unnoticed by the xenos death-machines that stalked the landscape. Here they were penned in and slaughtered. The enemy had no remorse. It felt no mercy. They had set out to cleanse this world for their obscure purposes, and if any moral compunctions entered their equations then Allectius had not been able to discern them.

All were long gone now. Only the bodies remained. Those who had fallen in the streets had long since mummified. Bodies left in the shade had decayed down to dry bones. Those caught by the most powerful weapons had disintegrated completely. Their dust layered the interiors of the buildings and blew in clouds through the streets. All of them, those the Ultramarines had not been able to protect. Adeptus Astartes were hardened, their minds reinforced by years of hypno-conditioning and training. For all that, it ate at Allectius. A helplessness that he could only express through fury.

The citizenry were evacuating now, transports taking them and any resources they could carry away as fast as possible. That was the purpose of the patrol today, and others like it. Try to find what survivors and abandoned materiel they could and get them off-world. Perhaps if they had known the odds from the beginning, more might have been saved. Perhaps not. The crusade's leadership had said this world must be saved, and so they had tried. Failure was not something Space Marines were accustomed to.

They were approaching the walls of the fortress now. Allectius had never been to Macragge, the home world of the Ultramarines – awoken from stasis by Archmagos Cawl with the Imperium torn asunder, he had been on crusade ever since. He had seen pict-captures, however. Even the fortifications there were beautiful, built with strength and aesthetics both. There was nothing pleasing about the sight of Redoubt Primus. It was squat and undecorated. Only thick walls could withstand the molecular stripping of gauss weapons.

Tarantula sentry guns bristled from emplacements. They came in a variety of shapes: assault cannons and heavy bolters for the enemy infantry, lascannons and multi-meltas for the armour. There were even missile launchers to help defend against aerial attack. It all looked quite formidable. Unfortunately, looks could deceive. Ammo supplies were running low. Most of these guns would fall silent within minutes of an attack beginning.

The sergeant paused as the auspexes scanned him and his men. He pulled his helmet off with a hiss of depressurisation, the brush of a cool breeze on his sweaty face welcome. Once their identities were confirmed, the great adamantine gates began to slide open. More than a dozen serfs rushed out to help get the wounded inside, overseen by Apothecary Calvus. The white-armoured brother handled the medicae needs of the Space Marines, and when necessary harvested the gene-seed from the bodies of the fallen. Only by carefully preserving the Chapter's due in this way could future initiates be raised to the transhuman level of the Space Marines.

'It is good to see you again, Brother Allectius,' said Calvus.

'The same to you, Brother-Apothecary,' the sergeant replied. They clasped gauntlets briefly. 'Do you know why we were recalled?'

'I do.' It was not the Apothecary's way to mince words.

'Yet I have work to attend to seeing to your casualties. Find Chaplain Sisenna. He will explain.'

Allectius nodded. 'I will leave them in your capable hands and seek him out.' He turned to the rest of his squad. 'Take the time to resupply. We may be fighting again at any moment.'

Each pressed a fist to their chests in response and the sergeant turned away to stride into the dark of the base. The structure had, by necessity, been sized to accommodate the build of a Space Marine, but the rush of construction left it a tight fit nevertheless. Glow-globes fixed on the ceiling brushed his head as he passed under them, nearly forcing him to duck aside. Most were kept dim; power supplies were just as rationed as everything else these days.

Allectius passed the refectory on his right. It was quiet save the murmur of conversation and the clink of dinner-ware. The briny scent of hard rations was on the air – fresh food had become an unthinkable luxury as the xenos noose tightened. He could spot his brothers easily enough, of course; their stature made them stand out if nothing else would. The rest of those gathered were a mix of serfs and locals, but it was becoming hard to tell them apart. Heraldry was greying into unrecognisability by weathering and grime.

The sergeant could not help but notice the reaction his presence drew. A hush of conversation, stares. It added to his disquiet and he hurried on. The sounds and smells faded as he continued, replaced by the growing spice-and-lemon scent of incense.

As he drew closer to the chapel, the hallway began to be lined by posts. Each held a token of some sort. Here, the shattered fragments of a plasma gun. There, a purity seal that had nearly burned away. It had begun as a stop gap, temporary honours for fallen brothers. Whole suits of armour then. Now all that remained was what could not be salvaged and repurposed.

There had been ninety-three warriors in the company when they had arrived at Cassothea. There had been talk of picking up reinforcements before proceeding to the next campaign. That had been fifty-six dead brothers ago. Their totems had overrun the chapel and spilled out into the passageways. There was nothing faceless about their memories. He had known these men for years, fought alongside them. Now they were gone.

Allectius could hear the words now, in Sisenna's powerful rumble.

Lord Guilliman, Avenging Son,
Guide us in battle.
Steel us against the trickery of the xenos.
Make of us scourges of the Emperor's foes.
Aid us, O gene-father and primarch,
As we lay our righteous fury upon the alien.
For our enemies are many,
And seek the ruin of all mankind.

The sergeant stepped into the chapel. Six Ultramarines knelt before the Chaplain, their heads bowed. Allectius recognised the men of Squad Two, led by Sergeant Proclus. Another patrol, preparing to continue the search. Sisenna stood before them, a compelling sight in his black armour and skull-mask. His staff of office, the crozius arcanum, was held in front of him as he intoned the rite. He met Allectius' gaze and gave him a slight nod of recognition. The sergeant returned the gesture and stood to the back to wait.

Each member of Squad Two stepped forward to be blessed, touched on each pauldron by the aquila of the crozius. Then they stepped past the Chaplain to a particular totem. A helmet hung there, surmounted by a crest of once-brilliant red and white. Now it was faded and dingy. The headgear itself would have been salvageable. It had been left in place nonetheless, the only small honour the company could still offer its fallen commander.

Each saluted in turn to the memory of the company commander, and turned to depart. Proclus himself was the last to step forward and accept his blessings. The other sergeant turned when he was done and offered Allectius a sad smile. He paused only to briefly rest a gauntlet on Allectius' shoulder. He departed with his squad. The Squad Four sergeant watched him go uneasily.

'Brother Allectius, how are you?' The Chaplain's voice brought his head around. Sisenna removed his skull-helm and set it aside. The face revealed was broad and tawny, broken by lighter streaks of a number of scars. One marked through his eye – that orb had been replaced by the cold red light of a bionic.

'Ill at ease, Brother-Chaplain, if I am to be honest with you,' replied the sergeant.

Sisenna stepped over to light new incense. The flicker of flame cast his face into a sharp divide of light and shadow. 'What troubles you?'

Allectius laughed without humour at that. 'What does not? Our enemy closes in. I am recalled from duty early, my mission incomplete. I am the subject of whispers and stares. Even the Apothecary tells me merely to seek you out.'

The Chaplain turned to face him once more and waited patiently.

Allectius flexed his hands, then the words tore out of him. 'Is my honour called into question?'

'Ah, there it is,' said Sisenna quietly. 'No.' He gestured away. 'We must always strive to do better than the day before. Our calling is the highest. If we are not improving, we are dying. All of that said, you are not here to be reproached.'

The sergeant took a calming breath. 'Then what is the matter? If we were being reassigned, word would come from the lieutenant.'

'That strikes to the very heart of the matter,' said the Chaplain. He paused, an uncharacteristic hesitation, before continuing, 'Falerius is dead.'

'No,' breathed Allectius. Another wound on his soul, another loss to be borne. Lieutenant Falerius had been forced to take command when the senior lieutenant died in the opening days of the conflict. He had held the company together through the tough fighting of the past months. 'How?'

'Squad Three was pinned down by hostiles in the city ruins. Falerius led the Bladeguard into battle to rescue them. They could get the brothers out, but the enemy had posted Deathmarks in the surrounding buildings.' Deathmarks were the deadly snipers of the necron forces. The rest the sergeant could imagine.

Allectius closed his eyes. 'An honourable death,' was all he could manage.

Sisenna nodded. 'It also leads to your involvement. With all the officer cadre dead, command would usually fall to the senior sergeant.'

'As the Codex Astartes dictates,' agreed Allectius. 'I am fully prepared to accept Sergeant Fulgentius' command.'

The Chaplain shook his head now. 'That is not to be. Falerius left specific instructions on what should happen in the case of his death.' He locked eyes with Allectius. 'He named you, Allectius. You are hereby promoted to lieutenant, pending the confirmation of the Chapter Master to make it official, of course.'

Allectius could only stare at him for a moment. Finally, he managed, 'What?'

'You are in command of the company now, lieutenant.' Sisenna stepped forward and rested a hand on his shoulder. 'I believe you will rise to this challenge. The sergeants have agreed to abide by the decision. We are behind you, one and all.'

The newly minted lieutenant searched for words. 'I–'

Before he could find them, something fundamental in the cosmos shifted. An oppressive weight fell upon the very essence of the world. Colours faded and lights dimmed. It hit Allectius like suffocation, as if the air was too still to be able to breathe. He had to force it into his lungs, and could feel his hearts pound. There was no question it went beyond him – he could see that Chaplain Sisenna had staggered a step, his face twisted in his surprise.

That was when his vox-rig crackled. *'Forgive me, but we need the lieutenant in the command centre right now.'* The communication serf sounded strained, in real pain. *'We're getting distress calls from the evacuation ships. Something has gone wrong.'*

CHAPTER 2

Gnaeus staggered through the darkened corridors of Redoubt Primus. He was doing his best to hurry. It was easier said than done. There was no escaping the wrongness that now pervaded the world. Everything took more effort now. Even the basic functions, like walking or breathing. He had seen it on the faces of everyone he met, stumbling through their tasks with blank faces.

The serf crashed into the wall as another wave of dizziness washed over him. The world seemed to spin, the solidity of the rockcrete against him the only anchor. His mouth watered as his gorge rose, and he struggled to fight it back down. He breathed through his nose slowly and evenly, focused on it. The nausea slowly receded. This time. He couldn't escape the feeling that it was getting worse.

His weakness frustrated and angered him. There was no time for it. Everyone in the fortress was in mortal danger, and all he wanted to do was crawl into a dark corner and lie still. He held on to the fiercer emotions tightly. They would have to drive him. One foot in front of the other. Keep moving. Don't let it drag you down.

Remember, remember the danger.

The necrons were coming.

They needed all hands. Gnaeus had to be ready. He was moving again, plodding forward. The corridor seemed to waver around him, but he pushed on. The armoury was nearby. He could picture it – the sacred chambers where the holy wargear of the company was kept. He had toiled in such places for nine years, since his tutelage had begun at age ten. He had been taught by the masters, while the whole workshop was overseen by the distant authority of their Techmarine overlords.

He had worked with weapons all his life, and been required to train with them should he ever need to help defend the holdings of his masters. Adeptus Astartes were few in the galaxy, after all, and spread thin confronting all the horrors that it held for mankind. To crew their ships, guard their monasteries and perform their labour, they depended on the serfs. In return, Gnaeus and his people were given a good life, full of purpose.

He had reached the archway into the armoury. It was divided into two sections. One path led into where the mighty Space Marines were clad for war. The other was smaller, shabbier. It was where the wargear for their mortal servants was kept. Gnaeus took another deep breath and headed for the latter.

Then he saw movement down the Astartes pathway and turned his head with a frown. There was no question it was not one of the masters. They were distinctive to say the least, their presence overwhelming at times.

He stepped into the holy chambers. They were drenched in shadow. Tools of the artificer's craft hung on racks nearby. Gnaeus picked up a hammer warily, calling out, 'Is someone there?' There was a rustling sound but no response. The young serf tightened his grip on his makeshift weapon. 'Come out now!'

A figure emerged from the darkness. They were stooped with age, with a shuffling gait. 'Be at peace, young one. Forgive me. I was lost in my thoughts and did not hear you approach.' There was a terrible weariness in that creaky voice.

More importantly, Gnaeus recognised it. He lowered his hammer with a sigh. 'Tulla, you frightened me.' He returned the tool carefully to its proper resting place. His frown promptly returned. 'What are you still doing here? You were supposed to leave on the last transport.'

The old woman came forward. She carried a multitool in one hand. 'There is no leaving, Gnaeus. I do not know why, but the ships are trapped here.' She shook her head. 'It is as though the path between the stars is closed to us. Some said that ships that tried to depart were badly damaged, or even destroyed.'

The words hit hard. If it were true, and the exodus from Cassothea had been cut off somehow, what were they to do? With effort, the young serf pushed his fears aside. 'Surely they could have made arrangements to keep you on the ship, at least.' He stepped forward and guided her to a seat on a nearby bench. 'It's dangerous down here, mistress.'

Tulla gave him a sad smile. He could hear how laboured her breath was. Her arm seemed painfully thin as he moved her to sit down. 'You were always a kind boy, Gnaeus. I am sorry you had to come to this dreadful place.' She looked away. 'The soul-sickness was up there too. All amongst the crews and the passengers. There is nowhere safe left.'

'So you came back to the armoury? To perform rites of repair?' he asked wryly, nodding to her multitool.

Tulla looked around wistfully. 'I have spent my whole life fixing the sacred armaments, that they might better serve the masters. I have kept their armour polished and painted, and applied the sacred unguents to their bolters.' She sighed softly. 'Such things seem to fall by the wayside in desperate times. It is all I know to do, however. I am... content here.'

'I–'

The alert klaxon sounded. Its wail was dampened by the strange pressure on the world. Normally ear-piercing, it seemed somehow distant. Meaningless. Gnaeus shook that listless response off.

'Forgive me, elder. The enemy approaches. I must gather my equipment and go help with the defences.'

She patted his hand. 'Go. Do what you must. It is all any of us can do in such times.'

Gnaeus hurried back into the antechamber and on into where the serfs kept their armament. He put on his flak armour as quickly as he could, tightening the straps to get a good fit. He collected his shotgun and the bandoliers of shells he'd been issued. He was no exception to the strained supply situation; shells might be more plentiful than bolt-rounds, but a few more pitched battles, and he'd be trying to fight the xenos with the weapon's reinforced stock as a makeshift club.

It was a thought that didn't bear lingering on. Others were straggling in now to gather their gear. Too few, too slow. This soul-sickness was eating at them all. There was nothing he could do about that, either. All he could do was make his way to his place in the defences, and do his best to hold it.

On his way out, Gnaeus glanced over his shoulder. Tulla was still sitting where he'd left her, staring into the dark. It gave him a sense of purpose that lengthened his stride and broadened his shoulders. As long as he was between her and the enemy, he swore to himself, no harm would come to her.

The klaxon chased him all the way to his station. It was not the classic image of manning the walls, shoulder to shoulder with your brave comrades. The necrons were a curious combination of mindless and dangerously intelligent. Waves of their skeletal warriors would march into the massed guns at the walls, but that was not the only avenue of attack. They would come from above, and below, and within. All the defenders could do was spread out and try to catch them as they arrived.

As for Gnaeus, his gear had originally been assigned to him to help defend the *In Nomine Imperator* from boarders. It was not suited to long-range engagement. Thus, he had been given the task of patrolling the deep corridors of the base. He was not alone in his work, of course. It would be too easy to silence a single sentry. The lords did not make such foolish mistakes.

Nevertheless, the patrol was nerve-wracking. He paced out his patrol route through the darkened passageways. It began with the thunder of the great sentry guns. Even this deep in the complex they vibrated the rockcrete and made dust rain from the ceiling. Gnaeus could hear his breath, loud in his void-sealed helmet. He knew what was coming next.

The howl.

It didn't seem to matter how many walls lay between him and the necron aircraft as they made their runs. The scream of their passing cut through barriers. Even if he was foolish enough to stop up his ears, he'd feel it in his bones. The sheer dread that it provoked was impossible to describe.

Every time it was a struggle to not cast down his weapon and flee. It was even harder now, with this vile pall they had laid over everything. Gnaeus was shaking uncontrollably. It chilled him down to his core. Once again he found himself desperately fighting back vomit, lest he flood his helmet.

Then he heard it. The scratching sound around the corner of the next T intersection. That rasp, metal on the rough stonework. He needed to vox in. He needed to investigate. His legs felt frozen, and he could feel his lip trembling.

'Coward,' he whispered. Tears were in his eyes. He pounded his fist into his thigh.

Someone screamed around the corner, a shrill noise of terror. It ended as swiftly as it started, in a wet gurgle.

Somehow that sound washed away the sharp edges of his own fear. There was someone who needed help, and Gnaeus couldn't just abandon them to whatever grisly fate had found them. His steps were halting, but he moved forward. The sounds of squelching awaited him as he turned the corner.

For a moment, he couldn't make out what he was looking at. It was just a mass of twitching limbs and raw, wet meat. Ribbons of slick skin flapped with each spasm, spattering drops of blood against the walls and floor. It all snapped into focus. The hunched shape of a skeletal frame, wrapped in ghoulish charnel. The body of the guard, pinned to the ground by long blades. It was *peeling* him with its other scythe-hand, inch by bloody inch.

Worse, the other guard wasn't dead. He was pinned through the chest, but he was still moving. Even as Gnaeus stared the fallen man reached out a desperate hand towards him, managing only a choking wheeze that blew a bubble of blood through his lips. The thing noticed the movement and turned, and the serf found himself under a cold emerald gaze that gleamed from a metal skull.

He took a step back, his boots slipping in blood. There was too much of it in the hallway. It was as though some had leaked into this world with the horrid thing, from wherever it came. The horror rose to its full height, pulling its blades from the dying man with a slurping sound. Gnaeus wanted to scream, but it just came out a terrified whimper. *Shoot!* some part of him yelled. *Shoot it!*

He convulsively pulled the trigger, firing from the hip. The shotgun blast went wide, blasting chips of rockcrete from the wall beside the necron. It tilted its head, studying the near impact with an almost animalistic lack of recognition. It returned its cruel gaze to him and lunged into sudden movement. It rushed up the hallway towards him, releasing a shrill keen as it came.

Training took over. Gnaeus brought the shotgun to his shoulder and worked the slide. The spent shell tumbled away. He fired again, and this time caught the charging thing in the centre of its torso. Gibbets of pilfered flesh sprayed off in a bloody arc and it staggered under the impact. He didn't relent, hammering it with shot after shot. Each round impacted with a sound somewhere between the wet thump of pounded meat and the dull tolling of struck metal.

His magazine was empty. The flayer was slumped against the wall, the green light of its eyes gone dim. Gnaeus wasted no time, frantically reloading his weapon with shaking hands. One of the shells slipped between his fingers to hit the floor.

'Emperor's blood and bones,' he hissed furiously and ignored it, pulling another from the bandolier instead of wasting time.

Gnaeus wasn't ready when he heard that sound. It was the soft *clink... clink... clink...* of shot hitting the ground. He looked over and confirmed his fears. The pellets were being extruded from the damaged flayer. The quasi-liquid metal that made up each necron's body was pushing them out, slowly at first but with increasing speed. The light of its eyes shimmered back on and it began to push itself upright once more.

The serf began to backpedal as fast as he could. If he could just finish reloading, then–

Blood began to gush down the walls, flowing along the floor. Chunks of meat and bone were swept along in the cascade. Gnaeus saw them start to come through. The great bladed hands first, dragging the wet, gore-soaked body out behind it. Four more of the monsters. They weren't digging their way in – nothing so prosaic. They were extruding into this world impossibly, birthed from some unknown hell-realm.

The serf turned and ran. He could hear the keening start behind him, the clatter of their metal talons against the floor as they took up the chase. He felt like his heart was going to pound out of his chest. He fumbled to activate his vox as he sprinted through the corridors.

'Command, this is south-west sector four reporting! Xenos intrusion! At least five of them! They're portalling in somehow!'

All he got in return was static. He had to hope the transmission had got through. Perhaps someone had heard his shotgun. His lungs were already burning from his head-long flight. He didn't have to look to know they were still after him. That uncanny shrill scream of unnatural hunger was ceaseless behind him.

Gnaeus turned a corner going too fast. His legs nearly went out from under him as he tried to come around. He hit the far wall with a crash of flak plate against rockcrete. Air rushed from his lungs in a wheeze. He nearly fell, caught himself on his hands. He was scrambling down the hall when he became aware that there was something ahead of him. All he got was a moment's impression of massive figures in lapis lazuli blue.

'Down, mortal!' rumbled a thunderous voice.

Gnaeus had been trained from birth to obey such commands. He spared no time for thought, just lunged to the ground. Even so, he could not help but turn and look. They came around the corner, shrieking for blood. Their stolen skins flapped wetly around them as they ran. Their reaper's claws were held out before them imploringly, anxious to find flesh to rend and carve. Monsters from a nightmare.

A tremendous roar filled the air. Thick beams of white-hot melta energy tore through the air above him. Their passing heated the hallway so much that he could feel it through his armour, like standing before an open oven. His void-safe visor polarised to protect his eyes, throwing everything into artificial shadow. The beams struck the oncoming necrons with annihilating force. They disintegrated stolen flesh and metal structure alike, liquefying what fragments they did not reduce to ash instantly.

Gnaeus lay there, huddled on the ground and trembling. He was afraid to move, just waiting for the rush of blood that would announce more of the hideous foe arriving.

Nothing came. Instead, the heavy tread of armoured boots approached him.

'The mortal is intact,' came another resonant voice. 'On your feet, serf. The xenos are destroyed.'

On shaking hands, Gnaeus lifted himself off the ground. He scarcely dared to look at his rescuers. Three mighty figures in the ceramite war-plate of the Adeptus Astartes. They towered head and shoulders above him, their great melta rifles still held at the ready. The emitters glowed red-hot. The one who had come to him stared down at him, ruby lenses gleaming.

'Your weapon,' the lord said flatly.

Gnaeus glanced down. His shotgun lay where it had tumbled from his hands as he threw himself down. His cheeks burned as he hastily collected it. 'Thank you for saving my life, my lords,' he managed to rattle out unsteadily.

'We heard the fighting,' was the simple reply. The helmet turned, that inscrutable gaze falling on the destroyed xenos instead. 'Flayed ones.' Disgust was redolent in the Ultramarine's tone now. 'Carrion fiends, drawn to the assaults of their cannier brethren.' The mighty warrior glanced to the serf. 'You are fortunate to be alive.'

Gnaeus looked to the ruined monsters himself. Puddles of melted metal lay amidst scorched flesh and heaps of ash. He swallowed hard. 'The Emperor protects, my lord.'

'He does.' The Space Marine seemed to lose interest in him. 'Find your way to a command post for reassignment. We shall scour this sector and ensure it is cleansed of xenos taint.'

The young serf bowed immediately. 'As you command, my lord.'

The Space Marines had not waited for his response. The

one who'd spoken to him was already continuing down the tunnel, with the other two following in his wake. They did not look at Gnaeus as they passed. They turned the corner and were gone.

Gnaeus slumped against the wall, breathing hard. He had seen the great lords before, of course. He had even witnessed them fight occasionally, here on Cassothea. It had always been from a distance, though. The casual ease with which they had obliterated those monstrosities astounded him.

As long as the Ultramarines stood, there was still hope.

He had his orders to follow. The serf hurried off down the corridor to find the command post.

Hours later, Gnaeus trudged back to the armoury once more. He was weary, no mistaking it. That pall over existence – the Pariah field, they were calling it – pushed it into a listless exhaustion. He wanted nothing so much as to lie down and stop moving. Perhaps never move again.

They had driven the necrons away again. Some had said this was nothing more than a probing attack, testing their defences. It did not feel like a victory. They were still trapped, still weakening. Defeat as many xenos as they liked, there was no end to the horde. The outcome was no longer in question. It was just a matter of time.

Gnaeus shook the thought away with a burst of anger. His helmet felt suffocating suddenly. He pried it away convulsively, narrowly resisting the urge to hurl it down the hallway. He longed for movement, for a breeze on his skin. The air was scarcely less stifling in the tunnel. He could smell the blood and filth.

He wasn't alone in the tunnel, he realised. It was an odd moment of sudden clarity. Others stumbled on around him in their own wargear. Each was isolated in their thoughts, as wrapped in a shroud of misery as Gnaeus himself had been. At times, they would stumble to a halt, staring vacantly, only to stumble on again a minute later. It recalled nothing so much as a procession of the dead.

'We're alive,' Gnaeus whispered. At first he just wanted to reassure himself. When no one nearby so much as moved, he raised his voice to all of them and said forcefully, 'We're still alive, damn you!'

No one stirred. Empty gazes slid past him. Repugnance welled up in him, like blood in a deep cut. He hurried on, swerving around those he could and shouldering past them when they were pressed too close. At last, he broke out ahead of the assembly and stepped into the armoury itself. Here, at least, were familiar scents to cut through the stink of his armour and his fear. Clean, honourable scents. Polish and unguents, grease and metal.

His weariness had returned. Gnaeus made his way towards the mortal chambers. It would be a relief to be shed of his flak suit and weapon. A shape on the bench caught his eye as he passed the arch into the lords' chambers. It was still dark in there, unsurprisingly – the masters would fight long beyond when a mortal's endurance would give out. They must be out harrying the withdrawing enemy even now.

He stepped into the entrance. 'Mistress Tulla, still cleaning? You should have sought sanctuary during the assault.'

There was no response. Fear sparked in Gnaeus anew. There was no blood on the floor, but what assurance was that? Could not something just as terrible as the 'flayed ones' have come here? He eased his shotgun up and took a step forward towards the shape of the old woman.

'Mistress Tulla? Are you well?'

He activated the stablight on his helmet. The elder serf did not even startle at the sudden brightness. She sat there, staring into the distance with vacant eyes. Her mouth was slack and a sickly greyness had stolen all colour from her cheeks. He could see the slow rise and fall of her chest, but that was the only evidence that she was still alive.

Gnaeus swept the beam around the chamber. There was no sign of any foe. Then he hurried to her side, taking her hand in his. Even that slight pressure tipped her, made her slide towards the floor like a puppet with its strings cut. He caught her hastily and eased her to the ground. There was nothing in her gaze. It was as though something vital was simply gone from her, some spark smothered out.

'Medicae,' he rasped. He activated his vox, 'Medicae! Medicae team to the lords' armoury! We have… a casualty. Some sort of illness. Something is wrong.'

CHAPTER 3

Allectius surveyed the apothecarion. It would have been put to shame by the true facilities that could be found in the Fortress of Hera on Macragge, of course, but it had been the best they could assemble on this world. Bunks lined the walls, patrolled by mortal medicae staff keeping an eye on the patients. Many were attendees of the Apothecary, others were local chirurgeons and physicks contributing their talents. A few were merely volunteers, carrying censers of cleansing incense to encourage healing and suppress the smell of illness and death. All worked towards the common goal of saving as many human lives as they could.

'Volusius is on the mend. He will be fit to return to duty within a matter of days,' said Calvus, where he stood beside the new lieutenant. Chaplain Sisenna was nearby, observing. 'The three brothers who were wounded during the necron attack yesterday will soon be healed as well.'

'That is welcome news,' replied Allectius. 'We will need

every warrior we can get in the days to come.' He turned his gaze on the Apothecary. 'Tell me of this sickness running rampant among the mortals.'

Calvus frowned. 'It is no plague. Instead, it matches what reports we have had from other areas of the front. It is the soul death.'

Allectius took a deep breath. 'That is the confirmation of our worst projections. We have fallen under the veil of the Pariah Nexus.'

'Indeed,' Calvus said grimly. 'From what I know, it is the first time an Imperial force has witnessed the assimilation of a world into the Nexus.'

'There is nothing that we can do for those afflicted?' asked the lieutenant.

'Tend to them. Force-feed them. There is no record of any who succumb to the soul death recovering.'

Another tragedy playing out to the bitter end. War was full of those. 'We cannot afford such a drain on our resources. Provide them with the Emperor's Peace.' Allectius started to turn away, paused. 'Treat them with respect, Apothecary.'

Calvus inclined his head. 'Of course, brother-lieutenant. As they honoured us with their service, we shall honour them in death.' He departed to attend to his duties.

'The Ecclesiarchal representatives among the populace request permission to hold daily gatherings, to implore the Emperor's protection on their flock,' said the Chaplain as he fell in beside Allectius on the way out.

'If it will provide the mortals some comfort, so be it,' replied Allectius. 'Arrange work shifts to enable it.'

'It shall be done,' said Sisenna. They walked on through the corridors in silence for a span, before he said, 'We must also discuss the disposition of the company's relics.'

Allectius stopped, causing the Chaplain to do likewise. 'We have already resolved this matter.'

'A matter of perspective. I understand your wishes, that the items be kept with the body of Falerius until we can rejoin the crusade fleet.' The Chaplain's eyes and voice were steady. 'I ask you to reconsider.'

'They belong with the company's last true commander,' said Allectius. 'My tasking is a temporary measure, in response to a crisis. Until we have confirmation from Lord Calgar that my promotion is to stand, I am not a fit wielder.'

'An impossible criterion,' said Sisenna. 'The shroud of the Nexus does not allow for astropathic commune. We cannot confirm your new rank until such time as we escape this system.'

'Honour does not bend before circumstance,' said Allectius flatly and turned away to continue on.

'Your honour must extend beyond yourself now, lieutenant.'

There was a sharpness to the remark that drew Allectius' head around with anger in his eyes. 'Think carefully on your next words, Chaplain. I did not ask for this position, but I am in command now.'

Sisenna crossed his arms. 'That is exactly my point. You fear what our brothers will think of you if you take up the sword and shield. I ask you now, what will they think if you do not? We find ourselves in dark straits. The darkest I have seen in this crusade. If you do not have faith in yourself, how will they believe in you?'

The lieutenant bit back his first heated response. His untrammelled fury had served him well as an Assault Intercessor, but those days were done. Command demanded a more level head. He closed his eyes and forced himself to consider the Chaplain's words impartially.

'You are correct, though I may not wish it. What do I need to do?'

'Come with me,' answered the Chaplain.

He led the way through the corridors of the base to the chapel. People stepped aside at their passing; Space Marines with a bowed head of respect, mortals with genuflection. The deference of the latter was something Allectius was accustomed to, but seeing it from the former was still surprising. Sergeants were ultimately among the warriors. Officers were set apart, more distant figures of absolute authority.

Even the baseline humans looked at him differently now. None of them looked him in the eye, but he saw it in his peripheral vision as he passed them. That desperate hope. Imperial citizens were raised on tales of the mighty Space Marines, unconquerable paragons of virtue. They were waiting for a miracle, and who better to deliver than the Emperor's Angels of Death?

Allectius knew nothing of miracles. His training was decades of warfare, and by all the principles he knew, their situation had crossed over into a last stand. It would not be the first, or the last, time in history that Astartes fought to the last against an unstoppable foe. From Calth to Macragge, the Ultramarines had sacrificed themselves against terrible threats in the name of the Imperium. It did sadden him, however, that he could not save their charges.

They arrived at the chapel. A handful of other Ultramarines were present. It was not uncommon for members of the company to come here to meditate during what little recuperation time they received. These were the veterans of the Bladeguard, elite warriors of the First Company seconded to the Chapter to serve as an inspirational spearhead force. Each had fought in thousands of battles and honoured the Chapter by their glorious deeds.

Still, Sisenna showed no hesitation to intrude on their thoughts. 'Arise, brothers. I have need of you to act as witnesses.'

The Chaplain continued on from there, trailed by Allectius and the roused Bladeguard. The lieutenant saw the mild curiosity on their faces as they stood to follow, but could do nothing to satisfy it. He had never proceeded to the sacred rear chambers of the chapel. His duties as a sergeant had never demanded it of him, and he knew nothing of what Sisenna had in mind.

The room they entered was a simple one. Braziers of incense burned at each of the corners, tended by serfs in dedicated service to the Chaplain. A handful of great marble slabs lay in the centre. On two lay the bodies of fallen brothers. Allectius recognised Brother Landrian from his old squad and Lieutenant Falerius. Beyond these biers, at the far end of the room, were a few ornate chests.

The Chaplain noticed where his gaze had rested. 'I honour our dead with as many of the rites as we can manage here. Their treated bodies must lie in state for a matter of days, before the cremation. Their ashes will be returned to Macragge if possible. If not, they will be interred here.'

'It pleases me to see them accorded the respect they deserve, now that their service has ended. Both were good men,' Allectius said.

'It is an honour to see them beyond the veil of this world,' said Sisenna.

He opened two of the chests. With reverent care he retrieved an item from each, placing them in turn upon one of the unoccupied slabs. The first was a power sword of baroque design, its blade gleaming in the light. The second was an ornate storm shield, a mighty aegis large enough to stretch from a Space Marines' shoulder to the ground. Bones suspended in stasis fields decorated the surface, recognisable as those of a dead Space Marine by their size.

'Behold,' intoned the Chaplain. 'Conciliator and Veritas.'

Allectius fell to one knee immediately, accompanied by the rustling sound of the Bladeguard doing likewise. These artefacts were sacred, entrusted to the care of their company as they had gone to war beside their primarch. They had been passed down through millennia of service, laid low enemies by the thousands and saved the life of their bearers from as many deadly blows. The relic shield's power was said to be of such moment that its protection extended even to those who fought near the bearer.

'Brothers, this warrior has been elected to bear these holy arms. Do you judge him to be worthy?' asked Sisenna.

'We do,' chorused the Ultramarines.

Allectius struggled to hide his surprise. These honoured warriors surely had not known this was coming, yet they had shown no hesitation in their answer. He found it difficult to accept. Surely they could not approve of him taking up this mantle from better men? The circumstances were dire. It must simply be that they realised this.

'We do this in honour of the Emperor, and guided by the wisdom handed down by our Father, Roboute Guilliman,' continued the Chaplain.

'Ave Imperator,' replied the gathered brethren. Allectius

said the words fervently, adding his own silent plea: *Gene-father, help me lead these men as well as they deserve.*

'Rise, Lieutenant Allectius.' Allectius stood, that new rank feeling real for the first time. Sisenna turned and lifted the shield from the slab. 'This shield I entrust to you. It will guard against those who would see the destruction of your flesh. Let its weight forever remind you to be the guardian of your soul. Its name is Veritas, and none who have borne it have sullied their tongue with a lie. Do you, Allectius, swear to honour their memory and follow their example?'

'I do,' replied the lieutenant. The Chaplain placed the shield upon his arm, and he shifted to take it. The heft of it was impressive, as though he carried with him the very wall of a fort.

'This blade I entrust to you,' said Sisenna as he lifted the sword. 'It will serve you well in war, but let its name, Conciliator, remind you always of the heart of what it is to be an Ultramarine. We are raised above our fellow men to safeguard them. Let no innocent blood stain it, and abandon none who need your protection. That is your oath. Do you so swear?'

'I do,' said Allectius again. The sword, too, was handed over to him. It was surprisingly light and balanced in his grip, the hallmark of a design older than the Imperium itself. Between the two of them, he had not felt so invincible since the day he had first been raised from the Scout Company and been garbed in his war-plate.

Sisenna took up his crozius arcanum and touched it to Allectius' brow. The metal of the sacred aquila was cold against his skin. 'Emperor, hear us, we entreat you. Guide this warrior. Grant him but a measure of your wisdom and foresight, that he may serve you well. Give us the strength to stand at his side and bring down your wrath upon all who would stand against us. We do this in your name. Ave Imperator.'

'Ave Imperator,' echoed those gathered once more.

'Thank you, brothers. You may return to your meditation,' said Sisenna warmly. The Bladeguard each stepped forward and clapped Allectius upon the pauldron before departing.

Allectius caught his reflection in the surface of the blade. He thought little of his appearance, yet it struck him at that moment. The fair hair and skin. A face of aquiline features, pockmarked and torn by a dozen scars. What captured his attention the most, however, was the tears in his pale blue eyes. He had never felt so honoured. It was an exaltation beyond any he had imagined, but also a burden of responsibility unlike any he had known.

Then his vox crackled.

The voice of the communications serf came through. *'Forgive me for interrupting, my lord. We have received a communiqué from the ship-captain of the* In Nomine Imperator. *She requests an audience with you at your earliest convenience. She says she has urgent news.'*

Allectius could see the same grim worry on Sisenna's face that he himself felt. What news could there be save that of the worst kind, in these times? 'Very well. Tell her we will be in contact shortly. Reach out to Librarian Tertulus and Apothecary Calvus as well. Let them know I wish them to be present in the command centre for the conference.'

'As you command, my lord,' replied the serf.

'I will want you there as well, Chaplain,' said Allectius.

'Of course, lieutenant. I shall accompany you,' replied Sisenna.

Allectius turned to set out. *What could it be now?* he wondered.

The command centre was forever bustling with activity. Serfs and local populace intermingled in work here, making sure the redoubt's defenders operated in a unified manner. Cogitators lined the walls, humming and chattering. Auguries were fed into servitors, the mindless cyborgs mumbling as they moved markers on maps to indicate the latest positioning reports. The air was unpleasantly warm, a combination of too many machines and people, and not enough ventilation.

'Give praise unto the Emperor for the presence of His Angels!' called someone as Allectius strode into the room. The activity paused as the gathered mortals turned and bowed, hands fanned in the sign of the aquila.

'Continue your labours in His name,' said Allectius, and the work resumed.

'Tertulus is already here,' said Sisenna at his elbow.

The Librarian stood amid the room with a gloomy expression on his dark-skinned face. When Archmagos Cawl had gathered the recruits for the Primaris project millennia ago, Tertulus had come from Prandium. Awakening from stasis in modern times to find his home world destroyed by the alien menace known as the tyranids had given him a morose turn of mind. It suited his armour, a darker shade of blue than the standard Ultramarine plate to denote his role.

The Librarium was responsible for keeping the history and traditions of the Chapter. They were also selected for having psychic potential, and were trained to use those supernatural talents in battle. Their unnatural ways sometimes set them apart from the rest of their brethren, but few could argue against their efficacy in destroying the enemy. Tertulus had achieved only the first rank of Lexicanium among his kindred, and was tasked with reporting on the company's deeds.

'Any word on the situation, Brother-Librarian?' asked Allectius as the pair approached him.

The psyker's gaze remained fixed on the distance, not so much as flicking towards them. His lips moved ceaselessly in some silent tirade.

Nonplussed, Allectius glanced to Sisenna, who responded with a slight frown.

'Tertulus? Are you well?' asked the Chaplain, his voice raised slightly.

The Librarian's head snapped to face them, his expression twisted for a moment. It smoothed and he took a deep breath. 'Forgive me, brothers. The effects of the Pariah Nexus are felt most keenly by those touched by the immaterium. It is… unpleasant.'

'I had heard such reports.' Sisenna searched the other man's face for a moment. 'I encourage you to come to the chapel if it wears upon you. The rituals of old offer strength in dark times.'

'I will keep that in mind,' replied the psyker.

An approaching sound drew Allectius' attention – the heavy footfall of Mark X armour boots, in a familiar tread.

'The Apothecary joins us,' he announced.

A moment later the medicae made his way through the parting crowds to join them. He offered a terse nod to the other three. 'I am here as requested. What is the matter?'

'We shall find out now.' The lieutenant directed his

attention to the communications serf manning the long-range vox-station. 'Contact the *In Nomine Imperator*. The ship-captain should be awaiting us.'

'As you command, my lord.' The mortal worked the controls of the console.

'Greetings, honoured lords. This is the In Nomine Imperator. *I thank you for gathering so quickly to hear what we've discovered.'* Damasippa's voice was overlaid with some static, though not enough to keep her from being understood. Allectius thought there was strain in her voice, underneath that professional calm. *'We have completed our interpretation of the latest planetary auguries, and have discovered two pieces of information deemed to be of significant note.'*

'Have you learned anything regarding this system falling into the Pariah Nexus?' asked Tertulus eagerly.

Allectius gave the Librarian a stern look for interjecting, but Damasippa's answer came before he could take control of the conversation again.

'We believe we may have, lord Librarian. I will explain, and send a noospheric feed of information as well.'

The comms serf pointed to the central hololith in the chamber so as to not intrude on their discussion, indicating where the feed would come through. It sparked to life with a clatter and a hum, projecting the three-dimensional display above. The machine was a relic, its pict-quality imperfect and images coming through only in shades of green, but for rapid data display it was useful.

'By refining the augur-feeds to the timestamp of the first reported symptoms of the Nexus-field, we located an anomaly.' The hololith resolved to show a survey of the main landmass of Cassothea. One set of coordinates was highlighted, on a plateau over one hundred and fifty miles north-west

of Redoubt Primus. *'A massive energy surge of unknown provenance.'*

'A necron installation coming online?' asked Sisenna.

'What enemy forces we have encountered have been transported in by ships. We have not had the naval strength to interdict them. That implies this is not one of their slumbering tomb worlds, and we have seen nothing to contradict it. That would mean this is something they have newly built,' replied Allectius.

'What of orbital bombardment?' queried Tertulus.

'The area shows auspex signatures that align with reinforced quantum shielding. According to records, our vessel would have difficulty getting through a field of this magnitude,' answered the ship-captain.

Allectius pushed it to the back of his mind for the time being. 'You said there were two things you needed to convey. What is the other?'

'Nothing you will be pleased to hear, my lord.' The ship-captain sounded regretful. *'In the time since the anomaly mentioned, we have detected a spike in necron activity worldwide. Multiple battle group-sized formations are closing in on Redoubt Primus, including full vehicular and aerial support elements.'* As before, her words were illustrated by the display. Though the highlighted portions were little more than smudges against the terrain, there was no doubt as to what they were looking at.

'Thousands upon thousands of necrons,' said Calvus flatly.

A stillness settled over the room as mortals stared at the images and absorbed what they meant. It would have been difficult for the redoubt to withstand such an assault when it was at full strength. Depleted in numbers and ammunition, and waning under the influence of the Nexus, these were grim prognostications.

'Can you estimate how long we have?' asked Allectius into the silence.

'There is obviously an overall command element at work, as the varied forces are moving for a synchronised arrival. Based on current speeds of the slowest forces, the attack will begin in thirty-three hours.'

'They have trapped us by blinding our Navigators completely and stifling the warp currents, and now they move to extinguish resistance once and for all.' Sisenna's hand gripped the hilt of his crozius, the leather-wrapped hold creaking with the force exerted.

Allectius stepped forward. The hololith was showing the projected movement of the necron forces closing in, with a counting chronometer beside it. The lieutenant's head tilted as he contemplated the pattern. An idea began to emerge, though it seemed a fool's gambit at first glance.

'Ship-captain, freeze this strategic prognostication at twenty-three hours from now,' he said.

He was the focus of their attention now.

The projection rewound to the indicated time, showing the xenos forces beginning to congeal into a single formation. Once the naval command serf had completed the request, the Chaplain spoke up. 'You have a plan, lieutenant?'

Allectius could not escape a certain level of unease. He had been satisfied as the sergeant of a squad. This was a trial by fire beyond anything he had imagined. There was no escaping the need to act, however.

'A thought,' he allowed. He pointed to a gap in the enemy's line. 'There is an opening here.' The display fizzled then stabilised at the proximity of his gauntlet.

Tertulus contemplated it. 'A possibility to break out of the cordon? It would do no good. The Nexus encompasses the world and beyond. The entire star system, at the very least.'

'A breakthrough, yes,' said Allectius. 'Not to escape, however. It is time that we returned to what we do best.'

'You mean to go on the offensive,' said Sisenna with a note of surprise.

Allectius steeled himself before the judgment of his brothers. 'Yes.' He indicated the gap again. 'We leave one squad to help hold the redoubt. The remainder of the company marshal for a mechanised advance. We hit this point at this time and punch through.' He stepped back and studied the map. 'Once on the other side of the necron encroachment, we will have a clear path to our primary objective – the destruction of the installation the *Nomine* detected.'

'Only one squad to stay? Will that not compromise the defences?' asked the Lexicanium.

'A possibility,' admitted Allectius. 'Yet the bitter truth is staying with the whole company would not change the ultimate outcome. If we do this, we may enable the withdrawal from the system to resume.'

'Should we not at least attempt bombardment before we turn to this?' asked Calvus.

'If we launch an orbital strike and fail, we will have revealed what we know and doomed any other approach. The enemy has enough forces to defend that base and destroy us at the same time.' Allectius addressed the ship-captain. 'In all of our records, has a bombardment against a quantum field of this magnitude succeeded?'

'*Never*,' said Damasippa regretfully.

'They will attempt to intercept the strike force,' said Sisenna.

Allectius nodded. 'They will. Yet both neighbouring forces

are necron infantry, and for all the powers our foes possess, they are not quick on the uptake. We will move fast and strike hard, as Astartes are meant to.'

'A bold strategy,' opined Calvus thoughtfully.

'A dangerous one,' replied Allectius. 'Our chances of success will be low. It is, however, the only way I see to give the people of this world any chance at all.'

'It is preferable to lingering here under this pall, waiting for death.' A muscle in Tertulus' cheek spasmed.

Sisenna crossed his arms, armour creaking. 'I have faith in you, lieutenant. If you believe this is the wisest course forward, we shall see it through to the end.'

'I will need all of your support in what is to come. We must prepare to strike out immediately,' said Allectius.

'I will see to it that the serfs prep the Outriders and Repulsors that will be needed,' said Tertulus.

'I must make sure the plans for treating and transporting the wounded are in place, that the mortals may carry on in my absence.' Calvus turned to depart.

'Come, lieutenant,' said the Chaplain. 'We can adjourn to the chapel to discuss assignments for each squad. I have some insights into their fortes you may find useful.'

'Of course, Brother-Chaplain. Your counsel will be most appreciated. Ship-captain, continue to conduct auguries of the surface. Any information you can gather from orbit may mean the difference between victory and defeat,' said Allectius.

'It shall be as you command, my lord.' Damasippa signed off.

Allectius moved to follow Sisenna out of the command centre, but he could not stop from looking back at the doorway. The projection still hung there, glowing in the air. The genesis of a desperate plan, whose only virtue was being the best of bad options. His deepest instincts told him that to do nothing but stand their ground was to fail this world. The Emperor had created the Space Marines to take the fight to the enemy, not to sit idly by.

All he could do was hope he was leading them to something more than just another place to die.

CHAPTER 4

Gnaeus pushed his way through the gathered crowd. It seemed that everyone not busy with duties had gathered to see the Ultramarines depart. They stood in a mass outside the main gate, talking uneasily with each other and craning to get a look. Serfs and locals alike, faces grim and hands wringing. There was fear in the air, and not a little despair. He could practically smell it.

'They're abandoning us. Leaving us to be slaughtered,' he heard someone murmur. A stubble-cheeked person, hair styled like a local with neatly shaved rows.

'Don't say that,' a woman dressed like a medicae worker replied. 'If they hear you…'

Swallowing hard, Gnaeus continued on. It took the application of his elbows to a few people, but the artificer serf-turned-armsman at last reached the front of the crowd. He pulled up short as the wall of people abruptly ended. None had the audacity to push in close to the lords as they prepared to leave. That unspoken reverence was like a force field, keeping those present arranged in a rough semicircle.

He saw them. The mighty figures of the Ultramarines, resplendent even now in the bright blue of their war-plate. They were organised by mode of transportation, and engaged in checking their vehicles and wargear. Twenty-one of them gathered around the large Repulsor armoured transport and its more firepower-focused Repulsor Executioner cousins. Ten more on the Outrider bikes, providing an armed and highly mobile escort. Thirty-one Space Marines gathering for battle, an awesome sight in any circumstances. Even more serfs hurried amongst them, agents of the armoury, chanting the rites, burning incense and applying sacred unguents needed to awaken the machine-spirits to battle readiness.

'It's not given to us to question the will of the lords.' This time it was a man in old manufactorum leathers. There was no telling what work he did now. He seemed to be talking to himself.

Gnaeus knew that he should agree with the man. More, he should encourage him. Reach out and affirm his faith. Instead, he stood by with his stomach churning. Word had spread fast of the coming attack. No sooner had that sunk in than came the announcement that all but six of the Ultramarines would be departing to strike back at the enemy.

No one doubted the consummate warfare skill of the lords. Gnaeus had seen their sheer power first-hand, hadn't he? It was hard not to feel like they were being written off, however. The worst attack that Redoubt Primus had ever faced, and they would do it without the greatest source of their strength. What outcome was possible save annihilation?

A stillness fell across the gathered crowd and shook Gnaeus from his gloomy thoughts. The reason for the silence quickly became apparent: one of the lords was approaching, a mighty storm shield on one arm, a power sword at his back and a plasma pistol at his hip. He carried his helmet under one arm, leaving his scarred, patrician face visible. With his short hair combed forward about his brow, he was the picture of a warrior. The ominous figure of the Chaplain in his black armour and skull helm followed in his wake, like a reminder of mortality.

The approaching Space Marine stopped and surveyed the crowd. Then he spoke, a powerful voice that washed over them, amplified by his war-plate's vox-mitter. 'Greetings to all, citizens and serfs. A difficult time lies ahead. The enemy comes in force, and we find our backs to the wall. I see the fear in your eyes and hear it in your words. The enemy means to break you before they even arrive. They would rip the very soul from your body with their technomancy rather than face you in battle.

'I scorn them and their xenos cowardice.' The warrior drew the power sword sheathed at his back. It flashed in the sunlight. 'Do you see this blade? It has been borne by better men than I. They have fallen in righteous battle with our foe, yet the sword remains. Battered, but unbroken. I take up their cause as I took up this blade, and should I find my end another will do the same.'

Everyone was listening intently. Gnaeus could practically feel the held breath all around him.

'We go to confront the enemy in their lair, and break the chains that bind us here. It falls to you. Every moment that you buy, with las and with shell and with blood, will be another life saved to escape to orbit. The shuttles and the

Thunderhawks shall run to the end. No one will be abandoned. Not while you still draw breath and fight in the Emperor's name.'

The Space Marine ran his piercing blue gaze over the crowd. It was electric to lock eyes with the transhuman warrior, even for a brief second. 'If you stand and fight, you may die. Yet your memory will be carried to a thousand worlds, on the lips of a thousand saved souls, and set ablaze the spirit of the million worlds of the Imperium. Humanity stands as long as we stand together. You will live forever, and your vengeance will rise up and hurl these aliens back into the darkness that spawned them. Will you be the blade? Will you give me your oath?'

There was a moment of silence. Gnaeus wanted to step forward, to make a brave proclamation. He found himself frozen. The memory of those things in the hall, the blood that ran from them. It tied his tongue into knots.

'I will, my lord!' called someone else further along the gathering.

Gnaeus flushed with embarrassment. He hastened to add his voice, 'So will I, lord!', but it had become a chorus by then, and he was merely part of it.

The Ultramarines commander gave them a solemn nod in response, his voice punching through the shouts with ease. 'I did not doubt you. You have honoured the Emperor with your service these past months. Hold fast but a few days longer, and you shall join the line of heroes upon whom the Imperium was built.' He held up a hand in farewell. 'If the Emperor is willing, we shall see each other again. Until then, remember your oath.'

The Space Marine turned away then and returned to the vehicles. As he approached, the rest of the elite warriors began to board, either piling into the personnel carriers or mounting their dirtcycles. Engines roared, the hot wind of the Repulsors' turbines washing over the crowd and pulling at clothes and hair. A wave of grit came with it, forcing people to cover their eyes and look away. By the time it was safe to watch again, the Ultramarines were already down the road, headed off into enemy territory.

Some left immediately, but many in the crowd lingered, watching them shrink to specks that vanished into the distance. Gnaeus stood amongst them, arms crossed over his chest as if warding off cold. All he could hope was that this was not his last time watching the lords ride off to war.

With a sigh, the young artificer serf turned away to head back into the redoubt. There was work to be done.

The Ultramarines convoy pulled away from Redoubt Primus and set off through the dusty streets of the ruined city. Allectius did not glance back. Nevertheless, the memory of the mortals they left behind stayed with him. The experience of command had thus far been one of a steadily growing burden of responsibility. Duty was a heavy weight on any Space Marine, but it increased exponentially as his charges grew. No more could he concern himself only with his squad. Now the whole company, the whole world, the whole system, the fate of all hung in the balance of his decisions.

Mortals always imagined themselves discreet, and rarely were. Their low conversations and fearful whispers had been easy pickings for his keen hearing, even before the further enhancement of his armour's auto-senses. They imagined themselves abandoned to a grim fate. It was not a factual assessment, but was the outcome likely to be much different? Allectius was leading his forces on an assault whose chances were bleak at best, on the thin hope it would save more than a futile garrison.

His brothers were not confused about their prospects. It showed in the demeanour of those aboard the transport. The Ultramarines were never the most boisterous of the Adeptus Astartes, but the air here was downright grim. Each Space Marine was looking death in the eye and refusing to flinch. They waited with silent resolve, performing rites of maintenance on their wargear or meditating. He knew each of them by name and face, and had fought alongside them for decades now in service to the lord commander.

If this was to be the end, he was pleased to face it with warriors like these.

The assignment post was located near the gate to allow easy access to both exterior and interior work parties. The power feeds had been damaged during the last attack and the repairs were not complete yet, so the room was lit only by several dozen candles. It was always busy. People came and went constantly, reporting task completions and seeking new work to do.

At the centre of all this activity sat Ordinate Xavis at his desk. His grey Administratum robes were a bit worn around the edges, but his desk was as fastidiously arranged as always. He was eternally focused on the papers before him, scribbling away with both an ordinary pen and two autoquills attached to a body harness. Originally he had come to this world to oversee the allocation of resources during Cassothea's fortification. Once that ambition had crumbled under xenos assault, the Space Marines had swiftly put him to work organising the populace instead.

He glowered at Gnaeus through a pair of thick spectacles perched on the end of his sharp nose. 'Relocation duty.'

'What does that mean? Where do I report?'

Xavis huffed wearily. 'You will report to the underground storage facilities. There are still non-combatants sheltering in the redoubt. Even with the accelerated orbital evacuation schedule, some will remain by the time the enemy arrives, and they are being moved below to safeguard them against the coming assault.'

'When does your transport leave, adept?' called someone from the rear of the line mockingly.

Xavis' eyes narrowed. 'For your information, I was labelled essential personnel by the lords, so I will not be going off-world. You, however, Marrum…' The clerk made a note on a form without even looking. 'You will enjoy waste disposal duty, I trust.' He focused on Gnaeus again. 'Now, *move*. Next!'

Gnaeus hurried from the chamber and back into the dim corridors before he got an unfortunate reassignment of his own. He hadn't ever visited the deep storage vaults during his duties here, but he had patrolled the halls near them and knew where they were. Before he got there, however, he began to pass people lined up against the wall. Elders, children, the severely disabled. Some dragged bags of belongings with them, or carried them in crates.

They had fled here when the onslaught started, as necrons swept through lesser protected settlements. There was nowhere left to run. In some parts of the Imperium, they would have been abandoned as useless in the face of what was coming. That was not how the Ultramarines saw things, however. They would be protected as best they could, for as long as they could.

Most of them looked stricken, lost in their own worlds of misery. Few even glanced at him as he passed by. He couldn't blame them; the weight of the Nexus dragged everyone down. Those whose constitutions were already weakened had been especially hard hit. The grim tidings that followed the fall of the shroud hadn't helped spirits. He wondered how Elder Tulla was getting on in the care of the apothecarion. It would have been good to visit her and see how she was doing, but duty demanded most of his time.

He reached the head of the queue shortly thereafter, where a woman in local garb stood with a dataslate. She was middle-aged and rough-built, perhaps an agri-labourer or manufactorum worker. Either way, she was the one marking off the non-combatants as they arrived. Unfortunately, he saw that wasn't the total extent of her duties as he approached.

'What's in the bag?' she was asking the person before her. An old man with white hair, two children clinging to his legs.

The old man looked down at the sack. 'Everything we could carry when we left home.' His hoarse voice was listless.

'Sentimental goods,' she said brusquely and made a note on her slate. She reached out and grabbed the bag with one hand, tossing it onto a pile behind her.

This stirred some measure of emotion in the man, who took a half step forward and reached out a hand. 'But–'

'There's no room for anything but necessities,' she said flatly. 'You'll be provided what you need, everything else must be disposed of.' Noticing Gnaeus standing there she raised an eyebrow. 'You here to work?'

'I am,' the serf replied uneasily.

'Good,' she said flatly. 'Take these thirty down into the chambers and find them empty billets. Then report back.'

'Right,' Gnaeus said. He looked to the group, and it was hard not to focus on the tears in the old man's eyes. 'Come on then.' He tried to keep his voice as gentle as he could. 'Let's find all of you a safe place to sleep.'

He began to lead them down the circling stairs into the storage vaults. There were great lifts available, but those were reserved for large-scale supply movement. They followed along compliantly. There wasn't any fight left in these people. What good would struggling have done them, anyway, he mused. The Imperium might be protecting them at the moment, but no one ever imagined it was soft. Even when it was holding back the blade above your head, it was still the iron fist. Obey or be crushed.

They stepped off the staircase and into the vault. It was immediately clear why there was no room for belongings. People were being jammed in down here. The chamber was tremendous, designed for mass storage of supplies and materiel, but it had been converted wholesale into a hab block to make a hive-worlder sweat. Cots were stacked in bunks and laid end to end. A clothing dispensary lay at one end, where simple grey work garb was dispensed by orderlies. In the corner, a sanitation centre had been established, where the people were cleansed and deloused every day.

It was all painfully impersonal. No concession had been made to privacy or comfort. It was only about a third full at this point, but people were coming in at multiple entry points, guided by workers like Gnaeus himself. No one was being boisterous, but the rustle and murmur was constant by sheer weight of numbers. The acrid stink of too many bodies crammed into too small a space was inescapable.

The air circulators were running nonstop and each breath felt stale anyway. The only procedure seemed to be taking new arrivals to an empty bed and making a note of which number the cot was labelled with.

For just a moment, the young serf imagined being down here when the attack came. The flickering of the lights, maybe even darkness. The thunder above, dust raining down from the ceiling. Nothing to do but wait for the enemy to inevitably break through and find them. For the slaughter to begin.

Gnaeus swallowed hard. 'Come with me,' he said to the people he was leading again, and set off towards the nearest open spot.

One of the children left their elder to hurry up next to him as he walked. She couldn't have been more than six or seven years of age. Her hair was buzzed down to her skull to help avoid parasites, and her brown eyes seemed huge in her face.

'Are the xenos going to kill us all?' she asked.

Gnaeus was caught off guard and nearly tripped himself up on the leg of a cot. Her voice was so matter of fact. He glanced back, but those he was guiding were lost in their own miserable thoughts. No one was paying attention.

Once he'd recovered, he shook his head. 'No. We're going to kill all of them instead.'

The child took a moment to think this over. 'Aren't there a lot of them?'

Gnaeus nodded. 'There are. They're not a match for us though.' He tried to keep his voice full of a confidence he didn't feel.

'Why not?' she asked.

'Because the Emperor is with us,' he told her firmly. 'As

long as we stay in His light, no heretic or xenos can defeat us.'

'Oh,' she said uncertainly.

'What's wrong?' the serf asked.

'I just... I heard someone say it's all over. That we were all going to die here.' The girl had lowered her eyes to the floor ahead again.

Gnaeus stopped and dropped to one knee to look her in the face. 'Listen to me.' Once she was looking him in the eyes, he continued. 'The Emperor does not abandon the faithful. As long as there is courage and faith in your heart, He will be there with you.' He mustered a smile for her. 'I will be up there for you, and you will be down here handling the believing for me. Together, we'll drive these xenos back. What do you say?'

The girl nodded sombrely.

'The Emperor protects,' he told her, and squeezed her shoulder. He stood and looked back to the other two. 'Your bunk is here. For now the little ones can share.'

Gnaeus turned and hurried on, not wanting their thanks. He worked his way through the rest of his group as fast as he could. Part of him didn't want to remember their faces. He wished he believed what he had told her, that if they just held strong they would triumph. It might have been true for the Imperium as a whole. This was only one battle in a greater crusade, after all, and soldiers would flood towards the front by the millions as it went on. That would not save the souls of Cassothea over the days to follow, however.

'Hey, you! Serf!' The call snatched him from his thoughts, and he turned with a frown.

Another man was standing there, perhaps a decade older than Gnaeus himself. He had the look of someone who had not lived an easy life; a lined face and weathered skin. He was standing next to one of the cots, on which lay a still form. An older person, grey-haired and shrunken.

Gnaeus walked over to him. 'What's the situation?'

The man shook his head wearily. 'Another one. Give me a hand carrying him over.' He moved to get a hold of the person, seemingly sleeping.

'What?' Gnaeus asked. 'What's going on? Another what?'

The other worker looked exasperated for a moment, then peered at him and said, 'Ah. You're new to this assignment, huh?'

'Yes,' Gnaeus replied.

'Soul death,' the man said. 'People down here have been succumbing left and right. By the time the aliens get here, they're all going to be dead anyway.' There was an exhausted bitterness to the words.

'We have to keep faith,' said Gnaeus softly.

'Yeah, sure. Now grab the other side.'

They hefted the form of the old person between them. There was something curiously nondescript about the body now. It breathed, if shallowly, but there was something doll-like and empty about its face. Whoever this was was gone now, and only the crude clay of their existence remained. All Gnaeus could hope was that they'd gone to the Emperor's side.

They moved on through the rows of beds, hauling the limp form. It was also curiously light, as if when the soul had gone it had taken something material with it. That, or perhaps the person had simply been starving for some time anyway. Rationing was strict to make sure everyone had enough, but it was hard to make sure some took what was meant for them.

'Are we taking them to the apothecarion?' Gnaeus asked.

The other man snorted. He glanced over. 'Oh, you're not… no. I heard at first they were checking them all, making sure there was nothing to be done. But then the Lord Apothecary left, and now…' He shook his head.

'So where are we taking them?' Gnaeus honestly wasn't sure he wanted to know.

'We're almost there,' the other said and nodded ahead.

Gnaeus looked and realised they were approaching one of the freight lifts. More bodies were already stacked in the space, listlessly sprawled against each other. The lights of the cab were off, either from a malfunction or to keep people from having to stare at the heaped forms. The serf found himself trying not to look any of them in the eyes, hollow and sightless as they were.

'Here we go,' said the other man, and they added the body they'd carried to the macabre collection. He turned to leave.

'Wait,' Gnaeus called. 'We can't just leave them here, right? There has to be more to it?'

'Once the lift is full, we'll send it up and other people will offload them, take them elsewhere.'

'Where?' asked the serf.

The man paused. 'I don't know. I didn't ask,' he said flatly. He left without another word.

Gnaeus swept his gaze over the surrounding bodies. He could find out, perhaps. Go demand answers. A chill ran up his spine. They would be well taken care of, wherever they were going, he told himself.

Every second spent here was time spent not doing his duty. He had work to do.

Gnaeus worked for hours upon hours. By the time his shift ended, he was struggling to put one foot in front of the other on the way to his quarters. On a physical level, the work was not particularly gruelling, but the shroud of the Nexus made everything weigh heavier. Emotions were where the real burden had lain. These helpless people, waiting for a fate that seemed inevitably grim. Others had already succumbed even where they should have been safe, slain by the machinations of the xenos.

He wanted to scream it out in the hallway, to just cave and collapse. Instead, he shoved it all down. It was a knot in his stomach, a roiling nausea that wouldn't go away. *One foot in front of the other,* he told himself. *One day after the next. It will all be over soon, one way or another.*

That was when the sound of music pulled him from his thoughts. Gnaeus followed the sound, winding through the corridors of the redoubt. It cleared as he came closer to the source. The familiar strains of pyrophonic music, accompanied by dozens of voices raised in chorus. The comforting sounds of the Imperial Creed. His steps sped up as if of their own volition, carrying him on to the threshold of the chamber itself.

Light poured out into the corridor from the great hall. It had been set up as a cathedral to the God-Emperor. Statuary honouring the Master of Mankind and His primarchs and saints lined the sides, and the pews were already crowded with a number of people. At the front a priest of the Ecclesiarchy led a chorus in their song, praising the Emperor. The front of the altar showed the scene of Him being interred upon the Golden Throne, the moment of His ascension.

Gnaeus walked forward unsteadily, finding his way into a pew and falling to his knees next to others already there. His chest ached and his stomach still turned, pressure built up inside him with no release. Then he heard the choked sob next to him, and realised that everyone was in tears. Some wept with their heads down in silence, others wracked by helpless sobs.

His own eyes prickled and his throat felt tight. He leaned forward until his forehead rested against the wood of the pew before him, cold against his skin. There was no holding it back now. The pain was real, but he wasn't alone.

The first tears streamed down Gnaeus' face, and he raised his eyes to the altar.

God-Emperor, help us, he mouthed. *For we are lost and afraid.*

CHAPTER 5

'Necron signatures incoming on auspex!' came the call from the Repulsor pilot, Brother Accidus.

Lieutenant Allectius clenched his fist. That was the end of the best-case scenario. They were hurtling along at high speeds across broken terrain, accompanied by the surrounding Outrider bikes. Now they were reaching the point directly between the nearest masses of enemy units. He had allowed himself to hope they were going to slip through unnoticed. Fortune did not favour them today, it seemed.

He accessed the transport's noospheric connection to pull the auspex readings up on his optical overlays. There was no denying the readings: enemy energy signatures coming in fast, quickly enough that the transport had no chance of escaping them.

'Tomb blades,' he muttered. Few necron forces moved with such speed, and their erratic approach pattern sealed the identification. Repulsors had many virtues, but overwhelming speed was not one of them. This foe would catch them. In such a situation, the Codex Astartes prescribed pushing on; to slow down in an effort to purge this first wave of threats would be to allow deadlier elements to be brought to bear.

The lieutenant sent a vox-burst to the transport pilots and the Outriders. 'Repulsors, you are to continue towards the objective regardless of enemy activity. Outriders, engage any enemies that threaten the transports. Reduce incoming fire to the transports by any means necessary.' As acknowledgments rolled in, he cued the squad vox-net with a thought. 'Sergeant Fulgentius, get your men on the vehicle's weapons. I will take the gatling cannon for myself.'

'That's the most exposed gunnery position, brother-lieutenant!' the sergeant protested.

Allectius paused part of the way up the ladder, injecting a wry note into his reply. 'Then I suggest you prepare yourself to take command.' All humour faded. 'I will not allow others to take risks in this battle while I hide in the transport.' Without waiting for a response he finished scaling up to the turret.

His helmet broke through into sunlight. It seemed incongruous against the grim weight of the Nexus; even the Space Marines felt the pall, though they bore up under it better than their mortal auxiliaries. They were entering a mountain pass, lush with plant life and run through with rivers. Beautiful, were it not for the dark figures racing down the side of the mountain on the left side towards them. His interface with the vehicle's sensor suite painted them in reds: hostile targets. The tomb blades, closing fast to engagement range.

Each was a nearly complete circle of alien alloy. The

outer edge was marked by technosorcerous outthrusts of unknown purpose and a weapon hung under the front end. Within lay part of the skeletal figure of a necron warrior, oddly subsumed into the structure of the vehicle itself. They zipped along several feet above the ground, quick and agile. Their xenos technology seemed to echo the anti-gravity field of the Repulsor itself, but if it was similar then theirs was capable of a nimble precision that the transport lacked.

The rangefinder on his auto-senses flashed a green rune. 'All gunners, engage at your discretion,' Allectius broadcast.

The lieutenant turned his attention to his own weapon. The heavy onslaught gatling cannon was a formidable device. The receiver was as big as his torso, handles mounted on either side. He took hold and the mount connected with his optical overlays, marking a reticule on them with supplementary targeting data available. Faded ghostmarks indicated other gunners choosing their targets, ensuring a minimum of wasted fire. He slid the crosshairs over the first of the oncoming enemies and squeezed the trigger.

The gun's multiple barrels spun into action. Within a beat of his hearts it spoke with a thunderous roar, a tongue of fire marking a stream of rounds being unleashed. It shook the form of even the mighty Primaris Marine wielding it. Other weapons on both transports were coming to life simultaneously, spewing a devastating wave of munitions towards the enemy. Stub bullets, bolt-rounds, Icarus rockets, las-beams and more were unleashed.

The first of the hovering necron skirmishers was torn apart in the blink of an eye. Green fire washed the landscape and shattered chunks of unknown alloys tumbled away. The rest scattered instantly, their close-knit closing formation dissolving into evasive manoeuvres. It was not swift enough.

Two more spun away, ragged holes punched in their frame. Another vanished into an explosion as a rocket struck home.

Some of the tomb blades were harder to kill, upgraded with strange technomantic defences. One came under a rain of Ironhail stubber rounds. None of them landed, scattered away by a powerful gravitic field. The focused beams of a laser destroyer mount slashed towards another. Such a weapon would have shredded a far more formidable vehicle. Instead the annihilating energies vanished in a flash of dark energy, shunted away by unknown mechanisms.

Allectius swept the rattling onslaught cannon in their wake, doing his best to track the fast-moving attackers. They had entered their own weapons range now, and counterfire had begun lashing at the Ultramarines convoy. Gauss streams like green lightning flensed through metal and flesh in an eye-blink. Caught in a conflux of such attacks, an Outrider dissolved into their constituent particles before they knew they had been hit. A stream of particle beams, flickering in blue-white and so fast that they were scarcely visible, stitched up the side of the Repulsor towards Allectius. Each impact scattered sparks. It stopped only a foot away when a lascannon shot plucked that enemy from mid-air, shearing it into molten halves.

Outriders began peeling away to engage the tomb blades, keeping the transports as safe as they could. They were caught up in whirling grounded dogfights with the enemy in moments, manoeuvring desperately for advantage. Their dual bolt rifles spat fire the moment they got a targeting lock on one of the tomb blades. Even as the lieutenant manned his weapon, he saw such an engagement play out. An Outrider came in from the side of a hovering necron, bolt-fire punching out the middle section and leaving it to spin itself apart.

The Ultramarine had his own pursuer, however, coming up fast on his six. Allectius swung the gatling cannon around to try to cover his warrior. Just before he got there, green energy struck out and evaporated the rear third of the dirtcycle and most of the biker along with it. The lieutenant's hands tightened in fury on the weapon's grips. He tracked his fire after the xenos responsible. The cannonade fire swept across the necron and pulverised it, leaving only scrap in its wake.

A red rune of warning flashed on his overlays. 'Significant energy build-up detected,' announced the dull voice of an alarm servitor. Still new to the command interface, the lieutenant had become distracted by the raging battle around him. Allectius whirled to the indicated spot and his eyes widened. A Doomsday Ark and a pair of Annihilation Barges had closed in while the Ultramarines were engaged.

The ark was a great skeletal-framed craft, underslung by a massive cannon and lined with gauss flayers. The barges appeared like nothing so much as upsized and up-gunned tomb blades. The former was losing ground, but the cannon beneath it was already glowing an ominous green in the depths. A full-charge blast, draining its engines but devastating when unleashed.

'Brace for impact!' Allectius shouted into the vox.

An emerald lance stabbed out from that great gun. The lieutenant's auto-senses were forced to polarise for a moment to keep the brilliance from damaging his eyes. Thus, he only heard the impact rather than saw it: a series of explosive blasts that rattled the ground and threw him against the side of the turret. When his vision cleared, he saw where it had hit. One of the Repulsor Executioners, the *Fortitude of Calth*, had a great blackened scar carved into it.

Smoke poured from the damage, and the vehicle was listing and swerving.

The other Executioner, *Relief of Corillia*, brought its turret around and returned fire with a heavy laser destroyer mount. The ruby energy struck home against the ark, but one of the beams was deflected by the shimmering dome of the necron vehicle's quantum shielding. The other scored only minimal damage, raking a glowing line down the hostile craft's side.

'Initialise a hunter-slayer missile, Brother Accidus,' Allectius sent to the pilot of his own craft, *Agnathio the Unifier*. Without waiting, he switched to a vox-link with the *In Nomine Imperator* in orbit. 'Ship-Captain Damasippa, are you monitoring our situation?'

'I am, lord lieutenant. We are maintaining position above your location,' came the quick, if staticky, reply.

'I am providing you an auspex link. Prepare for immediate bombardment at the indicated coordinates,' Allectius said.

'That is close to your forces, my lord. There is a chance–'

A low-power beam swept forth from the Doomsday Ark, scything one of the Outriders into atomised oblivion in the blink of an eye.

'Obey, ship-captain!' commanded the lieutenant. He triggered a burst of fire that swept another of the tomb blades from the air. They were scattering now, their numbers depleted but their task complete.

'As you command, my lord,' she replied.

Accidus had finished carrying out his orders by that point. The hunter-slayer launched on a tail of smoke and fire, howling off in an arc towards the enemy. A single-shot weapon, it was guided by a machine-spirit capable of tracking priority targets. It struck home dead-on against the ark, punching through the hull and detonating in an eruption of arcane internal workings. The *Relief* added its own las-fire to the attack, scoring another glancing hit against the enemy vehicle.

Then a series of massive explosions began to walk their way down the mountainside, sweeping across the three enemy vehicles – fire from orbit, the *Nomine* bringing its formidable bombardment cannon to bear. While it could not be called a precision weapon at this scale, even being caught in the blast zone of one of the macrocannon shells was enough to wreak havoc among the necron armour. They were lost from sight in a cloud of smoke and dust that followed.

As they emerged from the debris back into view, it was clear that the ark was in a bad way. It was slewing back and forth, green fire crawling across its battered frame. They were pulling away from it now. All of them, that is, save the *Fortitude*. The gravitic battle tank was falling away from her allies just as quickly, turbines damaged. Worse, while the necron machinery would repair itself in due time, they had no such capability.

The tactical calculations were swift and simple. The conclusion bitter.

'*Fortitude*,' began Allectius into the vox.

'*We see it too, lieutenant,*' came the swift response. '*We will buy you the time you need to break away.*'

The Ultramarines commander could not repress a spark of self-recrimination burning in his chest. If he had seen the ark sooner… 'Courage and honour, *Fortitude*.'

'*In Guilliman's name!*' came the reply.

The *Fortitude of Calth* broke from the formation immediately, coming around to face the oncoming enemies. The sharp turn drove up a cloud of dirt from the force of the gravitic fields and the howling wind of the turbine. The hatch slammed down and the battle-brothers within poured out, disembarking to join the fight. Eradicators with their melta rifles held ready, led by Sergeant Proclus. Lexicanium Tertulus emerged with them, force sword and bolt pistol already drawn. Arcs of warp-fire crawled about his head and arms as he prepared to bring his powers to bear.

The last thing Allectius saw of them was the *Fortitude* firing its devastating macro plasma incinerator as the enemy came into range. One of the annihilation barges came apart under the stream of white starfire, evaporating like water under a hot sun. Then they swerved around the next foothill in the valley and their brethren were lost to sight. Outnumbered and outgunned, they could be relied upon to stand until the end against the xenos.

'Courage and honour,' whispered Allectius again, to himself alone this time. Then he turned to clamber back down the ladder from the turret. Activating a wide vox, he said, 'All remaining forces, full speed ahead. We must not waste the time that is given to us.'

'It's a distress signal,' said Chaplain Sisenna.

It had been a few hours since the battle in the valley, and they seemed to have left behind their pursuers thanks to the sacrifice of the *Fortitude* and those aboard her. Now, rumbling across the open plains beyond the mountains, they had picked up the beacon Sisenna spoke of.

'From where?' asked Allectius. They were on different vehicles, but a private vox-loop allowed the command cadre to confer easily.

'The wreck of the Memory of Vega,' said Apothecary Calvus. Even he seemed nonplussed by this development.

The *Memory of Vega* was a Gladius-class frigate that had entered Cassothea's system a little over a month ago. It had not belonged to the Ultramarines, but rather to one of their successor Chapters, the Doom Eagles. They were also of the line of the Primarch Guilliman, but had separated thousands of years ago after the end of the Horus Heresy. The bond was still a strong one, and the Ultramarines would have gladly helped their kinsmen.

Unfortunately, the *Memory* had been badly damaged when it arrived. It had lost control as it proceeded in-system, and the local fleet elements had not been able to scramble fast enough to save it. Lost to the planet's gravity well, it had plummeted to the surface in a catastrophic crash. Ground rescue attempts had been made, but it was far beyond the company's reach by that time. None had managed to get there successfully.

'Why is this the first we are hearing of it?' asked the lieutenant.

'The signal is not a strong one,' replied Sisenna. 'It is far smaller than the ship's own transponder. No one would have heard it from orbit. The mountains blocked the signal from reaching Redoubt Primus. We are the first force to get beyond them.'

'Is there any chance of it being a trap?'

'It is not impossible,' admitted the Chaplain. 'The ident-tags are in line with crusade records, however.'

Allectius mulled this over. He had originally intended to avoid the wreck. It was directly in the shortest path to the plateau, but no one knew what hazards might linger there. They could little afford more losses.

He pulled Brother Accidus into their vox-net. 'How long will a diversion around these coordinates take?'

'An hour and a half,' said the pilot promptly.

The lieutenant took a deep breath. The decision was ultimately his, he reminded himself. He was in command of the company now. 'We will investigate this signal. If there is a chance our cousins are still alive, I will not abandon them.'

Gnaeus followed along beside Watch-Lieutenant Seria. She was one of the militia officers, the original defenders of Cassothea before the Ultramarines and their auxiliaries had arrived. She was dressed in a dark blue uniform with a stub pistol belted at her side. Half of her head was swathed in bandages, including one of her eyes. Fresh blood stained the fabric. Whatever had hit her, she was lucky – even glancing hits from the xenos weapons were often mortal.

All of the redoubt's defences were being braced against the coming onslaught. The officer led the way back to the tunnel at the opposite end of the courtyard from the gate. It was big enough to allow the passage of armour from the redoubt's internal armoury. They did not travel far up the great causeway, however. Instead they turned almost immediately into a side corridor that led to a spiral staircase going up. This level was where the sentry guns were kept, each one in its own small outward-facing bunker.

Most of said arsenal consisted of the Tarantulas brought by the Ultramarines. Each was a squat construction, almost five feet tall and twenty feet wide. Each one mounted a specific armament. A pair of heavy bolters was the standard, but assault cannons, lascannons and multi-meltas were also available. Their simplistic machine-spirit automatically targeted foes that came within range. They had served well for months, but ammo supplies ran thin and powercells were wearing out.

Seria brought him to one of the assault cannon platforms. There was no obvious damage to it. Activation runes glowed green on its interface panel, all save one. The targeting function was a blinking red. Gnaeus knelt next to the weapon and rapped the rune with his knuckles. It didn't change.

Gnaeus sighed. He had hoped to avoid opening the machine up. There was a certain decorum to be observed. 'I need you to turn away,' he said.

She seemed a bit relieved to do so, truth be told. He turned back to the machine and opened one of the side panels. Within lay a complicated technomantic mess where the machine-spirit slept. The problem was immediately clear. One of the pathways was burnt out.

The proper rites to interact with such a thing were in binharic, beyond his ability to replicate. Instead he hummed quietly to himself in the closest approximation he could. Hopefully the spirit would appreciate the effort rather than be affronted at how far it fell short. He rerouted the path as quickly as he could. As he established the connection a spark leapt to his fingers with a distinct pop. He yanked his stinging hand back with a hiss.

'Are you okay?' Seria asked anxiously.

'I'm fine, I'm fine. Almost done.' Gnaeus closed the panel up and reactivated the turret. The activation runes blinked on green one by one. The last one came on amber now and he sighed. 'That's what I was afraid of.'

She turned around and studied it. 'What does that mean?'

'All I've been able to do is patch it. Any target-rich environment and it's going to burn out again within minutes.'

'Ah,' she said, and gave a weary laugh.

Gnaeus raised an eyebrow questioningly.

Seria waved her hand at the ammo drums. 'It only has a

couple thousand rounds left, artificer. It'll run empty before it ever burns out.'

Gnaeus huffed a laugh too. 'Consider it fixed, then.'

He stepped up to the firing slit on the bunker. Shadows were growing throughout the rusted ruins of the city as the sun slipped towards the horizon. This was the last sunset he was ever going to see, he realised. It didn't feel real, even so. Maybe some things didn't sink in until the very end.

A klaxon sounded then. His heart pounded, and he heard the intake of her breath. She stepped up beside him as the lonely wail echoed through the streets.

'They've reached the edge of the city,' she said.

'I'd better get back to the gate and gear up.' Gnaeus offered her a hand. 'The Emperor protects, watch-lieutenant.'

Seria accepted the grip. 'The Emperor protects, artificer.'

Allectius could not deny that command was resting heavily on him. They had lost half of their Outriders and one of their battle transports in their first clash with the necrons. It seemed dubious that Lieutenants Triarius or Falerius would have made these mistakes. The company had taken losses under their leadership, it was true, but Allectius had lost almost a third of his command in a single clash, losses he could ill afford.

Could they still succeed when they reached the enemy installation? Had they ever stood a chance? There was no way to know until the matter was already decided. The Codex Astartes contained great wisdom on warfare, but nothing he had read told him how to confront this uncertainty. It had been simpler as a sergeant; he had led his men into battle and trusted those above him. Now the gap to his superiors was so great they might as well not exist. There was only him.

The lieutenant's mind was still uneasy when a rune flashed on his visual overlays, indicating they were close to the crash site. He rose from his seat in the transport, clambering up into the turret once more to get a view on what lay before them. Auspex feeds were all well and good, but there was a lot to be said for direct observation. Wind whistled around him as he emerged into the sunlight once more.

The open plains lay all around him, marked here by waving grass several feet tall. A crumpled trail lay behind the Ultramarines forces where the grav-field had smashed it flat. The enemy would have no problem following them if they found it. Allectius welcomed that. Even if the xenos had not assuredly had more esoteric means of tracking them, any hope of evading their foes was gone. Better now to draw as many away from the redoubt as they could.

Ahead of them lay what they had come to find, however, and it dominated the landscape in that direction. A Gladius-class frigate was just under a mile long when intact. This one was not. It had come apart as it fell through the atmosphere. Multiple fragments, each one hundreds of feet in length, lay in massive craters. Some were marked by great pillars of black smoke, still burning even a month after the impact.

The nearest section appeared to be a chunk of one of the macrocannon turrets. Only one of the barrels had survived the descent even remotely intact, and it was bent badly. Even twisted so, it was bigger than either of the tanks in the convoy. The mechanisms of the turret itself were displayed, a ravaged mess of mechanical innards as big as a hab unit. It was strange to see such secrets exposed to crude daylight.

Allectius tapped into the *Unifier*'s auspex readings again.

The vox-beacon they had followed to this place was coming from one of the fragments – a piece of the ship near the middle of the debris field, itself nearly a thousand feet long. It jutted up into the sky like the haft of a broken spear, keeping its shape only due to the vessel's adamantium keel.

They were crossing a sharp transition now, the thick grass dying away into ash and dirt. The fires from the initial impact must have spread this far before rains could put them out. Their target rose before them.

Allectius began to climb back down. 'Sergeant Fulgentius, detail a fire-team of your men to accompany me in investigating.'

The sergeant nodded and selected a handful of his brothers.

'Apothecary Calvus,' said Allectius.

'Yes, lieutenant?' replied the medicae specialist.

'You will accompany me as well. If some of our cousins are still alive, they may need your attention. If not, at least we can try to retrieve their gene-seed.'

'As you command,' Calvus replied.

The Repulsor pulled to a halt and the hatch opened, allowing the knot of seven Astartes to emerge. They set off towards the looming shape of the broken ship, ash crunching beneath the heavy tread of their boots. As the loud engines of their vehicles fell behind them, the lieutenant listened closely, alert for any sign of a hostile presence. Instead, all that greeted him was grim silence. The only sounds beyond the presence of the Space Marines were creaking groans from within the fragment. No birds flew overhead, no small animals scampered about.

'Lieutenant,' said Brother Marcellus to get his attention.

One of the members of the fire-team that accompanied them, he motioned to the ground nearby.

Allectius walked over to look for himself. Fragments of destroyed necrons littered the dirt. Each was burnt or scoured into unrecognisable lumps. He only knew what they were because he had seen such refuse before. Such pieces were often left when one of the xenos was teleported away, the unsalvageable parts abandoned. The ground was trampled with marks, too muddled to identify.

'Someone is alive here. And fighting,' observed Calvus.

'Or something,' Allectius replied. 'We push on.'

A direct path seemed wisest; there was no time to waste. Allectius led them straight towards the signal. A shadowed rent in the hull allowed ingress into the ruined ship. The darkness of the interior swallowed them, and his auto-senses switched over to preysight to compensate for a lightless environment. The groans of the hull were louder now, echoing around them ominously. A reminder that this place was not stable, if he needed one.

They made their way up into the belly of the broken vessel. This place was ravaged – whatever had not been destroyed before impact had been crushed on landing. Some corridors had collapsed completely, forcing them to navigate around as best they could. Everything was burned and scarred. The substance of the walls was melted and shaped in unpleasant organic fractals.

Apothecary Calvus was monitoring an auspex as they went. As they approached a turn, he spoke up. 'The interference here is serious, but there appears to be movement ahead.'

Allectius glanced back at him. The approach of the Ultramarines was not subtle: if there was anyone up ahead, they would have heard the heavy tread of boots on decking.

'To any survivors of the *Memory of Vega*, we are not your foes. I am Allectius of the Ultramarines.'

Only the moans and sighs of the broken vessel answered him.

The lieutenant motioned two of the fire-team forward. They went around the corner with their weapons at the ready.

'Emperor be merciful,' said Brother Opiter.

Allectius followed in their wake. What had the battle-brother's attention was a nightmare. The scorched bones of mortals filled the corridor ahead. They were conjoined with each other in impossible ways, and even fused into the walls. Skeletal jaws were locked in eternal screams, and grasping fingers were frozen, clawing for release.

'A failure of the Geller field?' asked Opiter.

A thought to give even a Space Marine pause. The Geller field was all that kept out the inchoate madness when a ship travelled via warp drive. Without it, energies of unfathomable corruption and merciless predators of the immaterium flooded in unchecked. Oblivion was the kindest fate that waited for those who suffered such a misfortune.

'Not a complete failure, or the ship would not have survived to reach the planet.' Calvus stepped up to survey the horror. 'But even a flicker can cause untold damage, especially if it forces a ship to make an emergency translation to the materium.'

'It would explain the crash. If too many of the crew serfs were lost, they would struggle to maintain control even once the immediate danger had passed,' said Allectius. He activated his vox to report the potential of warp contamination to the Chaplain, but the only response was a howl of static. Shrieks and screams echoed through the white noise. They spoke of a torment beyond reckoning. He terminated the link with a thought.

'Keep moving.' Allectius kept his pistol in his hand as he walked, Veritas at the ready on his other arm. Dangers could linger long in a place so contaminated.

'We approach the signal,' noted Brother Marcellus.

It was a curious effect as they got closer, as though something in this part of the ship had held the worst of the destruction at bay. Dead bodies were still strewn about, but here at least they seemed more natural. Less twisted into macabre insanity. There were signs here too of a more familiar sort of destruction – rents carved in the walls, and blast marks from bolter-rounds. Allectius quickened his steps but stayed alert.

They turned the next corner and there they were: the fallen forms of six Space Marines clad in their ceramite war-plate. Each was of the Second Generation, just like the Primaris Marines of Allectius' own company. Where the Ultramarines were clad in brilliant blue, white and gold, their successor kin wore silver with red. All save one, that is: the last of them wore the black of the Chaplaincy, but for the silver of his left shoulder pad that still bore the skull and wings heraldry of his Chapter. His crozius arcanum was laid across his chest. All of the bodies were arranged with similar reverence.

'Apothecary,' said Allectius.

Calvus hurried forward, stopping at each body to interface with their armour and check for life signs. The wounds a few of them bore were obviously lethal even for a Space Marine: staved in chests, or holes melted clean through their heads. They would have fought to the end, as any Space Marine did when no other option remained. Especially those of this line; the Doom Eagles were of a morbid bent, known to proclaim themselves already dead when they entered the Emperor's service. They would hesitate little to sacrifice a life that was already lost.

Whatever foe they had battled, no trace of it remained. More confirmation of the foulness of the warp. Allectius pressed a fist to the aquila on his chestplate reverently. To fall battling the Archenemy was the best end a Space Marine could–

'Step away from my fallen brothers.' It was a cold and forceful demand, accompanied by the sizzle of a power field's activation.

Calvus froze, and the lieutenant motioned to him to move away from the bodies as demanded. Allectius looked up slowly, keeping his hands away from his weapons. Another Space Marine stood there, clad in the colours of a Doom Eagles Chaplain. He carried no crozius, however. Instead, a great sword was held out before him threateningly, the arcs of disruption energy crawling up and down the blade.

'Be at ease, cousin.' Allectius did his best to keep his voice firm but calming. 'You are among allies, kin of Guilliman's line.'

The Chaplain examined each of them, his sword unwavering. Allectius took the chance to study him in turn. He was struck by some differences from the commonly seen Chaplain garb. He was a Judiciar instead, a subset of new Chaplains training to lead by example. His helmet was sealed over the mouth with a solid welded plate, symbolic of his oath of silence observed in the press of battle. A great hourglass hung from his hip, next to the holster of his bolt pistol. The glimmering grains ran through it with a curious slowness. His armour was battered in a dozen places, signs of fierce fighting.

'Are you hurt, cousin?' asked the lieutenant. 'We have an Apothecary with us.'

'I…' The Chaplain shook his head. 'You are Ultramarines. After all this time?'

'We are. We detected your signal when we crossed the mountains. We could not reach this place before, and did not know of any survivors. Are you the only one left?'

The sword slowly lowered. 'Yes. Five were lost in the crash, and we never found them. Three others succumbed to their wounds in the day that followed. We had purged this place of the worst warp spawn by then, but it was not long before the xenos attacked thereafter.' The Doom Eagle walked forward slowly and knelt next to the dead Chaplain. 'I envy them.'

Allectius looked to Calvus, but the Apothecary could only gesture a lack of comprehension. The successor Chapter was known to have a morose mien; there was no way to tell what was normal here.

The lieutenant cleared this throat. 'Come then. At the very least, let us leave this place behind. We will explain our situation to you, and you will be welcome among us.'

They passed back through the dark corridors of the lost ship. Allectius was not sorry to leave it behind. Had he the means, he would have consigned it to destruction lest the taint spread from it. As it was, all he could do was hope that someday they would have the opportunity they lacked today, and be glad they rescued their kinsman from the wreckage.

Chaplain Sisenna strode from his transport to meet them as they emerged once more into daylight. He paused as he saw who accompanied them. 'We lost contact with you.

Grim news has arrived. The necron onslaught against Redoubt Primus has begun. I was preparing a retrieval force.'

'Not necessary, Brother-Chaplain,' replied Allectius. Knowing that the enemy even now besieged their allies filled him with an unease he did his best to conceal. So many choices had been made, their effects unfolding all around them. He motioned to their companion, who pressed a fist to his chest in salute. 'We found our cousin within, though sadly the rest of his brothers were lost in battle.'

'An unfortunate loss, but a tremendous boon to see a fellow dedicate of the Reclusiam as well.' Sisenna stepped forward and took the Judiciar's arm in a firm warrior's grip. 'What is your name, cousin?'

'Bittrien,' the younger Chaplain replied. He took in the armoured vehicles with their Outrider escorts. 'You go to war.'

'Yes,' Allectius said. 'Were it in my power, I would return you to your Chapter. Instead we have come upon you as we move to strike against the very heart of xenos power on this world.'

Bittrien absorbed this with a moment of thoughtful silence. 'It is well it is not within your power to send me away then, for I have no wish to go. I am alone, and must honour my Chapter with my deeds. I will not have it said that the Doom Eagles were not there when their kinsmen needed them most.' He squared his shoulders. 'Whatever battle you face today, it is my battle as well. In Guilliman's name.'

Allectius could not help but be moved by this display of fidelity. He reached out to clap the Judiciar on the pauldron. 'We are honoured to have you.'

Sisenna motioned for him to follow. 'Come, cousin. I

shall explain the details of our situation aboard the Executioner as we continue towards our objective.'

The lieutenant glanced around. 'Yes. It is past time we were back about our labours. Come, brothers.' He set out for his own transport with the fire-team and the Apothecary following him.

Allectius watched as the tall grass of the plains raced by once again. It was not far now to the plateau where the necron energy signature had been detected. Soon they left the flat lands behind again, ascending once more into rocky, mountainous terrain. The sun was beginning to sink low on the horizon, dyeing the land in delicate pinks, oranges and yellows. It should have been a beautiful sight, but it seemed dark and empty somehow. The pall of the Pariah Nexus was growing in strength, either by time or proximity.

Then he saw it, silhouetted against the setting sun – a great spike, slender and black, that rose into the sky from upon the plateau that lay ahead. The rangefinder on his overlays reported that it was over fifteen hundred feet tall. Looking at it made his eyes ache strangely, as if it was bright on some spectrum that he could not perceive.

'Sisenna, do you see this?' he asked into his vox.

'Yes, lieutenant,' came the grim voice of the Chaplain. 'The shroud upon the immaterium strengthens as well.'

'We draw close to the objective,' agreed Allectius.

Allectius could see the drain on the rest of the brothers in his transport, too, a weariness that showed in their biologis feeds, a slumping of their helmets. The Space Marines had been resistant to the effects of the Nexus thus far, perhaps due to the fierce faith they all possessed. Not in the God-Emperor of the Ecclesiarchy, of course, but in the principles that drove them. Even this transhuman drive had its limits, however. This increased effect would begin to wear them down.

As they drew closer smaller structures began to become visible as well, in the tell-tale geometric shapes of necron architecture. There was no sign of enemy forces, but the xenos manipulated dimensions the way that a forge-master shaped metal. The lieutenant had no doubt in his mind that when they struck the vile machina would defend their technomantic creation.

Waiting would only play into enemy hands. Necrons never rested or wavered. They would never be vulnerable. The Space Marines would only weaken against the powers of the Nexus, and even now their comrades were sorely pressed at Redoubt Primus.

Allectius took a deep breath and opened a vox to all of his brothers in the convoy.

'Ultramarines, prepare for assault. We march for Macragge!'

CHAPTER 6

Gnaeus gripped the shotgun tightly, trying to ignore the tremble in his hands and the slickness of the sweat against the inside of his gloves.

'Steady!' called one of the officers from the Cassothean militia.

They were gathered in the great entry hall, more than a hundred serfs and locals banded together. They huddled behind rockcrete blocks and whatever other makeshift cover had been hurried into place. A woman in labourer garb clutching a lasgun stood next to Gnaeus, hastily conscripted to fight like many here. The shrieks of strafing necron craft were constant, a terrible accompaniment to the thud of gunnery and the hiss and crackle of xenos weapons. Ahead lay the great plasteel gates, the last obstacle between the ruined city overrun with the twisted constructs and the corridors of the redoubt.

They could hear the Tarantula sentry guns hammering

away. Gnaeus could imagine it. A constant flood of bolter shells and more, slashing back and forth across an encroaching wave of silver forms lit by lurid green. Technomantic bodies would fall, sparking and thrashing, only to rise again and rejoin the flood. The defenders all knew the reality. The guns had been low on ammo even when the fight began. Soon they would–

Silence. It was one Tarantula, then another, a spreading quiet that washed over the gathered soldiery. Rattling to a halt as their ammo stores depleted. Eyes showed white in fear as they searched the ceiling above, begging the guns to spring to life once more. It didn't happen.

'Steady!' that officer called again. His voice wavered. Gnaeus couldn't blame him. Who wouldn't be scared? The necrons were death, and they were coming for them all.

Any reassured by the plasteel slab before them embraced a false comfort. The serf had heard the reports, seen the eldritch weapons of the necrons at work. Soon his fears were confirmed. The gate began to spark and fizzle. It was like some strange time-lapsed hololith of a stone eroded by water. Eerie emerald light began to eke through cracks and gaps, dyeing the faces of the waiting Imperials in sickly colours. The metal layers gave way completely in one section, and he saw the first skull-face and hunched frame beyond.

The necrons were inside.

People panicked, and the first of the xenos to come through was the focus of a veritable barrage of firepower. The skeletal figure juddered as las-blasts and stub rounds impacted on its surface. It didn't even get to fall before the teleport field began to shimmer around it for extraction. Unfortunately, the focus was misplaced. Too many shots were wasted on a single target as a dozen more breaches hissed open in the gate and more of the necron warriors began to walk through.

Gnaeus fired his shotgun into one of these other invaders. It dropped to one knee, a crackling crater blasted into its side. The shot was extruded and the ribcage regrew, the hole sealing shut within moments. Then it rose to rejoin the assault. More simply stepped past it, continuing their cold advance without fear or self-regard.

'Spread your fire! Spre–'

The officer's desperate attempts to restore order to the firing line ended abruptly as a tesla blast arced out from a heavily armoured Immortal among the warriors. The bolt of lightning seemed alive as it crawled over the man, melting his flesh and flak armour into a single mass. He collapsed, dead and burning, but the energy of the attack only seemed hungrier. It leapt from the toppling corpse to two other militia soldiers nearby, incinerating them in turn.

Gnaeus tried to avenge him, firing a pair of shots into the xenos machine. It made no effort to avoid the attack, ignoring the pellets rattling from its armour-plated body. It did, however, turn its glowing eyes upon him, if only briefly. It must have signalled on unknown spectra to its underlings. A few turned in mindless obedience to this directive, and the serf threw himself down behind the rockcrete barrier.

Green light flared all around his defence. The woman standing next to him scarcely had time to scream before she slumped against the cover. Gnaeus pulled her down in a desperate attempt to save her. She slid to the ground next to him and Gnaeus recoiled in horror; her face was simply gone, revealing wet bone and muscle locked in that final shriek. He shoved the body away and struggled not to vomit.

The same scene played out all around him. Gauss flayers stripped away the armour and flesh of defending soldiers with equal disregard. Occasional tesla blasts leapt among clustered groups, reducing them to smouldering husks. The warriors might be attacking in mindless mass, but the Immortals laced among them were smarter. They guided their hollow kindred in destroying high-value targets; heavy weapons teams were swiftly silenced in bursts of green rays and lightning.

The courtyard could not hold.

The first black-armoured Stalker toppled as the *Relief's* laser destroyer beams scythed it up the middle. The quantum field absorbed much of the attack but enough got through to slice the hexapodal war-walker into uneven halves. The two pieces of the towering xenos war machine toppled away, still twitching. The second Stalker scrambled closer on its insectile legs, heat ray flashing as it engaged the *Unifier*. Having managed to get in close, the thermal weapon was at its most powerful. It carved a deep rent into the transport's hull, which blazed white-hot under the onslaught.

The gatling cannon returned fire at point-blank range. Even with the necron walker's armour deflecting some of the assault, plenty of the rounds punched through. The barrage effectively chewed the alien war machine apart, emerald energy erupting from its shattered chassis. It slumped backwards before detonating, a wash of jade fire that enveloped the Repulsor. In the wake of the blast, the Astartes vehicle was a smouldering ruin as well.

The only thing that saved it from being an absolute disaster in Lieutenant Allectius' mind was that all the infantry had disembarked already. He had no further time to ponder their grim situation, however. More of the xenos were pouring from their unhallowed Eternity Gates, an implacable horde bent on destroying the Ultramarines invaders. Two of the glowing portals were mounted on the pyramidal structures that made up the complex. They faced inwards, towards the route that led right up to the great spire. Gauss beams and tesla bolts crackled from the shimmering force field projected by Veritas. Without that protective energy, he would have been slain a dozen times over already.

The Ultramarines commander returned fire with his plasma pistol, expertly placed shots destroying the mindless necron foot soldiers left and right. He did not fight alone. The Bladeguard veterans stood shoulder to shoulder with him, their towering storm shields joining with Veritas to make a shield wall. Their power swords blazed, rending asunder any xenos that dared to close the gap. Outriders harried the necron flanks, bolt rifles spraying fire into the mass of their foes. Intercessors fought from cover, adding their own explosive rounds to the fusillade.

A bellowed litany caught his attention. He could not make out the words over the cacophony, but a glance revealed Sisenna exhorting the brethren forward. He smote a warrior that dared to get too close with a single blow. Judiciar Bittrien fought by his side, safeguarding the older Chaplain. The two were each a force of nature unto themselves.

The Judiciar was a living example. A mighty swing of his greatsword cleaved through an Immortal with a single blow, leaving two halves to fall away. Sisenna's exhortations honed the strength of his allies, even as his crozius arcanum shattered a necron with every swing. The heroic efforts of the rest of the command cadre could not be ignored either. Apothecary Calvus fought and healed at once, saving lives and taking them with equal ease.

A gauss beam slashed across the throat of a nearby Inter-cessor, stripping armour and flesh away in the blink of an eye. Apothecary Calvus was there instantly. He eased the Space Marine to the ground and brought him peace with a single round from his absolver pistol. A second shot felled a charging necron, as his other hand applied the narthecium to retrieve the precious gene-seed from the slain warrior.

But the sheer mass of the necron forces opposing them threatened to grind all their efforts away to nothing.

The courtyard could not hold.

The thought came to Gnaeus in a burst of icy clarity. This was not the hall with the flayed ones. Wherever the Ultramarines were, they were fighting a battle even more desperate. No one was coming to save him and purge the horrors he faced. Those gathered here were barely slowing the xenos advance, much less pushing it back. All their fears were true. Redoubt Primus would fall.

For a single second the idea paralysed him with terror.

'This is the launching ground! Where is the next load of non-combatants to be shuttled off-world? We've lost contact with the vaults!'

It was just a burst of comms traffic on the vox-net, but it cut through all of his fear. The thought of those children and their grandfather, abandoned to an unknown fate down in the depths... It couldn't be borne. The whole point of all this horror had been to save as many as possible. Some-one had to go. Someone...

Gnaeus looked to the back of the hall. A corridor into the rest of the fortress – it couldn't have been more than fifty feet away, though right now that seemed as impossible as a hundred miles. A green beam ripped away the belly of a

nearby man, spilling his innards in a sudden rush. Screaming in a mix of terror and fury, someone scrambled over
their barrier with a bayonet fixed to their lasgun. They didn't
make it three steps before a tesla bolt cut them down. The
hall stank of ozone and blood.

Their numbers were thinning rapidly. Waiting would only
worsen his chances. Gnaeus gathered his legs underneath
him and took a deep breath. With his teeth bared in terror he sprinted for the corridor. A gauss blast crackled past
him and struck a rockcrete lump, evaporating a chunk of
it. Another soldier saw him running and seemed about to
yell out in fury when a beam caught her in the chest. For
a moment, exposed lungs fluttered within patchwork ribs,
and then she slid to the ground, mouth working silently
as blood sheeted down her front.

Gnaeus was into the corridor. His breath was loud in
his ears, almost as loud as the pounding of his heart. The
sounds of the onslaught continued behind him, human
weaponry fading out to be replaced only by screams and
the ominous hums and sizzles of the alien devices. This was
no shelter. He ran headlong into the dimly lit corridor. A
brighter light shone ahead – the second line of defences.
He would have to–

They were screaming. He tried to stop and skidded in
blood, his feet nearly going out from under him. The second
line was already under attack. Structured much like the gate
to confront a forward attack, it had instead been assaulted
from all sides. The only reason it had not collapsed completely was because one of the handful of Ultramarines that
remained behind fought here, anchoring the defenders with
his thundering bolter. Monstrous constructs on serpentine
bodies slithered through the walls as though they didn't

exist, lashing beams and whipping coils destroying human bodies left and right. Gore-drenched flayed ones dragged themselves free of their unknown demesne to bring carnage to this one.

One turned its face to Gnaeus, only feet away. He emptied the rest of his magazine directly into its head, shattering the cranium completely. Arcane innards sparked and sizzled as the body toppled backwards. There was no way back, only forward. He ran into the madness, vaulting a barricade. His boots came down on the gooey remnants of a human body, the head and limbs ripped away.

The serf's feet slid out from under him. He hit the ground scrambling. The fall was the only thing that saved his life, as a particle beam sliced through the air where his head had been. One of the constructs was slithering after him. He crawled as fast as he could for the next tunnel entrance, too terrified to manage a scream. It was unnaturally quick, faster than he would have been at a dead run. He could hear the rasp of its coils scraping the floor as it rushed towards his back.

An overcharged plasma beam burned through the air right about his head. It passed so close to him that he could feel it through his armour, a flash pain as skin cooked in a line across the top of his head and down his back. It bored a white-hot hole through the blasphemous machine's abdomen, sending it thrashing to the floor.

The gunner was a local militia fighter carrying a plasma gun. It was startling to see such precious technology in the hands of a random fighter. There was no telling where she'd gotten it from.

She was screaming. 'Come on then, you xenos filth! Come and be purged!'

Wild beams obliterated necrons left and right, disintegrating chunks of them with starfire. She had set it to overcharge and was firing as fast as she could.

Gnaeus scrambled past her legs, his hands and knees slick with the blood that ran across the floor. No one was sparing him a glance now. He pulled himself to his feet on a nearby barricade and staggered on towards the waiting corridor. He was a few feet in when a brilliant flash behind him threw his shadow out ahead for a split-second. He could feel the heat on the back of his neck and risked a single glance back.

She was a bonfire in the shape of a human being. Thrashing, writhing, screaming. The overheated plasma gun had fallen to the ground, where it still glowed red-hot. Betrayed by her own weapon, she was saved from her agonies by an enemy. A construct lunged in and ripped the head from her shoulders with a whipping coil. A cold mercy, motivated by a mechanical indifference.

The Ultramarines' advance had been stymied mere moments after entering the blackstone complex of the xenos. The technomantic aliens had boiled forth from benighted buildings and extradimensional vortices the moment they had arrived. Either they had been expected, or even now the Space Marines were underestimating how responsive the enemy legions could be. It had only been warriors leavened with Immortals at first, but now more potent foes like the Triarch Stalkers had begun to arrive.

As if to confirm the thought, a wave of praetorians leapt in on their anti-gravity packs. With one hand they blazed away with particle casters; with the other they struck with black-wreathed voidblades. Allectius caught a swordstroke on his shield, deadly energies meeting with a sizzling flash. He surged forward, smashing into the mechanical body of his foe and sending it staggering. He fired a plasma shot into the opening, boiling away the skull-face of his opponent.

They could not afford to be bogged down here. They were holding, but the pressure would grow unto annihilation. Despite the risks, they had to break through.

'Forward!' Allectius bellowed.

The Bladeguard surged in a disciplined rank, smashing into the xenos with crushing force. The less-defended brethren advanced in their wake. Nevertheless, the march forwards exposed them to greater risks. A new quartet of praetorians soared overhead, coming down in the vulnerable core of the Astartes formation. Their rods of covenant sprayed exotic energies as they swept in, doubling as deadly melee weapons once they had landed. Both forms of attack had little trouble penetrating the ceramite of the Space Marines' war-plate.

An Intercessor fell, struck to the ground with the sweep of a necron weapon. A burst of fire ended his life a split-second later, his life rune flashing and fading on the lieutenant's biologis feeds. The Judiciar swept in a heartbeat later and engaged the whole of the enemy unit. He dismantled them with consummate skill, but paid a cost in blood as a burst of energy tore through his side. Calvus hastened to the side of the fallen Intercessor to secure his gene-seed, while the Judiciar continued forward despite his injury.

Another Stalker approached, looming over the Space Marines. Its heat ray fired on the dispersed setting, washing deadly thermal energy over the Bladeguard. Runes of warning flashed on Allectius' displays as the heat spiked, but his defences held. It found a gap in the defences of another brother, the deadly heat punching through his armour to incinerate the flesh within. The *Relief* counter-fired with all of its weapons, staggering the enemy vehicle. An Eradicator finished the job, lunging forward to fire his melta rifle into it from the other side. The lance of power punched through the cockpit and destroyed the necron inside.

An Immortal put a gauss blaster beam through that brave brother's face, evaporating most of his head in a single shot. Blood spurted from the crater as the Space Marine toppled backwards, his melta rifle falling from nerveless hands. Allectius destroyed the offending Immortal himself with a supercharged plasma blast to the side; a bitter exchange of losses that the enemy could afford, but he could not.

They broke through. It was sudden, a crumpling of the last layer of necron forces, and there the spire was. From this perspective it towered about them, a spear tip aimed at the heavens. There was a terrible presence to it. It vibrated on some unheard frequency, a ringing felt in the soul. Even for the lieutenant's psyche, reinforced by psycho-conditioning, it was a heavy weight trying to drive him to his knees. He bared his teeth and pushed through it.

'Demolitions forward!' he barked. 'Defensive perimeter!'

Gnaeus ran for everything he was worth. He was deep into the fortress now, keeping to little-used tunnels to try to avoid drawing any more attention. His legs ached from running, and his lungs burned. He stopped, slumping against the wall for a moment. He coughed and wheezed, struggling to catch his breath. Nausea surged. He pried his helmet off, biting his lip to keep from crying out as it rubbed against the blistered flesh on his scalp. The near passage of that plasma blast alone had burned through it. It came away just in time. He threw up, spraying vomit down the rock-crete wall.

An explosion rocked the redoubt, shaking the floor under his feet and raining dust from the ceiling. The lights in the hallway flickered and went out, plunging everything into absolute darkness. Gnaeus froze. The sudden blindness made him focus on what he could hear – the distant sounds of battle and the screams of the dying. Fumbling, he managed to turn on the stablight mounted on his helmet and swept it up and down the corridor. Nothing moved.

The serf wiped a sleeve across his face, clearing away spittle and tears. A large part of him wanted to just curl up here and wait for the end. He wasn't sure at this point if that was the darkness of the Nexus upon him, or just his exhaustion. All he could do was push on. He seated his helmet again with a wince and reloaded his shotgun. He couldn't even fill the magazine any more; he had only six shells left on his bandolier out of the eight needed.

Gnaeus gathered himself and hurried on through the darkness. He was close to where the vaults were now. He hadn't travelled far before the lights flickered back to life with a hum, dull and red now. Backup generatoria must have kicked in to provide emergency power. If the enemy was searching out power signatures and destroying them that wouldn't last long either. It would be better if he was done before the darkness returned.

Fortunately, he had arrived at the vault access sector. The beam of his stablight showed the area abandoned. The doors topping the staircases were sealed, and the cargo lifters were locked at the top. There was no sign of fighting. He wasn't sure if that was better or worse; the idea of the people who should have been working here simply abandoning their posts to try to save themselves made him sick to his soul.

Was that really any different from him abandoning the gate defence?

Gnaeus gritted his teeth. They were nothing alike. He had come here to save these people, and he was going to do so. He stepped up to the control panel for the lift and deactivated the lock, then opened the door.

Bodies. The cargo lift was full of bodies.

Of course it was. In the madness of the attack the quieter horror of soul death had slipped his mind. Whoever had fled this place hadn't bothered to move these people either. He swallowed hard and stepped over them to reach the control panel. He hit the interior descent rune and waited as the cab creaked and hissed into slow movement.

Gnaeus could hear the people all around him, breathing shallowly. It made his skin pebble and crawl. For a moment he couldn't help but imagine the power dying again and leaving him stranded in this carriage, with nothing but these lifeless half-dead for company as he slowly suffocated. He closed his eyes tightly and tried to make himself breathe slowly.

The lift creaked to a halt and the doors slid open again, revealing the vault with its ranks of bunks. Everything was lit only by the same dull red light, spread thin in this great chamber. All he could see were the silhouettes of people huddled and hiding as best they could. His stablight could only pick out a few drawn faces at a time, fearful eyes gleaming.

'You–' Gnaeus' voice creaked as he tried to call, and he swallowed and started again. 'All of you, listen up! You don't have to be afraid.'

They were just staring at him. His thought on coming here

had been to save those specific children, but just looking around, he could see many more.

'I'm here to help you get out of here. As many of you as I can. We'll load this lift with one group, take them up, and then send it back down for the next.'

His words were sinking in. There was the beginning of a surge. People started to rush towards him. The serf swept his shotgun across them hastily and shouted. 'No! Orderly! We do this right, or I swear to the Emperor I will leave and lock this lift down again!' He wasn't sure if it was an empty threat. He couldn't imagine abandoning these people to such a horrid fate, but he couldn't afford a riot here, either.

His threat cowed the people with ease. They meekly followed his instructions and clambered into the lift. He could hear their gasps and whimpers as they manoeuvred around the limp figures already piled on board. He wanted to say something comforting, but there wasn't anything to say. It was ghoulish and there was no way around it.

Once they'd squeezed as many people in as they could, he started the cab moving back up to the floor above. Dismayed cries sounded as the doors slid shut, but he steeled himself. There was no other way. Once they emerged back onto the next floor, he hurried over to the staircases and unsealed the doors, then motioned to one of the people he'd brought up.

'Send it back down. There's no time to waste. I have to take all of you now. There's a shuttle holding on for you as long as it can.'

'I'll stay,' volunteered a man with a soldier's haircut and a missing leg, leaning on a crutch. 'I know the way to the pad too. I'll lead the next group.'

Gnaeus hesitated, then offered the man his hand. 'Thank you. May the Emperor watch over you.'

The wounded fighter gripped the offered hand briefly. 'The Emperor protects. As you said, there's no time to waste.'

The serf gave him a firm nod and turned to the others gathered around fearfully. 'Come on then! We're going to have to move quickly. No matter what you see, just keep moving.'

They just stared at him, caught between dull and terrified. The damn Nexus had bled these people nearly dry. He took a deep breath and set off at a jog. He would have to trust that they understood. When he glanced over his shoulder, they were following, at least. It would have to be enough.

The emergency power died just as he had feared it would when they were only about halfway to the landing pads. There were terrified noises from his followers, and he called back. 'Follow my light! Stay with me!' He refused to think about the people who must still be down in the vault, plunged into absolute darkness. The stairs up were open now, at least. It was fast approaching the time when everyone would have to fend for themselves as best they could.

At last they headed up the stairs to the landing pads. Gnaeus stopped at the bottom and motioned them on ahead of him. 'Go!' They ran past, some of them stumbling in their haste. The more alert and capable helped them back to their feet to hurry on. Once the last of the non-combatants had passed, the serf followed them up.

He broke out to the cool air of the evening. The sun had just finished setting beyond the horizon, and the sky was grey. Craft howled by overhead, both the sharp crescents of the necrons and the bulkier form of Imperial aircraft engaging them to try to keep the airspace clear for the shuttles.

The shuttle itself was starkly visible up ahead thanks to its lights. The people he'd brought were already streaming towards the waiting vehicle where a crewman stood in the hatch waving them on.

Screaming erupted without warning and people began to scatter.

CHAPTER 7

A pair of Ultramarines rushed forward carrying melta bombs to bring the spire down with. The rest arrayed themselves to hold off the enemy. Allectius turned his attention to helping with the defence. A plasma blast scattered fragments of a warrior across several feet. His pistol coughed, its fuel expended once and for all. Reverently he holstered the ancient weapon and reached over his shoulder. Conciliator drew smoothly, the power field igniting in a flash of brilliant blue-white.

The pressure was only growing. A strange construct picked its way among the wreckage of the dead. It was tall, a smallish body mounted on great gangling legs. Grasping claws dangled before it, collecting shattered remnants. Silvery beams flickered from an orb on the abdomen. Everywhere they touched, destroyed necrons knitted themselves back together. They staggered to their feet and marched to rejoin the onslaught.

'Reanimator!' Allectius called, unable to reach it himself.

The Judiciar was there. Heedless of the mortal danger he was in, Bittrien cleaved his way through the enemy ranks. The sheer impact of his charge scattered warriors. A green beam plucked at his shoulder, dissolving armour and flesh at a go. The arm fell limp, but the warrior of the Reclusiam did not even slow. He forged ahead, tearing free of the mob to reach the construct. A mighty sweep of his great sword hacked away two of the legs in a single strike. The body toppled, and Bittrien planted one foot on it before driving his blade in. The construct spasmed uncontrollably before going still.

A storm of catastrophic energy struck the Doom Eagle. One moment the grim champion stood, the next he was simply gone, disintegrated. Ash upon a bitter wind.

'Vermin,' sneered a cold voice that echoed over the battlefield.

That ravening power and the voice tracked to the same place. A figure had emerged from a nearby Eternity Gate. It hovered above the ground as if disdaining anything so mundane as walking, writhing coils under its torso projecting some strange field that held it aloft. Esoteric bolts arced from technomantic nodules on its back. It spun an eldritch staff, still burning with the energies that had destroyed the Judiciar, and glared about the battlefield with a single emerald optical orb.

'Vermin,' it repeated. It spoke perfect Gothic, in mechanised tones bereft of any hint of a soul. 'Scrabbling little nothings, clawing at the works of your betters. You survive only so long as you escape our attention, and now *you have it.*'

* * *

Gnaeus felt that senseless terror well up in him even before he saw them. Warriors marched in rank, their gauss flayers held before them. The green beams were already flickering out, stripping flesh and life from the refugees as they desperately sought somewhere to run to.

A larger one walked behind them, even more heavily armoured and intricately decorated than the Immortals he had seen. There was something in the gleam of its optics and the way it carried itself that spoke of not just intelligence but personality. It carried a gauss weapon of its own, but held it up with an air of contempt, as if unwilling to waste its talents on such paltry targets. It seemed willing to leave its servants to slaughter the helpless humans.

For one eternal moment, the question of what drove him confronted him again. Amidst all these easy, scattering targets Gnaeus likely wouldn't even draw attention. He could flee to the shuttle himself, demand they take off. Save himself. The other option, some desperate effort to save these battered souls, would likely only result in death. To sacrifice himself for a goal was one thing, but to die for nothing?

The Space Marines had asked them to be the blade, however. To make a stand, regardless of the cost.

'Get on board the shuttle!' Gnaeus roared. It startled him, as if it wasn't even his voice.

It was enough to shake some of them from their terror, to get them funnelling towards the waiting hatch. They were still getting slaughtered, however. He had to draw the necrons' attention. Even if only for a moment. Even if he only saved one life by doing so.

Gnaeus grasped his shotgun with both hands and blasted the nearest warrior. It staggered, and the second round put it on the ground. He switched to the next target as fast as he could, tearing off one of its arms with two shells before the third smashed into its torso and knocked it to the ground as well. The armoured one was looking at him now, eyes cold. He fired a shell right at it, a desperate act of defiance, sparks flashing where the pellets glanced from its plating.

The serf pulled the trigger again, and all it did was click. The last of his shells was gone, and the warriors were turning to eliminate this threat to their commander. He closed his eyes tightly and waited for the emerald flash that would end his life. If he was lucky, it would be quick.

It didn't come.

He opened his eyes to find the necrons standing by, their weapons held low. Their commander was walking towards him, the relaxed pace of the supremely confident, one hand held up to the warriors in a staying gesture. The lesser forms seemed bound to its will. Seeing it had Gnaeus' attention again, the leader motioned to him. It tapped its chestplate, a clear challenge. It held its gun out away from itself insouciantly, inviting him to strike first. He couldn't help but stare at the strange glowing hieroglyphs that decorated its chest and collar. Where its servants appeared scuffed and lifeless, this one shone as though it had been burnished.

The serf could see people boarding the shuttle now out of the corner of his eye. It bolstered his courage. He discarded his fear and charged in, reversing his grip on his shotgun to swing it like a club. There was a terrible presence to the xenos. It beat at him like a physical force as he drew close, trying to drive him to his knees. He gritted his teeth and forced his way through it, swinging with all his might.

It was a dead-on strike. The alien made no attempt to avoid the attack. The butt of the shotgun caught directly on its sculpted jaw, with a dull ringing sound. The impact made Gnaeus stagger backwards, his arms numb. The only result otherwise was the necron's head turning slightly with the blow. Slowly it shifted to focus on him again, emerald optics gleaming.

Desperately he swung again. It caught the shotgun this time with its free hand. The movement wasn't fast so much as preternaturally efficient and timed perfectly. The serf struggled to retrieve his weapon from that grasp, but he might as well have been trying to pry it out from under an autocarriage. It swung the blade mounted on the underside of its gun, a swift stroke with that same precision.

Gnaeus snatched his arms back and stumbled back a few steps. For a split-second he thought he'd been fast enough. Then he saw his hands still gripping the gun, and the pain of the amputations hit him. He looked down and saw his truncated wrists spurting blood, and a cry of anguish tore its way free of him.

The kick caught him in the side and hurled him to the ground, knocking the air out of him. He coughed and wheezed, trying to roll over, but a cold metallic foot planted on his chest and pinned him in place. He was staring into the emitter of the necron commander's energy weapon. Its little diversion was clearly over.

There was no heroism in this moment. All he could do was sob in pain, beating at the weapon with his maimed limbs in an effort to move that terminal aim.

Allectius had seen reports of the twisted crypteks that were the masters of the blasphemous technomancy of the xenos. This one must be of their ilk, though it blazed with power unlike any description he'd encountered. Strange thralls loped into battle all around it. They looked like necrons of a sort, but *altered*. Their lower bodies seemed normal enough, but their heads and arms were twisted by a silvery overgrowth. The faces had been restructured into dull orbs, perhaps in mimicry of their master, and their arms now ended in scythe blades suitable only for slashing.

The cryptek swept its staff over the assembled necrons, and emerald energies boiled over them. Even with the reanimator destroyed, their wounds began to close faster. Damage that should have felled them instead sealed and allowed them to fight on. Allectius put his power sword through the chest of one and kicked it off the spire's dais, only for it to rise and spear at him with the blade on its gauss weapon. The sharp tip scraped from his armour. Another blast of plasma roared from the necron technomancer's staff, obliterating a nearby Bladeguard with contemptuous ease.

'Demolitions team!' snapped the lieutenant into the vox.

'We are ready, brother!' came the reply after a strained moment. *'Brace for detonation!'*

Allectius and his brethren steadied themselves as instructed. For one brief second the world was divided into black and white, hot air washing over them in a rush. The necrons, not forewarned, stumbled or fell as the ground trembled.

'That is impossible,' said one of the brothers on the vox, sounding shaken in a way that Space Marines rarely were.

The laughter of the cryptek pealed over the battlefield as Allectius dared a look back. The ground around the base of the spire had been reduced to molten lava, glowing red-hot. The shaped blasts had ballooned outward, carving a crater out all around and revealing the structure sunk deep into the planet. Yet the blackstone obelisk itself was untouched. The melta bombs had done nothing to it.

'Emperor on the Throne,' breathed the lieutenant. Space Marines were still dying all around him. Their numbers were thinning fast. Calvus tried to drag a wounded Intercessor back to treat his wounds, and received half a dozen gauss blasts for his trouble. They tore him apart in the blink of an eye. Great swathes of his armour evaporated under the first beams, leaving him vulnerable to the next few that devoured huge chunks of his body.

Those who remained were desperately fighting for their lives.

'Ship-captain,' Allectius said fiercely into the vox.

He parried the sweeps of one of the blade-armed thralls. It followed up with a blast of energy from its eye which he caught on his shield before riposting right through the orb, destroying its head.

'*I see you, my lord,*' came the despairing reply of the serf leader on their strike cruiser.

'If we could drop the quantum shielding–' he began.

Damasippa cut him off, a startling breach at any other time. '*To drop it fully you would need to be able to search the area for what is powering it, and destroy it. There is no time or…*'

'What is it? Speak!' he demanded as she trailed off.

'*There is an odd augury marker in the area. Individual-mass, but the power signature is extremis. The tech-priests believe it could be interfaced with their power supply on some level.*'

Plasma arced into Veritas and drove Allectius back a step with the impact. The shield held the devouring energy away from him. He glanced past the bulk of it to see the hovering cryptek. There could be little doubt which individual among the enemy was drawing that much power. Sergeant Fulgentius fired a spray of bolt shells at the enemy leader, which were deflected by a shimmering field at the last second.

One of the cryptek's thralls used the chance to put both blades through his chest. His biologis feed vanished in an instant, the wound too grievous even for a Space Marine.

'If I can fell it?' he panted into the vox.

She sounded anguished, to the verge of tears. *'It might only be a temporary disruption, my lord. A single macrocannon shell would not suffice, even if we managed a direct hit. Which I cannot guarantee.'*

'A standard shell,' he said. 'We have Exterminatus-grade weaponry aboard.'

'Yes,' she said reluctantly. *'It should not be used unless authorised by crusade leadership, and there is no way to get you out of the–'*

'We are dead, ship-captain.' His words were matter of fact. There was no joy in the declaration. There was only a duty to be fulfilled. 'You will obey my order in this matter. You have no right to refuse the commander of the company, and that is what you will tell the crusade when they ask.'

There was sorrow in her voice, but to her credit she did not hesitate. *'I hear and obey, my lord.'*

'You will have one shot at this, ship-captain. Do not fail us.' Allectius switched his vox to the company net. 'Brothers! The cryptek must fall!'

It was all the lieutenant had to say. No one stopped to count the cost. They were Adeptus Astartes. They were Ultramarines. If this was the end, they would see it through with strength and honour. They surged forward, abandoning all defences for their final charge.

They bought yards with blood and bolt shells. The first to lunge into the teeth of the enemy horde were hurled back, broken. That bought room for those on their heels to come to grips with the enemy. Allectius hacked and cleaved his way forward. Gauss beams plucked at him, but he paid them no mind. A thrall leapt for him, blades gleaming, and he smashed it from the air with his shield. The power field tore it apart and spat forth the remnants.

A Destroyer, larger than any the lieutenant had seen, swept towards his side. Sisenna lunged into the gap. The Chaplain met the charge with a swing of his mace, and sparks flew under the impact.

'Onward! Onward for Guilliman! Onward for the Emperor!' thundered the Chaplain, and then he was lost to sight in the havoc of battle.

The cryptek could see him coming now. It drove its staff towards him, and terrible power washed forth. It split on the field of Veritas, but Allectius could feel even the storied relic heating under the onslaught. It saved him from annihilation, but the very edges of that devastating power were enough to burn his arm right through his armour, flesh cooking and boiling. He drove on into it, like a man into the winds of a hurricane.

He was there.

Allectius leapt, his blade raised. The necron technomancer had only enough time to throw its hands up in a desperate last defence, then his power sword was plunging through. Conciliator sheared through living metal and arcane workings alike, erupting from the xenos' back in a burst. They fell together, Astartes and alien, tumbling back to the ground.

Waves of power erupted from the mortally wounded alien. They tore at the lieutenant, ripped his shield away and left him bare to the dangers all around. He bore down with all his strength, driving the necron into the dirt. The cryptek thrashed and screamed, a mechanical howl that wavered from bone-rattling depths to ear-piercing heights. It was done. It lay still, and the unholy green glow all around flickered.

The enemy fell upon him, a methodical destruction from which there would be no escape. It did not matter now. Allectius pulled his sword free with the last of his strength and held it high, gleaming and proud.

A star fell to meet him.

A bolt-round struck the xenos in the chest. The detonation sprayed Gnaeus' face with hot shards of metal, slicing his cheeks and brow. It caught the necron off-guard and sent it staggering back a few steps. The serf desperately tried to use the moment to scramble up and run, boots slipping in his own blood.

A powerful hand seized the back of his shirt and hurled him bodily towards the shuttle. He hit the ground rolling.

'Get him aboard that shuttle!' boomed a stentorian voice.

Smaller hands collected Gnaeus and half dragged, half carried him towards the waiting hatch. More of the refugees. They were the ones bringing him now. He looked back and saw the massive form of one of the Space Marines. His helmet was red, a sharp contrast with the blue of his armour, and he carried a pistol and a roaring chainsword.

More of them, blue-armoured blurs, were smashing into the warriors. The crimson-helmed sergeant turned back to face the xenos commander and pointed at it with a sword.

'If it is a challenge you seek, alien, you have found it.'

That was the last Gnaeus heard of him as he was dragged aboard the shuttle and the hatch hissed shut behind him. The world was blurry and grey. Desperate hands were squeezing his wrists, tying them. It should have been agonising but everything was getting numb and cold. They draped a blanket over him as the world began to shake.

He could see a viewport from where he lay. Cassothea was falling away, the grey of the evening sky fading to a star-speckled black. The curve of the world came into view. Even as he watched, a brilliant light flashed on that surface, dazzling to his eyes even so far away.

It was beautiful, and he tried to tell the others about it. No one seemed to listen.

Darkness took him.

EPILOGUE

They had brought Gnaeus to the apothecarion on board the ship. The 'medicae deck', they called it, as this wasn't an Astartes vessel. Eventually, they promised him, he would be returned to the Ultramarines. They would likely see his hands replaced by bionics so that he could return to his work in the armoury. For now, the priority had to be getting out of the system.

It had been deemed an impossibility mere days ago. He could remember it clearly. They were trapped, and that was the end of it. He had felt the fear then, especially as the Space Marines had departed on their desperate assault. He was ashamed of it now as he lay in his bed and looked out of the viewport at the stars beyond.

It was still not a day for celebration. Cassothea was lost. The shroud of the Nexus was gone, but they said it would only be a matter of time before it returned. The war would continue, across a hundred systems. Some of those battles would make this one pale to insignificance.

Yet as Gnaeus held his bandaged arms close to his chest and waited for the ship to slip into the warp, all he could think of was the blade. Held aloft by that lord, a symbol. Picked up and carried forward despite grievous losses. A symbol of the Imperial cause.

The blade had not broken. It had served unto the very end, and it had saved Gnaeus and all the tens of thousands of people aboard these ships. They would fight another day.

We will carry your sacrifice forth and return it a thousandfold, he promised all of those they had lost. From Elder Tulla to the great lords themselves, no loss would be in vain. The cause would continue because it was more than any one person, great or small.

The cause – and Gnaeus' faith – were unbroken.

YOUR
NEXT READ

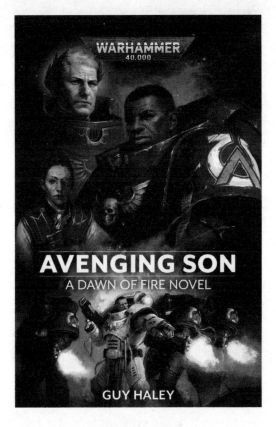

AVENGING SON
by Guy Haley

By the will of the reborn primarch Roboute Guilliman, the Indomitus Crusade spreads across the galaxy, bringing the Emperor's light back to the Dark Imperium. In the Machorta Sound, a desperate mission could determine the fate of the crusade – and battle is joined...

YOUR
NEXT READ

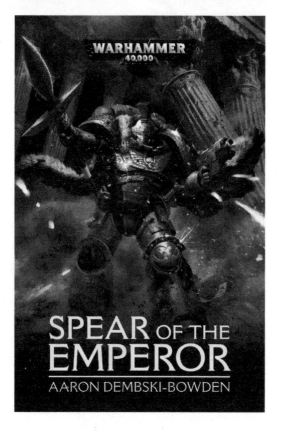

SPEAR OF THE EMPEROR
by Aaron Dembski-Bowden

The Emperor's Spears are a Chapter on the edge of destruction, last watchmen over the Elara's Veil nebula. Now, the decisions of one man, Amadeus Kaias Incarius of the Mentor Legion, will determine the Chapter's fate…

KRAKEN
CHRIS WRAIGHT

Hailing from the icy death world of Fenris, there are few brotherhoods among the Adeptus Astartes as noble or fierce as the **Space Wolves**. These warriors, often thought more beast than man, have defended the Imperium of Mankind with bolt, blade and fang for over ten thousand years.

In *Kraken*, Chris Wraight weaves the poignant tale of Kvara. The lone survivor of his pack, he heads into the storm-tossed oceans to slay a great beast and meet a mighty death so he may join his comrades in the feasting halls of the afterlife forevermore.

He wore their names on his armour. The words had been graven deeply; a parting gift from the Iron Priest before he'd left Fenris. Nearly a centimetre deep, now crusted with the filth of years, just like the rest of him.

Eight names: four on the right side of his dented breast-plate, four on the left. One was barely legible, scraped away by some massive, crunching impact a long time ago. The others were all faded, or obscured by burn marks, or bisected with scratches.

He remembered them all anyway. They came to him when he slept, whispering to him in old voices. He saw their faces, looming up out of the dark well of memory, their flesh still marked by tattoos, scars and studs. Sometimes they were angry, sometimes mournful. Their purpose in appearing, so he'd realised, was always the same: to urge him on, to stir him into action.

And so he never rested, not truly. He respected the

demands of his vocation and kept moving. Oaths had been sworn, and they bound him more tightly than bands of adamantium. One world after another, blurring into a morass of sense impressions; some cold, some hot, all struggling, all playing their tiny part in the galaxy-wide war that had long since ceased to have boundaries.

It would have been easy to lose his sense of significance in all of that. It would have been easy, after twenty years of it, to give in to the darkness that lurked behind his eyes and forget the faces. He'd seen it happen to mortals. Their mouths drooped, their eyes went dull, even as they still clutched their weapons and made a show of walking towards the enemy. Then, as sure as ice follows fire, they died.

That was why he had the names put on his armour. The carvings would continue to fade or sustain damage, but some mark would always be there, some small impression to register what had once been lives as vital as his life.

And as long as there were marks to remind him, he would not slope off into despair. He would keep moving, seeking the final trial that would restore lost honour and still the whispers in the dark.

One world after another, blurring into a morass of sense impressions; some cold, some hot. None that made much of an impression on his sullen mind; since their wars gave no opportunity to achieve the goal he craved.

None, that was, until the last of them.

None of those worlds made an impression on Aj Kvara until, following the eddies of fate, he came to Lyses, and the raw beauty of it stirred even his old, cold soul.

Morren Oen shaded his eyes against the morning glare, squinting as the green light flashed from the waves. Fifty metres below him, the downdraft of the flyer's four rotors churned the water.

There shouldn't even have been water down there. There should have been several thousand tons of dirt-grey plasteel, designation Megaera VI, humming with life and machinery. There should have been lights blinking along the smoothly curved tidewalls to beckon the flyer down to land, and the low grind of algal processors working their way through the endless harvest.

Instead there was a thin skin of floating debris bobbing on the emerald water. He saw a plastic hopper tumble by, rolling amid a web of tangled fibres. Below the surface, there were dark shadows, perhaps the outlines of struts and flotation booms, still half-operative even after the main structure had gone down.

'Emperor,' he swore, sweeping the scene of devastation for something, some sign of resistance or survival.

Four other flyers hung low over the water, each one full of men with lasguns. They pointed their barrels uselessly down at the debris. Whatever had happened to Megaera VI had moved on long before they got there.

Preja Eim leaned a long way over the edge of the flyer's open-sided crew bay and took a few more picts. Her auburn hair fluttered in the warm breeze, catching on the upturned collar of her uniform.

'Have enough yet?' asked Oen, turning away from the view and leaning back against the juddering metal of his seat-back.

Eim carried on clicking.

'Information,' she said, her face screwed up in concentration. 'There might be something. Some clue.'

Oen looked at her wearily. She was so young. Her freckled

skin looked healthy in the sun, almost translucent. Perhaps, once, he'd been as enthusiastic in his work.

For the first time since joining up, he felt too old. Forty years of service on Lyses, rising steadily through the ranks, had taken its toll. Rejuve was expensive, and he had other commitments that prevented him splashing out. And so he felt the skin of his jawline sag a little and his stomach bulge out over his heavy old regimental belt. Watching Eim made him feel worse. It reminded him of what he had been, and how long ago that was.

'Snap away,' he said. 'Don't think you'll get anything we haven't already scanned for.'

He looked out aimlessly, keeping his hand over his eyes. The curve of the ocean ran unbroken across the horizon, deep green and smooth. The pale rose sky shimmered above it, warmed by the diffuse light of both suns.

Oen was used to the view of open seas. All of Lyses was open seas. All of it, that was, except for the floating hubs, strewn across the endless ocean like motes of dust, separated by thousands of kilometres and gently drifting.

And they were being picked off, one by one. That thought, when he chose to entertain it, was quite thrillingly disquieting.

'Procurator,' came a voice over his earpiece.

'Go ahead,' said Oen, welcoming the distraction. Whatever news there was, it was unlikely to make him feel worse.

'Grid Nine have a comm-signal. Ship entering the orbital exclusion zone. The hails all check out, but they thought you ought to know.'

'Nice of them. Why, especially?'

'It's not in-system, nor Navy. They think it might be Adeptus Astartes, but they're not sure.'

At the mention of the magic triplet of syllables, *as-tar-tes*, Oen felt his heart miss a beat. He didn't know whether that was born of fear or excitement. Probably a bit of both.

'They're not sure? What are they not sure about?'

'Perhaps you'd better get back to Nyx, procurator. They're not going to try to stop it, and by the time you get back it'll be in geostat.'

'Fine. Keep them quiet until I get there. We're just about done here.'

The link broke. By then Eim had stopped taking picts and was looking intently at the wreckage.

'No signs of explosions,' she murmured, watching the pieces float by. 'It's like some giant hand just... pulled it apart.'

'Did you hear all that?' asked Oen, ignoring her. 'We're going back in. You can take another flyer out here if you want to keep at it.'

Eim looked at him, and her freckled face was wide-eyed. There was a strangely childlike look of desolation in them.

'What's doing this, procurator? Why can't we stop it?'

'If I knew that, do you not think I'd have ordered something more potent than overflights?' He smiled, trying to be reassuring, and knowing he'd probably failed. 'Listen, the distress signals have been picked up. Trust in grace, Eim. There's probably a whole company of Space Marines lining up on Nyx as we speak, and, believe me, there's no more impressive sight in the Emperor's own galaxy.'

He slumped in the chair in the reception chamber, leaning both hands on the only table, smelling like old meat. His scraggly beard spilled over the breastplate of his enormous armour, snarled and tangled. Grey streaks shot through it, making him look like an old, sick man.

Do they get old? thought Oen, observing him through the one-way plex-glass viewport in the corridor outside. *Would they die of age, if given long enough?*

Accounts of the newcomer's landing from atmospheric control had been garbled. One transmission implied that the newcomer had blasted his way through the upper defensive cordon without warning, while another, from a low-order servitor-controlled station, indicated nothing but impeccable orbital manners.

One way or another, though, he'd got through, and his ship, now standing five hundred metres up on the landing stages, was like nothing Oen had ever seen – dirty, angular, covered in plasma burns and with a blocky aquila picked out in bronze on the sloping nose. It didn't look big enough for inter-system travel, though it must have been, since its occupant certainly wasn't from Lyses.

From the look of it the ship's crew was entirely composed of servitors. They were strange looking creatures, with clunking servos and spikes and animal bones hanging from their pearl-white flesh. They'd stayed on board the ship after the pilot had stomped down the landing ramp, which Oen couldn't be too sorry about. Not that the pilot was any less strange.

'I thought you said…' began Eim, gazing through the viewer, fascinated. Her query trailed off.

Oen knew what she meant.

'I've been told they vary,' he said, rather stiffly. 'The only picts I saw were from a rogue trader who'd run a squadron out through Ultramar. Those ones were… different.'

Eim nodded slowly, running her eyes over the bulky figure sitting at the metal desk on the other side of the viewport.

His head was bare and bald. A knotwork tattoo ran across

the tanned flesh from behind one ear, over the skull and down towards one eye. His face seemed to have several metal studs in it, each one a slightly different shape. His armour was pale grey, like dirty snow, and had carvings all over it. The lettering wasn't standard Gothic – it was angular and close-typed, covered in marks and bisected with slashes like those made by animal claws.

Oen had imagined the armour of a Space Marine to be clean, polished and flawless, just like the ones in the devotional holos sent out by the Ecclesiarchy's Office of Truth Distribution. He'd imagined bronze shoulder-guards and bright cobalt breastplates glimmering under the white lumens.

He hadn't imagined the mess, and the dirt. He certainly hadn't imagined the smell.

'Finished gawping?'

Both Oen and Eim jumped. He'd spoken. The words were thickly accented, as if Low Gothic were a foreign language, and muffled by the dividing wall. He hadn't looked up. His strange yellow eyes remained fixed on his loosely clasped hands.

Oen readied himself, shot Eim a reassuring glance, and went round the corner to open the door. As he entered the room, the newcomer looked up at him.

'I'm sorry, lord,' said Oen, bowing before taking a seat opposite. 'Standard observational procedure. We have to be careful.'

The newcomer, massive in his armour, gazed at him with a profoundly disinterested expression on his savage face. He didn't smile. His scarred and tattooed features looked almost incapable of smiling.

'A pointless gesture,' he said quietly. 'If I'd wanted to kill you, you'd be dead already. But since you've started, observe away.'

Oen swallowed. The newcomer's voice was worryingly deep, underlined with a permanent, breathy growl and made eerie by the unusual pronunciation.

'Do you have, er, a designation? Something I can use for the reports?'

'A designation?'

'A title, lord. Something I can–'

The huge figure leaned back, and Oen could see the metal chair flex under the enormous strain.

'I am a Space Wolf, Procurator Morren Oen,' he said. As he spoke, Oen caught sight of long, yellow fangs flashing out from behind the hairy lips. 'Have you heard of us?'

Oen shook his head meekly. He felt his heart beating a little too quickly. Something about the man in front of him made it very hard to retain composure.

Except he wasn't a *man*. Not like Oen was a man, anyway.

'Good,' said the newcomer. 'Probably for the best.'

Oen cleared his throat, trying to remain something close to professional.

'And your name, lord?'

'My name is Kvara.'

Oen nodded. He was aware he was gesturing too much, but he couldn't stop it.

'I'd expected… more of you.'

That had come out wrong. Kvara looked at him with amusement. His eyes were circles of gold. Animal's eyes, lodged in a lined, worn and battered face.

'You do not need more of us. One of us is more than enough.'

Oen nodded again.

'Quite so,' he said, casting around for something more intelligent to say.

Kvara stepped in then, tiring of Oen's stammering enquiries.

'The data in your sending was clear,' he said. As he spoke, he lifted a gauntlet and flexed the fingers of it absently. Oen stared at it, distracted by the casual, supple movement. 'You've lost five of your harvester stations in five local months. No survivors, no readings. Nothing but debris. Something is coming out of the water. A beast.'

Kvara let his gauntlet fall to the tabletop with a dull clang.

'I have hunted beasts before.'

'We've men assigned to this already,' Oen said. 'I'd hoped that–'

'That I might join them?' Kvara shook his head. 'No. Tell your men to stand down. In this, as in everything, I work alone.'

Oen looked up into the golden eyes, and thought about protesting. Perhaps this... *Space Wolf* didn't know how big a hub harvester was. Anything that could take down one of those things must be massive, far bigger than the flyer he'd returned to Nyx in. The security detail he'd had on alert for three months consisted of nine hundred men, and he'd been considering expanding it.

'I'm not sure–'

'You're not sure I can handle whatever it is you've got attacking your people,' said Kvara. 'You're not sure something looking as dishevelled and terrible as me could do much more than get himself killed.'

He leaned forward, and the metal of the table bowed under the pressure of his forearms. Oen recoiled, feeling the hot-meat breath wash over him.

'This is not about you, Morren Oen,' whispered Kvara, taking a cold pleasure in running his tongue around the words. 'This has nothing to do with you.'

Oen tried to hold the gaze from those animal eyes, and failed. He looked down at the rivets on the table, ashamed of himself.

'I need a flyer,' said Kvara, sitting back. 'Fastest you have. Then you can forget about me, and forget about your problem.'

Oen nodded for a third time. Being in the presence of Kvara was intensely tiring. He found himself happy to do almost anything to get the encounter over with.

'It will be done, lord,' he said, knowing that, whatever he'd expected to get out of that first meeting, he'd failed badly. 'I'll get straight on it.'

Eim looked sympathetic as Oen emerged from the room. She placed a hand lightly on his shoulder.

'How'd it go?'

Oen shrugged and smiled wryly.

'Not what I expected,' he said, shaking off the hand and walking down the corridor. He went quickly, keen to be out of there. 'Though I don't really know what I thought would happen.'

Eim trotted after him, looking up anxiously.

'How many of them have come?'

'Just him.'

'You're joking.'

'No.'

Eim snorted.

'I'll get the 'paths sending again.'

'That may not be necessary.'

'Of course it'll be necessary,' said Eim, scowling. 'We need men. There must be Guard somewhere within range – they'd send a whole company soon enough if they thought tithe production was about to fall.'

Oen halted, looking thoughtful. Now that he was out of Kvara's intimidating presence, he was beginning to think more clearly.

'He doesn't think he needs help.'

'That's his problem. I mean, did you *see* what he looked like?'

'Right up close,' said Oen, ruefully. 'It wasn't pretty.'

Eim shook her head irritably.

'*One!*' she snorted. 'I didn't think they ever worked on their own. I thought they came in squads – you know, like you see on the holos.'

Oen shrugged.

'So did I,' he said. 'Maybe different types have different ways. He's a Space Wolf. Heard of them?'

Eim shook her head.

'Nice name,' she said. 'Suits his looks.'

'Careful what you say,' warned Oen, looking over his shoulder and back down the corridor. 'His hearing's very good.'

'Okay, okay.' Eim sighed, and ran a weary hand through her hair. 'But, procurator, this is the last thing we needed. We lose another hub, and we'll miss the next quota even if I keep the crews on triple rotation. For a minute there I was daring to hope we'd find a way out of this.'

This time it was Oen who put a reassuring hand on her shoulder.

'You never know,' he said. 'He may be more impressive than he looks.'

He leaned closer to her, and lowered his voice.

'He's taking a flyer out, soon as I can requisition one,' he said, covering his mouth. 'And, whatever he says, I want it tracked and a team placed ready for rapid deployment, just in case he finds anything. Can you do that?'

Eim shot him a tolerant, affectionate look.

'Sure I can,' she said. 'Just in case.'

The flyer skimmed low over the ocean, casting a deep green shadow on the waves. Kvara drove it hard, irritated by the lack of the explosive speed he was used to. One engine was already burning close to capacity, and the dashboard in front of him was active with red warning runes.

Kvara ignored them and concentrated on the view from the cockpit. Lyses stretched away in every direction, formless and empty, a wasteland of pure water and pure sky. The first sun was up, and the arc of the atmosphere was bleached salmon pink. The ocean was calm, veined with lines of white where the massive swells rolled under him.

It was pristine. In an Imperium where the hand of man fell heavily on everything it touched, Lyses was a rare jewel. In its inviolability it reminded Kvara of Fenris. On the death world, everything below the Asaheim parallel was barely touched by humanity. Lyses was more benign, but had the same vast, untouched quality.

Despite everything, that spoke to his soul. It had been a long time since anything had done that, and he found the experience, on the whole, uncomfortable.

There is one objective left, one mission, one task. Remember it.

He pushed the flyer down further, skimming it barely a man's height above the waves. Spray flashed down the sleek flanks of the machine, spinning and frothing as he banked around in a long arc. Then he powered it up, sweeping along the trajectory the procurator had given him. For a moment, just a moment, he could have been back on a *drekkar*, relishing the steep pitch and yaw of the heavy wooden hull as it ploughed through the endlessly violent seas of his home.

But Lyses was too beautiful for that. Too beautiful, and too forgiving.

Below him, the algal blooms began to intensify. Deep green and cloudy, they hung just below the surface, bathed by the light of the sun. They extended for hundreds of kilometres, a vast mat of nutrient-rich matter, stuffed with proteins.

It was for them that mankind had come to Lyses, to suck up the endless stream of life-giving algae, to process it into foodstuffs ready to be transported off-world to the famished hives and forges elsewhere in the sector. Hub harvesters, mobile floating industrial behemoths, prowled the waters endlessly, slowly ploughing furrows through the infinite bounty, dragging it up and packing it into billions upon billions of dried and pressed pellets ready for transport to gigantic processing manufactoria on other planets.

According to the records Kvara had accessed in Nyx, Lyses hadn't had a serious security incident for over five hundred years. The harvesters had just kept on going, criss-crossing the ocean, working the algae and scooping it into their maw-like hoppers, as if it would go on forever.

But nothing lasted forever – everything decayed, everything was tainted.

Kvara allowed himself a grunt of cynical satisfaction. A world without strife was an affront to his battle-hardened sensibilities. All that could exist in such a place was softness, and softness opened the door to corruption.

The blooms grew ever thicker as the flyer sped on. The green darkened, forming a solid mass under the waves. If things had been working properly, he guessed, it would never have been left to become so overgrown.

A green rune blinked on the forward scanner. Kvara sat back in the pilot's seat, cramped in his bulky armour, and watched the ruin of the hub approach. He came in low, observing the way the broken struts still speared up from the waves.

The harvester had been massive. Wreckage littered the surface for a square kilometre or more, floating on the gentle swell or lodged in thick knots of algae. Kvara applied the air brakes, swivelling the engines forward to arrest his speed and achieve a low hover. He flicked a dial on the dashboard, and the bubble-cockpit slid back.

Warm, softly fragranced air rolled over him. The smell of the algae was rich and faintly sweet. Kvara hauled himself out of the seat and leaned over the side. His weight caused the flyer to tip violently and the engines whined as they compensated.

He narrowed his eyes, poring over the debris. No burn marks or signs of explosions marked the surfaces. Where the plasteel was broken, it looked like it had been snapped cleanly. Other pieces had the jagged evidence of claw-rakes on them.

Kvara studied each piece carefully, spending time observing the angle of the impacts, the force used, the frequency of them.

Is it worthy? Is it enough?

Early signs were promising. He felt a tremor of excitement in his hearts, and swiftly suppressed it. There had been too many disappointments for him to start thinking along those lines.

Keeping the cockpit-bubble open, Kvara sat back in the pilot's seat and started a slow circle of the wreckage. As he did so, he abstracted his mind from the particular, and drifted into the general.

There were huge channels gouged through the algae blooms, marking the passage of something truly massive. Though there were several of them, Kvara had the sense that only one beast had made them.

Prey.

He closed his eyes, just as he would have done on Fenris where the spirits of hunter and hunted intertwined closely, haunting the high mountain airs and staining the unbroken snow.

I see you. I see your path. I will follow it, and then comes the test.

He saw the trail of the beast in his mind, just as if it were a herd of *konungur*, twisting away into possible futures. He saw it plunge down into the frigid depths, as dark as the void of space, writhing along the jagged ocean floor.

He opened his eyes. Below him, a wide furrow in the algal carpet stretched off into the distance, jagging back and forth.

I see you.

Kvara nudged the flyer after it, following the trail. As he did during every hunt, he put himself in the mind of his prey, imagining the mental processes of the beast and the strange, sluggish thoughts in that giant mind. He had learned to do it with such acuity that, for a moment at least, he might have been one himself.

As he travelled, his certainty grew. He powered the flyer back into full propulsion.

Kvara sat back, eyes half-closed, the warm wind racing past him. He let his instincts play loose, running down the prey, chasing after it as if a physical scent had lodged in his nostrils.

It was the same then as it had always been. For a moment, the hunt took over, the quest became everything.

In simpler, harsher times, that was all there had been.

In the past that was now faded and hard to recall, he had lived for nothing else.

I see you.

The drekkar took a heavy hit and buckled over to starboard. It rolled across the heavy, gun-grey sea, lashed by the torrential rain. The deluge lanced down from the low cloud line, spears of liquid that bounced and rattled from the deck.

Everything moved. Waves crashed against the high flanks and cascaded down the deck, as cold as mountain-ice and hard as bullwhips. The masts screamed against the rigging, taut with ice crystals and shivering.

'I see you!' roared Thenge, bounding up to the prow with his long, white pelt in tow.

Olekk and Regg followed him, clasping tight to the railing, their boots slipping on the sodden deck-boards. Each one of them carried a long spear in their hands, crowned with a biting edge ground out of the iron by the priests.

Lightning flickered across the northern sky, followed by the crack, roll and boom of thunder.

Fenrys was angry, just as ever, and the seas boiled with that anger.

Aj Kvara hung from the high foremast by one hand, swaying far out over the water as the ship tilted and tipped. He hadn't seen anything but the driving rain and riot of moving water.

He swore to himself, and hurried down the rigging. If Thenge had seen something from the prow, then his eyes had been the keener. That was bad. Kvara's youth was supposed to be his advantage.

Then, before he was halfway to the deck, the sea off to port boiled up in a mass of bubbles and lashing, slapping fronds.

'Here it comes!' yelled Rakki, his voice high with excitement. From somewhere else in the longship, furious laughter broke out. Kvara dropped to the deck, grabbed a spear and raced to the side.

Ahead of them, breaking the surface a dozen fathoms off, something vast and black slipped above the turmoil of the waves before sloping back down again. Kvara saw a glossy shell, pock-marked with barnacles, rolling away from the pursuing hunters and diving smoothly. A geyser of water puffed up as the beast exhaled and drew in more air.

'*Hvaluri!*' roared Olekk, laughing like the others.

Kvara felt excitement spur up within him, and he leaned further over, craning for another glimpse. The drekkar carried over thirty warriors. Taking a hvaluri would feed them and their families for weeks, as well as providing much else of value to the tribe.

'Faster!' Kvara shouted, up at old Rakki who was master of the ship.

The big man, one-eyed and scar-faced, glared back at him from the tiller.

'You hunt!' he blurted, outraged. 'I sail!'

The creature broke the surface again, closer that time, sweeping up through the choppy water and letting out a muffled bellow of anger.

Maggr was still up in the rigging, and was first to throw. His spear shot down through the rain, spinning on its axis. It hit hard, burying the jagged iron blade deep into the hvaluri's armoured hide. The beast roared and went down again.

'*Hjolda!*' Maggr bellowed, balling his fists and sending his face red with fervour.

Other spears shot down, missing the target and splashing into the walls of moving water.

Kvara bided his time, waiting for the hvaluri to surface again. The ship slipped steeply down a precipitous leading wave, wallowing at the base of it before climbing up the next one. The deck rolled and swung like a berserker's axe-lunge, testing the warriors' precarious footing. They braced themselves against the ropes, edging closer to the tilting side of the ship, peering into the storm-lashed murk for a glimpse of the prey they hunted.

'Round left!' bellowed Thenge, getting frustrated and reaching for a second throwing spear.

The drekkar shivered as its prow came across, buffeted by the crashing seas. The skinsails, those had hadn't been furled against the storm, stretched out taut, making the ship race through the spray like a loosed crossbow bolt.

'I have it!' crowed Olekk, leaping up on to the sharply pitching rail and taking aim.

Something long and sinuous flashed out of the water, lashing across at Olekk with spiked barbs and dragging him over.

There was no scream. He was gone in an instant, pulled down into the icy depths from which no living man ever returned.

Kvara ran across the deck, springing up to where Olekk had been standing. He had a brief glimpse of black tentacles thrashing in the water, covering a foaming patch of dark red before that was swept astern by the racing sea.

He hurled his spear down, but the edge of the ship bucked wildly, sending his aim wide.

'*Skítja*,' he swore, jumping down and reaching for another spear.

Then the drekkar shuddered heavily, as if something vast had hit it from below. Thenge lost his footing and sprawled across the deck like a drunkard. The whole ship shot up, briefly thrown clear of the waves, before crashing back down again, snapping whole lengths of rigging and making the loose ropes flail like scourges.

Maggr jumped from the broken ropes, still flushed from his success, and barrelled up to the prow, leaping over the grappling form of Thenge.

'Ha!' he crowed, grabbing two throwing spears and taking the lead warrior's place.

Kvara chuckled at the presumption of it, leaping away from the rolling edge and grabbing a fresh spear of his own.

Everyone was still laughing and roaring – the ragged, caustic laugh of hunters gripped by the manic touch of the kill-urge. The whole ship was febrile with it, spilling over with savage, raw energy.

'I *want* this kill,' spat Kvara. His blond hair had come loose of its plaits, and lashed round his clean, ruddy face in the wind. He grinned as he spoke, and his white teeth flashed in the storm.

'Then throw quicker, lad,' said Maggr, taking up a spearing position and scouring the churning waves.

It came up again then, huge and glistening. Kvara saw a single eye the size of his chest, as round as the moon and grey like an oyster. It glared at them, burning with bestial hatred and fury.

He didn't hesitate. Fast as a whip-snap, Kvara hurled the spear. It whistled through the air, striking straight through the heart of the eye. The shaft trembled, and it lodged fast.

The hvaluri bellowed, its roars making the water drum and vibrate, before rolling heavily away from the boat.

'It won't go down!' shouted Thenge, back on his feet and braced for another throw. 'Not now!'

Kvara raced to fetch another spear. His heart was thumping with glorious, brutal energy. Every muscle ached, every sinew was taut, but his heart sang.

I speared the eye! I did it!

The creature reared up, thundering out of the boiling sea, throwing water across its hunched, gnarled back in huge tumbling sheets.

'*Morkai!*' swore Regg, hurling a spear at it and somehow managing to miss.

The beast was massive, at least the size of the drekkar and much, much heavier. It thrashed around in a wallow of agony, the spears still protruding from its body. A huge shell of barnacle-crusted blackness rolled around, crowned with spines and bone-ridges. A mass of tentacles flashed out from under the skirts of the shell, twisting and writhing like a nest of prehensile tongues. Spray shot out, splattering against the masts and cascading down on to the warriors.

'Too close!' warned Rakki, heaving on the tiller.

The ship came round, but not quickly enough. Tentacles shot out, latching on to the railings and dragging the drekkar back. It tilted heavily, listing over nearly to the tipping point.

Thenge lost his footing again, raging and cursing as he slipped down the steepling deck. A tentacle spun out, clamping on to his ankle and gripping tight. He grabbed his axe from his belt and hacked down, severing it cleanly and freeing himself.

Other warriors charged, hurling their spears at the exposed underbelly of the beast. Some of the blades bit deep, disappearing into the forest of thrashing members, provoking fresh roars of pain. The sea frothed with a thick black sludge as the monster began to bleed. Some of it splashed out across Kvara's face, hot and salty.

'It'll drag us down!' shouted Rakki, toiling uselessly at the tiller.

More tentacles latched on to the ship, some reaching all the way across to the far side. The drekkar listed further, and water began to lap across the lower edge of the deck, washing up across the already drenched planks.

Thenge raced over to the nearest tendril, hacking away with his axe. He cut through it sharply, but two more fronds quickly whipped across. All across the ship, warriors swapped their throwing spears for short-handled axes and began chopping frantically at the strangling lengths of tentacle. Even as they worked, the ship slipped further down, dragged through the mountainous swell by the wounded beast.

Kvara drew his throwing arm back, only to feel a viscous, slimy wall of flesh hit him full in the face. He crashed back heavily, cracking his head on something unyielding on the way down. He had the blurred impression of a black tube the width of his arm snaking across his field of vision and falling over him. A hot wash of pain ran through his skull, and he felt blood running down the back of his neck.

Acting on instinct, he swept up his spear, still grasped in his right hand, shoving the blade of it up through the tentacle. It carved through sweetly, separating it into two pieces. The broken-off end continued to writhe on its own, jerking and spasming across the sodden wood.

Kvara staggered to his feet. The ship was going down. Waves rushed up the tilted deck, flooding into the hold below. For every tentacle the warriors slashed apart, more shot out, wrapping the drekkar in a morass of dripping, slippery tendrils.

'Hjolda!' he roared, grabbing his axe from his belt and throwing his arms back in challenge.

The beast loomed up at him, sweeping up out of the waves and roaring its own booming call of anger.

Kvara sprinted down the listing deck, leaping over the bodies of the fallen and veering past the flickering ends of searching tentacles, ignoring the hammering pain in his head. He ran straight at the huge domed shell, hacking away the snaking tubes of meat as they swept into his path.

It felt like he was running down a cliff-edge, straight into the depths of the bottomless ocean. He could see the bulk of the hvaluri below him, wallowing in a messy broth of broken spars and bloody water.

He leapt, flying away from the ship and through the air, plummeting for a moment, his long hair streaming behind him and his axe held high.

Then he landed, crunching on to the shell of the beast, feeling the hard surface flex from the impact.

He nearly skidded straight across it and over the far side, but managed to clutch at a bone-ridge with his trailing hand. He yanked to a halt, nearly blinded with spray and buffeted by the gusting wind.

The creature let out a deafening roar and hauled itself further out of the boiling sea. Tentacles shot up, trailing across its shell, reaching out to rip him from its back and hurl him into the water.

Kvara pulled himself to his knees, balancing precariously on the bucking, rolling curve, hacking at any tentacles that reached him. Blood still ran from his head wound, making him dizzy. Through the clouds of spray, he could just make out the drekkar rolling away, righting itself as the hold of the tentacles was released.

Kvara batted away a flailing length of tentacle, then slammed the axe-head down. It cracked open the shell, plunging deep into the translucent, sticky matter beneath.

The beast bellowed, thrashing and yawing in the waves. Jets of black ink spouted up, splashing across Kvara's chest. He pulled the axe free, drew it up and chopped down again. The blade cracked open a new wound, shattering the beast's armoured covering and tearing up the soft flesh beneath. More ink welled up, boiling hot and fizzing.

Kvara kept attacking it, ripping up the outer layers and burying the axe-head deep into the yielding blubber beneath. The tentacles lashed out, feebly now. The cries of the beast became plaintive rather than angry. Gouts of black murk pumped from its wounds, turning the roiling waves dark and viscous.

Kvara heard a heavy crunch close by. He looked up and saw Thenge by his side, scrabbling for purchase on the shell before getting to his knees. The big warrior grinned at him, an axe in each hand.

'Brave work, pup!' he laughed, whirling the blades in his hands before hacking them down. 'We'll make you a man yet!'

Then the two of them got to work, gripping the tilting shell and hacking it open, burrowing down, slicing through the hide of the beast, breaking up what remained of the hard barrier between them and the pulpy mass beneath. Out of the corner of his eye, Kvara saw the grappling hooks fly out from the drekkar, latching on the foundering creature, ready to haul it to the side of the ship. Other warriors were preparing to make the leap across, brandishing hooks and cleavers.

Kvara kept his head down after that, working hard. His

pain at the back of his head wouldn't abate, though it didn't stop him working.

Amid all of it, he still grinned. He couldn't help himself. The flush of victory ran through his veins, keeping his arms moving and giving his legs the strength to hold him in position.

This is my kill, he thought as he hacked away furiously, trying not to let his stupid, childish grin show too much.

My kill.

A day later and the storm lessened in its fury, though the seas ran hard for much longer. The drekkar made heavy work of it, labouring in the deep swell. The central mast still stood but much of the rigging had been ripped away. Several holes had been punched below the waterline, and no matter how fast the crew bailed it out, the bilges sloshed with seawater where the makeshift repairs had been hammered on.

Aside from Olekk, three other warriors had been dragged over the edge. That was a heavy toll for the tribe, though the scale of the prize compensated for that. The meat of the hvaluri would keep them fed for many months once the women had smoked and salted it. The tough shell would provide tools for them and the beast's blood would be distilled into both fuel and food.

The ship ran low in the water, laden down with every piece of hide and blubber the warriors could fit aboard. It stank of the sea, acrid and salty, but no one minded that. It was a good haul, worth setting out across the blade-dark ocean for.

As they neared home Thenge sat with Kvara in the prow, chewing on a long piece of sinew and letting the grease run down his beard.

'Feeling better?' he asked good-naturedly.

Kvara nodded. He'd broken his arm on the leap back to the ship after the hvaluri had given up the fight, much to the raucous amusement of the rest of the crew. Even after it had been bound up with a rough splint, it still ached – not that he would ever show it.

His head was the worst of it. He didn't dare to get it looked at by the priests. The blood still oozed thickly from the wound, and the pain grew with every passing hour. His vision was beginning to blur. It wasn't healing.

'I mean what I say,' said Thenge, jabbing his finger at the blond warrior. 'That was brave. The test of manhood awaits, and you're ready.'

Kvara took up a string of sinew himself and chewed on it.

'Not sure?' asked Thenge.

'I'll do it,' he said. 'Not now.'

Thenge snorted.

'Why wait?'

Kvara looked away from him, down the longship where the rest of the crew laboured. They were his people, the ones he'd lived with all his short life. They'd never made him feel anything less than part of their world. The test of manhood – the long, solitary hunt across the icy wastes, daunted him. He didn't fear death, and certainly didn't fear danger, but something about the ordeal made him hang back.

He would do it, but not soon. The time wasn't right.

'I don't know,' he said, truthfully enough. He took another bite of the sinew, feeling the slippery flesh slide around his mouth. The action of eating dulled the pain slightly. 'I'm not ready.'

He looked up then, up at the grey walls of cloud that shrouded Fenrys. In a rare break, where the sheets of occlusion gave way slightly, he thought he saw something up there, shadowing them. A huge bird, perhaps, but its profile was strangely angular. It seemed to hang motionless in the air.

'Perhaps you're not ready to be out on your own,' said Thenge, resignedly.

Kvara nodded, not really paying attention. His head was getting worse. The clouds closed back together, hiding whatever it was that he'd seen.

'Yes,' he said. 'Perhaps that's right.'

Kvara ran his finger over the names on his armour. The snow-grey metal was softened in Lyses' warm light. Even the blade marks, the scorches and the dents looked a little less jagged.

He didn't need to read the names in order to remember them. They were carved on to his mind just as deeply as they were etched into the ceramite.

Mór, his thick-set face framed by black, dense sideburns. Dark hair, pale skin, like a vision of an underverse spectre with the sardonic humours to match.

Grimbjard Lek, the polar opposite. Sunny, blond, his mouth twitching up into a wicked smile at the first excuse. He'd killed with a smile on his face, that one, glorying the Allfather with every swing of his axe.

Vrakk, the one they'd all called Backhand, bulky and blunt with his power fist thrumming, a dirty fighter but useful enough to make up for it.

Aerjak and Rann, brothers-in-arms, inseparable and possessed of that uncanny awareness of the other's state. Kvara had always had Aerjak down for the Rune Priests. He'd had a strange way about him, something tied to the wyrd, for all the good it had done him on Deneth Teros.

Frorl, the blade-master, swinging his frostblade with that unconscious, mocking ease, disdaining ranged weapons for the thrill of disruptors and steel-edge.

Rijal Svensson, wiry and fast, quick to anger and equally quick to laugh, his nose broken so many times that it had almost been not worth bothering with. He'd never accepted augmetic replacements, preferring to keep the stub of gristle and bone-shards in place to remind him not to get carried away.

Finally, Beorth, the quiet one. Only happy when hoisting his heavy bolter into position or at the controls of something huge and slung with big guns. He'd have been a Long Fang before he made Grey Hunter, if they'd let him. He'd laughed rarely, never sharing the coarse jokes the rest of them let spill from their profane lips, but when he had done, that rolling, rich, mirthful rumble had made Kvara grin unconsciously along with him.

Beorth had been the hardest, out of all of them. He'd been the one they'd never noticed unless he wasn't there.

Kvara let his armoured finger trace out the names, clicking softly as it passed over the runic grooves.

Perhaps you're not ready to be out on your own.

A warning light blinked on the dashboard. Kvara snapped out of his memories and took in the data.

The hub was in visual range and racing towards him fast. It was a small installation, a few hundred metres in diameter on the surface and crowned with a couple of comms towers, a few landing stages and a squat ops centre. Lights still blinked at the summit, flashing piercingly in the heat of day. The algae stretched away from it, sparse in patches and thick in others. Four lines of oily smoke rose from the harvester processing nodes, indicating that it was still working.

Kvara's face wrinkled in disapproval. He could smell the thick stench of promethium already, a low-grade variant, greasy and sour.

His armoured fingers ran over the console, keying in the landing codes from the databank Oen had uploaded to the flyer. A pict over to his left immediately updated with the response. The protective cover of one of the landing stages withdrew, unfurling like an iron rosebud, and he banked the flyer towards it.

Nothing obviously wrong.

He touched the flyer down on the platform and jumped down from the open cockpit. Smoke poured from one of the engines, and the others wound down slowly, as if their bearings had been ground away.

Kvara strode across the apron, unconsciously checking his weapons. The bolt pistol at his waist was fully loaded and primed with the appropriate blessing. Blood, his own blood, ceremonially stained the muzzle. Across his back was strapped Djalik, his blade. It was a short, stabbing sword, notched and serrated along one of the cutting edges and with inset runes lodged under the bronze-lined hilt. Over the years the metal had been dulled with burns from the weapon's disruptor field, making it as dark as charcoal.

Kvara sniffed the air, going watchfully. Everything was quiet. The installation barely moved on the placid waters. The warm wind blew across the towers and manufactoria units, washing over the grey plasteel in an endless, placid sigh.

Ahead of him, two doors slid soundlessly open, opening the way into the hub's interior. Orange lights blinked on, illuminating a bare, clean corridor. Everything smelled of the algae – a mulchy, briny tang that lingered at the back of the throat.

Kvara paused before entering, taking a final look across the hub. Aside from the low growl of automating processors, all was calm. The green waters lapped softly at the flanks of the harvester, a hundred metres down from the landing platforms.

Where are the men?

Reluctantly, having got used to the clean, unfiltered taste of the air, Kvara retrieved his battered helm from its mag-lock and screwed it in place. The balmy atmosphere of Lyses disappeared, replaced by the filtered, sterile environment of his armour-shell.

Kvara took up his bolt pistol, and breathed a prayer, the same prayer he'd uttered during every quest since Deneth Teros.

Allfather, deliver me from safety and bring me into peril.

Then he walked inside.

'Where is he now?'

'Alecto XI. He's landed.'

'That's a long way from the last site. Have we got anything from the crew?'

'Nothing. Not a thing.'

'When was the last transmit?'

'Uh, hang on.'

Eim steadied herself against the sway of the flyer. It was a big one, capable of spending several days out over the water and accommodating a full assault company. She didn't like using craft that big – their judder and yaw, as well as the fuel-tinged air, made her nauseous, and the grunts got restive cooped up in the holds.

'We don't have anything from them for six days, ma'am.'

Eim turned to the comms officer and raised an eyebrow.

'Why wasn't that picked up? They're meant to be checking in daily.'

The comms officer, a grey-faced man with deep-sunk eyes and an unfortunate overbite, shrugged apologetically.

'There are a lot to monitor.'

Eim swore and rubbed her eyes with the balls of his fists. Throne of Earth, she felt tired. Oen would owe her for this when she got back.

'Okay, run a scan. Check for anything.'

'I can't see… whoa. I really don't know… what is that?'

Eim pushed him aside and leaned over the augur console. As she watched the shapes clarify, she felt a sudden, cold thrill shudder through her body.

'How close are we to him?'

'A long way. Procurator Oen insisted on a range of–'

'Forget that. We're going in. Signal Nyx, but don't wait for a response.'

She turned away from the comms officer and looked out across the cramped bridge space. Other officers looked up from their stations. Their expressions had switched from mild boredom into nervous expectation.

'Get the men armed and ready to deploy,' she said, speaking to the company commander, a squat, low-browed man called Frehis Aerem. 'All squads, assault order, ready to drop on my word.'

Eim looked back at the console before he'd had a chance to respond. As she watched the augur line sweep round for another pass, she felt her heart start to thump faster within her chest.

'Damn you, Oen,' she muttered, shaking her head as she

watched the data stream in. 'You let him go out there – this is on *your* conscience.'

The corridors were quiet and lit only by dim orange light. Every metre of them was pristine, scrubbed clean and glistening. Octagonal hatches appeared at regular intervals along the walls, all closed. Kvara tried one of the handles, and it clicked against the bolt lock. He punched through the mechanism, cracking the handle, and the hatch swung open.

The chamber on the far side was empty. There was a desk, two metal chairs, a scale model of the harvester station on a sideboard. More orange light flickered from a semi-functional lumen, catching the jewels in a cheap devotional image of some primarch or other. No one was inside and, from the sterile smell of it, no one had been inside for some time.

Kvara turned back, walking through the network of corridors. Despite his heavy boots, his footfalls were soft. The power armour hummed – a low, grinding noise at the edge of mortal hearing – the only thing that broke the dense fog of silence.

Kvara paused, inclining his head, listening carefully. For a second, there was a trace sound, right on the edge of his audible range. Nothing he could latch on to, and not enough data for the helm to augment.

He started walking again, keeping his pistol held high. The grey hair along the back of his neck stood erect, brushing against the collar of his armour. He could feel his thick blood pumping vigorously around his bulky frame. His awareness had sharpened up, causing his muscles to loosen and his pupils to dilate. He heard his own breathing resonate within the helm, close and hot.

I come for you. You know I am here.

At the end of the corridor was another intersection. He waited again, watching, listening, absorbing.

Show yourself.

The lights blew.

The corridor plunged into darkness. Something raced up out of the shadows, phenomenally fast, scrabbling on the metal floor as it came.

In the nanosecond before Kvara's helm compensated, it swerved around the corner and out at him. A hellish face, obscenely long and crested, lashed up out of the dark.

Kvara loosed two bolts, aiming fast. They impacted with a crack and flash of light, shattering a brittle shell. High screams, alien screams, echoed from the walls.

More of them arrived, leaping over the fallen outrider. Jointed limbs clattered over metal, flashing ice-white as more bolt-flares lit them up. They came in a tangled rush, jostling each other, jaws wide and biting.

Kvara pulled back, firing all the time. His arm moved only by fractions, picking out target after target, cracking apart the growing swarm of xenos creatures. The intersection clogged quickly with smashed shells and oozing pulp, but he kept coolly firing.

Just as the ammo counter ran down, the onslaught ceased. The last of the chittering screams died away, leaving a pile of twisted, snapped and cracked shells in front of him.

Kvara ejected the old magazine, slammed a fresh one into the pistol housing and drew his blade with his left hand. Djalik's disruptor field fizzed into life, throwing an electric blue aura out from the cutting edge.

He strode out into the intersection, wading through a swamp of broken, twitching carcasses, watching for more of the xenos to come at him.

He knew what they were. He'd fought such beasts on a dozen worlds.

Hormagaunts, the Imperium called them.

Kvara liked fighting tyranids. Unlike Traitors, for whom he could feel nothing but a blind, disgusted fury, or the greenskins, which were contemptible, tyranids were a force he could respect.

They were pure. They suffered from neither fear nor corruption nor fatigue. Like the native beasts of his own world, they lashed out with an unsullied primal aggression, driven to kill out of hammered-in instinct and never stopping until death took them or the task was completed.

They saw him as prey. He saw them as prey. That made things even.

Ahead of Kvara the corridor opened out into a wide, square room. Banks of equipment were arranged in long rows, all still clean and unsullied. Across them lay the bodies of the hub's crew, very much not clean and unsullied.

They had been ripped open. Their bodies, what was left of them, hung in glistening loops of gristle and sinew all across the room. A few had tried to get out, running for the double doors on the far side of the space. The trails of blood, as thick and dark as engine oil, didn't reach very far. The corpses still had looks of horrified surprise on their faces – those, at any rate, who still had faces.

Kvara swept the room with his pistol. The lights were still down, and his helm picked the outlines of the bodies in fuzzy grey light.

He sensed them coming before his armour's equipment did. A skittering, scraping run, muffled by the closed doors to the corridor beyond, punctuated by the high-pitched rattle of xenos vocal cords. They were racing towards him – dozens of them, maybe more.

Kvara grinned.

The doors burst apart, thrown aside by a press of straining bodies. Blurred xenos outlines, skeletal and reptilian, swarmed through the gap and into the room, screaming at him with stretched-wide jaws, pouring over the surfaces in a rolling wave of needle-teeth and hooked claws.

'Fenrys!'

Kvara charged straight back at them, leaping over a slumped pile of eviscerated bodies and bringing his blade round in a wide, blistering arc. He hurled himself into the tide, loosing volleys of bolt-fire that flashed out in the dark like storm lightning.

They came on, lashing out at him, and he shattered their talons. They leapt up to maul him, and he broke their snapping jaws. He spun round, shifting from one foot to another, punching out, slicing back with the blade, firing all the while. Scrawny xenos bodies smashed apart, bursting open and spraying fluid across his whirling, gyrating armour.

More of them poured in through the broken doors, streaming into the chamber and leaping up to make contact with him. They bounded over the bodies of their own dead, desperate to draw blood.

Kvara smashed his pistol-hand round, caving in a swollen xenos skull, before sending two more rounds spinning into two more targets, jabbing up with the blade and hauling it back through the entrails of another flailing monster.

They were all over him, tearing and screaming, but he was faster, bigger and stronger. As they howled with agonised frustration, he grunted with coarse satisfaction. His gauntlets were heavy and sticky with fluids, but he kept them moving. The liquid splattered over his breastplate, dousing the graven names under layers of filth.

He had been bred to do this. There was nothing left for him but this. Only in such work could his soul find a measure of peace even as his body pushed itself to the extremes of performance.

He was back where he belonged. Back in the fight.

'Kvara!'

Mór's voice was strained over the comm, broken up by the crackle of ordnance. Huge, thumping crashes distorted the feed.

'Position, brother,' snapped Kvara, running hard, feeling the sweat run down his temple.

'Rann… all gone…'

And that was it. The comm spat a fog of static. Kvara kept running, keeping his head low, weaving through the rubble. Solid rounds fizzed over his head, impacting against the rockcrete and showering him with rubble.

Blood of Russ – where are they?

He sensed a detonation to his left, and leapt clear. The already ruined wall exploded, hurling out an orb of fire and rusty shrapnel. The blast wave threw him from his feet, slamming him into the nearside bulwark. His armour crunched through it, tearing up the stone and showering him in dust.

'Position!' he spat, righting himself and breaking into a run again.

Nothing but hissing came over the comm. The fractured sky of Deneth Teros rumbled with electric storms, and a fork of violet lightning licked the burning horizon.

'Lek. Svensson. *Position.'*

He ducked down again and started to run. Above him, huge artillery trails lanced between the shells of the spires, exploding in a cacophony of overlaid, shuddering booms.

The static mocked him, and he blinked the feed closed. Far ahead of him, the city core was tearing itself apart. A vast hab-spire, hundreds of metres tall and crested with jagged towers, toppled over with eerie, magisterial slowness. Already broken open by a hundred major impacts, the walls imploded as it crashed down amongst the ruins, throwing up a bow wave of burning dust. The screams of those inside were lost in the ripping, flickering wind, burned away by the igniting promethium in the air.

Kvara raced across a narrow transit corridor, dodging the smoking craters and leaping over the lines of barbed stranglewire. Explosive rounds followed him, puffing up as they hit the tarmac. Since he'd left Vrakk, coughing up his own blood in the gutter with his lower body on the other side of the street, Kvara's tactical display had showed nothing but interference. The location runes of his pack all showed blank.

We're being torn apart.

He spotted movement, right on the edge of his left visual field, and swerved after it. Something – something big – ducked under a huge, low-hanging metal beam.

Kvara fired. The bolts screamed off into the fire-flecked murk, exploding as they demolished the beam in a cloud of spinning metal shards.

Then he was running again, leaping past smoking mortar holes and sweeping around smouldering heaps of twisted slag. He hadn't killed it. He'd have known if he had killed it.

Warned by some inner sense, he skidded to a halt, dropping down to a crouch.

A ball of plasma seared out of the gloom, missing by centimetres, slamming into the wall behind him. Kvara lurched forward, feeling the heat as another plasma bolt flew across his back.

He rolled to one side, bringing up his pistol and firing blind. The bolts connected with something, there was a shrill shriek, and the plasma torrent ceased.

Kvara sprang up, bounding after the source of the noise, ducking and swooping across the broken ground. As he went, his senses processed a thousand minor events in every direction – Guardsmen howling and weeping with fear and pain, juddering fire from dug-in positions over by the refineries, the grind and crack of armoured formations coming up from the transit hub along what remained of the Joslynssbahn. He processed those sounds, but did nothing about them. Everything was focussed on the elusive shadow, the shape that stayed one step ahead, the shape that had come among them and summoned blood.

Kvara tore round the shell of a burned-out Chimera, tasting the sweet taste of the hunt in his cloyed saliva.

Ahead, two hundred metres, he saw it again, dark between clouds of engine smoke. Huge, edged with spikes, loping like a maddened devil of the Helwinter. Corruption rolled from its carapace in a stink of oily shadow.

It turned, and eyes the colour of newborn flesh blazed at him.

Kvara fired as he ran, loosing a rolling column of explosive rounds and zigzagging through the broken remnants of the 576th Armoured Falchions.

The bolts connected, and the creature rocked back on huge, cloven feet. It cast aside a charred and broken plasma cannon and reached for a glittering blade. A scream sliced through the air, echoing in nightmarish polyphony.

Kvara didn't slow down. The pistol clicked empty, and he cast it aside, drawing up his blade Rothgeril and activating the lashing disruptors.

The thing he faced had once been a man. After that, it had been a Space Marine. After that, it had become a living altar of sadism, a prophet of the darkest corner of insanity and depravity in a galaxy already drenched in it.

Its armour, a grotesque blasphemy of Tactical Dreadnought plate, had burst out and split from the pulsing flesh beneath. Translucent tumours swelled up in the cracks, glowing and leaking and trembling. A face – part helm-grille, part skeletal rictus – grinned out from under a cowl of whip-curl bronze snakes. Eldritch energy rippled across the warped ceramite like meltwater. Blood flecked and speckled the pale pink tracery, boiling and hissing as the raw ether touched it and recoiled.

Kvara swung the blade low, driving it with frightening speed and precision. He could sense the acuity of his own movements, and gloried in it. Every nanometre of his body was straining for the kill. His hearts thudded, his blood raged, his lungs burned with a cleansing pain.

The blades clashed, and a boom of power discharged, throwing Kvara back and blunting his charge. The monster reared over him, pulling its pulsing sword-edge round for another blow.

Kvara pulled away, opening up a narrow space and spinning round to build up fresh momentum. The creature sliced its own blade across at him, tearing the very air itself asunder and leaving a trail of agonised matter in its wake.

Kvara ducked under it, feeling the charged edge tear a

chunk from his backpack. He thrust up, ignoring the sickly stench of filth that poured from the corrupted horror, grabbing the hilt of Rothgeril two-handed.

The sword bit deep, blazing like a field of stars as it crashed through the distorted ceramite and warp-addled flesh.

Then it was hauled away, dragged from his hands by a wrench so hard that Kvara lost his feet and was dragged, face-down, into the ash and dust of the ruined city. He recovered instantly, rolling away to evade the downward killing plunge before jumping back to his feet and backing away, disgusted at how easily his weapon had been taken from him.

Now the creature held two swords. One, its own, blazed with sick, overripe energy. The other, Kvara's, held upside-down by the blade-tip. The beast's long fingers squeezed through the furious disruptor field, bleeding dark purple blood where Rothgeril's biting edge sunk deep into its twisted flesh.

It laughed, and the sound was like the screaming of children.

Weaponless, Kvara clenched his gauntlets and snarled, ready for the onslaught. The creature was nearly twice his height, mutated and imbued with the essence of the Ruinous Powers. The Grey Hunter gazed up at it through red helm lenses, fearless and desperate, judging whether any blow he landed could do any damage to such a monster, tensing to sell his life with as much blood and fire as could still be mustered.

But not yet. A hurricane of heavy bolter fire slammed into the towering monster, smashing up the twisted armour and churning deep into the rose-pink muscle. It reeled, flailing against the bludgeoning hail of exploding projectiles.

Beorth limped out of the roiling clouds, his underslung bolter thundering from his two-handed grip. The comm-link was still a hiss of nothing. In broken bursts, Kvara could only hear a strangled, desperate sound from Beorth's feed.

The man, the big man, was *roaring*.

'A blade, brother!' shouted Kvara, stretching out a hand imploringly.

Beorth ignored him. He strode towards the staggering creature, firing all the while, ripping the armour-shell free of its sickening sigils and unholy signs. His own armour was as black as night, burned and rent open, and blood still poured from a dozen mortal wounds. He walked on regardless, massive and implacable, pouring a steady stream of withering, searing destruction from the red-hot muzzle of his huge weapon.

The monster waded through it, clawing at the bolts even as they punched into it, blowing shards from its armour and spraying plumes of purple. It staggered towards Beorth, screaming the whole time in a paroxysm of outrage and madness.

Then it leapt, streaming out in trails of blood and shell-discharge, arms outstretched and jaws open. It crashed into Beorth, knocking them both to the ground and rolling over. It savaged at his neck, tore at the cracks in his armour, stamped down with cloven hooves on to his prone limbs.

Kvara raced after them, pouncing on to the back of the creature. He grabbed the ornate lip of its armour and heaved, pulling it away from Beorth. The horror snarled and lashed round, trying to throw him off. Kvara clung on, digging his fingers deep into the exposed flesh under the ceramite, tearing it up and pulling it out in strips.

Beorth clambered back to his feet, drawing his blade. The heavy bolter thudded to the floor, spent and smoking.

The creature of Chaos threw Kvara off, hurling him to one side and swinging the twin swords down at his prone body. Kvara rolled away, evading them by centimetres, before Beorth charged back, slashing with his own combat blade, whirling and dancing with all the skill of Frorl.

Together, the two of them rocked back and forth, hacking and blocking. The Traitor was reeling now, weeping blood in rivulets down its shattered armour. Beorth's left arm hung limply by his side, awkwardly twisted, his every move radiating agony.

Kvara lurched to his feet in time to witness his brother's sword knocked away with a vicious swipe from the Traitor's warp-tainted blade. It spun away, glittering in the firelight, clattering across the stone. Spurred on by desperation, Kvara scrambled after it, grabbing the hilt just as it came to rest.

He whirled back round, only to see the creature break Beorth's neck with a final, horrifying lunge. The huge warrior was hoisted into the air and cast aside with a sickening crunch of bone.

Then it turned to Kvara, and grinned.

Kvara ignited the disruptor on Beorth's blade, barely noticing the runes signifying 'Djalik' along the blade. It felt light in his hand, balanced the way a combat sword should be.

'For the Allfather,' Kvara breathed softly, staring at the murderer of his pack, sensing the death-spirit locked tight in the killing blade.

The creature charged at him, both swords flailing, but its movements were jerky and erratic. Massive wounds had opened out across its body from Beorth's onslaught, all bleeding torrents.

Kvara darted forward, ducking under the first incoming swipe before jabbing up with the point of Djalik, twisting as the edge punched up through the outstretched chin of the Traitor.

The point cleaved cleanly, thrusting up through bone and brain. The monster, impaled on the lashing, spitting energy blade, jerked like a marionette, lashing out blindly with its twin weapons.

Huge fists battered Kvara, buffeting him from either side, but he remained firm. He fed power to Djalik's disruptors, and the creature's head bulged, cracked, and exploded.

A rain of pulp and bone shot outward, blinding Kvara and sending him reeling backwards again. Disorientated, he stumbled, landing heavily on his back. A sharp pain radiated from his side, and he caught sight of the Traitor's blade lodged in his torso. Runes flashed red across his helm display, giving him a tediously thorough summary of just how badly hurt that made him.

The headless body of the Traitor toppled, thudding dully against the tortured earth of Deneth Teros. Tendrils of warp-matter flickered across its ruined corpse, dancing like grave-sprites.

Still on his back, Kvara grabbed hold of the corrupted blade, gritted his teeth, and pulled. It came free with a wet squelch, dragging strands of muscle and skin with it through the jagged gash in his armour. He could feel the poison in the wound already, hot and boiling away like a swarm of insects. He tried to rise, and failed. Blood was leaking out of him freely, defying the clotting agents in his body. His vision blurred, going black, and his head fell back against the hot soil.

Above him, the sky was scored with trails of fire. As if from far away, he heard the rush and clamour of warfare.

The ground trembled underfoot as huge war engines trundled towards one another. High up in the dark skies, black silhouettes of drop-ships hung, shaky in the heatwash from their labouring engines.

Kvara watched it all mutely, feeling paralysis creep up to his lips. He could feel his consciousness slipping away, even as his ravaged body rallied against the poison frothing in his blood.

'Position...' he murmured, automatically, repeating the word he'd used so often over the last hour, feeling the bitter futility of it even as his mind lost its grip on the world of the senses.

Beorth was dead. Vrakk was dead. Rann and Aerjak had died together, just as they had surely been fated to do. The pack – all of them – were dead.

Kvara felt a solitary tear of rage run down his burned cheek. He wanted to take his helm off, to taste the air of the world that had done this, but his hands no longer obeyed his commands.

Night closed in on him, the night of oblivion. The last thing he saw was the helm display, functional and stark. The eight runes, eight identifier marks, were all blank, like empty holes into the void.

All dead.

The thought burned at his mind even as it retreated in nothingness. It stabbed at him, far sharper than the wound in his side, sharper than the many wounds across his battle-worn body, sharper than the knowledge, coming to him even as he lost everything else, that he was equal to the poisons, and that this would not be the last fight he would live to see.

That didn't matter. For the first time since coming off the ice and taking the Helix, that didn't matter.

Nothing mattered.
All dead.

'This is your choice.'

'I have made it.'

'Not yet. You need more time.'

'My decision won't change.'

'It may. I've seen it before.'

The eyes in the dark were red and slanted. If he had died, he would have expected eyes like those.

But he hadn't died, not physically. The eyes behind those lenses were like his. They were sunk deep into a black wolf skull mask with teeth set around the helm-grille.

Around him, the isolation chamber of the *Vrafnki* hummed with the grind of sub-warp travel. He didn't know where it was going, or how long it would be in transit. Much still had to be explained to him, though he was in no hurry to ask for information.

'It's a privilege, not a right,' said the Rune Priest, though less harshly than he might have done.

Kvara let his head sink back to the metal surface of the medicae cot. Every part of him still ached. His blood felt painfully hot, as if he'd been given a transfusion of molten lead.

'With all respect, lord,' he said, working his swollen lips painfully, 'I don't believe you. It's never been refused.'

For a moment, the skull mask remained static. Then a low, grating chuckle broke out from behind the black armour.

'Maybe.'

The mask drew closer, looming over him, coming to within a few centimetres of his face. Kvara looked up through the translucent mask of the medicae shroud with the one eye that still worked. He felt the soft pulse of the machinery around him, cycling his blood, working his hearts, filling his lungs, keeping him shackled to life.

'What do you think taking the lone path will be like, Hunter?' he asked. 'How long do you think it will take to find a prize big enough to extinguish your grief? When we pulled you from the ice, as near to death as you are now, you'd killed a hvaluri. How much bigger would your beast have to be, Aj Kvara, before its death would be enough?'

Kvara smiled grimly.

'When I was a child, I dreamed of killing a *krakken*. That's what I thought it took to become a Sky Warrior.'

'Then you are a fool. The krakken cannot be killed.'

'But Jarl Engir–'

'The krakken cannot be killed. It will tear at the roots of the world for eternity, weakening them, making them frail.'

The Rune Priest withdrew his skull mask. Kvara closed his eye. He felt the drugs in his system dragging him back to unconsciousness, and fought against it.

'It can be killed,' he said, feeling his words slur. 'I know it, and you know it. Everything that lives can be killed.'

He kept moving, heading down, ever down, fighting through the hormagaunts as they swarmed up from the lower levels, relishing every wave of them as they crashed and broke against his armour. Djalik was slick with their fluid, as was the muzzle of his bolt pistol, now dangerously low on ammunition.

The creatures had come from below. They'd run up the sensor shafts from the underwater sections, fast and silent. The human crew would have had no warning – no time even to send off a panicked transmission before the living wall of teeth and claws ripped into them. Before Kvara had arrived they'd been dispersing again, falling back down in scattered packs, making way for the monster whose appearance they'd heralded. Only his intervention had stirred them again, rousing them back into the slavering, indignant fury they'd shown before.

Now, once again, their numbers had been thinned. Kvara wheeled around smoothly, knocking three of the creatures bodily into the chamber walls. Two thumped wetly against the plasteel, slumping to the floor. The other managed to get up, and he grabbed it, snapping its neck with a contemptuous twist.

The floor rocked as something collided with the outside wall. The collisions were getting more violent, and he braced himself against them. A hormagaunt, one of the last remaining, skittered into the chamber and threw itself at him. Kvara cracked his fist into its oncoming jaws, not bothering to use the blade.

The chamber lurched again, and a crack snaked across the wall. Kvara backed away from it, running a quick check over his armour's integrity seals, knowing full well that he was several hundred metres below sea level.

The structure around him groaned and the walls began to bulge inwards. The cracks grew, as if something huge and prehensile had wrapped itself around the chamber and was pulling tight.

Kvara braced himself, gauging from the creaks and snaps of breaking struts how big the thing outside was.

The walls bulged further, breaking into a lattice of fractures, then broke. Seawater, opaque with bubbles, cascaded in, hitting him hard and knocking him off balance. Kvara thrust himself upward, kicking out against the sudden influx, rotating in the torrent and lashing out with his blade.

Its edge connected with something viscous and mobile, snagging on it before cutting through.

He kept moving, pushing out from the rapidly disintegrating walls, powering through the rushing water. More tendrils snaked inside, thrashing after him. As he moved, he fought against a dizzying whirl of disorientation. Everything was in motion, frothing and racing. Water poured rapidly into what remained of the chamber's outer casing, rushing up to waist-height, then shoulder-height, then over his head.

Through a blurred curtain of moving water Kvara saw a huge length of sucker-clad skin race past him, ripping away a length of armour-casing from the hub's exterior. He kicked himself towards it. As he pushed off the crumbling floor gave way entirely, dissolving into a bubbling foam of broken mesh and cladding. More water bloomed up from under it, chasing out the last of the chamber's air in a glistening bubble.

Kvara brought Djalik round in a curve, aiming at the tentacle snaking through the breach. The blade sliced into it cleanly, and a huge cry echoed throughout the water – a shuddering, booming bellow of pain.

Then the last remnants of the chamber caved in, bringing with them a fresh deluge of churning, bloody water from all directions. Kvara ducked down under a collapsing wall section, lurching away from it in slow motion even as he fell down deeper, supported now by nothing but collapsing struts and spars. He tumbled into the centre of the zone of destruction, dragged further into the abyss as the metal around him was crushed and whipped into nothing more than splinters.

The last of the air shot up in columns of glittering silver, leaving him plummeting through rapidly darkening seawater. His helm-visor partially compensated, rendering the scene around him into a riot of false-colour targets.

Kvara spun away from the forest of needle-thin sensor prongs jutting below the disintegrating harvester, still falling rapidly, still trying to get some kind of lock on the creature that was doing this. He had a vague impression of something vast moving just above him. He spun cumbersomely on to his back and fired upward. The bolts shot through the water leaving long trails of bubbles. A series of muffled thuds rang out and impact shocks rippled through the water.

Then Kvara hit the algae. He was dragged into a sticky, cloying morass of thick vegetation. It grasped at him, pulling on his limbs. He twisted around again, slicing out with his blade to clear it, still falling deeper. He reached out with his bolter-arm, ready to fire upward again, only to have a tentacle shoot down and lash round his wrist, wrenching it out of position.

With a violent jerk, he stopped falling. The algae rolled away from him and more tendrils snaked down, grabbing him and pulling him back up. He cut himself free, only for more suckers to grab on. Kvara felt his second heart thumping hard. His breath echoed, fast and regular, in the enclosed space of his helm.

He looked up, and saw the creature in full for the first time. A huge serrated crest of armour reared up in the gloom, ridged and pocked with barnacles. Jaws protruded from under the crest, lined with flashing lines of needle teeth. A massive torso, segmented and flexible, hung down from a spike-ringed neck. Tentacles flowed out from joints along the torso, writhing in the water as if they had sentience of their own. A long tail trailed back into the depths, terminated with a scorpion-like sting. The beast's hide was glossy and streamlined, and it moved through the water with a ponderous, muscular grace.

As Kvara stared up at it, struggling against the tendrils that clutched at him, its huge jaws opened to reveal several flicking tongues, each one the length of his forearm. Six multi-jointed arms uncurled out from the forest of tentacles, stretching out to grab at him. As Kvara saw the claws extend towards him, he remembered the shattered pieces of plasteel floating on the water.

He wrenched his bolt pistol free of the tentacles and fired straight at the creature's looming face. The rounds shot off through the water, leaving trails of bubbles in their wake.

With a mighty whiplash movement, the leviathan surged away from them, evading the projectiles with a sinuous ease. While it was moving, Kvara brought his blade to bear, severing the tendrils that still bound him and breaking free of their hold.

He dropped deeper, spinning around as his heavy armour dragged him down. The creature swam around and swept down after him, undulating through the blooms of algae like a colossal sea-serpent of Fenrisian myth.

Kvara tried to control his cartwheeling descent and failed. The thick liquid dragged at his limbs and the turbulence buffeted him. The wrecked hub was now far above him and out of his eyeline. Even with his helm lenses compensating, it was hard to make out much through the murk other than the vast serrated shadow pursuing him.

Then he reached the bottom. The sea floor rushed up at him, dark and jagged. Huge rocks, each as sharp as butcher's knives and many metres high, cut up into the fog of algae. Kvara arched his back, missing the tip of the nearest stalagmite by a finger's width. He spun away from it and collided with the flank of another one. As he rebounded clear, he managed to mag-lock his blade and stretch out with his free hand. His fingers clutched at the sharp edge of another rock column and he clamped his gauntlet tightly over the rock. His body swung after it, crashing into the unyielding stone and grinding to a standstill.

The stalagmite held him, and his boots lodged firm against a narrow ledge on the stone. Locking himself in place with his free hand, Kvara swung his pistol up again and loosed another volley of bolts.

The creature had been close on his tail the whole time – too close to evade the point-blank shots. The bolts span into its bony crest, detonating once they penetrated the hard casing and exploding with a series of blunt thuds. The beast screamed and jerked sharply back up, sending a backdraught of water washing over him.

He spotted the tail sweeping round at him almost too late. Kvara pressed himself back against the rock-edge and the bulbous sting swam past just in front of him, lashing furiously as it passed.

Then the creature was coming at him again, surging through the water, multiple arms outstretched. Kvara squeezed the trigger again, but the pistol jammed.

Spitting a curse, he let it drop and brought his blade up. His movements were as fast as he could make them in the thick soup of algae, but still too slow, too cumbersome. The first tentacles clamped on to his weapon-arm, pinning him back to the rock. Then more shot out, wrapping themselves around his midriff. They squeezed tight, and Kvara felt his breastplate flex under the pressure.

A clawed hand reached for him, aimed at his head. Kvara managed to pull himself out of its path, wrestling hard against the drag of the tendrils. The beast's talons smashed into the rock behind him, shattering it and sending a cloud of dust floating out and up.

Kvara felt the first crack on his armour even before the warning runes started to flash. It ran transverse across the list of names on his right side, breaking up the inscriptions.

Then the creature went for him again, this time at his torso. Kvara kicked back against the rock, pushing himself upwards. He wrenched his blade-arm free and lashed out at the tendrils around him, briefly clearing a space to operate in. He struck deep, cutting into solid flesh and staining the water with the beast's dark blood, before rolling away and down, sliding down the sheer rock in a flurry of kicked-up dust.

But the beast was far faster, and the abyss was its element. It shot after him, moving with unhurried undulations. The creature's outstretched claws grasped at him, gouging new rents in the ceramite of his backpack where they made contact. More warning indicators flared red across his lens display.

Kvara rolled clumsily on to his back, swinging his blade round and slashing at the scrabbling talons. The beast clutched its claws back up away from the flashing blade before punching them back down after it had swept across. Talons punched down, through Kvara's guard, cutting into his trailing leg like a stud being shot into leather.

Kvara grimaced, wrenching his leg away as the flesh punctured. The leg-plate cracked open, leaving clouds of blood in the water behind him. Valves shut closed at his knee socket and his armour's greave filled with water as the rents in the ceramite spun apart.

The creature swooped in closer, black against the shadow

of the deep waters. Off-balanced and unsighted, Kvara crashed and wheeled down the sheer face of the pinnacle. He hit a jutting outcrop in mid-spin that arched his spine and sent him reeling in the opposite direction. Then he collided with another wall of rock face-first, cracking his weakened breastplate further. For a second he could see nothing but flashes of red light. He swung out blindly as he fell further and the sword bit into pursuing claws, darkening the water with the beast's oil-black blood.

Then his boots connected with something solid and his dizzying plummet thumped abruptly to a halt. His vision cleared, though he could feel blood running down the inside of his helm. The cracks in his plate were leaking water and it sloshed around, freezing and pressurised, in the cavities between his skin and the armour.

He was lodged in a narrow cleft between two sheer peaks of rock. Frustrated for a moment, the beast scratched frantically at the pinnacles above him, pulling them apart to get at him. One elongated talon stabbed down clean through the gap, carving through the protection of his upraised sword-arm and severing it nearly clean through.

Kvara roared with pain, watching helplessly as his blade floated free of his control. Blood ballooned out from the wound, pluming in jets through the water.

Another claw shot down through the narrow cleft, reaching for his head and shoulders. Dizzy with pain and incipient shock, Kvara only just managed to punch up with his good hand. His gauntlet closed over the incoming talons and he twisted, using his whole body to leverage the manoeuvre. The talons ripped free, and the creature roared in turn, sending pulsating shivers radiating through the water.

By then Kvara's armour had sealed off the severed vambrace. His blood had already started clotting, and his vision had cleared. Above him, the huge creature withdrew its tentative strikes and broke into a frenzy of pain-filled destruction. Its tail crashed round, demolishing the fragile peaks of the two pinnacles. Another pass, and the last of his protection would be ripped away. His sword-arm was useless, his armour was compromised, and his weapons were gone.

Kvara pulled two krak grenades from his belt and primed them. He clutched them both in his good hand and crouched down, coiled to spring.

Something like elation coursed through his heavily damaged body – the elation felt by a master swordsman having at last met his match in battle.

The beast had the measure of him. It was worthy.

I have found it.

Its tail crashed back across, demolishing the pinnacles on either side of the cleft, exposing him again to the full wrath of the wounded creature. When the debris cleared, Kvara just had time to see an enraged, bleeding face hurtling straight at him. It was obscenely stretched, utterly alien, devoid of anything but animal hatred and a primal lust for the coming kill.

Kvara pounced, propelling himself upward into the oncoming jaws, holding the twin grenades tightly in his one working gauntlet and thrusting them forward. The beast snapped its jaws closed out of instinct, ripping Kvara's arm off at the shoulder.

He bellowed with pain. Dark stars exploded before his eyes, quickly lost in a blur of shock and agony. He saw his own blood stream out in a long, viscous trail as he fell back, hanging in the water like a slick of promethium. He felt more water rushing into the breaches in his battleplate, cracking open the ravaged protection and sending him tumbling back down into the shadow of the rock-cleft.

Above it all was the face of the beast, grinning with alien malice, triumphant and malevolent. It came in close, its teeth stained with his blood, ready to finish him.

Then the grenades went off.

Kvara was hurled down against the rock as the twin booms rocked the sea floor. The creature spasmed and bulged as the explosions tore through its innards. A shockwave swept out from the epicentre of the blast carrying scraps of flesh and carapace with it and carpeting the stark rock needles. The swirling mass of tentacles seemed to implode, shrinking back in towards the bony ridge of the creature's spine before going suddenly limp. A long, echoing scream resonated through the water, hanging there until the beast, flailing for a moment longer in a desperate attempt to cling on to life, slumped immobile.

It still hung, buoyant and huge, drifting a little on the cold, dark currents, before beginning to tilt away, trailing lines of gore from its punctured torso.

With what little awareness that remained to him, Kvara gazed up at it. Though wracked by pain and feeling the frigid clutch of unconscious rush up to grasp him, he could still marvel at the beast's size.

My kill.

Kvara's head fell back on to the rock. Water had got into his helm, which was slowly filling up. Pain throbbed throughout his whole body, acute and blinding. He felt heady with stimms and adrenaline. Before they did their work, dragging him into the oblivion of the Red Dream,

he only had one more thought – a correction – recognising
the nature of the beast he had killed and the significance it
possessed. The voices no longer echoed in his mind, and
he could no longer see them as they had been. Death, next
to that, seemed of little consequence.

Our kill.

The wound in his head never healed. He became sick, then
dizzy, falling over the deck as the drekkar pitched with the
winter sea. They laughed at him right until the time he
couldn't get up.

Kvara saw the world through a mist of confusion, nauseous and slurring. The sea went flat, and the wind came
hurling down from the heavens in a blaze of fire and
smoke.

He cried out for Thenge, looking for the big man through
the rushing noise. Thenge wasn't there. In his place stood
a giant wearing a black metal skin and the mask of a wolf.
His dried pelt cloak shook in the downdraught and he carried a skull-topped staff.

I am dead. This is the spectre of Morkai.

He felt hands reach out for him – human hands. He was
pulled on to some kind of stretcher. He recognised the smell
of those hands. Preja Eim, perhaps, the human female who
had stood outside the interrogation chamber. Where was
her superior, the man called Oen? There were others there,
clad in environment suits and talking in low voices.

This is not real. I am not on Fenris.

The drekkar reeled, nearly sending him into the sea. He
managed to lift his head, and saw the shaky outline of a
huge metal casket in the sky. It was as grey as the clouds,
and hung above the ship in defiance of all law. Gigantic

rings of bronze thundered with flame, breaking through the storm and making the air shake with heat.

The giant with the black metal skin made a gesture, and more metal-clad warriors leapt down from the hovering casket. They wore snow-grey armour with runes hammered into it and none of their faces were visible. They lumbered up to Kvara, walking smoothly even as the ship plunged through the swell.

I have killed the krakken, and it has killed me. Now they come to take me to Halls of the Slain.

Kvara felt the water drain from his helm. In the distance, sounding as if still underwater, drills rang out, removing the surviving sections of battleplate. Lights flashed painfully in his eyes, surgical and piercing. He heard voices with the accent of Lyses Gothic coming in and out of hearing. A man came to the forefront, his forehead creased with concern.

That is Oen. He fears me still. What is he doing here?

They took him up into the hovering casket of fire. The pain in his head grew worse. Kvara looked down from his impossible position for a final time, seeing his own blood on the decks below. Then, at last, he saw Thenge and the others, huddled at the far end of the ship, gazing up, open-mouthed.

They were afraid. He had never seen them afraid of anything before.

Huge doors closed with an echoing clang, sealing him in. The lights dimmed. He heard the sound of medicae equipment being dragged closer.

Someone leaned over him. It might have been the black wolf-mask. It might have been the man Oen.

It didn't matter. They both said the same thing.

'You will not die, warrior.'

* * *

'Could you not have got here quicker?'

'Throne, Preja, I do have other things to worry about.'

'He's scaring the hell out of everybody.'

'I don't doubt it. Is he up and walking?'

'No, he can't get up. But he's still fething scary, procurator.'

Oen walked as fast as he could down the corridors of the medicae unit, ignoring the nervous glances from the apothecary's staff as he went. Eim trotted along at his side, irritable and tense.

'What has he said?'

'He wants his armour. He wants to know what we've done with his ship.'

'And you told him?'

'That he can have it, and that we left it the hell alone.'

'Good.'

The pair of them reached the secure ward. Two sentries in full assault armour stood guard outside. They saluted briskly before opening the metal-banded doors.

The ward was spacious enough, but its lone occupant made it seem cramped. He lay on his back, his huge limbs barely fitting onto the reinforced slab of plasteel that served as a bed. Wires ran from his chest, his face and his limbs. One arm had been severed just below the shoulder and the stump was crowned with a metal cap.

As they entered, Kvara lifted his head. Even after so long, his face was still swollen with bruises. He looked at Oen and Eim with those strange, luminous gold eyes.

'I came as soon as I could, lord,' said Oen, bowing.

Eim stood to one side, chewing her lip nervously.

The Space Wolf took a long time to speak. When he did, his thick, growling voice had gone. His throat shook, and the sound that emerged was little more than a pale whisper.

'How long?' he rasped.

'Two standard months,' said Oen. 'I'm told you've been in some kind of deep coma. We've done what we can, so I'm glad to see you awake again.'

Kvara ran his eyes over the wires jutting from his body, and grunted.

Oen watched him carefully. Kvara looked even more ravaged than he had done on arrival. His long hair and beard hung in grey straggles over the edge of the cot. His massive barrel chest, covered in scars and tattoos, rose and fell under a thin coverlet. His skin was studded with metal devices, none of which the surgeons had made any attempt to investigate. They'd been terrified of doing anything invasive to him and had been half-appalled, half-fascinated by his outlandish physiology. As far as Oen could tell from their reports, the Space Marine had essentially cured himself.

'You recovered the creature?' Kvara asked. His eyes met Oen's blearily. Even with Kvara in such a state, the procurator found it hard to meet that gaze.

'What was left of it, lord. The remains are preserved.'

'The head?'

'I... er, the what?'

'Did you retrieve the head?'

'We did.'

Kvara let his head fall back. His breath was ragged and shallow.

Oen looked at Eim, who shrugged. He had no idea what to say.

'My armour,' said Kvara. His voice had slurred, as if he were fighting against sleep. 'Where is it?'

'Here, lord,' said Eim, motioning over to the far corner

of the room. 'We brought it here, just as you asked, when you were sleeping.'

Kvara lifted his head again with difficulty, screwing his eyes up and peering out as if through a thick fog.

The armour had been hung on a reinforced metal scaffold. Even the broken pieces had been mounted on the rig, each one carefully hoisted into place by a team of engineers who'd been every bit as reverent and afraid as the surgeons.

The breastplate hung in the centre. Where once the surface had been covered in eight lines of runes, it was now almost bare. A series of huge impacts had scoured the surface clear, wearing away the grey paint and boring deep into whatever material it had been constructed out of. The curved surface glinted sharply in the light of the medicae chamber, as raw as newly-tempered steel.

'The names,' whispered Kvara, looking at it intently.

'Your pardon?'

Then the Space Wolf issued a dry, cracking chuckle. It seemed to pain him, and he looked away from the armour and back at Oen.

'Come here, mortal,' he ordered.

His throat dry, Oen shuffled closer. Kvara winced as he turned his head, exposing a pair of fangs between chapped lips.

'How did you locate me?' he asked.

Oen swallowed.

'I disobeyed your instruction, and your movements were tracked. By the time our flyers arrived, you'd destroyed the creature.'

Kvara nodded.

'I should add,' said Oen haltingly, remembering how he'd felt when Kvara's body had been retrieved, 'that we're sorry.

We came too late. But, you should know, we did what we could for you. You were never alone. We couldn't keep up with you, but you were never alone.'

Kvara smiled at that. Unlike the weary, sardonic smile he'd worn on arrival at Lyses, the gesture was natural, almost human.

'Never alone,' he echoed thoughtfully.

Oen swallowed again, uncertain of what to say to that. An uneasy silence fell over the chamber.

'I don't expect you to understand the ways of my kind, human,' said Kvara at last, his voice low. 'I don't expect you to understand why I came here, nor why I must take the head of that beast back to Fenris, nor what that will mean for the blood-debt of my pack.'

His bestial eyes shone wetly as he spoke.

'Their names have been erased, and it eases the torment of my soul. But we'll remember them in the sagas for as long as such songs are remembered. And among them, in the position of honour, will be yours, human. Take that as you will, but there are those in the galaxy who would see it as a compliment.'

Out of the corner of his eye, Oen saw Eim raise her eyebrows and give a little shrug. He tried to think of something suitably polite to respond with.

It was difficult. For all the reputation of the Adeptus Astartes, the reality of them was hard to come to terms with. Perhaps the Space Wolves were a minor Chapter, a fringe example of the species with more eccentricities than the others. Maybe the other ones he'd seen on the devotional holos with their gleaming cobalt armour and gold-lined pauldrons looked down on them as quaint or inferior.

By the time Oen had thought of something, though, Kvara

seemed to have drifted back into an exhausted sleep, and to say anything further felt rather superfluous. For the sake of form, though, Oen bowed courteously and gave his reply.

'That's very kind, lord,' he said. 'What a nice tradition.'

He had learned to use his new body out in the wilds of Asaheim, and it gave him the strength and poise of a demi-god. Even out of his armour he could withstand the biting air of the Fang with barely a flicker of discomfort. He had been changed, dragged beyond himself and into the realm of legend.

For all that, the first time he met them his tongue felt thick and useless. He'd never been much of a talker, and they already knew one another as well as mortal broth-ers. He envied the way they were with each other – easy, casual, close.

'So they've sent us a whelp,' said the one they called Mór, scowling at him as he entered the hearth chamber with his false-confident strut.

The one they called Lek laughed at that, grinding the edge of his axe with a whetstone. He stopped the wheel and pushed a loose strand of blond hair back behind his ear.

'So they have.'

Vrakk, Aerjak and Rann looked up from their game of bones. Vrakk shook his head wearily and went back to it. Aerjak and Rann exchanged a knowing smile, but said nothing.

'Can you use a blade, whelp?' asked Frorl, walking up to him and whirling a practice-sword expertly in his left hand.

'Of course he can't,' snorted Svensson, wrinkling his ruined nose sceptically. 'He's just been pulled off the ice.'

He felt his anger rising at that. Since the changes in his

blood, he could be made angry so quickly. The Rune Priest had warned him of that, but still he struggled to control it. Perhaps he would never control it. Perhaps, having been shown the realm of the gods and his place within it, he would still stumble at the final hurdle.

'He'll learn,' said the big one, the one they called Beorth.

Of all of them, he was first to clap his hand on his shoulder. His rough palm fell heavily, like a blow, and he staggered.

'You'll learn, won't you, whelp?'

He looked into Beorth's eyes, and saw the calm, effortless strength there.

'Don't call me whelp,' he said, holding Beorth's gaze.

'Oh?' Beorth looked amused. 'What do you want to be called?'

'Brother.'

Vrakk snorted, still engrossed in his game.

'You have to earn that,' he said.

Aj Kvara didn't look at him. He looked at Beorth, whose hand still rested on his shoulder.

The big warrior seemed like he was going to say something, then paused. He looked down at Kvara, who was still bristling with youth and anger and uncertainty.

'Perhaps you will,' he said. 'For now, though, you need to learn to fight.'

Beorth grinned, and pulled out his blade. It was a short, stabbing sword, notched and serrated along one of the cutting edges and with inset runes lodged under the bronze-lined hilt.

'Let me show you,' he said.

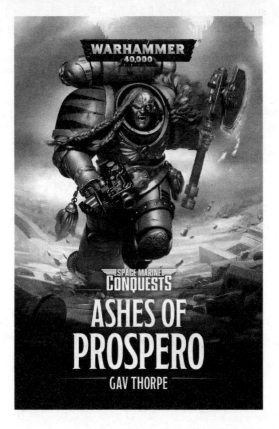

REDEEMER

GUY HALEY

The **Blood Angels** have long been the most valiant defenders of the Imperium. Yet for all their selfless sacrifice, they suffer from a fatal flaw: the Black Rage. These Space Marines must constantly strive to resist this darkness, lest the madness consume them and monsters be made of men.

In *Redeemer*, High Chaplain Astorath travels to the world of Asque, where a brother of the Blood has succumbed to the Black Rage. It falls to the Redeemer of the Lost to hunt down the benighted warrior, and deliver the peace that only death can bring.

There were chords of pain that played for Astorath alone to hear. Music that troubled the dreams of insane composers haunted his waking hours. If it played anywhere, anywhere at all, then he would hear it. Most often he heard a lonely tune wrung from one miserable instrument, but at times these soloists would be joined by others to make quartets or sections, and in the worst of days an entire, melancholic orchestra would gather. Then the music would sing most urgently to him across time and space. Always it was discordant, tragic, full of pain and anger, notes played out of sequence as less-talented hands fumbled their way over a maestro's work. The music recalled something great nonetheless, and was all the more painful for imperfection.

These outpourings were for others to tame. The duty of his brother Chaplains was to get the strains to play in tune, to conduct the suffering towards a last crescendo. When the brothers in black and bone took the lead, the music would climax and cease, and in the ceasing Astorath the Grim would know that all had returned to rightness.

Sometimes the music did not stop. Sometimes it rose to unbearable heights, past all hope of redemption, down to the blackest pits of despair, where it continued, polluting all around it with pain.

It was Astorath's role, as Blood Angels High Chaplain, to end these painful discords. His solemn duty was fratricide. His axe tasted noble Space Marine blood as often as it did the vitae of the Imperium's enemies. 'The Ender of Songs', the aeldari called him, and apt though that was, he had a better-known title.

To the Chapters of the Blood, he was the Redeemer of the Lost, and he was loved and loathed in equal measure for his excellence at his duty.

Astorath slept his way across the light years. Wherever he went, his sarcophagus travelled with him, seated in the place of honour at the heart of the *Eminence Sanguis*.

Only a few of the most high Blood Angels had their own personal sarcophagus. Astorath was naturally among them. The exterior of his sarcophagus was decorated with stylised sculpture that depicted the warrior inside. Although distorted by being wrapped around the lid, it was unmistakably Astorath rendered in the abyssal black of polished carbon.

The sarcophagus was set at an angle of forty-five degrees at the centre of a ring of carvings depicting the High Chaplain's responsibilities. In Astorath's chamber all was chill. Frost coated the carvings. Red lumens bathed the room in a bloody glow, and black shadows hid from it. The colours echoed Astorath's inner world. While Astorath slept, his dreams were of black and they were of red, and nothing else, until somewhere a warrior's soul broke, and the music began again.

Each song was different. He heard this one as a screeching passage that rose and stopped, and began again, over and over, a piece badly practised whose end could not be attained. It penetrated the bloody red; it sent ripples over the oily black. The music called to him for it could call to no one else. The song was a plea for mercy only he could grant. It woke him.

Stirred from his slumber, Astorath opened his eyes in the blood-threaded amnion nourishing his body. The sarcophagus' machine-spirit detected the movement, and began the process of full awakening. Drains opened at the base of the sarcophagus to suck the amnion away. The mask covering Astorath's mouth came free, the amnion level dropped past his chin, and he took his first free breath since he had lain down to rest. The needle interfaces of monitoring machines slid from the sockets of his black carapace. Thick tubes twisted like umbilical cords suckled greedily at the arteries in his forearms, thighs and neck as he slept. They throbbed now as they returned his purified blood to him, and detached from his skin with sorrowful kisses.

Light falling on the black sculpture changed, fading from sanguine to gentle red gold, the colour of the sunlight of Balor. Inset wheels spun within the sarcophagus' ornate decoration, locks disengaged, a heavy bar disguised as the figure's crossed arms lifted and rose. The lid slid up and away.

Astorath sat up. Pale skin and jet-black hair glistened with residual preservative fluid.

'Sergeant Dolomen,' he said. His voice was quiet yet filled

with authority. Vox-thieves hidden in the room's decoration opened up communication with the command deck.

'*My lord*,' Dolomen responded.

'A brother is lost. Prepare our Navigator for fresh directions. We have work to do.'

The *Eminence Sanguis* appeared on no roll of service for the Blood Angels. It was not expected to take part in the Chapter's battles and rarely did. It had been requested, built and commissioned solely as the personal transport of the High Chaplain, and had conveyed many holders of the office across the galaxy.

Sepulchral halls linked sombre chambers. Every being upon that craft, whether unmodified human, tech-priest or Angel of Death, understood the solemnity of their mission and carried themselves with utmost dignity. The *Eminence Sanguis* was a near-silent ship, where robed figures went on solitary errands. Its machine-spirit was as cold as the void outside its plasteel skin and as distant as the stars it sailed for.

It was a fast ship, quick in the void but swiftest in the warp. Although it was of low mass, in the realm of the warp concepts had more importance than physical truths, and the ship was heavy with duty. So singular was its purpose it cut easily through the conflicting currents of ideas that made the immaterium treacherous. Not even the madness of Chaos could deny the weight of Astorath's work. Aided by the importance of its mission and the faith of those aboard, it passed through the worst of storms, and made impressive speed whatever etheric tempests curdled the Sea of Souls.

In the nightmare of the warp, the *Eminence Sanguis* turned

aside from its prior destination towards the source of the song.

Astorath's armour terrified the mortals who came to greet him. There were only three of them stood at the edge of the landing platform when he emerged into the dank forest, and they were frightened, for death stood behind him. His battleplate's ceramite was carved to resemble musculature exposed by flaying, and was painted to match. His jump pack was an arcane design, its form dictated more by art than function, and to the cowering men and single woman, he appeared to be blessed with wings. The pinions were immobile, sculptures of metal as crow black as his hair, yet to them they seemed real. His pauldron was a field of skulls. His kneepads featured more of the same. The axe he carried was as tall and heavy as the largest of the mortals, with a haft fashioned to resemble a spine. All he carried and all he wore spoke of the ending of life.

The world of Asque only accentuated his deathly aspect. The Blood Angels Stormraven squatted on a rusted landing platform half overtaken by forest growth. Support pillars were engulfed by rippled grey wood. Slimy creepers strangled guard rails, and buried machinery in wet mats of giving flesh. The ship was black, covered in red saltires and glowering skulls. Upon the ancient pad it resembled the ornamentation on an overgrown tomb, peeking out through a cemetery's ruin.

Mould crawled up every surface of the arching roots holding the fungus-trees off the ground. Clouds of their spores floated past in granular mists. The three mortals wore heavy respirators to protect themselves against the spores, but Astorath had no need of such protection, and stood before them bareheaded, a winged giant clad in skinned muscle.

In the gloom of the fungal forest, his pale skin appeared blue. He was flanked by Sergeant Dolomen and the Sanguinary Priest Artemos, his only companions from the Chapter. Together they represented the triumvirate of bone, blood and death that shaped the Blood Angels' soul. They were doom incarnate.

Astorath did not look human, and he was not. The mortals were right to be afraid.

'Where are our brothers?' Astorath asked them through bloodless lips.

Despite their protection, the mortals' eyes were rimmed red with spore exposure. The leader, the female, spoke with a voice roughened by poor quality air. She was old, but had that wiry strength certain women keep until the end of their lives.

'They are this way, my lord,' she said, pointing a wavering arm behind her to tangles of roots and trunks receding into the spore-blue air.

Astorath looked into the forest. Far off, the music played.

'Take me there,' he said. 'Dolomen, guard the ship.'

The men and woman looked at each other nervously. None of them wished to be the one to start the march. The idea of telling Astorath what to do, even when asked to provide guidance, seemed to fill them with terror.

'Take me now,' Astorath said.

Relieved to be commanded, the civilians led the way down a run of rockcrete stairs that was so buried in rotted matter, fungal stands and roots it appeared no more than an animal track.

'You, female. Tell me what happened here.' Astorath's footsteps were heavy, thumping on the soft ground like dying heartbeats.

'Your brother took the ordes meat–' began the woman.

'From the beginning. Tell me of this place. Tell me what happened to you before my brothers came. It will help me understand what has befallen them.'

So she did. Her name, she said, was Srana. Astorath filed it away with a million other names, never to be forgotten.

'This world is not a bad world,' Srana began. 'I have read of others. I know there are worse places than Asque.'

They were obliged to duck through interlaced rubbery vines whose rough surfaces adhered to them. Astorath and Artemos shoved their way through with difficulty, for the vines would not break, and the paths the humans took were too small for them. As Astorath forced his way out, the woman glanced back, to see if she had spoken out of place. Astorath's return stare had her turning her face away twice as quickly.

'Before the silent ones came, we lived in sunlight, up there.' She pointed upwards, where arrow-straight trunks lifted off from their cradles of roots, though she did not look, too afraid or too saddened by what had happened. 'Up there are our homes. That is our world, not this place. Up there, there is no mould. The air is clear. The weather is warm. We had good lives.'

'The nature of this world's purpose?'

'The production and export of chemical products derived from the great fungi,' she said. 'Their wood is no good. It is black-hearted, rots quickly. No use for building, but when bled and boiled it gives useful liquors. We had our duties to the Imperium, and we fulfilled them.' She dared to look back again. 'All we wish is to do so again, to live in the sun and pay our dues to the God-Emperor. We worked hard. We prayed hard. I am so sorry about what has happened here. Please, let the Emperor know we are sorry for whatever we did to anger Him and bring this disaster on ourselves. I am so sorry the Red Angels came to help us, and this happened. I–'

'What happened here is not your fault,' said Astorath bluntly. 'You have done no wrong. If you had, I would kill you, but you need not fear punishment from me. Unless there is some element of your tale that is deserving of harsher judgement?'

She shook her head. 'None, no, my lord. We did nothing. We are victims. I think. Maybe the meat… Maybe we poisoned him?'

'All humanity is a victim in these dark times. If you speak the truth, you have nothing to fear. You did not poison him. Continue your tale.'

'The Rift came, and the sky turned sick. The silent ones came soon afterwards. They appeared in nightmares at first, pale, naked things, the size of half-grown children, pot-bellied, long arms, horrible in proportion, but their faces were the worst. They were blank, no eyes or nose, only a curved mouth full of jutting teeth. We all dreamt about them, standing in the corner of our sleeping chambers, staring at us.' She shuddered at the memory. 'It didn't take long for us to realise that we dreamed of the same things, of silent, pale faces with no eyes. A few panicked children was all it took. Word got round. We were afraid.

'We worked on as best we could. Then the tithe ships stopped coming. Then the merchantmen. We produce enough food for ourselves, but are dependent on outsiders for many other things. We sent out messages from our astropaths in the capital, but got no reply. They tried harder, until one by one they went mad, and so Count

Mannier ordered no more attempts be made, in order to save the last.'

'When was this?'

'Decades ago. I was young then, old enough to remember how things were. There are no sky-speakers now. Some of what I relay to you was told to me by my mother.'

'You speak of matters dealt with by the planetary government.'

'My mother was adviser to the count. I am of noble birth,' she cackled. 'Though you would not believe it now.'

'Continue.'

'The dreams became worse. Then they stopped being dreams. We woke in the night to find the silent ones looking at us. They'd vanish, after a while, but they were there. We had picts and vid-captures.' She went quiet. 'Then, after a little longer, they started to hunt us.'

They passed along a road broken to useless slabs by fungal roots.

'We killed a few, they were flesh and blood it seemed, and it gave us heart. But they came and went as they wished. We struggled to trap them. We couldn't see them. They picked us off at their leisure. We were afraid to sleep. So many of us died in nights of terror, and we were driven from our homes, down here. They didn't come down here so much, on account of the spores maybe. We managed to hold on, but we were dying slowly. The count took the chance with our last astropath and sent the message – I was a girl still then. It took so long to answer, we didn't think anyone would come. Then your brothers arrived, and they were cunning and brave and killed many of the silent ones. Everything looked like it would be good again. It was, for a while. They took back this township for us, so we could look on the sun. They drove the creatures deeper into the forest. We began to rebuild.'

They reached a stairway choked by the outgrowths of the tree it circled, and started to climb upwards.

'Then your brother took the ordes meat, and suddenly it wasn't good any more.' She smiled weakly. 'Come on, it's this way.'

When Astorath and Artemos arrived in the reclaimed township they found their brothers out on patrol, and so settled down to wait for their return in a room in a derelict habitat.

'We should consider the possibility that this entire planet must be purged,' said Artemos, speaking by private helm-to-helm vox. 'You heard what she said.'

'The old rules are not so rigidly applied,' said Astorath. 'Word of daemons has spread now. Once, even you would not have known of them, brother. How can knowledge of them be hidden when they walk openly across the galaxy?'

'Knowledge isn't what bothers me,' said Artemos. He lifted a ragged curtain and glanced out through a cracked window. The habitat overlooked a landscape of lacy branches that moved in the light of the planet's moon. 'This whole place might be tainted. You know what it's like when they get their fingers in the minds of men.'

'If every world that had known the touch of the daemon since the Rift opened was laid waste, there would be no Imperium left,' said Astorath. 'Purity of thought is the best safeguard. The question of whether this world is tainted is for others to answer. It is not obviously so, and we do not have the resources to deal with it if it is. Our mission is to secure our missing brother.'

Artemos shrugged. 'You are right. I speak prematurely. The

things here could have been Chaos-warped predators, rather than daemons. Or they could be a strange kind of xenos. Some of those things the aeldari consort with.' He shook his head and let the curtain drop. 'Xenos or daemon, they are filth, all of them. The galaxy is not what it was. The old evils come sneaking out of the shadows.'

'Put these questions from your mind, Brother-Priest,' said Astorath. 'Whatever they are, they are not our business. Mercy for the lost is our sole concern.'

They waited a few hours for the Blood Angels assigned to Asque to return to the outpost. A single half-squad had been sent, and there were three of them left, all Primaris Marines. They were not surprised to find Astorath at the township.

'I am Brother Fidelius, Eleventh Squad, Third Battle Company, acting sergeant,' said the warrior who led them. 'These are Edmun and Caspion. You are High Chaplain.'

'I am,' Astorath confirmed.

'Then I greet you as my lord.' Fidelius dropped to his knee and bowed his head.

'May the blessing of the Angel's virtues and graces fill you and carry you through battle, my brother. Now rise.'

Fidelius stood again.

'Who is the one who is afflicted?' Astorath asked.

'Brother-Sergeant Erasmus.'

Astorath paused before asking his next question.

'And is Brother-Sergeant Erasmus like you, or like me?' The gravity of his question seemed to distort space around them.

'He is not a Primaris brother, my lord, if that is what you mean,' said Fidelius.

'So you were deployed as a mixed squad?'

'At our captain's command,' said Fidelius. He looked at his brothers. 'We three were among those raised from the Great Blooding. We lack experience. Erasmus came to teach us.'

'You fought as mortals on the walls of the Arx Angelicum?'

'We did,' said Fidelius. 'There were four of us Primaris Marines, until the xenos things slew Brother Aelus. The four of us and Erasmus were deemed enough for the task at hand, but these things are slippery, and claimed their due in blood. Erasmus said…' He shared a look with his brothers. Astorath recognised it, for he had seen it many times – the look of a Blood Angel exposed for the first time to the effects of the Rage. 'Erasmus said Aelus made a grave error, and that we must learn from it. He said that Aelus' death was fair exchange for the thousands of their dead, and we will avenge him. We were looking for the silent ones when you arrived. They stay away from the population now. We've cleansed most of this sector. We'll get the rest.'

'Are they daemons?' asked Artemos.

'I know little of daemons, but I don't believe so,' said Fidelius. 'They are easy enough to kill, though they are stealthy. They're psychically able, they cloud the mind, they're never where you think they are, but they are of flesh and blood. There's not very many of them. Dangerous to unmodified humans, but little threat to us. I can imagine how easy it was for them to wreak havoc on a planet this sparsely populated, but we would have had this continent secure and been on our way to the other hemisphere if it weren't for…' He paused again. Disquiet showed in his eyes. 'If it weren't for this.'

'What became of Aelus' gene-seed?' asked Artemos.

'It was lost. We tried to save it, but we could not. We have no Priest with us. I apologise. Perhaps it could have been retrieved, but I do not have the skills.' Fidelius turned his attention back to Astorath. 'If you have responded to our message, then the worst has happened. I didn't believe it was possible. Erasmus was so noble.'

'You thought it something else?'

'I am no expert, and hope deceived me, perhaps, but I hoped so. If you are here, it is not some other thing. It is the Black Rage.'

'It is,' Astorath confirmed.

'I am surprised you arrived so swiftly. I sent word only days ago.'

'I did not get your summons,' said Astorath. 'I require no message. The music of torment called me, so I came.'

'It happened here,' said Brother Caspion. They were in a house built around the topmost trunk of the arrow-like trees. The spongy wood, slender as a man at that point, made a central pillar around which all else was constructed. Broken pots lay about, and a smear of blood darkened the wall. 'Brother-Sergeant Erasmus had been behaving erratically all day, but we did not know what we were seeing. If we had, we would have acted.'

'Be calm, young brother. This is not your doing,' said Astorath.

Caspion nodded gratefully. 'They were giving us a feast in our honour when Erasmus turned. He ate the meat, then something happened, and before we could react he had killed two of the mortals, shouting as he did about traitors and being trapped. We tried to restrain him but his strength was too great and he escaped. The natives have not returned here since it happened.'

'Relations seem good otherwise,' said Astorath.

'Fidelius convinced them Erasmus was influenced by the creatures. They were shocked a Space Marine could be so affected, but they believed it,' said Edmun.

'I do not like to trade in falsehood,' said Fidelius. 'Forgive me.'

'A lesser evil. Let them continue to believe it is so,' said Astorath. 'It would be for the best if that remains the story they tell after we are gone.'

'Better they fear the alien than their protectors, brothers,' said Artemos.

'Better still that the twin curses of our gene-line remain secret,' said Astorath.

'They feared that their meat offended us, and triggered his behaviour somehow,' said Edmun. 'Is that how it happens?' he asked tentatively.

Astorath watched the Primaris Marines closely. Though the new Space Marine breed seemed resistant to the flaw, they were still taught the rituals and the severity of the curse. To little effect, it seemed. So many had been inducted so quickly that they'd had no time to learn properly.

'The women, Srana, she mentioned this ordes meat. Was there anything unusual about it?'

'They said it was a delicacy. They were excited. The animal has to be hunted, and they have not been able to hunt since the creatures came. It was bloody, and tough, but of good savour,' said Fidelius. 'Could it have been the cause?'

'It is most unlikely,' said Astorath. He paced around the room and stopped by the bloodstain. 'Whose blood is this?'

'Brother Erasmus',' said Caspion, ashamed. 'I injured him.'

Astorath pulled a strip of spongy fungus wood from the wall. He chewed on it, letting snatches of experience be teased from the coagulated blood. There was little genetic material, and therefore little could be gleaned. Beneath the ponderous thoughts of trees, Astorath got impressions of bewilderment and fear, then the anguished tune of Erasmus' soul played loud and drowned out all else, and he spat the chewed wood out. 'The Rage comes unannounced. You all partook of the meat?'

Fidelius nodded.

'Then it was not the cause. You are unaffected? No increase in your thirst?'

'None, my lord. It does not affect us the same way,' Fidelius said, almost apologetically.

Astorath looked around the room. 'And Erasmus burst out of the door? After you wounded him?'

'Yes, my lord. Erasmus then dropped to the forest floor,' said Fidelius.

'One hundred and thirty feet,' Edmun said disbelievingly.

'He had his battleplate,' said Fidelius. 'No weapons except his combat knife. He vanished. We've combed the area thoroughly, grid by grid. Edmun is a good tracker.'

'I lost him,' Edmun said. 'We followed his trail to the bounds of the next settlement, where the trail gave out. The enemy tried a sortie against us there, and we were forced to fight. When it was done, I could not find his tracks again.'

Astorath nodded, still examining the room.

'I am finished here. Tell the people of this village they have nothing to fear. Soon you will be able to complete your mission, for the greater glory of the Emperor. First, you must direct me to where the greatest concentration of enemy are.'

'But why?' said Fidelius. 'They are to the north, Brother-Sergeant Erasmus ran south.'

'He will be where the enemy are,' said Astorath. 'We are

warriors. We suffer a warrior's curse. Though they may be violent towards their own, those under the influence of the Black Rage are still servants of the Emperor. They fight for Him until the end, however misguidedly.'

Astorath prepared for the giving of mercy. He had stripped the top portion of his armour off, and sat cross-legged in a habitat yet to be reclaimed by the planet's depleted people. Artemos held out his bare arm for Astorath to cut, and with the Sanguinary Priest's blood Astorath anointed his skin. He lapped at Artemos' wrist twice to blunt his Red Thirst, and, through the vitae of Sanguinius running through Artemos' veins, to remember the sacrifice of their primarch. The curse music sang in Astorath's mind as the blood filled his mouth.

'You can't go alone,' Artemos said. He wiped his arm and clad it in ceramite again. The ritual was a businesslike affair. Under such circumstances, the armouring of the soul was done with the same practical battlefield efficiency as the reloading of a boltgun. 'The settlement to the north is full of the enemy. We should all go.'

'I have fought some of the most celebrated heroes of the Blood, brother. These creatures are feeble. They will not slow me, and when I find Erasmus I will best him.' The blood symbols were drying on Astorath's skin. He sheathed his blade, and began to collect his armour pieces.

'Let me come with you.'

'This is my duty alone, brother.'

Artemos helped him don his backplate and breastplate, holding them in place while Astorath bolted them together with a sanctified power driver.

'Then take some of Erasmus' Primaris brothers with you,

as a precaution against mishap. We cannot afford to lose you, when we have lost so much already.'

Astorath looked over his shoulder into Artemos' eyes. 'Are you seriously suggesting a mere sergeant might get the better of me?'

'No, my lord.'

He returned to his armour. 'There will be no mishap. The Primaris Marines will remain here. It is inevitable that they will see the effects of the Black Rage first-hand one day, for we all do, whether as witnesses or sufferers. I would prefer them not to yet. The Primaris brethren brought hope to our Chapter. It is best if as few of them as possible see the curse that afflicts the rest of us. The Chapters of the Blood have been through much these last centuries. Allow us a moment of resurgence before we must face the monsters within again.'

'The truth will out.'

'Truth always does. However, it will be many years before these Primaris Marines return to Baal. They have done good work here, but this entire world must be freed. They may die before they can pass the information on to others of their kind.'

'Are you sure I cannot accompany you?'

Astorath ran his thumb lightly down the edge of the Executioner's Axe. Blood beaded on his skin.

'I go alone, Artemos.' He pushed his still-bleeding hand into his gauntlet and locked it into place. 'Do not ask again.'

The forest of Asque was silent. So dominant were the fungiforms and moulds that animal life was scarce. Astorath walked roads high over the ground choked by fungal growth. Symbiotic relationships with the fungi were common in the few animal species which thrived, and ever adaptable humanity had taken their lead. The road was carried on buttresses encouraged to grow from nearby fungus-trees, but the network required maintenance; in the years since the Rift the sky-roads had buckled and the marks of human habitation everywhere were vanishing.

It took so little to erase humanity's efforts from existence. Astorath's duties, though obscure, were ultimately a part of the fight against that, to prevent mankind vanishing from history like so many hundreds of species before it.

The town rose in delicate towers high above the canopy. Once he had passed under the shadow of the first, he encountered the enemy.

A pallid, bloated shape disentangled itself from the shadows and leapt at him. Astorath's head buzzed with psychic interference. He could not see it clearly at first, but the efforts undertaken to improve a Space Marine's mind were as great as those that went into rebuilding his body. He shook the thing's influence off, and its form was revealed to him.

It was vaguely humanoid, mushroom-pale, bloated, disgusting as so many xenos were. Hooked claws in its wrists squealed off his armour. The mouth snapped at him, every bit as hideous as Srana had said.

'Surprise is your chief weapon, creature,' said Astorath. He grabbed it by the throat and held it aloft. It was surprisingly strong, and would easily slay a mortal man. 'But you have little else, and nothing that can do harm to me.'

In his grip the beast was helpless. It thrashed about and hissed until its breath was spent and it was dead.

He dropped the pasty thing. It sank bonelessly into itself and began to emit clouds of yellow spores from its body.

Astorath strode on, following strains of a funereal tune only he could hear.

'Brother Erasmus!' he shouted. His amplified vox echoed down silent streets, scaring up rare aviforms and startling parasitic growths into shedding slimy seeds. 'Brother-Sergeant Erasmus! Return to us! Return to your Chapter! Return for the Emperor's mercy!'

His shouting attracted the creatures. En masse they clouded his mind more effectively, but he aimed his blows at the blurred shapes and cleaved them down anyway. They sought to bury him under a weight of their bodies, and did, but they could not penetrate his armour. Soft fingers pried at his seals. Sharp claws scraped at his ceramite. The Emperor's armament held firm against their efforts and they died by the dozen.

'You do not learn,' he said, striking them down. 'You cannot harm me.' He paced his blows to preserve his strength, weathering the soft drumming of their alien fists on his battleplate and chopping them down with a forester's steady rhythm.

Killing all the way, he passed into the inner districts of the town, where grand squares were upheaved by the unchecked movement of living supports. Towers were choked by the rubbery vines, great tangles of them bursting from every window. The further he went the more creatures appeared, all attacking without consideration for their feebleness. His boots crunched on human bones made soft by decay. Thousands had died here, and it sorrowed him.

Finally, a rune flicked into being upon his helm-plate. A chime announced his true quarry was near. He activated his jump pack and burst from a knot of the creatures.

Black wings spread, prolonging his short flight. He

directed himself to a broad platform overlooking a further square, and there he found Brother Erasmus.

The fallen sergeant raged and screamed, shouting imprecations at enemies ten thousand years dead. The blood red of his armour was obscured by milky alien blood and brilliant smears of yellow spores. His knife had broken halfway along the blade, but he wielded it as if it were the finest sword. A hundred of the fungoid creatures swarmed him. Astorath wondered how long Erasmus had fought. It was not unusual for a brother gripped by the Rage to fight until his hearts burst, the ferocity of the affliction being enough to overtax a Space Marine's body, but if Brother-Sergeant Erasmus had fought since the day he had fallen, he showed no signs of fatigue, and still killed with great efficiency.

Astorath watched awhile. Though the Black Rage was a terrible curse, those afflicted displayed an echo of the primarch's martial glory when they fought, and the sight never failed to move him. The music of Erasmus' suffering sang loudly in his mind.

'Terrible, and glorious,' Astorath said, then called out, 'Brother! I am coming to you. Stand fast! Soon your suffering shall be done.'

He ignited his jets, and thundered down into combat.

They fought side by side, purging the town of its infestation. Astorath's axe buzzed through the xenos trailing lightning, and in short time the battle was done.

The High Chaplain faced the lost brother.

'Father!' Erasmus cried, his voice choked with spiritual pain. 'Have you come? Is Horus dead?'

'He is long dead,' Astorath said calmly. He held his axe across his body in both hands. 'Come to me, and know an end to suffering.'

'If he is dead, why do I see him, standing over me? Why does my blood leave my body? Oh father, why have you forsaken me?'

The lost brother threw himself at Astorath, and the day's real fighting began.

Erasmus was possessed by the death memories of Sanguinius, and full of desperate strength. Astorath judged Erasmus too strong to grapple, so took his time, softly singing the hymns of ending as he struck away pieces of the warrior's armour and bled away his might with gentle cuts. There were quicker ways to end one of the lost, but Astorath would do so only in extremis; the warrior must be comforted, and blessed. The final rites of death were as important as the rites of apotheosis and must be correctly observed.

Astorath fought to preserve the secrets of his Chapter. He fought to end the rampages of those who could not find a noble end in battle, but most of all he fought to save their souls. Kindness guided his axe above all things.

'You are a traitor, a betrayer, a worm in the eye of father,' shouted Erasmus. 'You consort with evil for your own benefit while the Imperium burns! Why? Why? Why?' Erasmus directed a flurry of blows at Astorath. The High Chaplain stepped back, mindful that even a broken blade propelled with such strength could break his armour.

'I am not Horus, brother,' he said softly. 'I am your redemption.'

He stepped back and around, swinging his axe with the motion, and took Erasmus' leg off at the knee.

The Space Marine fell face forward and howled piteously with sorrow. He tried to rise.

'I die! I die! Slain at the hand of my brother!'

Astorath stepped in, kicked the knife from the Space Marine's hand and with another blow shattered his armour's power plant, expertly deactivating the battleplate without triggering an explosion. A good part of Erasmus' strength was thus denied him.

'Why?' sobbed Erasmus. 'Why does it have to end this way?'

Astorath squatted down, rolled Erasmus over onto his back and pulled free his helm. The warrior's face was swollen with vitae, his eyes blooming with burst blood vessels. His eye teeth were at their fullest length. But there was yet nobility in him. There always was in the lost.

Astorath rested his palm on the warrior's brow. 'Peace, brother. Be at peace. I am not Horus. I am not the Emperor. I am High Chaplain, and you are Brother-Sergeant Erasmus. The wars you speak of were over ten thousand years ago. Now your fight is, too.'

Erasmus' eyes cleared a little.

'What… what has happened to me?'

'The Black Rage. Our father's death, echoing down time.' He gave the Space Marine a solemn stare. 'Now, listen to me. We are Space Marines, we do not pray. We hold no person to be a god, and all gods to be monsters. We give praise to no one but mortal heroes, and we thank the Emperor as a man and not a divine being. But we will pray now, you and I, for peace in death.'

Astorath spoke sacred words. Through the fog of the Rage, Erasmus repeated them, and a little more lucidity returned.

'Our lord's anguish…' Erasmus said. Tears spilled down his cheeks. 'I feel what the Angel felt. I can't stand it. He is sorrowing for me, for all of us. End it swiftly, please!'

'Fear not, my brother, mercy is my purpose.'

Astorath rose. The Executioner's Axe descended.

The music stopped, and a new weight was added to the High Chaplain's burden.

He recovered Erasmus' head, and voxed Artemos.

Artemos performed his grisly work back in the village. The Primaris Marines guarded the habitat door. The people kept away. They knew something sacred was happening within. Reductor blades sawed through bone, and ribs cracked wetly to give up precious gene-seed.

'Fear not, brothers,' Astorath said to them. 'Your brother died as all Blood Angels should, in communion with the Great Angel, Sanguinius.'

'High Chaplain,' said Fidelius. 'May I have permission to ask your guidance?'

'You may.'

'Will this happen to us?'

Astorath answered thoughtfully. 'Your creator, Belisarius Cawl, has many qualities, but he is a braggart and wears hubris like a gown. It is impossible to eliminate Sanguinius' suffering from our souls. But it may be that you are immune from its effects.'

'Then, if we shall never see what the Angel saw, can we truly call ourselves Blood Angels?' asked Edmun.

'You are Primaris Marines, but you are Blood Angels first. The blood of Sanguinius flows in your veins as it does in mine. You may never suffer the way that Erasmus did, but rest assured, you are my brothers,' said Astorath.

He made sure to meet the eyes of each of them, and as he did he heard a few distant notes of pain – a foretaste, perhaps, of what might come to pass.

Artemos joined them. 'It is done. Erasmus' gene-seed is secure. We will return his armour to the Chapter.'

'Then we are finished here,' said Astorath. He looked to the sky, and opened his vox-link. 'Sergeant Dolomen, we are returning. Prepare the Stormraven for flight. Please inform the *Eminence Sanguis*, we depart immediately. More duty awaits us.'

Somewhere in the immensity of space, a new tune had begun to play.

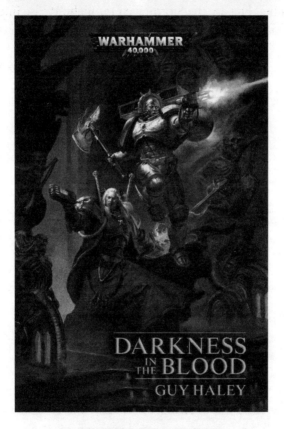

YOUR NEXT READ

DARKNESS IN THE BLOOD
by Guy Haley
(out November 2020)

Baal has been saved from the tyranids, yet the Blood Angels' greatest challenge awaits them. Reinforced by the new Primaris Space Marines, Commander Dante has been made warden of Imperium Nihilus. But to save the shattered Imperium, he and his brothers must first defeat the darkness within themselves.

YOUR NEXT READ

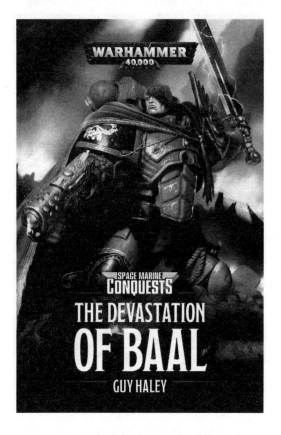

WARHAMMER 40,000

SPACE MARINE CONQUESTS

THE DEVASTATION OF BAAL

GUY HALEY

THE DEVASTATION OF BAAL
by Guy Haley

Baal is besieged! The alien horror of Hive Fleet Leviathan has reached
the Blood Angels home world, and their entire existence is under threat.
As the sons of Sanguinius gather, the battle for the fate of their bloodline begins…

THE TEST OF FAITH

THOMAS PARROTT

To be a **Dark Angel** is to be honoured as the First
Legion of Space Marines created by the God-Emperor
of Mankind. While this secretive Chapter bears an
unsettling mien, with its warriors shrouded in myth
and insinuation, the sons of the Lion know no fear,
for these grim Angels of Death will
never accept defeat.

In *The Test of Faith*, Thomas Parrott explores the
strained relationship between the Dark Angels and
their new Primaris brethren in a tale of brutal battle
and shocking betrayal.

'We have entered visual range, my lord Chaplain,' reported Sergeant Raum.

Interrogator-Chaplain Raguel looked up at being spoken to. The formal nature of the address struck him as a mixed blessing. The Reclusiam deserved respect, of course, and few more so than those who had risen to its highest echelons. Yet, none of the Primaris Marines had ever lost their solemnity with him. None save Hadariel. There was a distance there he was not certain how to help bridge. Regrettably, that was not his task for the day.

'Thank you, sergeant,' he replied steadily.

The inside of the Repulsor was kept in dim red lighting. It posed no difficulty for the enhanced eyes and war-plate auto-senses of a Space Marine. In the gloom he could see the squad of Intercessors standing by, their bolt rifles stowed on their armour for now. They exuded an easy calm. These were no fresh recruits, however the rest of the Chapter still spoke of them. Since they had joined, the Primaris Space Marines had been proven in combat time and again.

Still, it never hurt to bolster morale before a battle.

'Do you wish to address the brethren?' Raguel asked Chaplain Hadariel on a private vox-link.

They had fought alongside one another for years, ever since Hadariel had first begun to train in the Reclusiam. He was of the Second Generation, as were the rest of the troops on this mission. Only Raguel was of the original gene-seed line.

The Primaris Chaplain looked at him, red lenses gleaming coldly in the skull-mask of his helm. 'I do not,' he said.

Raguel frowned. 'As you wish.' He switched over to a unit-wide broadcast. 'Brothers of the Dark Angels! Sons of the Lion! Even now, we close in on those who have shattered the Imperial peace on this world!' As if on cue, stubber rounds began to rattle off the armour of the Repulsor. 'Stand firm and crush all resistance. They will break before us! For we are the Angels of Death, and we are the Emperor's vengeance!'

'For the Lion!' came the full-throated response from the gathered warriors.

'Intercessors, prepare for boarding,' barked Sergeant Raum.

The gathered warriors disengaged their restraints and rose to their feet. Simultaneously, the hatchway of the transport slid open. The odd orange light of this world came through the aperture, along with a rush of the cold, thick atmosphere. It contained toxic elements; no threat to a brother of the Adeptus Astartes, but there was also nothing to breathe. War-plate seals would have to be maintained until they were on board the target vehicle, at least.

One by one the Dark Angels aboard the transport leaped across the gap to the enemy vehicle. The sergeant was the first one to cross and the Chaplains brought up the rear. Raguel could see the exiting Space Marines coming under heavy stubber fire as they left the shelter of the tank. The hammering sound echoed throughout the area, even over the roar of the Repulsor's grav-engine. Sparks flew as rounds ricocheted from ceramite plates.

Then it was Raguel's turn to make the crossing. For one brief beat of his hearts he stood in the egress. The thick ice plates that formed the surface of Muz rushed past underneath both vehicles. Overhead hung the titian haze of the sky. Straight on was the corrugated surface of the enemy... 'vehicle' scarcely did the scale of it justice. The great tracked deep-miners of Muz were more like mobile hab-blocks than autocarriages. Entire clan populations lived out their lives on board, working the machine as it harvested crude promethium from beneath the ice plates.

The Interrogator-Chaplain leaped across in an easy bound, catching hold of the grooves and scars in the hull of the mining vehicle. Hadariel was only a step behind him. The wind howled and tore at them, exposed out here, but their transhuman strength was not so easily overcome. The squad had already spread out to allow room for them. Even as Raguel arrived, one of the Intercessors was planting melta charges on the metal skin of the great conveyance.

The demolition devices activated. Blinding light emanated as the thermal beams tore a sizzling hole straight through to the interior. Thick air howled in through the opening, just as it had with the Repulsor. Without hesitation the Dark Angels swung through the red-hot opening and pulled their bolt rifles out. All of it, from crossing over to punching the hole to entering ready for battle, happened in a matter of seconds.

It was enough to catch the vehicle's crew completely off guard. Pallid figures in heavy work leathers stared in shock as the hulking forms of the Space Marines poured into their workspace. It was some sort of storage area: great casks were stacked in rows, floor to ceiling in a chamber fifteen feet tall. The Dark Angels gave them no chance to recover. Their orders were clear: purge all occupants of the deep-miner known as *Meridian Secundus*.

Bolters began to roar immediately. Carnage followed in their wake. The workman's garb these traitors wore provided no protection. Everywhere shells hit, they punched right through into bodies and detonated within. Chests and heads exploded in gory bursts. Limbs were carved away in sprays of blood.

Raguel joined the onslaught the moment his boots connected with the deck, his plasma pistol flaring time after time. Each shot claimed a new soul, white-hot starfire scouring their flesh away in the blink of an eye. Hadariel followed in his wake, reaping his own harvest with cold efficiency. The thunder of the younger Chaplain's bolt pistol was a steady cadence of death.

Half of the locals were dead before they even managed to respond. Others were already choking and wheezing as the toxic fumes flooded the chamber. To Raguel's surprise, however, the handful that were still alive and wearing rebreathers did not break and flee. Instead, they turned and flung themselves towards the Space Marines in a frenzy. Most carried nothing more than heavy tools as makeshift melee weapons. A few carried autoguns or autopistols.

Five of them rushed directly for the pair of Chaplains. Bullets were deflected by the sacred energies of the rosarius in a series of blinding flashes. What shots got through glanced from power armour without doing harm beyond scratched paint. Raguel's plasma blasts annihilated two, and a bolt shell from Hadariel excavated the chest of another.

Then the enemy was on top of them. The first lunged directly at Raguel with a scream of fury, swinging a massive wrench like a club. The Interrogator-Chaplain drew and activated his crozius arcanum in a swift, smooth movement. It caught the wrench head-on. Heavy-duty metal met a crackling power field. The wrench shattered at the point of impact, spraying fragments in all directions.

The chunks popped and sparked off Raguel's armour harmlessly. The same could not be said for his assailant: one caught the traitor right in the eye, tearing through the orb in a spray of blood. The Dark Angel silenced his screams with a quick burst of plasma that evaporated two-thirds of his attacker's body. What gobbets of meat remained fell to the ground, burned and sizzling.

Silence had fallen over the area. The battle was done for the moment.

Raguel contemplated the ruined bodies strewn amongst the casks. 'It is a powerful emotion that would drive such rabble to attack Adeptus Astartes warriors. A deep loyalty, perhaps, or fear. What do you think?'

Hadariel stared straight ahead. 'I do not know.'

Three of the Intercessors approached. One of them, Battle-Brother Levian, held up a hand in greeting. 'It is good to have you fight alongside us once more, Brother-Chaplain Hadariel. We feared you might have lost your edge while gone on your special duty.' The tone was the jibe of an old friend.

Levian and Hadariel had served together even back amongst the Greyshields, Raguel knew. He remained stoic on the outside but listened closely to the exchange.

Hadariel turned his gaze on his old ally. Silence lingered. Finally, he said. 'No. I am fully capable of combat.'

Levian glanced to the two Dark Angels with him. 'Of course, Chaplain. I meant no disrespect.' His eyes darted to Raguel uneasily.

'I have taken none,' said Hadariel flatly. His head turned away.

Before Raguel could say anything, the sergeant's voice cut into everyone's vox. 'The enemy will not remain disorganised for long. We must push on towards the control centre. Rally at the western door.'

The squad and its pair of attached Chaplains moved to comply. They set up flanking the indicated exit. Most of the crew who had been unready for the flood of toxic air had fled in this direction. They could well have gathered rebreathers and weapons during the fighting to set up an ambush here. All the Dark Angels were poised and ready as the warrior on point opened the door.

Nothing happened. Only silence greeted them from the hallway beyond.

The man at the vanguard glanced through the opening and then looked back to the rest. 'No sign of hostile forces.'

'Push on,' Sergeant Raum instructed. 'We cannot afford to tarry here.'

They continued on into the corridor beyond in good order. Each of the Space Marines remained alert, constantly on the lookout for any sign of an enemy attack. This place was old and weathered, as befitted a machine of its great age. The floors were scuffed and worn by the passage of feet across centuries. Pipes on the walls dripped condensation, and old lights along the ceiling flickered where they were not burned out. Other passages branched off from this one from time to time.

Then the lights died.

It was only a momentary inconvenience. Even absolute blackness could not stop Space Marines in war-plate. Their auto-senses switched over to the thermal imaging of preysense in the blink of an eye. All it bought was the briefest pause.

It was enough.

They came scuttling in from the darkness. They were already moving the moment Raguel's vision cleared. Their blurred heat-shapes hurtled in from the side passages and along the ceiling and walls. They moved faster on their six limbs than any baseline human could hope to match. Shrieks of alien rage came only at the moment they struck, scarce warning for anyone caught off guard. Even with their enhanced reflexes, the Space Marines were embattled at close quarters before they could open fire.

One of the creatures leapt through the air and caught Raguel in the chest. The weight of it knocked him off balance into the wall behind him. Pipes caved under the impact, spewing hot steam over them both. Teeth bared, the Interrogator-Chaplain grappled with the many limbs of the xenos. Razored claws struck at him, carving through ceramite where they hit. One strike scraped along the side of his helmet, deflected from shredding his face only by Raguel hurling himself into the creature.

Raguel drove the beast into the far wall with all his might. Its grip on him loosened for a split second. He struggled to bring his plasma pistol to bear at that moment, but it writhed aside from the incandescent blast. A glowing hole melted into the wall was the only result. Teeth snapped inches from his helmet. He wedged a hand between their faces and drove its head into the red-hot edges of the impact point.

There was a hiss as xenos flesh met molten metal, and the creature shrieked. It was still alive and utterly deadly. There was one key benefit, though: he had bought enough freedom to bring his crozius to bear. The first blow crunched into its midsection, caving in its side. He did not stop there, smashing it repeatedly. It vomited pulped innards across him as its torso crumpled completely. Then it flopped to the floor with a final spasm.

Raguel spared himself a single breath to recuperate and tally his wounds. He was bleeding from a number of slashes, but none were life-threatening. Then he turned his attention to his comrades. The fight was still raging and Hadariel was nowhere to be seen. The Interrogator-Chaplain lunged into the fray without hesitation.

'Death to the xenos!' he thundered.

A surgically placed plasma blast here evaporated an alien talon as it pulled back to eviscerate a Space Marine. There, a brother held a beast at bay only with a combat knife between its gnashing jaws; Raguel applied his crozius arcanum to the back of the monster's skull, spurting liquefied brain matter in all directions and ending the stand-off.

Then it was over just as swiftly as it had begun. Dead xenos were strewn about, and the Dark Angels were reduced in number by four. Sprays of blood on the walls showed hot on the thermal imaging. Raguel turned on a helmet-mounted stablight and deactivated his preysense with a thought. The bodies of the aliens could be seen clearly now, with their elongated heads and excess of limbs. Their flesh was purple under the light, standing out from blue-black carapace. They bled a disturbingly human red, however.

'Genestealers,' said Raguel with disgust.

'That explains why this world rebelled against Imperial control,' said Sergeant Raum.

It was easy to imagine how it had played out. The insular clans that lived on the deep-miners made contact with Imperial authorities only when their tanks were full, to trade for fresh food, clean water and other necessities. No one from the outside would even know they were being infiltrated.

Raguel tried his vox-unit but only got static. 'Interference on the comms. Either the structure is a problem or we are being jammed. Either way, we need to alert the master as soon as we can.'

Raum nodded and turned to rally his forces to continue. Raguel went to locate his fellow Chaplain. He found Hadariel standing over the body of one of the Space Marines. Blood wept from a number of punctures to the chestplate. Both hearts torn apart along with two of the three lungs, the Interrogator-Chaplain assessed. His work required a keen knowledge of Adeptus Astartes physiology.

'I knew him,' Hadariel said without looking up.

It was Levian, Raguel realised. 'Yes,' he said.

'How long did we serve together?' the younger Chaplain asked.

'You fought together back unto the Indomitus Crusade,' replied Raguel levelly. 'A regrettable loss.'

'I do not feel it. I cannot…' Hadariel trailed off.

'You have been through a great ordeal, brother.' Raguel clapped him on the shoulder. 'Come. The squad is prepared to move on. They will need us in what is to come.'

The Primaris Chaplain nodded slowly and followed behind as Raguel rejoined the unit.

* * *

They pushed on into the dark tunnels. There was a palpable feeling of hostile eyes upon them. The Interrogator-Chaplain heard scuffling sounds down side passages and inside the very walls from time to time. The sounds were nearly lost in the rumble and grind of churning machinery all around them. Were his hearing not superhuman, he doubted he would have heard them at all. He kept his crozius free and ready, now. The foul xenos-worshipping cult that gene-stealers formed around themselves might not be any match for an Adeptus Astartes assault in open battle, but they had no shortage of underhanded tactics to help level the field.

They progressed up rusted stairs to the next level. Aged metal creaked under the heavy tread of the Space Marines. It did not give way, however. The deep-miners had been constructed in a different age. Benighted without the light of the Emperor, perhaps, but an era of remarkable feats of technological sorcery. Raguel knew that the Red Priests of Mars had demanded that the assault forces do as little damage to the great machines as possible. The master had suggested they bring their concerns to the traitors and heretics who had made these attacks necessary.

'We are not far from the command centre now. It will be difficult to coordinate a strike with the other boarding squads with the vox interference, however,' said Raum.

'Then we must attack as swiftly as possible. The sounds of righteous battle will draw our brethren on to aid us,' replied Raguel.

'As you say, my lord Chaplain,' said the sergeant.

The Interrogator-Chaplain switched to the private vox-link with his fellow Chaplain. That, at least, was working well with them in proximity. 'Are you prepared for battle, Hadariel?'

'Of course,' came the swift reply. There was a pause before

the other Chaplain continued more uncertainly. 'Our special tasking went well, did it not?'

An uneasy regret stirred in Raguel's chest at those words. 'I am certain you comported yourself in a way that honoured the Chapter. I would not concern yourself beyond that. Focus on the present. There is a battle to be won in the here and now.'

'Yes. You are right. I appreciate your guidance, my lord,' said Hadariel.

Soon they reached an armoured hatchway. It was tightly sealed, though that would prove no more of an obstacle than the miner's hull had. Raum took a moment to consult the schematics before nodding to all of them: this was their objective. The squad stepped up to prepare for the assault.

'Brothers Crispin, Herius,' said the sergeant. The two Dark Angels stepped forward, their bolt rifles equipped with the auxiliary grenade launchers. 'As soon as the hatch is breached, lay down a spread of frag grenades. We will clear the room from there.'

Raguel gave Hadariel a pointed look.

'Purge the unclean,' the younger Chaplain said, his voice as cold as ice.

Not exactly a speech to put the fire into their brothers, but it would have to do, mused Raguel. He watched as the Intercessor nearest the door applied another of the melta charges to the hatchway. It scythed through the armour plating in a brilliant flash. The hatch fell away amidst a swirl of smoke and debris. With twin *whoompf*s the grenadiers fired, their explosive payloads hurtling into the smoke and the bridge beyond. Before the detonations vibrated the plates under their feet, the rest of the Space Marines were already moving.

They erupted into a swarm of foes. The impact of the grenades was immediately obvious in torn flesh and spilt blood. It was the only thing that kept them from being mobbed instantly. Here, the true foulness of the genestealers was laid bare for all to see. Not just in subverting the loyalties of the populace, or in their own xenos nature. No, the worst of it was the corruption of the holy human form that they perpetrated.

The bulk of their foes were nightmare hybrids of various degrees. In some it showed merely in scaling around inhuman eyes, or tongues that hung from distended jaws. Others were far worse, with multiple arms and flesh bulging with alien carapace. The very sight of them filled Raguel with disgust and hatred.

He raised his plasma pistol as he strode forward, firing into the mass of horrors. Where the blazing blasts landed they superheated flesh, ripping bodies apart as the water in them erupted to steam. All around he could hear his brothers joining him, the roar of their bolters sending explosive rounds to scythe through the foe.

Then the enemy had recovered and the onslaught began. A woman in worker's garb charged him with a chattering autopistol, her flesh tinged with purple. Raguel caught her as she raised her blade to strike, his mace's power field flashing and smashing her to the ground a broken wreck.

'Emperor, bring ruin upon our foes!' the Interrogator-Chaplain shouted. It was the beginning of one of the Litanies of Hate taught in the Reclusiam.

'Ave Imperator!' bellowed the Dark Angels around him as they battled their twisted foes.

'Emperor, bring ruin upon our foes! Hear us, lord and master!' Raguel continued.

A snarling monster with three arms lunged at him, its lips punctured by the too many sharp teeth in its mouth. Its hands were full of a snarling, heavy ice-cutter. The Dark Angel sidestepped the charge, decapitating the hybrid with a well-placed pistol shot as it passed.

'Ave Imperator!' came the callback.

A small rag-wrapped figure with a muscled tail protruding from its covering hurled a demolition charge at him. The world turned white for a split second as his rosarius turned aside the force of the blast. One of his brothers nearby was not so fortunate, his armour shattered and his flesh pulped.

Raguel channelled his rage into his words. 'Emperor, Master of Mankind!'

'Let us be the ruin of your foes!' the Dark Angels chorused.

A deadly-looking brute with one hand clutching a sword of bone and the other wielding a fang-tipped flesh lash closed in. Raguel caught the sweep of the ossein blade on his crozius. When he tried to bring his pistol to bear, however, the lash whipped around his arm and snapped tight. Strange energies pulsed into his limb through the connection, bringing with it such agony that his muscles spasmed uncontrollably. The plasma pistol fell from nerveless fingers.

'Lord of Victory! Saviour of Humanity!' growled Raguel, disregarding the pain.

He exerted his transhuman strength with a heave, knocking the bonesword out wide. Then he lunged into the gap and hammered his skull-visage directly into the corrupted champion's face. Bone shattered and flesh pulped as blood spurted across his helmet and chest. It might have been dead already. He caught it with an upswing of his crozius, the blow lifting it clear off the ground and sending it hurtling back into its allies.

'Emperor upon the Golden Throne!' he thundered victori-
ously. Gore ran in rivulets down his mask.

'Grant us the power of your glory!' roared his brothers.

Raguel and his fellow Dark Angels were fighting as hard
as they could, but they were being overrun. There were
simply too many of their foes within the command centre.
Two more of the Intercessors were foundering in the flood,
dragged down by the mass of their enemies and cut apart
with weaponised tools. Hadariel was hard-pressed by a pack
of them lunging at him with razor knives. They swarmed
him in a frenzy, seeking weak places in his armour where
they could draw blood.

The Interrogator-Chaplain turned to move in that direction. 'Glory everlasting to the Master–'

His words were snatched from his lips as a wave of power
slammed into him. It had a terrible presence to it and carried with it a pain that made the feel of the alien lash pale
by comparison. Each nerve in his body was alight with
fire. Arcs of etheric power sizzled across the surface of his
armour as he staggered under the onslaught.

Through blurred vision he could barely make out his
assailant. It stood out from the crowd, its swollen cranium
pulsing with unholy power. A staff tipped in shimmering
gems was thrust in his direction, the tip of it crackling with
the same amethyst energies that had waylaid him. Raguel
took a step in its direction, pushing against the pain like
the current of a flooded river. Each movement carried a cost
in terrible suffering. He drove on anyway.

Without his pistol, there was no way to strike back from
afar. The Interrogator-Chaplain knew he had to close with
the xenos psyker if he was to survive. Yet it did not matter. There were limits even to what a Space Marine could

withstand. He fell to one knee with a crunch of ceramite and forced himself back up. His will was powerful, but it was only a matter of time before his mind collapsed.

'Raguel!' roared a familiar voice.

Hadariel, he thought, but his vision was going now, narrowing to a red point. Then suddenly the pain was gone. It was like surging up from the depths of icy waters to reach a sunlit surface. The alien presence in his mind vanished, and his vision cleared. Hadariel had abandoned defending himself to try to save him. He had fought his way towards the xenos witch, bleeding as he went from the knives that found gaps in his armour plates.

The enemy psyker had been forced to transfer its attention towards Raguel's pupil. Now the dreadful energies consumed Hadariel instead. Raguel was close now, however, his single-minded pursuit of his foe having driven him on through the melee and the pain. He lunged forward with all his might, smashing through the final rank of corrupted bodyguards. The xenos had only time to turn towards him with rising terror, its mouth opening and eyes blazing with arcane powers. Then his crozius rose and fell, shattering its body and sending it broken to the ground.

Raguel wasted no time in exultation now. He turned and charged anew into the swarm where Hadariel had collapsed. They scattered at the impact. Those who did not flee fast enough were hurried on their way with bone-shattering swings of his crozius. He caught one with his empty hand and slung it to the ground so hard that its head dashed open upon impact. Then he stood in the momentary gap he had created, arms wide in a challenge that dared any foe to try him.

That was when more of the hatches blew in. More Dark

Angels poured into the bridge, shattering the flanks of the genestealer onslaught. With this psyker-master dead and the tide turning, those that remained began to flee through whatever exits they could find. Escape into the darkness and strike again later, that was the way of the cult.

Raguel knelt and lifted his badly wounded friend. He carried him over to sit him gently against the wall.

'Raguel,' wheezed the younger Chaplain. He reached up and fumbled his helmet off, revealing a face matted with blood from his nose and mouth.

'Be at ease, brother. You fought with valour and are badly hurt.' Raguel rested his hand on Hadariel's shoulder for a moment before turning to face the approaching Sergeant Raum.

'My lord Chaplain,' said Raum. 'We must push on and continue to clear the miner.'

'Of course,' said Raguel. 'Hadariel is in no shape to continue. It is best that we remain here. That will allow me to ensure this place is cleansed of any moral contaminants as well.' The Interrogator-Chaplain swept his gaze across the bridge-turned-battleground, strewn with bodies and alien artefacts.

'As you say, my lord. I shall have an Apothecary sent as soon as we reach a place where the jamming has eased.' Raum made the sign of the aquila.

'Thank you, sergeant,' replied the Interrogator-Chaplain.

The sergeant departed, as did the rest of their brethren, to continue hunting the xenos throughout the vehicle. Raguel strode to where he could see his plasma pistol lying on the ground. He knelt to pick it up. It was covered in blood, but seemed otherwise undamaged.

'Raguel,' rasped Hadariel. 'I remember.'

The Interrogator-Chaplain froze.

'I remember… something. Something terrible. My head aches with the edges of it. I went to Malmar. The Chapter… There is a darkness eating us, Raguel. I cannot…' The younger Chaplain coughed, spraying blood down the front of his armour.

Raguel closed his eyes tightly. His hands closed around two objects from the floor, and he rose back to his full height. He holstered his pistol at his side and walked to kneel in front of his brother.

'You are merely hurt, Hadariel. That xenos filth got into your head. You cannot let it rattle you,' he said.

'No… It shook something loose. I can hear the waves. I can hear them… They did something to me, brother…' Hadariel reached up to grip Raguel by the upper arm.

'Be at ease,' soothed Raguel. 'All is well.'

Then he slashed across Hadariel's throat with the knife he had collected from the floor. Blood spilled, rich and red. The Interrogator-Chaplain gripped his brother tightly as the other Space Marine struggled. Then it was over.

Raguel sat back. He threw the knife away amongst the bodies with a convulsive movement. His hands were soaked with blood. It was all red. There was no way to tell this latest coat from that of the genestealers.

He knew, though. He would always know.

'Can we be certain that it was the exposure to the alien psyker that caused the lapse? Not merely a side effect of Primaris physiology?' Asmodai asked.

The chambers of the Rock were cold and dim. They were in the deep levels, where the screams could be heard at all hours.

Raguel glanced to the other Interrogator-Chaplain and frowned. 'We can never be certain of anything, save war and death.'

The senior Chaplain snorted. 'Either way it is a flaw. The mindwipe was broken too easily. We will have to be cautious in the future. More strenuous methods may be required to ensure silence amongst the failures.'

'Failures...' Raguel said quietly.

'Hadariel was given every opportunity to succeed,' Asmodai said flatly.

'I was not allowed to oversee his trial,' Raguel said.

'You knew him too well,' came the swift reply. 'We cannot permit personal bias to allow weakness into our highest echelons.'

'I was not even allowed to be present!' barked Raguel. He composed himself quickly. 'The first Primaris Chaplain to be tested to join our ranks, and he fails under mysterious circumstances. Some would call that suspect.'

'Do you question the wisdom of the Inner Circle?' rumbled Asmodai coldly.

'Spare me your intimidating theatrics, Asmodai. I did as I was ordered. Hadariel is dead. My commitment to our cause is not in question.' Raguel knew his hands had tightened into fists. He did not care. 'I merely regret the loss of a good warrior.'

'Of course. As we all do,' was all Asmodai said. 'You will be reassigned soon. There is work to be done.' He turned and departed.

'There always is,' Raguel said wearily to himself. 'The work never ends.' He departed as well, the screams of agony and horror ringing all around him.

YOUR
NEXT READ

WARHAMMER 40,000

SPACE MARINE CONQUESTS

WAR OF SECRETS

PHIL KELLY

WAR OF SECRETS
by Phil Kelly

Supporting the Dark Angels as they battle trauma-scarred t'au,
Lieutenant Farren and his Primaris Marines discover their allies have
many secrets they'll do anything to conceal…

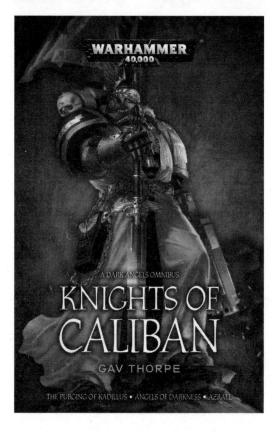

THE DARKLING HOURS

RACHEL HARRISON

Compiled of billions of soldiers from a million
different worlds, the **Astra Militarum** is, by sheer
number, the greatest army the galaxy has ever known.
These brave men and women hold nothing less than
the survival of humanity in their hands.
In *The Darkling Hours*, a powerful psyker lurks in
Termina. Commissar Severina Raine and her Antari
Rifles must root out the witch and save the city.

The city of Termina never stops singing.

Commissar Severina Raine knows that the sound is just the wind cutting through the city's many mineshafts and tunnels. It can be heard all over Termina, from the refineries on the surface to the processing plants far below, where Raine and her regiment, the Eleventh Antari Rifles, are billeted. There is no escaping the city's singing, but in the old overseer's watch room where Raine now sits and waits, it is at least a little quieter. The hanging lumens overhead turn in that same wind as it finds its way through cracks in the poorly plastered walls. Light glances off the casing of Raine's timepiece as she watches the hands tick around towards the crack in the top of the face. Her body aches from the previous day of fighting and her eyes are dry and gritty. She should be taking the time she has been given to sleep, but she finds that she cannot. Not while the fight goes on above her.

And certainly not with the city singing.

'It sounds like something living, don't you think?'

Raine clicks her timepiece closed and puts it back in the chest pocket of her coat. Andren Fel takes a seat on the opposite side of the overseer's table and hands her a tin cup with a loop of thorns scored into the rim. It is warm to the touch from the windfall tea inside it.

'I think it sounds like singing,' Raine says.

'Or howling,' Fel says. 'Either way, it is sorrowful.'

The storm trooper captain is unarmoured, clad in black fatigues that are sewn with the red bars that mark his rank. Fel's dark hair has got nearly to the length where it can tangle, and his face is cut and bruised. His densely tattooed hands are split badly across the knuckles. He is also meant to be taking the two hours they have been given to rest, but Raine knows that is as difficult for him as it is for her. That is why they often spend these hours talking.

'Shouldn't howling be a comfort for a Duskhound?' Raine asks.

Fel laughs at that, a low chuckle.

'True enough,' he says.

A tremor runs through the undercroft that makes the overhead lumens flicker and hum. Dust falls in fine columns from the ceiling and scatters on the wooden surface of the table.

'I saw Devri on the way up,' Fel says. 'He had to pull Blue Company out of the docks. The Sighted sank the lot to keep them from pushing up to the drilling fields.'

Raine nods and drinks from her tin cup. The windfall tea is bitter and spiced. It only grows on Antar, and only in the Northwilds, where Fel was raised before he was taken for the Schola Antari.

'Whatever the Sighted intend to take from Termina, it is in the mines,' Raine says. 'They have either abandoned or destroyed key locations all across the city, but they refuse to surrender the pits.'

'Seems a lot of blood to spend for the sake of promethium,' Fel says.

Raine nods.

'If they just wanted promethium they wouldn't have fled the refineries. It must be something else. Something they can twist and use.'

'Something buried deep,' Fel says.

A second, larger tremor shakes the room. More dust falls from the ceiling, and the lumens fail altogether for a moment. In the brief instant of absolute darkness Raine can't help thinking of the battle before this one, on Gholl, where she was captured by the Sighted and taken into the crystal caverns under the surface.

Buried, deep.

Raine pushes the memory – and the unease that comes with it – aside. She drinks from her tin cup again, nearly draining it. When she puts it down, the leaves cling to the enamel inside.

'You read the leaves before every fight, don't you?' she asks Fel.

He looks down at his own cup and nods.

'I do.'

'Would you show me how it's done?'

'I thought you didn't believe in omens or fates,' he says.

Raine shakes her head.

'I don't, but you do.'

Fel smiles.

'Alright,' he says. 'I'll show you.'

Raine holds out her cup to hand it to him, but he shakes his head.

'It has to be you that sets the leaves, so that our fates don't get crossed.' He shows her using his own cup. 'Turn the tea three times, and then tip out what's left.'

Raine does as he says, and tips the remains of her windfall tea out onto the floor before putting her cup back on the table between them.

'Where did you learn this?' Raine asks.

'My mother taught me,' Fel says simply.

Raine understands then why the ritual means so much, because it must remind him of home, and of the family he lost. Raine feels the timepiece ticking in her pocket like a second heartbeat.

Fel picks up the cup in his tattooed hand and frowns.

Raine cannot help it. She leans forward, just slightly.

'What do you see?' she asks.

'Hunting birds,' he says, turning the cup so that she can see. 'For a chase that ends in blood.'

Raine catches herself smiling.

'Not so surprising,' she says. 'And the rest?'

He turns the cup as if to look at it another way, still frowning.

'The duskhound,' he says, after a moment.

'The story that your squad is named for,' Raine says.

Fel nods.

'What does it mean?' Raine asks, though she can guess, because he's told her the old story.

Fel puts the cup down on the table.

'It means death, following close by.'

The overhead lumens stutter again.

'Isn't it always?' Raine asks.

The vox-bead Raine wears crackles in her ear before Fel can answer her. It is the Antari general, Juna Keene. From the way Fel reacts, Raine can tell he is receiving the same message.

'The timetable has moved up. Tactical briefing in ten minutes in the main control hub.'

'Acknowledged,' Raine says, into her vox-link. She hears Fel do the same.

'Back to duty, then, captain,' she says.

Fel nods and picks up the tin cups.

'Aye, commissar,' he says.

In the quiet that follows his words, Raine listens to the sound echoing from Termina's tunnels and hollows, and realises that she was wrong, and Fel was right.

It really does sound like howling.

The tactical briefing takes place in the old refinery control hub around a hololith projector that's been mounted on the main console. The other lights in the large, rust-stained chamber are switched off to allow the projection to show clearly, leaving most of the hub in shadows.

Andren Fel stands in those shadows and watches the hololith turn, memorising the details by habit. Distances and depth. The number of menial crew. Ingress points and exit options. It is how he always prepares for an operation, but today it is more than that. It is a welcome distraction from the shape he saw in the leaves. In Raine's fate.

The duskhound.

Death.

Raine stands on the opposite side of the hololith from him now, her angular face cast in hard shadows. The green light from the projection catches the edges of her Commissariat uniform, turning the golden braiding to jade and finding the edges of every dent and gouge in the silvered chestplate she wears. Fel meets Raine's eyes for a moment. They are dark, even in daylight, but in these shadows they could as well be the space between stars.

'What you're looking at is mine-pit designate Iota. It is the deepest mine in Termina, and the oldest.'

The words belong to Juna Keene. The general is sitting at ease on the edge of one of the secondary consoles. Her uniform is that of the regulars, green-and-grey splinter, with wear-worn pale leather gloves and boots. Only the white cuffs on her rolled-back sleeves mark her rank. That, and the easy authority in her voice.

'The pit-mouth is twelve-hundred metres across, side to side,' Keene says. 'Last recorded operating depth was around three thousand metres.'

Keene depresses a heavy key in the hololith's base. It resets to a different view, from above. Mine-pit Iota is a wide-open void in the face of the city, like a set of jaws for the world. Grooves made for lifters and transitways carved into the walls run around the edge of it, down into the depths.

'The Sighted have held the pit since the outset of the war,' she says. 'They have abandoned a dozen other key locations, but they refuse to leave Iota. There is something that they want down there. Something we cannot afford for them to find.'

'Iota is located in the western reaches,' Raine says. 'Which makes Karin Sun's Gold Company the closest for capture. Am I to assume that they have failed?'

'They tried,' Keene says. 'But the regulars cannot get close. The Sighted have a witch prowling Iota, and a powerful one at that. Sun chose to fall back, rather than lose his company to madness.'

Fel can't help but feel unease at the word *witch*. It's an old disquiet from home. One he is trained to act in spite of, that can never truly be erased.

'If the regulars cannot move in, the war in the western reaches will grind to a halt. We cannot let that happen.'

'Hunt-to-kill, then, general,' Fel says.

Keene nods.

'And you'll need to make it quick. According to Captain Sun, the witch's power grows stronger with proximity and exposure. It had Sun's troops all dreaming, running, or temporarily mad. Our witches,' Keene pauses, and frowns. 'Our *sanctioned psykers* fared twice as badly. Apparently Pharo clawed his own eyes out rather than get any closer.'

Fel shakes his head. Witch or not, he would never wish Pharo harm.

'If the witch's power grows with proximity, then that's how we'll hunt it,' he says. 'Go straight for the source of the fear.'

The general nods her head.

'Your Valkyrie is on standby. Once your boots hit the scaffolds, you will have six hours. If you miss your extraction, we will count you as lost. Is that clear?'

'As a springtime sky, general,' Fel says. 'Consider it done.'

Keene looks to Raine then.

'You will accompany them, commissar,' she says.

'Yes, general,' Raine says.

Keene doesn't say why, and Fel doesn't have to ask. There is only one reason to send a commissar along for a hunt-to-kill like this one. It will be Raine's duty to make sure that the Duskhounds don't lose themselves in dreams, like Sun's regulars did, and to deal with them if they do, with that pistol she carries or her sword's keen edge.

Fel catches Raine's dark eyes once more through the

hololith. The two of them have fought together countless times since her assignment to the regiment, and Fel has come to know her well, through stories shared and scars earned. He trusts Raine, even if his kinfolk don't, but he has no illusions. Just as Fel is made for the hunt and the kill, Raine is made for judgement, and for the hard choices. If it is necessary, she will not hesitate to pull the trigger. To do anything else would be to break faith.

And that is something that Fel knows Severina Raine will never do.

For the first time in days, Severina Raine cannot hear the sound of the city, because Jova's Valkyrie gunship is howling even more loudly than Termina can.

Raine keeps a steady grip on the handhold built into the Valkyrie's airframe as the pilot banks over the city on the approach to Iota. Cold wind rushes through the troop compartment from the open side doors, carrying with it the smell of fyceline and smoke. The wind stings Raine's eyes and catches at the collar of her buckled short-coat. She is wearing her funerary blacks and heavy, weatherproof gloves. Her silver chestplate is deliberately dulled to keep it from catching the light. She has strapped extra armour plates over her boots for the drop. The drop for which she needs the jump-mask slung around her neck, and the bulky grav-chute harness on her back.

'It will be quick,' Fel says. 'Straight down into Iota, and onto the eastward landing pad. It is only halfway down, but it's as far as we can go before there's too much strike risk from the scaffolding.'

Fel is standing beside her, with one hand on the airframe and his hellgun slung. He is fully kitted for the fight to come, with grenades and charges locked to his belt and the heavy-bladed knife he carries sheathed at his waist. Like Raine, he is wearing a grav-chute, though his is modified to be worn with storm trooper carapace. The tactical display built into Fel's vambrace shows the schematic of Iota rendered in green, and the landing pad as a bright white circle.

'The display in your jump-mask will keep the platform flagged,' he says. 'Once we hit the platform, we will shed the grav-chutes and move down towards Iota's heart. Clear?'

Raine nods. She has completed perhaps a tenth of the combat drops the Duskhounds have, but Raine has enough experience to know how to make it to the landing zone in one piece. The principles for use of a grav-chute are simple. Fire the thrusters as a method of aerobrake in adequate time before literally hitting the landing zone. Do not thrash your limbs. Do not panic. It is a matter of control and discipline under pressure, like many things.

'Completely,' she says. 'Just give the word, captain.'

Fel smiles at that.

'Aye, commissar,' he says.

The Valkyrie's internal vox crackles.

'*We are close to Iota,*' Jova says. '*I'll maintain at five hundred metres above the pit-mouth, but you'll want to make it quick.*'

'Understood,' Fel replies.

He pulls on his Duskhounds mask and locks it in place, the eye-lenses glowing red in the dim combat lighting of the troop compartment. Like the rest of his squad, Fel's mask is painted with a snarling hound's face to represent the creature of Antari folklore that gave the squad their name. Seeing it now, Raine can't help but think of the shape he saw in the leaves, back in the overseer's watch room.

Three loud thumps split the air, then, and the gunship's airframe shudders, rattling all of the way down Raine's arm.

'Well, now. There's no need for that,' Jova says, over the internal vox.

The pilot cuts speed and drops the Valkyrie into a curving dive. Inertia pulls at Raine's bones, and the airframe shakes and groans, but then the turbojets fire and Jova levels out again. Rol, Fel's second-in-command, whoops. The Duskhound is braced against the frame of one of the Valkyrie's open side doors with his hellgun raised. Rol has his mask in place too, but Raine can guess that he is grinning.

'Honestly, it's as if you wish for death,' Tyl says.

The Duskhounds' sharpshooter is braced in the other door, her rifle pointed out into the clouds and darkness. Tyl's rifle is modified for distance kills, with a variable scope and a longer, accurised barrel that she has scored with kill markings. Her tone is patient and good-natured. Tyl and Rol could be taken for true family. They are both lean and strong, with the same lilting accents. In a fight they are inseparable, each a spare shadow for the other.

'Glory, maybe,' Rol says, with a smile in his voice. 'The After can wait.'

Tyl laughs.

'I wish you wouldn't make light of it like that,' Jeth says. 'Death is no cause for laughter.'

Jeth is the only Duskhound built stronger than Fel is. His matt-black carapace is scored with words from hymnals written in the old Antari script, and he wears a loop of luckstones at his belt.

'You know I didn't mean it like that,' Rol says. 'Tell him, Myre.'

'Jeth is right,' Myre says, in her solemn voice. 'Mocking death will only bring it quicker.'

Myre is the youngest of Fel's Duskhounds, but you would not know it from her voice. It always sounds as though she has seen a sector's worth of sadness. Myre sits in one of the Valkyrie's restraint thrones, checking her gear briskly and locking it to her belt and thigh-plates. Raine sees heat-charges and blind grenades, and a loop of krak grenades that Myre passes straight to Jeth without needing to be asked. The Valkyrie thrums and shakes as more detonations light the clouds through the open side doors, and Raine sees the wide, dark mouth of Iota far below through the ashes and smoke.

'Do you all feel that?' Jeth asks. 'It's like knives running over my bones. I think we just crossed into the witch's circle.'

Raine realises then that she does feel it, the very edge of a creeping unease. She tightens her grip on the handhold above her head and takes a breath, pushing the feeling aside.

'We must deny it,' she says, over the roar of the Valkyrie's turbojets. 'It is the only way to defeat a psyker who intends to twist your own mind against you.'

Raine thinks back to Gholl. To the crystal caverns, and how her own mind was twisted against her. How she managed to deny it.

'There is a way to know the falsehoods from reality,' she says. 'There are always details amiss, even when the psyker is powerful. Hold to what you know to be true. Trust your instincts. It is much more difficult to fool the heart than it is the eyes.'

Fel looks to his Duskhounds.

'Listen well to the commissar's words,' he says. 'We hunt, we kill and we get out. All of us. Is that clear?'

'Aye, captain,' the Duskhounds say, as one.

Inertia pulls at Raine again as the Valkyrie cuts speed and holds position above the pit, its vectored engines roaring. Rol and Tyl slam their side doors closed and take position by the ramp with Myre and Jeth.

'You are good to go,' Jova says over the internal vox. *'I'll hold until you are clear.'*

'Understood,' Fel says.

Raine pulls her jump-mask on and secures it. It closes tight to her face. Her own breathing becomes very loud, contained by the mask. The air supply through the breather apparatus is stale and dry. Her visor lights with the simple guidance data that will guide her to the lifter platform and a drop distance counter flickers in the corner of the display.

Distance to target: 2134 metres.

'Ready?' Fel asks.

'Aye, captain,' the Duskhounds reply, and this time, Raine joins them in their response.

'Let's go make some fates,' Fel says, and he hits the release for the Valkyrie's rear ramp.

The ramp yawns open to reveal Termina's thunderous sky, underlit by the fires of war and the refineries that are still burning. Tyl and Rol go first, straight over into the dark. Then Myre and Jeth. The wind buffets Raine as she steps to the edge alongside Fel. She blinks. Breathes. Glances once more at the drop distance counter in her visor's display.

And then she jumps out into the war-torn sky.

As Raine falls through Termina's sky, towards the open void of Iota, she focuses on what she was taught.

Breathe. Don't stop breathing.

Arms and legs outstretched and stable.

Don't thrash. Don't blink.

Remain calm.

The sky lights with anti-aircraft fire and lightning flashes. The ground grows larger. Darker. Iota yawns wider. The wind tears at Raine's uniform and tugs on her limbs. Her fingers are cold and numb, despite the gloves. The drop distance counter tracks down quickly.

Distance to target: 1711 metres.

Breathe.

Don't stop breathing.

The landing zone in Raine's visor display is a bright white circle. Below, Iota grows wider and wider until there is no ground to see, and then she is below the line of the pit-mouth and falling into the darkness of Iota itself. Scaffolding and lifters blur past, and the counter tracks down. Raine cannot see the others, but then the pit is so dark and the wind is so strong. Her visor beads with water that runs in streaks to the edges.

Distance to target: 1226 metres.

The longer the freefall, the less likely it is you'll be seen. But the longer the freefall, the less control you have. The more likely it is you will hit something.

Don't blink.

Just breathe.

Her eyes sting and ache and Raine thinks for a moment of the shape in the leaves. She glimpses it again in the streaks of water beading on her visor. The Duskhound. Death. Her heart is racing.

'Breathe,' she says to herself.

Raine knows that it is the psyker's influence pushing at

the edges of her mind, making her see those things. Making her heart race even more than the fall does. She also knows that to panic is to die, so she keeps breathing deeply from the stale air of her mask and forces her limbs to stay locked as the counter keeps tracking down.

Distance to target: 914 metres.

But then there is a loud crack and Raine is dizzied. Her limbs go slack for an instant before she recovers her senses and realises that something struck her visor. An enemy round, or some kind of debris. She is falling fast, uncontrolled. Iota blurs around her. The wind is deafening. She can't catch her breath. She can't see. Can't stop spinning.

Just.

Breathe.

With the tactical display crazing in front of her eyes and the vox pickup hissing loudly in her ears, Raine fights the wind and the vertigo and the dizziness to right herself, and slow the fall before it kills her. She gets herself level, but she cannot tell if she is off-course. She cannot clearly see the white circle that marks the landing zone. In the corner of the display, the distance to target flickers and splinters.

It looks as though it says *Distance to target: 94 metres.*

Or is that *34 metres.*

'*Throne,*' Raine says, through her teeth.

She fires the grav-chute's jets. Inertia pulls hard on her limbs and jolts her spine. Raine's vision dizzies again for a moment, and when it clears she can see the landing zone below. Close. Coming up fast, despite the jets. What she was taught rushes through her mind. Use the fall. Don't lock your limbs. Roll with the speed of it.

Don't close your eyes.

Raine kills the grav-chute jets a moment before she hits

the deck of the landing platform and rolls. She doesn't lock her limbs, or close her eyes, which is how she sees that she hit at a poor angle, right by the edge of the platform.

And that she's about to go over it.

Raine twists as her body slides over the platform lip and manages to snag hold of the grating of the floor, though it nearly pulls her arm from its socket and she can't help but cry out. She hits the release for the grav-chute and lets it fall away into the pit below as two figures clad in black carapace drop to their knees and help to drag her back up onto the platform. Fel and Myre.

'Hells,' Fel says. 'That was close.'

Raine gets to her feet and pulls the jump-mask off. Iota's howling is even louder without it. The crystalflex of the jump-mask is crazed with cracks that burst outwards from a hole the size of a trade-coin. Raine becomes aware of her face stinging where she has been cut, and of warm lines of blood painting their way down her cheek. For a moment, she almost sees a shape in the damage to the visor. Teeth and eyes.

Raine shakes her head to clear it and drops the damaged jump-mask on the deck. Fel meets her eyes for a moment.

'Ready?' he asks her.

Raine nods and draws her bolt pistol from the mag-secured holster at her belt. The cold weight of Penance is comforting.

'Let's go,' she says.

Andren Fel was taught many things at the Schola Antari. He was taught how to lead others. How to memorise and strategise. He was taught how to survive with very little, and how to fight and kill with even less, but Fel's scholam training also granted him another skill.

Something that the masters would call *resilience*.

Those days are distant now, but Fel remembers them as clearly as any other. He remembers being bound and blindfolded. He remembers shocks and lashes, knives and blood, and the masters asking him the same question over and over again and expecting him to break.

Do you want it to stop?

Every cadet finds a different way to endure the resilience trials, and to keep themselves from answering *yes* to that question. The method is always secret, and personal, so that it cannot be broken. Fel's is a simple thing. An old evensong that his mother used to sing when he was a child.

Beware the darkling hours, my son,
For that is when the duskhounds come.
Keep within the light as the fire burns,
Until the morning sun returns.

Andren Fel thinks of those words again now as he follows the wide, rocky slope down into Iota. Down into the darkness. The words help to keep the witch's work at bay. The unease, as if he is being followed. The shadows, coiling and twisting and making shapes at the edges of his sight.

The glint of watchful eyes in the darkness.

The path down into Iota is wide and set with scuffed steel rails for excavation trains. Line of sight is fouled by large piles of rubble and the still, silent drilling machines that creak in the ceaseless wind. Iota's howling is louder the deeper they go. More than loud enough to cover any sound Fel might make as he gets shadow-close to the two Sighted scouts patrolling the path ahead. The two of them are wearing fully enclosed reflective helmets and dull blue flak armour marked with that sigil they all wear. The spiral, with the eye at the centre.

Not unlike the spiral of Iota, seen from above.

The shards of mirrored glass hanging from cords on the Sighted's flak armour knock together as Fel grabs hold of the scout and breaks his neck with a twist of his hands. Beside him, Rol quiets the other with the edge of his combat blade, then the two of them drag the bodies to where they will be hidden by the darkness and debris, before moving further down the slope.

Fel drops into the shadow of a mining machine, and Rol does the same. Ahead, the slope leads down onto a rubble-strewn plateau that is lit by oil lanterns strung between poles driven into the stone. The dim lights dance like faerie fires in the wind, painting long, restless shadows on the ground. A tunnel yawns in Iota's wall that wasn't on Keene's schematics. It has been cut jagged, leaving shards of rock pointing inwards. Outside it, an excavation trolley sits empty on the tracks. Iota's howling is much louder here. Twinned, almost.

'Well, that looks the sort of place you might hide a witch. Don't you think, captain?'

Rol's voice is without a smile, for once.

'I'd say so,' Fel says.

It's not just the look of the tunnel. Fel can see his Duskhounds' vitals in the corner of his display. Their heart rates are all reading as elevated, the price of resisting the witch. Fel feels it just as much as they do, unease welling up inside him like blood from a bad wound.

Beware the darkling hours, my son, says his mother's voice.

Fel shakes his head, hard. It's getting worse, which is proof that they are on the right track.

He sends a burst of vox, and the rest of his Duskhounds approach with Raine. She drops into cover beside him with her sabre drawn. Raine has dulled Evenfall's blade to stop it catching the light. In the darkness, the blood drying on her face looks black.

'We've got movement, captain,' Rol says.

Fel looks back around the cover to see a group of Sighted come up and out of the tunnel. A dozen of them, wearing those reflective masks, just like the others. Fel marks the leader by the mirrored cloak he wears, and the finely made sword at his hip. Eight of the Sighted are working together to carry a heavy, sealed casket over to the excavation trolley, where they set it down with a dull thud.

'We cannot let whatever that is reach the surface,' Raine says.

Fel shakes his head.

'Pattern?' Rol asks.

Fel watches as two of the Sighted stay behind to guard the trolley, and the rest turn back for the tunnel.

'Hangman's noose,' he says.

The first Antari story that Andren Fel ever told Raine was that of the duskhounds. The story goes that the hounds come to take the souls of those fated to die and drag them to the After for judgement. He told her that duskhounds can appear in the slimmest of shadows, even that of those they are sent to take.

In the moment that the hangman's noose closes, Raine believes every word of the old Antari story.

Raine is moving from cover to cover across the plateau with Fel when Myre and Jeth resolve from the shadows around the Sighted guarding the trolley. The Duskhounds grab hold of the two scouts and drag them from their feet into the darkness before reappearing moments later, without a sound. Myre drops to one knee and sets to work attaching her burn-charges to the trolley. The rest of the Sighted do not turn back. They just keep moving towards the tunnel mouth, as good as deafened by Iota's howling.

Fel sends a single burst of vox, then. The signal that means *close the noose.*

Near-silent flashes of hellgun fire lance from the darkness as Raine breaks cover alongside Fel. Three of the Sighted fall in rapid succession, masks shattered and coiling smoke from Cassia Tyl's pin-accurate kill shots. The rest of the Sighted turn and shout and scatter and raise their own weapons to fire back, only to find that death is already much too close.

Raine draws her blade through the first of them. Evenfall sings, cutting through the Sighted's blue-grey flak armour with ease. Black blood mists Raine's face as the woman spills over backwards without a sound. Raine lets her momentum carry her forward as the Duskhounds engage around her. Rol shoots one of the Sighted, centre-mass, before burying his combat blade in another. The Sighted staggers backwards but refuses to die. He raises his shotgun to fire on Rol, point-blank. Before he can pull the trigger, another whisper of hellgun fire cuts the space between the two of them and sends the Sighted spinning to the ground.

'*Good eyes, Cass,*' Rol says, over the vox.

'*It's like you said,*' she replies, from her sharpshooter's position. '*The After can wait.*'

Raine sees one of the Sighted go for Fel with a jagged, hooked blade. He lets his rifle swing by the strap so that he can catch the Sighted's arm and break it. Fel twists the scout off his feet, before taking up his hellgun again for the kill shot in one swift movement.

'You will see.'

The words come from the Sighted's leader, as he charges Raine with his sword raised. Her reflection grows larger in his mirrored mask. The Sighted is quick, the shards of glass on his cloak catching the lumen light as he ducks and parries and swings for her. Raine catches the Sighted's blade on her own and turns it aside before plunging Evenfall into his chest.

'You will see the truth,' the Sighted rasps, from behind his mask. 'All of your fears.'

'Fear means nothing when you have faith,' Raine snarls, pulling her sabre free.

The Sighted falls to his knees.

'You will see,' he gurgles. 'You are beheld.'

Then the Sighted collapses and dies, black blood spreading around him on the stone like outstretched wings. With the remaining Sighted dead, Myre and Jeth approach and the Duskhounds gather around Raine, their armour scored and gouged by blades.

'Beheld,' Rol says. 'That cannot be good.'

And then another sound overtakes even Iota's ceaseless howling.

Laughter.

The sound echoes from every surface, mad and cruel and almost songlike. The Duskhounds point their rifles into the darkness and Raine raises her sabre, but there is nothing to fight. Nothing to kill. The laughter grows louder and the shadows seem to draw closer, spilling over the stone like oil. Jeth mutters the Antari word for *ghosts* with horror in his voice and Raine catches a glimpse of a figure amongst the shadows. Her ghost is clad in Commissariat black with her arm outstretched, as if to take Raine's hand. The timepiece in Raine's pocket thunders like a second heart.

Severina, says the ghost.

Raine shakes her head.

Breathe, she thinks, just as she did during the fall. *Just keep breathing.*

'We have to move,' she says, through her teeth.

'I hear you,' Fel says. 'Myre, burn their prize.'

Myre nods and keys the bracer on her wrist. The Sighted's casket lights with heat-charges, silently burning. The laughter becomes strangled and angry and the ghosts turn away.

'Everyone into the tunnel,' Fel says. 'Now.'

The tunnel is cut steeply and jaggedly, as if it was made by claws, or frantic hands. Oil lanterns hang from ropes overhead and a thick, iridescent fog drifts along the tunnel, coiling around Andren Fel's feet as he follows the path. Contact risk down here is high. Field of fire is restricted, and line of is sight is limited by the steep grade and the curve of the tunnel as it loops downwards. Hollows have been blasted and cut into the walls all around Fel and new tunnels splinter off left and right. Eyes burn in the shadows, only to vanish when Fel draws sight on them. Claws click against the stone.

You are beheld.

'Watch careful,' Fel says. 'Don't stray, or separate.'

His Duskhounds vox affirmatives as they move swiftly at a ragged spread, their targeting lasers glancing off the fog. Raine keeps pace with Fel easily, her pistol drawn in steady hands. Her breathing mists the air. Fel checks the readout on his monitron's display. The ambient temperature in the tunnel reads as near-freezing.

'It shouldn't be this cold down here,' he says. 'Not so far underground.'

Raine shakes her head.

'It is the psyker's doing,' she says. 'We must be getting close.'

Fel nods. Iota's howling sounds almost joyful now, and much closer. He catches the smell of coalfires.

'Captain, we've got Sighted dead.'

The voice is Tyl's. She is a short distance ahead with Rol, crouching down in the fog. She straightens up as Fel approaches and shakes her head.

'Looks as though they kept digging until they died,' she says with disgust.

The Sighted at their feet is lying curled on his side. He wears one of their masks, but no armour, just worker's coveralls painted with their spiral mark. The Sighted's bare arms are cut with fate-marks in jagged whorls. As the fog stirs with Jeth and Myre approaching, Fel sees that the Sighted's hand is closed tightly around something that glitters, blood-red and iridescent like the fog. Fel has seen the like before, given to the Sighted's witches and commanders in place of their eyes.

'They are digging for crystals,' Fel says. 'For seeing stones.'

Jeth snarls a curse and takes a step back from the Sighted's body.

'That's what we burned,' Myre says softly. 'Seeing stones.'

Raine nods. The look in her dark eyes is midwinter cold.

'That must be how the psyker can reach so far and hurt so many,' she says. 'The crystals are acting as a psychic amplifier.'

Such clever puppets.

The voice echoes from every wall of the tunnel, and inside of Fel's head, too. It makes his vision run at the edges. He tastes blood.

'Go,' he says to his squad and to Raine.

The witch starts to laugh again as they move down the steep tunnel at pace. The walls seem to billow and swell like sails, studded with jagged chunks of that same crystal, burning red.

'The psyker will try to turn your senses against you. To trick and unnerve you with falsehoods and fears, but you must deny it,' Raine says, her voice ringing clear, even with the laughter and all of Iota's howling. 'Hold to what you know to be true.'

Fel does as she says. He takes a slow breath and holds to his truths. To the words of the evensong, and the cold weight of his hellgun, braced against his shoulder. The swift, quiet tread of his Duskhounds all around him.

And to Severina Raine, and the depths of her dark eyes.

Fel keeps his footing despite the scree and the steepness and the psyker's laughing, and rounds a sharp turn in the tunnel with the others beside him, stepping into a vaulted cavern filled with crates and barrels. Fuel, for the lanterns. A single figure stands in the middle of it, clad in a mirrored mask and holding something in an outstretched hand. A flare.

'You are beheld,' the Sighted says with glee. 'You will burn.'

Fel fires his hellgun, hitting the Sighted's mask dead centre and shattering it, but it is too late.

The flare is already lit.

'*Shit,*' Jeth says as the flare drops and the cavern lights, and everything is lost to fire and smoke.

Fel is staggered by it. Momentarily blinded. Even with his respirator kit he finds he can't breathe. Over the roar of the flames, Raine's voice echoes in his head.

Hold to what you know to be true.

Fel realises that there is smoke and fire, but no heat. No pain. The fire isn't real. He squeezes his eyes closed and takes another slow breath. When he opens his eyes again the cavern is empty. There are no barrels. No crates. Just a shadowed space where jagged crystals jut from every surface.

'Are you with me, captain?'

Fel looks at Raine. She is breathing hard, and blood is running from her nose, but her dark eyes are clear.

'I'm with you,' Fel says, with the taste of blood in his mouth.

Around him, his Duskhounds are reeling. Fel helps Tyl pull Rol back to his feet. He is murmuring something about fire.

Such well-made puppets.

Fel snaps his rifle up and trains it on the source of the voice. He doesn't know how he couldn't see it before. The nest of shattered crystal on the far side of the cavern, arranged in a glittering spiral, and the Sighted witch, sitting in the centre of it. It is a pale thing, clad in blood-spattered silks, with crimson seeing stone eyes.

Fel fires on the witch in a heartbeat, and his Duskhounds do the same. Raine's bolt pistol bellows. Crystal dust and smoke fouls the air, but when it clears, the witch is nowhere to be seen.

Fierce, too, the witch says. *Much more so than your kin who came before.*

The voice comes from everywhere now. Fel can't find the source of it. He backs into formation with his Dusk-hounds on instinct as the witch's laughter echoes from the seeing stones set into the walls. Fel loses the nest again, as if it has passed out of sight. All that he can see now is the witch, reflected in the facets of the crystals, distorted and fractured and grinning with blackened, blunted teeth.

Such strong cords you were given to move your limbs, the witch says. *Your minds cut and shaped for killing.*

The reflections shift and change and a flock of identical ghosts take shape around them. The witch, repeated a hundred times over. He is as thin as springtime ice, with feathers threaded into his skin by the quills. Like the other Sighted, he has cut dozens of times and dates into his face and throat. Fate-marks. They bleed afresh as he smiles.

Made never to question, the witch says. *Only to blindly obey.*

The shadows around the witch's reflections coil and unspool, lengthening and reaching for Fel and the others like hooked claws. The seeing stones in the walls burn even brighter. Fel's nose starts bleeding.

'The stones,' he manages to say. 'Break the stones.'

His Duskhounds fire, and the cavern fills with light and crystal dust and angry shadows. The witch hisses and snarls like an animal.

You might have been cut and shaped and strung with cord, but you are still mortal.

Fel's vision smears.

You are still human.

The smell of coalfires is overwhelming, despite Fel's respirator kit.

And just like the crystals, the witch hisses, *finding the fear in you is just a matter of digging.*

The shadows boil towards Severina Raine like an angry tide, nearly knocking her from her feet. A whole host of fears snag at her, aiming to find purchase in her soul. Fire roars, scorching her skin. The thunder of guns echoes in her ears. Raine smells the stink of the dead. She glimpses teeth and claws glinting in the half-dark. Tastes blood. Around her, the Duskhounds stagger.

'Deny it,' Raine manages to say. 'Hold to what you know to be true.'

Fool.

The word hits Raine hard, pinning her in place. The cavern and the crystals and the psyker's many images smear through her pistol's sights.

Fear cannot be banished by the truth, the psyker says. *Fear is truth.*

Raine fires her pistol on the closest image of the psyker, but it just blows away like smoke. The others all smile.

'Fear means nothing when you have faith,' Raine says.

The psyker laughs and it sounds like breaking glass.

We will see about that.

The cavern falls completely dark. Fel's optics don't touch it. He can hear his Duskhounds shouting for him, but he can't see them.

'Hold your ground,' Fel says. 'Remember it isn't real.'

Several sets of coalfire eyes bloom around Fel and he hears a snarl that sounds like logs breaking as they burn. Fel keeps his rifle braced as his mother's words echo around him, spoken in the witch's sing-song, mocking voice.

Beware the darkling hours, my son,

For that is when the duskhounds come.

'I am not afraid of death,' Andren Fel says, as the shadowed hounds circle closer, baring their teeth.

Perhaps not your own, the witch says.

And the hounds lunge past him.

Fel tries to turn and draw sight on them, but something in the shadows snags him and holds him still. His rifle hisses and locks when he tries to fire it. His Duskhounds are shouting again. Cursing. Screaming. Fel catches sight of them by flashes of las-fire and the glow of coals.

Tyl is caught in the jaws of one of the hounds.

Do you want it to stop?

Rol is a ragged mess, trying to drag himself to help Tyl.

Do you want it to stop?

Myre is crawling, leaving a painted line of blood along the stone.

Do you want it to stop?

Jeth is lying still and silent, his carapace torn open.

Do you want it to stop?

Fel hears Raine cry out. The last of the hounds has her by the throat, worrying and tearing. There is so much blood. Fel tries to get to her, but the shadows refuse to let go, pulling him to his knees.

'*Severina,*' he says.

Raine sees Andren Fel go to his knees with a crash of armour plates. Over the howling of Iota, she hears him say her name, an agonised rasp. Raine blinks and tries to move towards him, but her limbs are frozen. She can do nothing but watch the Duskhounds suffer. Watch Fel suffer. The Sighted psyker laughs and his many reflections clap their hands together. It sounds like thunder rolling.

See, he says. *Fear is truth.*

He smiles widely.

But you already know that, don't you, Severina Raine? That is why you have locked away your fears, deep inside.

Raine blinks, and on the backs of her eyelids, she sees a cell door, closed and bolted. A heavy quiet falls and Raine can no longer hear the Duskhounds suffering, or even the howling of Iota.

All that remains is the ticking of the timepiece in her pocket.

It grows louder as a figure steps from between the psyker's repeated images and approaches Raine. No, not a figure. A ghost. One clad in Commissariat black with her hand outstretched. She is tawny-skinned and scarred, with eyes as dark as ocean stones. It is like looking into a mirror.

But then, it always was, when Raine looked at her sister.

Try as he might, Fel can't find the words of the evensong. He can't distance himself from the stink of blood and the screams. From his Duskhounds breathing their last, and Raine, bleeding out on the stone.

Do you want it to stop?

Fel fights and struggles but the shadows twist tighter and his heart is beating out of time. The words are a roar that surround him.

Do you want it to stop?

'You are not my sister,' Raine says. 'Lucia is dead.'

She is, isn't she?

A bloodstain blooms on Lucia's tunic, then, spreading slowly from her heart outwards. Lucia's dark eyes turn glassy and blank, but she still walks closer. Her bootsteps sound like gunshots.

And tell me, Severina Raine, why is that?

Raine's heart burns. Blood trickles down the back of her throat. Lucia is almost close enough to touch her. Close enough for the barrel of Raine's pistol to press against her chest, right at the heart of that dark circle of blood.

What was it that killed your sister?

Fel can only watch Raine struggle in the hound's jaws and the pool of blood growing around her, black as a starless sky.

Do you want it to stop?

He takes a breath, and the word takes shape. The answer that will end the trial.

But then he catches Raine's eyes.

Fel knows the depths and darkness of those eyes. In these shadows, they should be like the spaces between stars.

'This isn't real,' Fel slurs.

The timepiece in Raine's pocket is deafening.

Say it.

Raine can't see anything, save for Lucia's face.

SAY. IT.

'My sister is dead because she failed,' Raine says.

And that is what you fear the most, isn't it, Severina Raine? Failure. You are afraid of sharing your sister's fate.

Raine's pistol shakes in her hands.

But it is unavoidable, the psyker says. *You will fail, just as she did. Your faith will break. Your fate is written into your blood. That is the truth. Your truth.*

Raine's mind is alight. Her vision failing. There is blood in her mouth and a tremor on her limbs.

You should end it, the psyker says. *For yourself and your puppet hounds. It would be a mercy.*

'End it,' Raine says, through chattering teeth. 'Yes, I will end it.'

And her fingers curl tight around her pistol's trigger.

Penance bucks in her hands. Blood hits her face. Lucia's blood, that might as well be her own. It is as cold as ocean spray. Her sister's image blows away like fog, and the psyker screams in rage, one hundred times over.

The shadows release Andren Fel, and he manages to get back to his feet. His Duskhounds are down, but alive. The witch's fractal reflections have become an angry storm, billowing around Raine like a flock of carrion birds.

'The nest,' Raine says, with effort.

Fel remembers the last words of the evensong.

Keep within the light as the fire burns,

Until the morning sun returns.

He has to make a fire.

He has to burn it.

But he can't see it from where he is standing. Fel remembers the way it vanished, as if passing out of sight. Hidden, like the knotwood homes of the fae in the old stories. They said you could only find them if you knew how to look. If you knew where to stand.

With his vision dazzling, and blood running from his nose, Fel staggers forwards through the witch's shrieking reflections until he reaches the place where he was standing before, and the shape of the cavern seems to change, revealing the nest. A heap of crystals, slick with witch's blood. Fel takes a charge from his belt, primes it and throws it into the crystal nest. It detonates with a blazing red light and a scream. Fel is thrown against the cavern wall hard enough to crack his armour. The witch's reflections shatter like glass until only one remains. A pale thing, clad in blood-spattered silks.

And then Raine's pistol bellows.

* * *

The Sighted psyker puts one pale, thin hand to the blood-stain spreading across his chest. Feathers fall to the ground, snapped at the quills.

Fool, he says again, but weaker this time. *You will see. You will fail. Your faith will break.*

'No. I refuse your so-called truth. I will not fail.' Raine fires again, and the psyker staggers backwards and falls, landing in the dust that's left of his nest of crystals. 'My faith cannot be broken.'

You will see, the psyker says, in a weak, blood-clotted voice. *A shadow grows, even in the firelight. You will not survive it. Death follows close by.*

'Not mine,' Raine says between breaths. 'Yours.'

And she fires the last round in her pistol's magazine.

Severina Raine stands on the landing platform, looking up, as Jova's Valkyrie descends through the darkness and the smoke. It casts a long shadow that grows to swallow them up. Only the Duskhounds' red eye-lenses light the gloom. The storm troopers are silent. There have been few words exchanged save for orders and answers since leaving the witch's cavern. The Valkyrie touches down on the landing platform, turbojets roaring, and the ramp lowers to the deck with a sound like a tolling bell. Dust kicks into the air in spirals. It billows in the push and pull of the mine-pit's breathing, and for a moment, Raine catches something like a shape in the dust.

Teeth, and eyes.

'Ready?'

She looks away from the falling dust at the sound of Fel's voice. He is standing at the foot of the Valkyrie's ramp, his black armour turned blood-red by the combat lighting.

'Let's go,' Raine says.

And she follows him up the ramp, with Iota's howling echoing after her.

YOUR
NEXT READ

HONOURBOUND
by Rachel Harrison

Commissar Severina Raine and the 11th Antari Rifles fight to subdue
the spreading threat of Chaos burning across the Bale Stars. Little does Raine
realise the key to victory lies in her own past, and in the ghosts that
she carries with her.

YOUR
NEXT READ

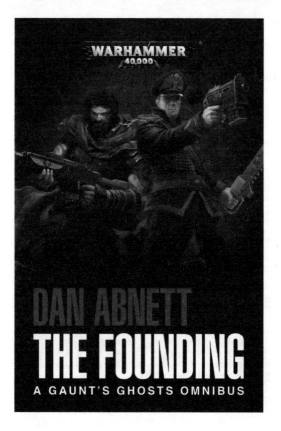

WARHAMMER
40,000

DAN ABNETT
THE FOUNDING
A GAUNT'S GHOSTS OMNIBUS

THE FOUNDING: A GAUNT'S GHOSTS OMNIBUS
by Dan Abnett

The opening trilogy of the Gaunt's Ghosts saga returns! From the destruction
of their world to their deadliest battle in the shattered hives of Verghast,
this is the first act in the long-running fan favourite series.

LIGHTNING RUN

PETER McLEAN

While the Astra Militarum defends holy ground,
the **Imperial Navy** rains down the Emperor's
fiery wrath from the skies.
In *Lightning Run*, Peter McLean tells the perilous
tale of pilot Salvatoria Grant, who is tasked with
transporting a venerable military general on a secret
mission. But when the journey goes wrong, Grant
finds herself in the greatest danger of her life.

Flight Officer Salvatoria Grant
Munitorum base Sigma
Elijan III

The thunder of the engines gave Sal life.

Her gloved hands played over the Valkyrie's controls, caressing the age-pitted steel and brass levers as the plane throbbed with potential on the landing pad. The powerful twin engines were idling, but she knew from long experience that it would only take her to pull *that* lever back, push *those* throttles forward, stamp on *this* pedal, and the assault carrier would rip free of the ground and into the air with a bellow of fury like the very wrath of the Emperor.

This Valkyrie had been Sal's plane for three years now, Terran standard. It wasn't *hers*, as such, of course. It belonged to the Imperial Fleet, Segmentum Pacificus, Fourth Flotilla, First Battle Group, troopship *Damocles*. Through those holy lines of command, it belonged to the divine God-Emperor Himself, and that was as it should be. The plane was her connection to the Emperor's divinity, her conduit to enacting His will on whatever world she had been sent to. The machine made her whole, gave her a purpose in the galaxy – to deliver death unending, in His name.

'Not long now,' she whispered to the Valkyrie. She felt as though she could feel its machine-spirit's need to be free of the ground, to fly the way it had been ordained to by the will of the Emperor. 'He'll be here soon, and when he comes he'll be in a hurry. They always are. Then we can fly and Emperor willing, we can kill His enemies.'

'You talking to yourself again, Grant?'

Second Flight Officer Herrion leaned into the cockpit behind her, his helmet dangling from its straps in his hand. They had been flying together for six months now and she still hadn't learned to like the man. He was unshaven, and an unlit lho-stick dangled from his mouth in open defiance of her rules. She let her right hand fall to her side and touched her father's ancient autopistol. She wore it at her hip on every mission, for luck and for her father's blessing.

'Ditch that smoke,' she ordered.

'Oh, come on, Grant…'

'Emperor, help me resist the temptation to shoot this fool,' Sal said, turning in her seat to fix Herrion with a savage glare.

There was no smoking on Sal's plane, no way. Not only because of the regulations, although she took those seriously, but also because you could actually smell the fumes of unburned promethium welling up from the Valkyrie's idling engines. One flame could be the end of both of them, and half the Munitorum base as well.

Herrion sighed and put his smoke away, unlit.

'Get in and buckle up,' Sal snapped, taking her hand off the gun. 'When he gets here we need to go *now*, not once you've got your kit together. And put your damn helmet on. Do you think you're some sort of mudfoot?'

Mudfoots, that was what the Navy flyers called the Astra Militarum infantry they usually ended up transporting in their Valkyries. Men and women who would nonchalantly take their helmets off and sit on them for protection against the occasional bursts of groundfire that were bound to come up through the floor of the plane sometimes. People who had never been in a crash-landing situation, in other words.

Mudfoots didn't belong in the air, but Salvatoria Grant did. Air was her element, the same as earth and mud was theirs. Her heavy Valkyrie felt like an extension of her own body. She wondered for a moment if the bridge crew of the *Damocles*, their desiccated bodies hardwired into the ancient spaceframe, felt the same way. She supposed they probably did, if they could still feel anything at all.

Herrion pulled a face but he buckled his helmet on as she had told him, and took his place in the co-pilot's seat behind her. Her two gunners were already aboard too, one at each of the side doors in the aft crew bay, where their heavy bolters protruded through the fuselage. The canopies were still up, and damp air blew into the cockpit. It smelled like it might rain later.

Elijan III was a temperate world, mostly forested on the surface but rich in deep underground promethium reserves. Sal had heard that when the wind blew from the right direction at night, the Munitorum base had reeked of promethium from the great refinery twenty miles up the river. That was before, though. Before the corruption.

Now the air only smelled of blood.

The corruption of Elijan III had come fast, and it had come hard. The vile taint of the Archenemy had spread like wildfire through the simple communities of pipemen and refinery workers, threatening to overtake all Imperial order on the world. That much Sal had learned at the Fleet briefing, at least. The rest of it, what the high command hadn't told them, she had learned in her time on the surface since the *Damocles* made orbit and disgorged four regiments of Guard and a hundred Valkyries to support them. Since her plane had first touched down on Elijan III, Sal had learned more about the hideous threat they faced than she had ever wanted to know.

The simple fact was, they weren't winning.

Oh, the Officio Prefectus would have it otherwise, of course, but Sal had eyes to see and she could think for herself. Not traits valued in the Guard, perhaps, but the Navy was different. In the Navy, you were expected to make command decisions based on the available information, to protect your plane and your passengers to the best of your ability. That meant not lying to yourself about the odds. The Munitorum base was crawling with troops, the walls manned with heavy autocannons and missile launchers, and still she thought it wouldn't be enough.

Elijan III had all but fallen to Chaos, and there was no lying to herself about that. Some terrible, blasphemous cult had overrun the planet, harvesting its rich natural resources for themselves in their endless pursuit of death and slaughter.

Now, though, there might be hope. She had been seconded to the Munitorum base, and although no hard intel had been revealed to her, it was clear enough to Sal that something of great importance to the war effort was coming to a head.

She took a deep breath and touched the controls in front of her again, taking strength from their holy construction and the connection she felt they gave her to the Emperor's divine will.

This control was for the nose-mounted multi-laser, *those* triggers would unleash her two Hellstrike missiles from their cradles under the wings. She could kill a main battle tank with those, if the Emperor willed it. She touched the triggers again, and slowly let out her breath. The plane calmed her. It was her spiritual anchor, her link to the ultimate divinity of mankind. Every shot fired was a prayer to the Emperor, every kill an offering to His glory.

She bowed her head and whispered the Emperor's catechism of devotion.

'Now what are you muttering about, you mad mare?' Herrion snorted. 'Emperor's blood, you're–'

'Use His name in vain again and I really will shoot you,' Sal snapped at him, twisting in her seat to glare at Herrion over her shoulder. She touched the pistol again. 'Not on my plane. Shut up and– They're here. Launch prep, right now!'

She wasn't looking at her co-pilot any more. Her attention was out of the side of the open cockpit, where a full general of the Astra Militarum was marching stiffly towards her boarding ramp at double time, with three aides and six heavily armed troopers hurrying after him. He was the hope of Elijan III, Sal knew, even if she wasn't privy to exactly why.

Herrion knew the art of aerial warfare well, which was the only reason she put up with him. His hands flew across the controls in front of him, running preflight checks with the practised skill that came from thousands of hours of flying time. He flicked switches, checked gauges, threw rockers, and the amber status runes on the main display turned to green in rapid succession as the twin canopies closed smoothly over their heads.

The Valkyrie shuddered with anticipation.

The crew bay intercom crackled in Sal's helmet vox.

'The general is aboard, pilot. Immediate dust off ordered. Proceed to Patroclus Base with all haste.'

'Aye, sir,' Sal said.

She could only assume she was speaking to one of the general's aides, but it didn't really matter. She knew a command when she heard one. She flicked to the Navy channel.

'Crew, secure doors, brace for dust off. Bolters to automatic,' she said, and flicked back to the open channel. 'Lock down and buckle up, sir.'

Two runes on her readout went from red to green as her gunners closed the side doors and made fast. That was it, they were ready.

'All systems green,' Herrion reported, his voice all business now they were working.

'Systems green,' she repeated.

The base channel clicked open in her ear.

'Transport, cleared for dust off.'

'Dust off,' Sal replied. 'Five by five.'

She reached out and threw a lever forwards.

Her gloved hand closed over the twin throttles and pushed them forward, and the thunder of the engines built to a piercing scream as the plane threatened to shake itself to pieces on the pad. She raised a clenched fist over her shoulder. Herrion leaned forwards for a moment, tapped his own against it. Good to go.

Sal stamped on the release pedal.

The Valkyrie hurled itself vertically into the air, the acceleration crushing her down into her padded leather flight seat until she thought her spine must surely be compacting on itself. That was the feeling of the Emperor's will being done, by her own mortal hand. Her connection to the divine, through His holy war machine.

A tight smile crossed Sal's face as she vectored the engines, channelling their furious power from lift into forward acceleration. The plane roared and blasted through the air with a howl of righteous fury, leaving Munitorum Sigma behind as she struck out over the thick forest below. Her head-up display layered information over her field of vision, the preset course to Patroclus Base showing her an endless hololithic tunnel of well-spaced green triangles that seemed to hang in the air in front of her.

Sal adjusted her flight yoke slightly, guiding the hurtling Valkyrie smoothly through the first triangle, which blinked out of existence as she passed it. She checked airspeed, altitude, wind shear, fuel and cargo weight, and keyed the passenger band again.

'ETA nine hours, sir,' she said.

A new voice came on the line. A man, older than the aide by the sound of him, with a voice that spoke with the gravitas of long-accustomed command. The general himself, she thought, and straightened with pride in her seat. She was honoured to be directly addressed by one of his illustrious rank.

'Make it eight. Can you do that for me, pilot?'

Sal looked at her readouts again, factored fuel tolerances,

reheat burn durations, structural fatigue risk. Always a risk, when you pushed a plane this old to its limits. She cleared her throat.

'Maybe, sir,' she said. 'But…'

'*I know,*' he said. '*We might blow up in the air. I have the authority to tell you this, pilot, but consider yourself sworn to crimson-level secrecy – if I can get what I carry there in time, we've won this war. If I don't, then it doesn't matter if I get there at all. Every minute counts. Do it.*'

'Aye, sir,' Sal said.

It would mean a course alteration, Sal realised. However hard she pushed the old plane, it couldn't be done otherwise. Not on their current heading. If she dropped them ten points east though…

That meant she would be flying them over a known enemy location. She didn't know exactly what was down there, but there was *something*. It was a gamble. Sal thought of the general's words, of the grim determination in his tone, and she made her decision.

She cancelled the preset course, vectored ten points east, and keyed in the afterburners. The plane kicked her in the base of her spine as it blasted through the air.

The Emperor's will be done. All their fates were in His hands, now and forever more.

The Valkyrie howled east over the forest on a flaming stream of afterburners, and a nine-hour estimate that became eight on their new heading, then became seven and a half. Sal hunched over the controls, milking every scrap of power from the overworked engines. She had felt the urgency in the general's words, the desperation he had been trying to hide. Whatever his mission was, whatever he carried, it was clear it *had* to reach Patroclus Base as soon as humanly possible.

They were flying over the enemy lines now. Great swathes of the forest were burning, where overland promethium pipelines had been ruptured in the fighting. Senseless waste and destruction, Sal thought. The vile cultists destroyed for the simple joy of watching things burn. All the same, they built as well. Already they had streaked over settlements and military bases, crude but effective looking. More than once, she had spotted tanks on the ground. Former Imperial tanks, to be sure, noble Leman Russ machines captured and corrupted by the abominations of the Archenemy. Another time, she would have been raining righteous Hellstrike fury down on them from her plane, but not now. The mission was all that mattered.

Runes were starting to flicker amber on the display as the strained Valkyrie began to complain, but Sal caressed her controls and whispered encouragement to the plane's machine-spirit.

'You're no tech-priest, the machine won't hear you,' Herrion reminded her. 'You'll kill us all if you keep pushing it this hard!'

'Shut up,' Sal growled, and ran a reassuring hand across the yoke. 'She can do this. She *has* to.'

Whether Sal's plane could do it or not became irrelevant precisely seven seconds later, when the surface-to-air missile blew her tail off. Warning klaxons wailed as though in physical pain, and the display lit up with flashing red runes across the board.

'Critical, critical!' Sal shouted into the open channel. 'Brace, brace, brace!'

Her Valkyrie was suddenly in a spinning nosedive, trailing

flames as it died screaming in the sky over Elijan III. Sal fought the controls with all her might, cutting the after-burners and vectoring what was left of her engines in a desperate attempt to turn their headlong plummet into something approaching a controlled descent. There was a clearing maybe two miles away, ferrocrete runway and armoured bunkers flashing in her vision as the Valkyrie spun wildly in its death throes.

Airbase, Sal thought. *Missile defences.*

It had always been a gamble; Sal had known that and she had accepted it. The enemy might be insane, but they weren't stupid. Of course they had air defences – and she had flown straight into them. Such was the Emperor's will for her that day, it seemed.

Wind screamed in her ears over the vox-channel from the crew bay, now torn open to the rush of air. A burst of flames ripped through the cockpit behind her from a rup-tured fuel line. Herrion shrieked, and Sal snatched a glance over her shoulder just in time to see him incinerated in his webbing. She slapped the big red fire suppressant switch on the console in front of her, but it was too late for him. The retardant foam sprayed uselessly across his reeking black-ened corpse.

'Anyone alive back there, brace and pray!' Sal yelled into the vox. 'We are landing *hard!*'

The first of the treetops hit them, and the Valkyrie rolled sickeningly as the great trees shattered in her wake. Sal screamed, and everything went black.

The pain hit Sal like a commissar's bullet to the temple. She forced her eyes open, barely able to move. There was a sec-tion of twisted airframe embedded in her helmet, maybe one polymer layer away from having gone through her skull. She reached up with shaking hands, found the buckle at her throat and released herself. She was stuck fast in the wreckage, and had to squirm down in her seat to get her head out of her ruined helmet.

It had saved her life – just.

She checked her father's autopistol was still at her belt, the three spare magazines in their leather pouches balancing its weight on her other hip, and hit the quick release that freed her from her webbing. She pitched sideways against the canopy, and only then realised that what was left of the Valkyrie was lying on its side on the forest floor. She yanked the canopy release handle, but the mechanism had been so badly crushed by the impact that it refused to move. Sal swallowed, realising she was effectively trapped in the cockpit.

She twisted in her seat and looked over her shoulder at the shattered remains of Herrion's console, his blackened corpse still strapped tightly into the webbing behind it. His canopy release looked undamaged.

She swallowed again.

Taking a deep breath, she braced with her legs and forced herself up and over Herrion's console, straining for the second canopy release handle. She pushed herself upwards with a grunt of effort and half fell onto the charred and foam-encrusted ruin of Herrion's corpse. Her gloved hand tore into his stomach cavity as she put her weight on him, rupturing his half-cooked insides.

When she stopped vomiting, Sal grasped his emergency canopy release and pulled it, blowing the entire top of the cockpit clear with a sharp crack of explosive bolts. She crawled gratefully over the roasted filth of her co-pilot and out of the plane, and threw up again on the churned loam of the forest floor.

She stayed there for some time, hugging the ground and retching with a mixture of shock and horror and sheer relief. She was Emperor only knew how far behind enemy lines, but she was somehow, miraculously, alive. There was nothing she wanted to do more than run, retrace her flight path on foot and try to find her way back to the Munitorum base. Find another plane, and just fly away. She belonged in the air, not here, not in some wild forest. She touched her father's pistol, and his words came back to her.

He had been a pilot himself, once, and he had given her his beloved sidearm on the day she came home and announced she had taken her oath and joined up with the Navy.

'The Emperor expects every woman to do her duty, however hard it may be,' her father had said to her that day. *'Make Him proud of you, Salvatoria. I already am.'*

'The Emperor expects,' she whispered.

She forced herself to her feet, made herself ignore the pain of a hundred cuts and scrapes and bruises. At least nothing seemed to be broken. She looked at her beloved Valkyrie, and wanted to weep. The whole rear section of the plane had been blasted away, and the fuselage had burst open where it had hit the ground.

One of her gunners was red paste under the wreckage.

She knew she had to try to complete the mission. Whatever the general's purpose had been, she knew it was vital to the war effort there on Elijan III. She had to have faith in the Emperor and *try*, however unlikely it may seem.

Both hatches were buckled and twisted but there was a gaping hole at the back of the plane where the tail had been, and Sal hauled herself painfully up and into the stinking interior of the crew bay. It was crimson with blood, reeking of ruptured guts and promethium. The upper fuselage had sheared off and come down onto the passengers like a guillotine, bisecting four of them and taking the others' legs off where they sat helpless in their flight webbing. They had all bled out from severed femoral arteries. The general looked up at her and smiled.

'Hell of a landing, pilot,' he said.

Sal almost died of fright.

In the Emperor's name, how…?

The general's legs were gone just below his groin, but… Sal blinked, and realised this wasn't the first time that had happened to him. The augmetics were ruined beyond repair and even now sparks were spitting dangerously from his dull metal stumps, daring the promethium in the air to explode and obliterate the entire wreck in a roaring fireball.

'Sir, we have to get you out of here,' she said, reaching for him.

He shook his head and tried to laugh, and blood ran out of his mouth and over his chin.

'My legs were augmetic, but my lungs aren't,' he said. 'There's some of your damn plane so deep in the right one I can taste the metal. I'm not going anywhere.'

'The mission…' Sal started.

The general nodded.

'That's yours now,' he said.

He reached into his uniform jacket with his left hand, and Sal realised the entire right side of his body wasn't working. He grimaced as he moved, and more blood ran out of his mouth and nose. He took something out of an inside pocket and held it out to her – an ornate ring, steel and brass with a gleaming gold bezel and a single clear crystal set into it.

'Take this,' he said. 'Wear it, if you have to, but keep it safe and get it to Patroclus Base.'

'What?' Sal asked, taking the offered jewellery with open bewilderment.

'Encrypter,' the general said, and coughed up more blood. 'Code level vermillion. It's got… their battle plans on it. I'm a Navy intelligencer. Get this… to Colonel Shrake at Patroclus, whatever it takes. The words are *Ave Imperator, in circulum arcanus trismegistus est*. Win… this war, pilot. The Emperor expects.'

Her father's words rang in her head.

The Emperor expects every woman to do her duty.

'Yes, sir,' Sal said, but he was already dead.

Sal peeled off her left glove, put the ring on and pulled the glove securely back over it to keep it in place. That done, she braved Herrion's corpse again to get back into the cockpit, and raided the emergency kit for bottled water and hard rations – and for the other thing she knew would be there, the thing every downed pilot hopes they never have to use.

She rigged the timed demolition mine to the Valkyrie and fled into the forest.

She was half a mile away when it blew. All the same she threw herself to the ground and covered her head with her hands, missing her helmet as burning debris rained down through the trees. After an explosion like that at the crash site, no one would come looking for any survivors, friend or foe. She was a ghost now, with no hope of rescue.

No pilot wanted to put themselves in that position, but it was the only way to be sure the cultists wouldn't come to investigate the downed plane and realise there was an Imperial pilot at large in the forest. The mission was everything, now.

Sal waited until the rain of twisted metal stopped, then sat up and touched her father's pistol. She was on foot and alone behind enemy lines, with two days' rations, one handgun, four magazines of ammunition, and over two thousand miles to cover in somewhere around six hours. There was nothing else for it.

She needed to steal a plane.

A fast one.

The enemy airbase was easy enough to find, even in the unfamiliar forest. She only had to follow the noise. The vile cultists delighted in wanton destruction, and the engines of war that enabled it.

Planes roared down the runway and into the air. They arced around to head back the way Sal had come, towards Munitorum Sigma. She recognised them from their silhouettes as they flashed west overhead. Lightnings. She knew then that the base was doomed.

Following my trail, backtracking us, she thought. *They've had it.*

The Munitorum base had missile defences, of course, but against a flight of Lightnings? No. No, they were too fast, too powerful. It would be a massacre.

Sal crept through the thinning screen of trees towards the cultist airbase, shuddering as she passed rows of broken skulls mounted on sharp stakes. There was a single fighter left on the runway, refuelling hoses trailing from its fuselage like limp tentacles. The beautiful machine had been defiled, Sal could see now, vile runes of Chaos etched into once-sleek flanks that looked as if they had been freshly anointed with blood.

She tasted bile, to witness such desecration of the Emperor's holy war machine.

She drew her father's pistol.

Cultists walked the perimeter, draped in blood-red robes daubed with evil black sigils. They had lasguns in their hands, no doubt stolen the same as the Lightnings were. As the base itself had been, probably. Looking at it, Sal reasoned this had to have originally been an Imperial facility before the corruption came and claimed it. No one but Imperial engineers had ever laid a runway so perfectly.

She narrowed her eyes as she thought about it. It was an Imperial facility, and an Imperial plane sitting there in front of her. She was no fighter pilot, no, but the Imperium ran on the principle of standard patterns. And she *was* a Navy flyer.

How different could it be?

The Lightning's cockpit canopy was open, and the boarding steps were still rolled up to its side. The fuel hoses were limp and flaccid, which either meant the plane was fuelled up and ready and just hadn't been uncoupled yet, or it had been hooked up only recently and refuelling hadn't started.

Fifty fifty on that, Sal, she told herself.

A fifty fifty chance, life or death on the flip of an Imperial Crown.

Whatever it takes, the general had said.

The Emperor expects.

She had faced worse odds.

Salvatoria Grant flicked off the safety of her father's pistol, said a prayer to the Emperor and sprinted for the grounded Lightning.

She got six yards before the first las-shot blew a chunk out of the rockcrete in front of her.

'Halt!' someone shouted, their voice guttural and somehow *wrong*.

Sal turned and fired on pure instinct. Her father's pistol kicked in her hand and twenty yards away a red-robed figure spun and dropped.

All hell broke loose.

Warning klaxons wailed across the airbase as someone triggered an intruder alarm, and then there was las-fire sizzling through the air all around her.

Sal fired again, missed, put her head down and ran like every enemy of mankind was on her heels.

The boarding steps were twenty yards away, then fifteen. Sal jinked and dodged, firing blindly over her shoulder as she ran as hard as she had ever run before in her life. The plane was waiting for her. The beautiful, crippled, *wounded* Imperial war machine, its hide so cruelly defiled with the foul sigils of the Archenemy.

The machine won't hear you, Herrion had said, and perhaps he was right about that, but Sal felt that she could hear the machine. In her mind, she could hear it weeping with shame and fury and the burning need for revenge.

She changed magazines at a full sprint and turned at the foot of the boarding steps, the pistol braced in both hands. She blazed into the charging cultists, dropping four, five, six, until they were just too close to miss her. At the last minute, she swarmed up into the plane like a simian, wincing as she felt the impact of las-rounds against the armoured fuselage.

Imperial standardisation was one thing, but the cockpit of a single-seater Lightning fighter was *nothing* like that of a Valkyrie. Panic gripped her as she saw the interior of the plane had been daubed with the same hideous glyphs that marred its outer fuselage – eye watering signs of abomination. A peeled human skull had been nailed to the top of the console, and the entire interior of the cockpit was drenched in blood. The seat under her was sodden with it, and she felt it soaking disgustingly into her flight suit.

Sal screamed and smashed the skull aside with a backhanded blow of her gloved left hand, feeling the general's ring dig into her finger with the impact. That ring was all that mattered, she reminded herself, fighting down hot vomit with every breath.

The mission, think of the mission.

She forced herself to ignore the blasphemous filth around her and *think*. A Lightning was an interceptor, designed to be scrambled at a moment's notice. There had to be an emergency action function, a way to override the need for preflights and just *go* when the Emperor called.

A big red button, in other words.

Everything in the cockpit was red, slathered with congealing blood, making it hard to distinguish one control from another. Not that one, that was the fire suppressant toggle. That was *always* in the middle of the console, on every plane Sal had ever been in. If not that, then... *there!*

The trigger grip was so obvious she almost missed it; it was just in the wrong place compared to what she was used to. It was over her head, hanging from the bottom of the canopy so it could be grabbed as a pilot vaulted into the plane.

Las-fire whined over her head under the open canopy, forcing her head down.

Stupid, stupid! How did I miss that?

She blasted three return shots out of the cockpit with her

father's pistol, until it clicked dry. She dropped it into the footwell, and risked losing her arm as she reached up and grabbed the big red grip.

Sal *pulled.*

Lots of things happened at once.

The canopy slammed down so hard it would have taken her hand off at the wrist if she had been a fraction of a second slower, and she heard the violent hiss of pressure seals engaging. Something coughed behind her, then roared like a native Elijanian vhorbeast as her engines lit up. Sal swiped a gloved hand over the console, clearing away enough blood for her to see the whole display illuminated in a blaze of coloured runes. The external monitor showed her a screaming trail of jet backwash incinerating the cultists who had been pursuing her. Her hands fell to the controls: throttle and stick, not the yoke she was used to her in big Valkyrie, but not so very different to the single-seater trainers she had used in the Navy flight scholam.

The Emperor bless standardisation, she thought.

The fuelling rune was flashing amber to tell her the hoses were still attached, but the brass gauge above it read reassuringly full. Again, there was a promising looking button under the flashing rune, so Sal reached out and stabbed it with one gloved finger. The fuelling hoses blew clear with a bang, and the flashing rune turned to steady green.

The Lightning was already pointed down the runway, so all Sal had to do was disengage the landing brake and push forward on the throttles. She whispered a prayer to the Emperor and shoved them forward hard.

That was a very bad idea.

The plane shrieked and almost flipped over backwards as *far* too much power was unleashed all at once. Only

Sal's honed reactions enabled her to control the wildly bucking machine, and now more las-rounds were slapping against the fuselage. She engaged ground manoeuvre mode and whipped the skittish plane around on its landing gear, using the jet exhaust to sweep the surrounding area like the mother of all heavy flamers until the gunfire stopped again.

'Gently now,' Sal whispered, half to herself and half to the plane's furious, tortured machine-spirit. 'We can do this. Together, we can.'

She got the plane angled onto the runway again and this time made herself pour the power on gradually, letting the engine note build from a rumble to a growing howl as the rockcrete sped past outside the canopy. The end of the runway was coming up far too quickly for comfort.

Sal hunted the blood-slick console frantically, looking for some sign of what was wrong. *It's a short-runway launch interceptor, there must be a way to…* There!

Her hand found the pull-toggle for the solid-fuel rocket assisted take-off and jerked it towards her. The resulting acceleration almost made her black out as the Lightning took off on a pillar of chemical flame, blasting into the air like a missile. The terrifying rush only lasted three or four seconds, by which time she was thousands of feet into the air with the spent rocket-fuel tank spinning silently away below her.

'Missile lock, missile lock,' the plane's servitor brain announced in a curiously emotionless voice. 'Incoming, two contacts.'

Two red contact runes were spiralling in on the head-up display now, closing with frightening speed. Sal cursed the cultists' missile air defences and slapped the chaff and flare icons simultaneously, pushing the throttle all the way forward and finding the afterburners with a grin of triumph.

The two incoming missiles blew themselves harmlessly apart in the cloud of chaff behind her as the Lightning went supersonic with a concussive boom fit to split the sky.

The Emperor's will be done.

Nothing could catch her now.

The base's other Lightnings had been heading in the opposite direction, towards the Munitorum base she had come from, and even if the cultists had recalled them, they were still no faster than she was, and probably a thousand miles behind her by now. She was home free.

The Lightning flashed over the endless forest far below, eating miles at a rate her Valkyrie could never have hoped to match. Sal used the time to work up a flight plan on the console's navigation cogitator, plotting a fresh course to Patroclus Base. She was maybe two hours out, at her current speed and heading. That put her ETA well within the general's original target.

She keyed the vox to send word ahead of her coming.

Static howled in her ears, intercut with the blasphemous ranting of one of the cultists' heretical preachers. She tried to change the band, got nothing but more of the same. It was unintelligible gibberish, to her ears, but still the harsh, guttural words made her feel ill. Just then she was suddenly, horribly aware of the vile sigils etched into the console and daubed over the surfaces inside the cockpit, of the skull she had knocked into the footwell, where it had sunk into the pooled blood that welled around her boots. She tried not to think about how wet her back and behind and legs were, her flight suit now saturated with blood from the sodden seat.

This plane had saved her life, but it was hideously

corrupted. Sal could feel the machine's once noble spirit still fighting somewhere inside the fuselage, but it was dying under the weight of the Chaos horrors that had been inflicted on it. The vox refused to change to any other channel.

Sal shut it off, and thought about what that meant.

She was coming up fast on Patroclus Base.

A Chaos-marked Lightning was coming up fast on Patroclus Base, with its surrounding cordon of heavy air defences.

They're going to shoot me out of the sky.

She shed altitude as fast as she could, bringing the Lightning as low as she dared, until she could be sure she was flying under their long-range auspex. The forested ground was a hurtling, insane blur of green at well over a thousand miles an hour and barely eight hundred feet up.

Sal's nerve gave out in the end, and she throttled back to under the sound barrier before the shock wave of her own passage could tear the plane to pieces around her. Patroclus Base was barely a hundred miles away now, and she was coming up fast on the outer ring of defences.

The plane blared a klaxon to tell her the first missile was coming at her. Sal launched more chaff and gave the throttle a blast to clear the area, dropping even lower until it seemed that the tops of the trees below were almost close enough to scrape the paint from the plane's desecrated fuselage.

Another alert, another burst of chaff, then the counter-measures icon was flashing to tell her that she was all out. She banked hard, throwing the plane into an arc that almost stood it on a wingtip, and keyed the main armament readout into her head-up display. The plane had two wing-mounted lascannons, but the primary weapon was a ventral-mounted long-barrelled autocannon that Sal knew had a truly awe-inspiring cyclic rate of fire.

The head-up display zeroed on the incoming missile as Sal righted the plane, closing at a speed that made sweat stand out on her forehead. Her finger slipped down the stick to the trigger, sticky with blood, and she forced herself to stay calm until the four red triangles overlaid on her display locked on to the rushing blur of the missile and flashed with target lock.

She squeezed down hard.

A one-second burst threw one hundred and twenty-seven high-velocity armour-piercing rounds at the missile with a sound like a ripsaw going through rockcrete. She flew the plane straight through the resulting explosion at close to eight hundred miles an hour, and banked hard once more.

The plane shuddered violently, and the flashing red runes on the console told a grim tale of structural damage.

'I'm Navy!' she shouted into the vox. 'Hold fire, you stupid mudfoots!'

The troops on the ground either couldn't hear her, or they simply didn't believe her. She was past the missile defences now, but there were Hydra batteries down there somewhere in the green. Several of them.

They opened up all at once, their quad-barrelled autocannons spitting an eruption of Imperial fury into her path. Sal swallowed in a dry mouth. She could climb above their effective range, of course, but not if she hoped to make a landing at Patroclus.

She *had* to get down there, and get down safe with the general's secrets intact.

A burst of rounds smacked into the belly of the plane, tearing more chunks out of the light armour and taking out half her electronics. The console display died.

Whatever it takes.

'O Emperor, forgive me,' Sal whispered.

Win this war, pilot. The Emperor expects.

She knew she had to. Whatever the general had given her, he believed the secrets contained on the encrypted crystal in that ring could carry the whole war on Elijan III. That would save tens of thousands, maybe *hundreds* of thousands of lives. What were a few mudfoot Hydra crews, compared to that?

They were human. They were, each and every one of them, the divine sparks of the Emperor's will. They were her comrades, her brothers and sisters in arms. They were shooting at her, yes, but only because they believed her to be an avatar of the Archenemy. They didn't know any better.

Sal *did* know better, she thought as she jinked the screaming plane around yet another burst of murderous anti-aircraft fire. The tortured airframe moaned in protest, and she knew the Lightning wouldn't survive much more of this. Not at this speed and altitude, not with the damage it had already taken. There was just no way.

She had no choice.

The Emperor expects every woman to do her duty, however hard it may be.

Sal keyed the head-up display and brought the plane around until the four triangles converged on the shape of a Hydra flak tank. There were tears in her eyes.

'Forgive me,' she whispered, and squeezed the trigger. 'Emperor forgive me, for I know exactly what I do.'

The ventral-mounted autocannon blew the machine apart with a two-second burst of supersonic munitions. There couldn't possibly have been any survivors.

'I'm Navy!' Sal screamed into the vox. 'For the Emperor's love, let me reach Patroclus Base!'

The vox returned a howl of static, but now she was this far away from the cultist base their signal jamming seemed to be out of range. Words fizzed in her ears, hardly intelligible.

'...*ing traitor! By...*'

'No!' Sal shouted, working the vox frequency shifter with her left hand even as she fought the stick with the other, narrowly avoiding another burst of anti-aircraft fire. 'Listen, *please! Navy Intelligence!* Colonel Shrake! Get me–'

One of the Hydras traversed its four swivel-mounted weapons and raked the side of her plane, punching rounds clean through the fuselage. Sal screamed as red-hot adamantium shot through the cockpit, taking a bloody chunk out of the meat of her left shoulder as it went. Her blood splattered against the inside of the canopy, running down the pane to mingle with the tainted, corrupt fluids that already profaned the Lightning. Sal tried hard not to think about what that meant. Wind howled around her as the cockpit violently depressurised.

She overshot the Hydra but there was small-arms fire snapping at her now, and she could see a four-man heavy weapons team hurriedly setting up a missile launcher.

She was out of chaff.

No choice, Salvatoria, she told herself. *There's no choice.*

The autocannon turned them into red mist against the green.

She brought the crippled plane around and zeroed in on the second Hydra battery. Her head-up display finally died.

Aiming by eye alone, Sal angled the nose of the Lightning down into a steep attack run and let rip with her ventral weapon. The Hydra erupted in a volcano of merciless fire as its magazine went up, and took its nearby Chimera munitions tender with it. Three of the Chimera crew bailed out, blazing like human torches as they died. Sal could hear their screams of agony, if only in her mind.

She hauled back on the stick and the Lightning creaked and groaned in protest as it came out of its dive, shedding chunks of metal into the air as she hauled it around and back onto course.

The vox fizzed in her ear, a new voice.

'...intelligencer. Col... Shrake... words?'

The shooting had stopped for the moment and now Patroclus Base was coming into view, the long runway waiting for her. It was lined with Hydras, and they were all pointed at her.

Sal wracked her brains for the general's words.

'Ave Imperator,' she said at last, 'in circulum arcanus trismegistus est!'

'Hold fire. All... hold fire.'

The vox signal was getting cleaner as she began her landing approach. There was no other option now – the Lightning was finished. It was a wonder it was still in the air at all, and Sal knew that her only choices were to attempt the landing and risk getting blown to pieces by the Hydras, or simply fall apart in the sky.

She took a shaky breath and keyed the landing gear.

Nothing happened.

Was this the Emperor's judgement, for the awful choice she had made? Was He about to smash her into the runway like a bug, in righteous retribution? No, she told herself. No, she did His work here.

His will be done.

She ripped open the emergency hatch to the left of her seat and found the crank handle. It was stiff, obviously too long since it had last been properly maintained, but it turned.

Wincing with pain and effort, Sal cranked the landing gear down by hand. The wound in her shoulder howled at her as it ripped further open, the broken bones grinding together under the torn flesh, and blood streamed down her arm and into the emergency cavity until the handle was slick with it.

She gave thanks to the Emperor that she still had enough hydraulic power to lower the flaps, at least, but all the same the crippled plane hit hard and bounced. The tearing agony in her shoulder made Sal scream as her crash webbing bit savagely into it, but she found the air brake lever through greying vision and threw it forward even as she slammed the throttles into reverse thrust.

The Lightning hit the ground again and slewed sideways for a moment, threatening to roll. Sal prayed and screamed and hauled it around at the last moment, righting it in a great, stinking cloud of promethium exhaust and vaporised tyre smoke.

She throttled back to idle, sagged in her webbing and passed out.

The after-action report was difficult, to say the least.

Colonel Shrake was a woman in her early one-twenties, with short, iron-grey hair and a badly scarred face that the patch over her left eye did little to hide.

She fixed her one remaining eye on Sal and said nothing.

Sal was sitting across a table from her in a small debriefing room, her shoulder field-dressed and her left arm bound to her chest in a tight sling. It hurt like murder, but it was nothing compared to the pain in her heart.

Two large men in the heavy carapace armour of the Militarum Tempestus stood behind the colonel's chair, matt-black hellguns in their hands.

The colonel looked down at her dataslate for a moment.

'So, one more time,' she said, her voice like a Fenrisian winter. 'You are not, in fact, an intelligencer. You are a Navy rating, rank of pilot flight officer, no more than that, and yet you are possessed of a crimson-level security passphrase and the single most important intelligence artefact in this entire theatre of war.'

Sal cleared her throat. She was very thirsty, but no one had offered her anything to drink.

'Yes, ma'am,' she said.

'You came into possession of these things after crashing the transport that carried my good friend and colleague General Gobrecht, leaving no survivors but yourself. After this you stole a Chaos-corrupted Lightning from an enemy airbase and flew here, murdering twenty-nine Imperial soldiers and destroying three valuable war machines in the process. Is that correct, Pilot Grant?'

'That's not–' she started, but the colonel's head snapped up and she glared at her until Sal's resolve crumbled. 'Yes, ma'am,' she whispered, and lowered her eyes in shame.

Here it comes, Sal thought. *I'm for the firing squad for sure.*

'Nonsense,' Colonel Shrake said.

Sal looked up in sudden shock as a slow, reptilian smile crossed the colonel's face.

'Ma'am?'

'Acceptable losses, pilot. They lived to serve the Emperor, and they died in service. Don't you understand? Dying is what soldiers are *for.* You are a heroine of the Imperium. You'd better get used to it.'

Sal wouldn't be leaving Elijan III on the *Damocles.*

She was done with Navy life, or so her handler told her.

When the time came, she would depart on a sleek, fast ship belonging to the Navy's intelligencers. What happened after that, she didn't know. Nobody would tell her.

Elijan III was over with, anyway. The Imperial victory had been decisive, crushing and brutally fast. Single-handedly, she had made that happen. Her, Salvatoria Grant, Heroine Pilot of the Imperium.

A heroine who cried herself drunkenly to sleep in her private room in the medicae block of the barracks every night.

Her handler knocked on the door of the room where she was still supposedly convalescing from her surgery. What she was really doing, most of the time, was drinking herself into oblivion. Nobody seemed to care, so long as she got her lines right. Her handler marched into the room, and gave her a stiff salute. He was a Militarum Tempestus sergeant, and he wore full dress uniform.

'Ma'am,' he said smoothly, pretending not to notice the raw redness of her eyes. 'They're ready for you now.'

Sal nodded and stood up, swaying slightly on her boot heels. Her knuckles were white around the glass of sacra in her hand. Her sixth that morning, she thought, or maybe her seventh, but she couldn't be sure. She never could, any more.

She was in full Navy dress herself, the starched jacket uncomfortably tight over her still-healing shoulder. They'd had to fit an augmetic joint to save her arm, in the end. It hurt all the time, every minute of the day and night. Especially the nights. Sal clung to that pain, embraced it.

Deserved it.

She gulped her sacra and put the glass unsteadily down on the low table in front of her.

It was time to face the massed ranks of the Astra Militarum again.

Time to be the heroine, again. The newest face of the Imperial propaganda machine.

Her handler reached into his uniform jacket and produced a pair of mirrored pilot's glasses, and handed them to her without a word.

She dutifully put them on to hide her red eyes, and followed the sergeant out of the medicae block. He led her down a corridor and out onto the square where the second Guard regiment awaited her, drawn up in parade formation.

Sal missed the Navy. She missed the freedom of flight, the furious glory of aerial assault. The space to breathe that was now denied to her.

Before her latest surgery, she had attended twenty-nine military funerals, closely watched at all times by two of Shrake's hulking Militarum Tempestus Scions.

She had sobbed like a child at every single one.

Once she had given her pre-prepared, pre-approved, heavily rehearsed speech to the assembled mudfoots and they had duly applauded and saluted and praised her in the Emperor's name, her handler escorted her back to her room in the medicae block.

'You should rest,' he said.

That wasn't a suggestion, Sal knew.

The sergeant turned on his heel and left the room, and she heard the key turn in the lock behind him. Sal poured herself a sacra and walked to the window, gazing out in despair.

It was getting dark outside now, and the barrack block's floodlights were coming on. Not that they were needed, not any more.

Outside, on the raked gravel in front of the building where the Chimeras were parked in long lines, a huge, flickering ten-storey hologram lit up the night. It showed a young

Imperial Navy pilot, taller and leaner and better-looking than Sal had ever been in her life, her hands braced on her hips as she stared into the distance with her chin raised in defiance. A caption hung in the air above it, the words fully twenty feet tall above the towering figure.

It read *Salvatoria Grant, Heroine of the Imperium!*

The key, turning in the door to lock her in – the newest tool of the Imperial propaganda effort.

The Militarum Tempestus troopers, never letting her out of their sight.

Twenty-nine funerals.

Salvatoria Grant sat down on her hospital bed, put her head in her hands, and she wept.

YOUR
NEXT READ

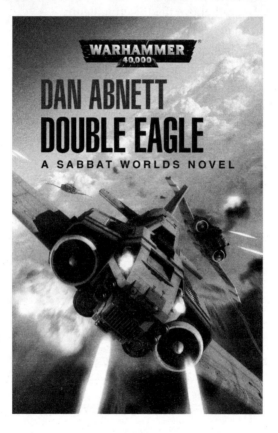

DOUBLE EAGLE
by Dan Abnett

The war on Enothis is almost lost. Chaos forces harry the defenders
on land and in the skies. Can the ace pilots of the Phantine
XX turn the tide and bring the Imperium victory?

YOUR
NEXT READ

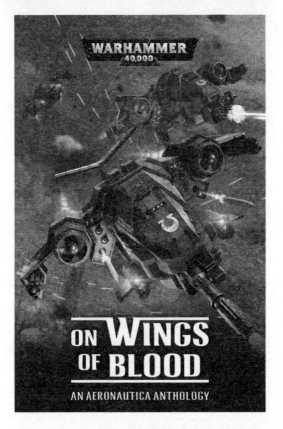

ON WINGS OF BLOOD
by various authors

Take the battle to the skies with stories of death-defying pilots
and devastating far-future aircraft! Brutal Space Marine gunships,
graceful alien fighters and hellforged Chaos craft fight for air supremacy
in a collection of aeronautical short fiction.

MISSING IN ACTION

DAN ABNETT

The Holy Orders of the Emperor's **Inquisition** are the Imperium's powerful secret police, responsible for guarding the souls of humanity and destroying any potential threat to the God-Emperor's realms. Investigating a series of murders leads fan-favourite Inquisitor Eisenhorn into a sinister series of ritual killings and the clutches of a terrifying Chaos cult.

I lost my left hand on Sameter. This is how it occurred. On the thirteenth day of Sagittar (local calendar), three days before the solstice, in the mid-rise district of the city of Urbitane, an itinerant evangelist called Lazlo Mombril was found shuffling aimlessly around the flat roof of a disused tannery lacking his eyes, his tongue, his nose and both of his hands.

Urbitane is the second city of Sameter, a declining agro-chemical planet in the Helican subsector, and it is no stranger to crimes of cruelty and spite brought on by the vicissitudes of neglect and social deprivation afflicting its tightly packed population.

But this act of barbarity stood out for two reasons. First, it was no hot-blooded assault or alcohol-fuelled manslaughter but a deliberate and systematic act of brutal, almost ritual mutilation.

Second, it was the fourth such crime discovered that month.

I had been on Sameter for just three weeks, investigating the links between a bonded trade federation and a secessionist movement on Hesperus at the request of Lord Inquisitor Rorken. The links proved to be nothing – Urbitane's economic slough had forced the federation to chase unwise business with unscrupulous ship masters, and the real meat of the case lay on Hesperus – but I believe this was the lord inquisitor's way of gently easing me back into active duties following the long and arduous affair of the Necroteuch.

By the Imperial calendar it was 241.M41, late in that year. I had just finished several self-imposed months of recuperation, meditation and study on Thracian Primaris. The eyes of the daemonhost Cherubael still woke me some nights, and I wore permanent scars from torture at the hands of the sadist Gorgone Locke. His strousine neural scourge had damaged my nervous system and paralysed my face. I would not smile again for the rest of my life. But the battle wounds sustained on KCX-1288 and 56-Izar had healed, and I was now itching to renew my work.

This idle task on Sameter had suited me, so I had taken it and closed the dossier after a swift and efficient investigation. But latterly, as I prepared to leave, officials of the Munitorum unexpectedly requested an audience.

I was staying with my associates in a suite of rooms in the Urbitane Excelsior, a shabby but well-appointed establishment in the high-rise district of the city. Through soot-stained, armoured roundels of glass twenty metres across, the suite looked out across the filthy grey towers of the city to the brackish waters of the polluted bay twenty kilometres away. Ornithopters and biplanes buzzed between the massive city structures, and the running lights of freighters and orbitals glowed in the smog as they swung down towards the landing port. Out on the isthmus, through a haze of yellow, stagnant air, promethium refineries belched brown smoke into the perpetual twilight.

'They're here,' said Bequin, entering the suite's lounge from the outer lobby. She had dressed in a demure gown of blue damask and a silk pashmeena, perfectly in keeping with my instruction that we should present a muted but powerful image.

I myself was clad in a suit of soft black linen with a waistcoat of grey velvet and a hip length black leather storm coat.

'Do you need me for this?' asked Midas Betancore, my pilot and confidant.

I shook my head. 'I don't intend to be delayed here. I just have to be polite. Go on to the landing port and make sure the gun-cutter's readied for departure.'

He nodded and left. Bequin showed the visitors in.

I had felt it necessary to be polite because Eskeen Hansaard, Urbitane's Minister of Security, had come to see me himself. He was a massive man in a double-breasted brown tunic, his big frame offset oddly by his finely featured, boyish face. He was escorted by two bodyguards in grey, armour-ribbed uniforms and a short but handsome, black-haired woman in a dark blue bodyglove.

I had made sure I was sitting in an armchair when Bequin showed them in so I could rise in a measured, respectful way. I wanted them to be in no doubt who was really in charge here.

'Minister Hansaard,' I said, shaking his hand. 'I am Inquisitor Gregor Eisenhorn of the Ordo Xenos. These are my associates Alizebeth Bequin, Arbites Chastener Godwyn Fischig and savant Uber Aemos. How may I help you?'

'I have no wish to waste your time, inquisitor,' he said, apparently nervous in my presence. That was good, just as I had intended it. 'A case has been brought to my attention that I believe is beyond the immediate purview of the city arbitrators. Frankly, it smacks of warp-corruption, and cries out for the attention of the Inquisition.'

He was direct. That impressed me. A ranking official of the Imperium, anxious to be seen to be doing the right thing. Nevertheless, I still expected his business might be a mere nothing, like the affair of the trade federation, a local crime requiring only my nod of approval that it was fine for him to continue and close. Men like Hansaard are often over-careful, in my experience.

'There have been four deaths in the city during the last month that we believe to be linked. I would appreciate your advice on them. They are connected by merit of the ritual mutilation involved.'

'Show me,' I said.

'Captain?' he responded.

Arbites Captain Hurlie Wrex was the handsome woman with the short black hair. She stepped forward, nodded respectfully, and gave me a dataslate with the gold crest of the Adeptus Arbites on it.

'I have prepared a digested summary of the facts,' she said.

I began to speed-read the slate, already preparing the gentle knock-back I was expecting to give to his case. Then I stopped, slowed, read back.

I felt a curious mix of elation and frustration. Even from this cursorial glance, there was no doubt this case required the immediate attention of the Imperial Inquisition. I could feel my instincts stiffen and my appetites whetten, for the first time in months. In bothering me with this, Minister

Hansaard was not being over careful at all. At the same time, my heart sank with the realisation that my departure from this miserable city would be delayed.

All four victims had been blinded and had their noses, tongues and hands removed. At the very least.

The evangelist, Mombril, had been the only one found alive. He had died from his injuries eight minutes after arriving at Urbitane Mid-rise Sector Infirmary. It seemed to me likely that he had escaped his ritual tormentors some-how before they could finish their work.

The other three were a different story.

Poul Grevan, a machinesmith; Luthar Hewall, a rug-maker; Idilane Fasple, a mid-wife.

Hewall had been found a week before by city sanita-tion servitors during routine maintenance to a soil stack in the mid-rise district. Someone had attempted to burn his remains and then flush them into the city's ancient waste system, but the human body is remarkably durable. The post could not prove his missing body parts had not simply succumbed to decay and been flushed away, but the damage to the ends of the forearm bones seemed to speak convincingly of a saw or chain-blade.

When Idilane Fasple's body was recovered from a crawl-space under the roof of a mid-rise tenement hab, it threw more light on the extent of Hewall's injuries. Not only had Fasple been mutilated in the manner of the evangelist Mom-bril, but her brain, brainstem and heart had been excised. The injuries were hideous. One of the roof workers who discovered her had subsequently committed suicide. Her bloodless, almost dessicated body, dried out – smoked, if you will – by the tenement's heating vents, had been wrapped in a dark green cloth similar to the material of an Imperial Guard-issue bedroll and stapled to the underside of the rafters with an industrial nail gun.

Cross-reference between her and Hewall convinced the Arbites that the rug-maker had very probably suffered the removal of his brain stem and heart too. Until that point, they had ascribed the identifiable lack of those soft organs to the almost toxic levels of organic decay in the liquiescent filth of the soil stack.

Graven, actually the first victim found, had been dredged from the waters of the bay by salvage ship. He had been presumed to be a suicide dismembered by the screws of a passing boat until Wrex's careful cross-checking had flagged up too many points of similarity.

Because of the peculiar circumstances of their various post mortem locations, it was pathologically impossible to determine any exact date or time of death. But Wrex could be certain of a window. Graven had been last seen on the nineteenth of Aquiarae, three days before his body had been dredged up. Hewall had delivered a finished rug to a high-rise customer on the twenty-fourth, and had dined that same evening with friends at a charcute in mid-rise. Fasple had failed to report for work on the fifth of Sagittar, although the night before she had seemed happy and looking forward to her next shift, according to friends.

'I thought at first we might have a serial predator loose in mid-rise,' said Wrex. 'But the pattern of mutilation seems to me more extreme than that. This is not feral murder, or even psychopathic, post-slaying depravity. This is specific, purposeful ritual.'

'How do you arrive at that?' asked my colleague, Fischig. Fischig was a senior arbitrator from Hubris, with plenty of experience in murder cases. Indeed, it was his fluency with procedure and familiarity with modus operandi that had convinced me to make him a part of my band. That, and his ferocious strength in a fight.

Wrex looked sidelong at him, as if he was questioning her ability.

'Because of the nature of the dismemberment. Because of the way the remains were disposed of.' She looked at me. 'In my experience, inquisitor, a serial killer secretly wants to be found, and certainly wants to be known. It will display its kills with wanton openness, declaring its power over the community. It thrives on the terror and fear it generates. Great efforts were made to hide these bodies. That suggest to me the killer was far more interested in the deaths themselves than in the reaction to the deaths.'

'Well put, captain,' I said. 'That has been my experience too. Cult killings are often hidden so that the cult can continue its work without fear of discovery.'

'Suggesting that there are other victims still to find...' said Bequin casually, a chilling prophecy as it now seems to me.

'Cult killings?' said the minister. 'I brought this to your attention because I feared as much, but do you really think–'

'On Alphex, the warp-cult removed their victims' hands and tongues because they were organs of communication,' Aemos began. 'On Brettaria, the brains were scooped out in order for the cult to ingest the spiritual matter – the anima, as you might say – of their prey. A number of other worlds have suffered cult predations where the eyes have been forfeit... Gulinglas, Pentari, Hesperus, Messina... windows of the soul, you see.

'The Heretics of Saint Scarif, in fact, severed their ritual victims' hands and then made them write out their last confessions using ink quills rammed into the stumps of–'

'Enough information, Aemos,' I said. The minister was looking pale.

'These are clearly cult killings, sir,' I said. 'There is a noxious cell of Chaos at liberty in your city. And I will find it.'

I went at once to the mid-rise district. Grevan, Hewall and Fasple had all been residents of that part of Urbitane, and Mombril, though a visitor to the metropolis, had been found there too. Aemos went to the Munitorum records spire in high-rise to search the local archives. I was particularly interested in historical cult activity on Sameter, and on date significance. Fischig, Bequin and Wrex accompanied me.

The genius loci of a place can often say much about the crimes committed therein. So far, my stay on Sameter had only introduced me to the cleaner, high-altitude regions of Urbitane's high-rise, up above the smog-cover.

Mid-rise was a dismal, wretched place of neglect and poverty. A tarry resin of pollution coated every surface, and acid rain poured down unremittingly. Raw-engined traffic crawled nose to tail down the poorly lit streets, and the very stone of the buildings seemed to be rotting. The smoggy darkness of mid-rise had a red, firelit quality, the backwash of the flares from giant gas processors. It reminded me of picture-slate engravings of the Inferno.

We stepped from Wrex's armoured speeder at the corner of Shearing Street and Pentecost. The captain pulled on her Arbites helmet and a quilted flak-coat. I began to wish for a hat of my own, or a rebreather mask. The rain stank like urine. Every thirty seconds or so an express flashed past on the elevated trackway, shaking the street.

'In here,' Wrex called, and led us through a shutter off the thoroughfare into the dank hallway of a tenement hab. Everything was stained with centuries of grime. The heating had been set too high, perhaps to combat the murky wetness outside, but the result was simply an overwhelming humidity and a smell like the fur of a mangy canine.

This was Idilane Fasple's last resting place. She'd been found in the roof. 'Where did she live?' asked Fischig.

'Two streets away. She had a parlour on one of the old court-habs.'

'Hewall?'

'His hab about a kilometre west. His remains were found five blocks east.'

I looked at the dataslate. The tannery where Mombril had been found was less than thirty minutes' walk from here, and Graven's home a short tram ride. The only thing that broke the geographical focus of these lives and deaths was the fact that Graven had been dumped in the bay.

'I hasn't escaped my notice that they all inhabited a remarkably specific area,' Wrex smiled.

'I never thought it had. But "remarkably" is the word. It isn't just the same quarter or district. It's a intensely close network of streets, a neighbourhood.'

'Suggesting?' asked Bequin.

'The killer or killers are local too,' said Fischig.

'Or someone from elsewhere has a particular hatred of this neighbourhood and comes into it to do his or her killing,' said Wrex.

'Like a hunting ground?' noted Fischig. I nodded. Both possibilities had merit.

'Look around,' I told Fischig and Bequin, well aware that Wrex's officers had already been all over the building. But she said nothing. Our expert appraisal might turn up something different.

I found a small office at the end of the entrance hall. It was clearly the cubbyhole of the habitat's superintendent. Sheaves of paper were pinned to the flak-board wall: rental dockets, maintenance rosters, notes of resident complaints. There was a box-tray of lost property, a partially disassembled mini-servitor in a tub of oil, a stale stink of cheap liquor. A faded ribbon and paper rosette from an Imperial shrine was pinned over the door with a regimental rank stud.

'What you doing in here?'

I looked round. The superintendent was a middle-aged man in a dirty overall suit. Details. I always look for details. The gold signet ring with the wheatear symbol. The row of permanent metal sutures closing the scar on his scalp where the hair had never grown back. The prematurely weathered skin. The guarded look in his eyes.

I told him who I was and he didn't seem impressed. Then I asked him who he was and he said 'The super. What you doing in here?'

I use my will sparingly. The psychic gift sometimes closes as many doors as it opens.

But there was something about this man. He needed a jolt. 'What is your name?' I asked, modulating my voice to carry the full weight of the psychic probe.

He rocked backwards, and his pupils dilated in surprise. 'Quater Traves,' he mumbled.

'Did you know the midwife Fasple?'

'I sin her around.'

'To speak to?'

He shook his head. His eyes never left mine.

'Did she have friends?'

He shrugged.

'What about strangers? Anyone been hanging around the hab?'

His eyes narrowed. A sullen, mocking look, as if I hadn't seen the streets outside.

'Who has access to the roofspace where her body was found?'

'Ain't nobody bin up there. Not since the place bin built. Then the heating packs in and the contractors has to break through the roof to get up there. They found her.'

'There isn't a hatch?'

'Shutter. Locked, and no one has a key. Easier to go through the plasterboard.'

Outside, we sheltered from the rain under the elevated railway.

'That's what Traves told me too,' Wrex confirmed. 'No one had been into the roof for years until the contractors broke their way in.'

'Someone had. Someone with the keys to the shutter. The killer.'

The soil stack where Hewall had been found was behind a row of commercial properties built into an ancient skin of scaffolding that cased the outside of a toolfitters' workshop like a cobweb. There was what seemed to be a bar two stages up, where a neon signed flicked between an Imperial aquila and a fleur-de-lys. Fischig and Wrex continued up to the next scaffolding level to peer in through the stained windows of the habs there. Bequin and I went into the bar.

The light was grey inside. At a high bar, four or five drinkers sat on ratchet-stools and ignored us. The scent of obscura smoke was in the air.

There was a woman behind the counter who took exception to us from the moment we came in. She was in her forties, with a powerful, almost masculine build. Her vest was cut off at the armpits and her arms were as muscular as Fischig's. There was the small tattoo of a skull and crossbones on her bicep. The skin of her face was weathered and coarse.

'Help you?' she asked, wiping the counter with a glass-cloth. As she did so I saw that her right arm, from the elbow down, was a prosthetic.

'Information,' I said.

She flicked her cloth at the row of bottles on the shelves behind her. 'Not a brand I know.'

'You know a man called Hewall?'

'No.'

'The guy they found in the waste pipes behind here.'

'Oh. Didn't know he had a name.'

Now I was closer I could see the tattoo on her arm wasn't a skull and crossbones. It was a wheatear.

'We all have names. What's yours?'

'Omin Lund.'

'You live around here?'

'Live is too strong a word.' She turned away to serve someone else.

'Scary bitch,' said Bequin as we went outside. 'Everyone acts like they've got something to hide.'

'Everyone does, even if it's simply how much they hate this town.'

The heart had gone out of Urbitane, out of Sameter itself, about seventy years before. The mill-hives of Thracian Primaris eclipsed Sameter's production, and export profits fell away. In an effort to compete, the authorities freed the

refineries to escalate production by stripping away the legal
restrictions on atmospheric pollution levels. For hundreds
of years, Urbitane had had problems controlling its smog
and air-pollutants. For the last few decades, it hadn't bothered any more.

My vox-earplug chimed. It was Aemos.

'What have you found?'

'*It's most perturbatory. Sameter has been clear of taint for a
goodly while. The last Inquisitorial investigation was thirty-one
years ago standard, and that wasn't here in Urbitane but in Aqui-
tane, the capital. A rogue psyker. The planet has its fair share
of criminal activity, usually narcotics trafficking and the conse-
quential mob-fighting. But nothing really markedly heretical.*'

'Nothing with similarities to the ritual methods?'

'*No, and I've gone back two centuries.*'

'What about the dates?'

'*Sagittar thirteenth is just shy of the solstice, but I can't make
any meaning out of that. The Purge of the Sarpetal Hives is usually commemorated by upswings of cult activity in the subsector,
but that's six weeks away. The only other thing I can find is that
this Sagittar fifth was the twenty-first anniversary of the Battle
of Klodeshi Heights.*'

'I don't know it.'

'*The sixth of seven full-scale engagements during the sixteen
month Imperial campaign on Surealis Six.*'

'Surealis... that's in the next damn subsector! Aemos,
every day of the year is the anniversary of an Imperial action
somewhere. What connection are you making?'

'*The Ninth Sameter Infantry saw service in the war on Surealis.*'

Fischig and Wrex had rejoined us from their prowl around
the upper stages of the scaffolding. Wrex was talking on
her own vox-set.

She signed off and looked at me, rain drizzling off her visor. 'They've found another one, inquisitor,' she said.

It wasn't one. It was three, and their discovery threw the affair wide open. An old warehouse in the mill zone, ten streets away from Fasple's hab, had been damaged by fire two months before, and now the municipal work-crews had moved in to tear it down and reuse the lot as a site for cheap, prefab habitat blocks. They'd found the bodies behind the wall insulation in a mouldering section untouched by the fire. A woman and two men, systematically mutilated in the manner of the other victims.

But these were much older. I could tell that even at a glance.

I crunched across the debris littering the floorspace of the warehouse shell. Rain streamed in through the roof holes, illuminated as a blizzard of white specks by the cold blue beams of the arbitrators' floodlights shining into the place.

Arbites officers were all around, but they hadn't touched the discovery itself.

Mummified and shriveled, these foetally curled, pitiful husks had been in the wall a long time.

'What's that?' I asked.

Fischig leaned forward for a closer look. 'Adhesive tape, wrapped around them to hold them against the partition. Old. The gum's decayed.'

'That pattern on it. The silver flecks.'

'I think it's military issue stuff. Matt-silver coating, you know the sort? The coating's coming off with age.'

'These bodies are different ages,' I said.

'I thought so too,' said Fischig.

* * *

We had to wait six hours for a preliminary report from the district Examiner Medicae, but it confirmed our guess. All three bodies had been in the wall for at least eight years, and then for different lengths of time. Decompositional anomalies showed that one of the males had been in position for as much as twelve years, the other two added subsequently, at different occasions. No identifications had yet been made.

'The warehouse was last used six years ago,' Wrex told me.

'I want a roster of workers employed there before it went out of business.'

Someone using the same m.o. and the same spools of adhesive tape had hidden bodies there over a period of years.

The disused tannery where poor Mombril had been found stood at the junction between Xerxes Street and a row of slum tenements known as the Pilings. It was a foetid place, with the stink of the lye and coroscutum used in the tanning process still pungent in the air. No amount of acid rain could wash that smell out.

There were no stairs. Fischig, Bequin and I climbed up to the roof via a metal fire-ladder.

'How long does a man survive mutilated like that?'

'From the severed wrists alone, he'd bleed out in twenty minutes, perhaps,' Fischig estimated. 'Clearly, if he had made an escape, he'd have the adrenaline of terror sustaining him a little.'

'So when he was found up here, he can have been no more than twenty minutes from the scene of his brutalisation.'

We looked around. The wretched city looked back at us, close packed and dense.

There were hundreds of possibilities. It might take days to search them all.

But we could narrow it down. 'How did he get on the roof?' I asked.

'I was wondering that,' said Fischig.

'The ladder we came up by...' Bequin trailed off as she realised her gaffe.

'Without hands?' Fischig smirked.

'Or sight,' I finished. 'Perhaps he didn't escape. Perhaps his abusers put him here.'

'Or perhaps he fell,' Bequin said, pointing.

The back of a tall warehouse over-shadowed the tannery to the east. Ten metres up there were shattered windows.

'If he was in there somewhere, fled blindly, and fell through onto this roof...'

'Well reasoned, Alizebeth,' I said.

The Arbites had done decent work, but not even Wrex had thought to consider this inconsistency.

We went round to the side entrance of the warehouse. The battered metal shutters were locked. A notice pasted to the wall told would-be intruders to stay out of the property of Hundlemas Agricultural Stowage.

I took out my multi-key and disengaged the padlock. I saw Fischig had drawn his sidearm.

'What's the matter?'

'I had a feeling just then... like we were being watched.'

We went inside. The air was cold and still and smelled of chemicals. Rows of storage vats filled with chemical fertilisers lined the echoing warehall.

The second floor was bare-boarded and hadn't been used in years. Wire mesh had been stapled over a doorway to the next floor, and rainwater dripped down. Fischig pulled at the mesh. It was cosmetic only, and folded aside neatly.

Now I drew my autopistol too.

On the street side of the third floor, which was divided into smaller rooms, we found a chamber ten metres by ten, on the floor of which was spread a sheet of plastic smeared with old blood and other organic deposits. There was a stink of fear.

'This is where they did him,' Fischig said with certainty.

'No sign of cult markings or Chaos symbology,' I mused.

'Maybe not,' said Bequin, crossing the room, being careful not to step on the smeared plastic sheet. For the sake of her shoes, not the crime scene, I was sure.

'What's this? Something was hung here.'

Two rusty hooks in the wall, scraped enough to show something had been hanging there recently. On the floor below was a curious cross drawn in yellow chalk.

'I've seen that before somewhere,' I said. My vox bleeped. It was Wrex.

'I've got that worker roster you asked for.'

'Good. Where are you?'

'Coming to find you at the tannery, if you're still there.'

'We'll meet you on the corner of Xerxes Street. Tell your staff we have a crime scene here in the agricultural warehouse.'

We walked out of the killing room towards the stairwell. Fischig froze, and brought up his gun.

'Again?' I whispered.

He nodded, and pushed Bequin into the cover of a door jamb.

Silence, apart from the rain and the scurry of vermin. Gun braced, Fischig looked up at the derelict roof. It may have been my imagination, but it seemed as if a shadow had moved across the bare rafters.

I moved forward, scanning the shadows with my pistol. Something creaked. A floorboard.

Fischig pointed to the stairs. I nodded I understood, but the last thing I wanted was a mistaken shooting. I carefully keyed my vox and whispered, 'Wrex. You're not coming into the warehouse to find us, are you?'

'*Negative, inquisitor.*'

'Standby.'

Fischig had reached the top of the staircase. He peered down, aiming his weapon. Las-fire erupted through the floorboards next to him and he threw himself flat.

I put a trio of shots into the mouth of the staircase, but my angle was bad.

Two hard round shots spat back up the stairs and then the roar and flash of the las came again, raking the floor.

From above, I realised belatedly. Whoever was on the stairs had a hard-slug side arm, but the las-fire was coming down from the roof.

I heard steps running on the floor below. Fischig scrambled up to give chase but another salvo of las-fire sent him ducking again.

I raised my aim and fired up into the roof tiles, blowing out holes through which the pale light poked.

Something slithered and scrambled on the roof.

Fischig was on the stairs now, running after the second assailant.

I hurried across the third floor, following the sounds of the man on the roof.

I saw a silhouette against the sky through a hole in the tiles and fired again. Las-fire replied in a bright burst, but then there was a thump and further slithering.

'Cease fire! Give yourself up! Inquisition!' I bellowed, using the will.

There came a much more substantial crash sounding like

a whole portion of the roof had come down. Tiles avalanched down and smashed in a room nearby.

I slammed into the doorway, gun aimed, about to yell out a further will command. But there was no one in the room. Piles of shattered roofslates and bricks covered the floor beneath a gaping hole in the roof itself, and a battered lasrifle lay amongst the debris.

On the far side of the room were some of the broken windows that Bequin had pointed out as overlooking the tannery roof.

I ran to one. Down below, a powerful figure in dark overalls was running for cover. The killer, escaping from me in just the same way his last victim had escaped him – through the windows onto the tannery roof.

The distance was too far to use the will again with any effect, but my aim and angle were good. I lined up on the back of the head a second before it disappeared, began to apply pressure–

– and the world exploded behind me.

I came round cradled in Bequin's arms. 'Don't move, Eisenhorn. The medics are coming.'

'What happened?' I asked.

'Booby trap. The gun that guy left behind? It exploded behind you. Powercell overload.'

'Did Fischig get his man?'

'Of course he did.'

He hadn't, in fact. He'd chased the man hard down two flights of stairs and through the main floor of the warehall. At the outer door onto the street, the man had wheeled around and emptied his autopistol's clip at the chastener, forcing him into cover.

Then Captain Wrex, approaching from outside, had gunned the man down in the doorway.

We assembled in Wrex's crowded office in the busy Arbites Mid-Rise Sector-house. Aemos joined us, laden down with papers and dataslates, and brought Midas Betancore with him.

'You all right?' Midas asked me. In his jacket of embroidered cerise silk, he was a vivid splash of colour in the muted gloom of mid-rise.

'Minor abrasions. I'm fine.'

'I thought we were leaving, and here you are having all the fun without me.'

'I thought we were leaving too until I saw this case. Review Bequin's notes. I need you up to speed.'

Aemos shuffled his ancient, augmetically assisted bulk over to Wrex's desk and dropped his books and papers in an unceremonious pile.

'I've been busy,' he said.

'Busy with results?' Bequin asked.

He looked at her sourly. 'No, actually. But I have gathered a commendable resource of information. As the discussion advances, I may be able to fill in blanks.'

'No results, Aemos? Most perturbatory,' grinned Midas, his white teeth gleaming against his dark skin. He was mocking the old savant by using Aemos' favourite phrase.

I had before me the work roster of the warehouse where the three bodies had been found, and another for the agricultural store where our fight had occurred. Quick comparison brought up two coincident names.

'Brell Sodakis. Vim Venik. Both worked as warehousemen before the place closed down. Now they're employed by Hundlemas Agricultural Stowage.'

'Backgrounds? Addresses?' I asked Wrex.

'I'll run checks,' she said.

'So… we have a cult here, eh?' Midas asked. 'You've got a series of ritual killings, at least one murder site, and now the names of two possible cultists.'

'Perhaps.' I wasn't convinced. There seemed both more and less to this than had first appeared. Inquisitorial hunch.

The remains of the lasrifle discarded by my assailant lay on an evidence tray. Even with the damage done by the overloading powercell, it was apparent that this was an old model.

'Did the powercell overload because it was dropped? It fell through the roof, didn't it?' Bequin asked.

'They're pretty solid,' Fischig answered.

'Forced overload,' I said. 'An old Imperial Guard trick. I've heard they learn how to set one off. As a last ditch in tight spots. Cornered. About to die anyway.'

'That's not standard,' said Fischig, poking at the trigger guard of the twisted weapon.

His knowledge of guns was sometimes unseemly. 'See this modification? It's been machine-tooled to widen the guard around the trigger.'

'Why?' I asked.

Fischig shrugged. 'Access? For an augmetic hand with rudimentary digits?'

We went through to a morgue room down the hall where the man Wrex had gunned down was lying on a slab. He was middle-aged, with a powerful frame going to seed. His skin was weatherbeaten and lined.

'Identity?'

'We're working on it.'

The body had been stripped by the morgue attendants. Fischig scrutinised it, rolling it with Wrex's help to study the back.

The man's clothes and effects were in plasteen bags in a tray at his feet. I lifted the bag of effects and held it up to the light.

'Tattoo,' reported Fischig. 'Imperial eagle, left shoulder. Crude, old. Letters underneath it... capital S period, capital I period, capital I, capital X.'

I'd just found the signet ring in the bag. Gold, with a wheatear motif. 'S.I. IX,' said Aemos. 'Sameter Infantry Nine.'

The Ninth Sameter Infantry had been founded in Urbitane twenty-three years before, and had served, as Aemos had already told me, in the brutal liberation war on Surealis Six. According to city records, five hundred and nineteen veterans of that war and that regiment had been repatriated to Sameter after mustering out thirteen years ago, coming back from the horrors of war to an increasingly depressed world beset by the blight of poverty and urban collapse. Their regimental emblem, as befitted a world once dominated by agriculture, was the wheatear.

'They came back thirteen years ago. The oldest victim we have dates from that time,' said Fischig.

'Surealis Six was a hard campaign, wasn't it?' I asked.

Aemos nodded. 'The enemy was dug in. It was ferocious, brutal. Brutalising. And the climate. Two white dwarf suns, no cloud cover. The most punishing heat and light, not to mention ultraviolet burning.'

'Ruins the skin,' I murmured. 'Makes it weatherbeaten and prematurely aged.' Everyone looked at the taut, lined face of the body on the slab.

'I'll get a list of the veterans,' volunteered Wrex.

'I already have one,' said Aemos.

'I'm betting you find the names Brell Sodakis and Vim Venik on it,' I said.

Aemos paused as he scanned. 'I do,' he agreed.

'What about Quater Traves?'

'Yes, he's here. Master Gunnery Sergeant Quater Traves.'

'What about Omin Lund?'

'Ummm… yes. Sniper first class. Invalided out of service.'

'The Sameter Ninth were a mixed unit, then?' asked Bequin.

'All our Guard foundings are,' Wrex said proudly.

'So, these men… and women…' Midas mused. 'Soldiers, been through hell. Fighting the corruption… your idea is they brought it back here with them? Some taint? You think they were infected by the touch of the warp on Surealis and have been ritually killing as a way of worship back here ever since?'

'No,' I said. 'I think they're still fighting the war.'

It remains a sad truth of the Imperium that virtually no veteran ever comes back from fighting its wars intact. Combat alone shreds nerves and shatters bodies. But the horrors of the warp, and of foul xenos forms like the tyranid, steal sanity forever, and leave veterans fearing the shadows, and the night and, sometimes, the nature of their friends and neighbours, for the rest of their lives.

The Guards of the Ninth Sameter Infantry had come home thirteen years before, broke by a savage war against mankind's Archenemy and, through their scars and their fear, brought their war back with them.

The Arbites mounted raids at once on the addresses of all the veterans on the list, those that could be traced, those that were still alive. It appeared that skin cancer had taken over two hundred of them in the years since their repatriation. Surealis had claimed them as surely as if they had fallen there in combat.

A number were rounded up. Bewildered drunks, cripples, addicts, a few honest men and women trying diligently to carry on with their lives. For those latter I felt especially sorry.

But about seventy could not be traced. Many may well have disappeared, moved on, or died without it coming to the attention of the authorities. But some had clearly fled. Lund, Traves, Sodakis, Venik for starters. Their habs were found abandoned, strewn with possessions as if the occupant had left in a hurry. So were the habs of twenty more belonging to names on the list.

The Arbites arrived at the hab of one, ex-corporal Geffin Sancto, in time to catch him in the act of flight. Sancto had been a flamer operator in the Guard, and like so many of his kind, had managed to keep his weapon as a memento. Screaming the battlecry of the Sameter Ninth, he torched four arbitrators in the stairwell of his building before the tactical squads of the judiciary vaporised him in a hail of gunshots.

'Why are they killing?' Bequin asked me. 'All these years, in secret ritual?'

'I don't know.'

'You do, Eisenhorn. You so do!'

'Very well. I can guess. The fellow worker who jokes at the Emperor's expense and makes your fragile sanity imagine he is tainted with the warp. The rug-maker whose patterns suggest to you the secret encoding of Chaos symbols. The midwife you decide is spawning the offspring of the Archenemy in the mid-rise maternity hall. The travelling evangelist who seems just too damn fired up to be safe.'

She looked down at the floor of the Land Speeder. 'They see daemons everywhere.'

'In everything. In every one. And, so help them, they

believe they are doing the Emperor's work by killing. They trust no one, so they daren't alert the authorities. They take the eyes, the hands and the tongue… all the organs of communication, any way the Archenemy might transmit his foul lies. And then they destroy the brain and heart, the organs which common soldier myth declares must harbour daemons.'

'So where are we going now?' she asked.

'Another hunch.'

The Guildhall of the Sameter Agricultural Fraternity was a massive ragstone building on Furnace Street, its facade decaying from the ministrations of smog and acid rain. It had been disused for over two decades.

Its last duty had been to serve as a recruitment post of the Sameter Ninth during the founding. In its long hallways, the men and women of the Ninth had signed their names, collected their starchy new fatigues, and pledged their battle oath to the God-Emperor of Mankind.

At certain times, under certain circumstances, when a proper altar to the Emperor is not available, Guard officers improvise in order to conduct their ceremonies. An Imperial eagle, an aquila standard, is suspended from a wall, and a sacred spot is marked on the floor beneath in yellow chalk.

The guildhall was not a consecrated building. The founding must have been the first time the young volunteers of Urbitane had seen that done. They'd made their vows to a yellow chalk cross and a dangling aquila.

Wrex was leading three fire-teams of armed arbitrators, but I went in with Midas and Fischig first, quietly. Bequin and Aemos stayed by our vehicle.

Midas was carrying his matched needle pistols, and Fischig an auto shotgun. I clipped a slab-pattern magazine full of fresh rounds into the precious bolt pistol given to me by Librarian Brytnoth of the Adeptus Astartes Deathwatch Chapter.

We pushed open the boarded doors of the decaying structure and edged down the dank corridors. Rainwater pattered from the roof and the marble floor was spotted and eaten by collected acid.

We could hear the singing. A couple of dozen voices voicing up the Battle Hymn of the Golden Throne.

I led my companions forward, hunched low. Through the crazed windows of an inner door we looked through into the main hall. Twenty-three dishevelled veterans in ragged clothes were knelt down in ranks on the filthy floor, their heads bowed to the rusty Imperial eagle hanging on the wall as they sang. There was a yellow chalk cross on the floor under the aquila. Each veteran had a backpack or rucksack and a weapon by their feet.

My heart ached. This was how it had gone over two decades before, when they came to the service, young and fresh and eager. Before the war. Before the horror.

'Let me try… try to give them a chance,' I said.

'Gregor!' Midas hissed.

'Let me try, for their sake. Cover me.'

I slipped into the back of the hall, my gun lowered at my side, and joined in the verse. One by one, the voices died away and bowed heads turned sideways to look at me.

Down the aisle, at the chalk cross of the altar, Lund, Traves and a bearded man I didn't know stood gazing at me.

In the absence of other voices, I finished the hymn.

'It's over,' I said. 'The war is over and you have all done your duty. Above and beyond the call.'

Silence.

'I am Inquisitor Eisenhorn. I'm here to relieve you. The careful war against the blight of Chaos that you have waged through Urbitane in secret is now over. The Inquisition is here to take over. You can stand down.'

Two or three of the hunched veterans began to weep. 'You lie,' said Lund, stepping forward.

'I do not. Surrender your weapons and I promise you will be treated fairly and with respect.'

'Will... will we get medals?' the bearded man asked, in a quavering voice.

'The gratitude of the God-Emperor will be with you always.'

More were weeping now. Out of fear, anxiety or plain relief.

'Don't trust him!' said Traves. 'It's another trick!'

'I saw you in my bar,' said Lund, stepping forward. 'You came in looking.' Her voice was empty, distant.

'I saw you on the tannery roof, Omin Lund. You're still a fine shot, despite the hand.'

She looked down at her prosthetic with a wince of shame.

'Will we get medals?' the bearded man repeated, eagerly. Traves turned on him.

'Of course we won't, Spake, you cretin! He's here to kill us!'

'I'm not–' I began.

'I want medals!' the bearded man, Spake, screamed suddenly, sliding his laspistol up from his belt with the fluid speed only a trained soldier can manage.

I had no choice.

His shot tore through the shoulder padding of my storm coat. My bolt exploded his head, spraying blood across the rusty metal eagle on the wall.

Pandemonium.

The veterans leapt to their feet firing wildly, scattering, running.

I threw myself flat as shots tore out the wall plaster behind me. At some point Fischig and Midas burst in, weapons blazing. I saw three or four veterans drop, sliced through by silent needles and another six tumble as shotgun rounds blew them apart.

Traves came down the aisle, blasting his old service-issue lasrifle at me. I rolled and fired, but my shot went wide. His face distorted as a needle round punched through it and he fell in a crumpled heap.

Wrex and her fire-teams exploded in. Flames from some spilled accelerants billowed up the wall.

I got up, and then was thrown back by a las-shot that blew off my left hand.

Spinning, falling, I saw Lund, struggling to make her prosthetic fingers work the unmodified trigger of Traves' lasgun.

My bolt round hit her with such force she flew back down the aisle, hit the wall, and tore the Imperial aquila down.

Not a single veteran escaped the guildhall alive. The firefight raged for two hours. Wrex lost five men to the experienced guns of the Sameter Ninth veterans. They stood to the last. No more can be said of any Imperial Guard unit.

The whole affair left me sour and troubled. I have devoted my life to the service of the Imperium, to protect it against its manifold foes, inside and out.

But not against its servants. However misguided, they were loyal and true. However wrong, they were shaped that way by the service they had endured in the Emperor's name.

Lund cost me my hand. A hand for a hand. They gave me a prosthetic on Sameter. I never used it. For two years, I made do with a fused stump. Surgeons on Messina finally gave me a fully functional graft.

I consider it still a small price to pay for them.

I have never been back to Sameter. Even today, they are still finding the secreted, hidden bodies. So very many, dead in the Emperor's name.

YOUR
NEXT READ

WARHAMMER 40,000

EISENHORN
XENOS
DAN ABNETT

XENOS
by Dan Abnett

Inquisitor Eisenhorn faces a vast interstellar cabal and the dark power
of daemons, all racing to recover an arcane text of abominable power –
an ancient tome known as the Necroteuch.

YOUR
NEXT READ

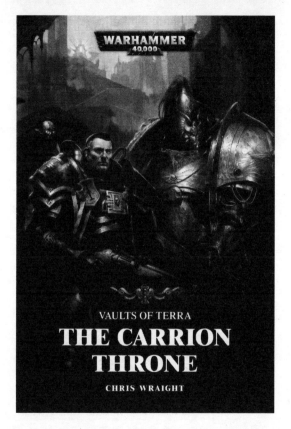

VAULTS OF TERRA: THE CARRION THRONE
by Chris Wraight

Inquisitor Crowl, who serves on Holy Terra itself, follows the trail of
a conspiracy that leads him to the corridors of the Imperial Palace…

THE CRYSTAL CATHEDRAL

DANIE WARE

As the galaxy darkens, the **Adepta Sororitas** – known more commonly throughout the Imperium as the Sisters of Battle – raise their battle-hymns, light their holy braziers and march to banish the blasphemous shadows that beset humanity.

In *The Crystal Cathedral*, the discovery of a long-lost cathedral brings joy to the Order of the Bloody Rose… until an unexpected attack turns their rejoicing into a desperate fight for survival.

Sister Augusta Santorus stood at the bottom of the wide stone steps, her scarlet armour gleaming, her head bared to the light. She had entrusted her weapons to the upheld tray of the little brass servitor and she carried only reverence and awe, as was proper in His presence. To bear arms in the house of the Emperor was blasphemy – after all, was His protection not enough?

In a line to her left stood her sisters, the squad's black-and-white cloaks stirring faintly, though there was little wind in this carefully carved valley. Its rock walls were almost sheer and they glittered with crystalline fragments, reflecting the blue-green gleam of the planet above, hazed in its own atmosphere and glorious to behold.

But that was not what held the Sisters' attention.

'Truly,' Sister Superior Veradis said softly, from the centre of the line, 'one finds His miracles in even the darkest of places. Sing with me, my Sisters…'

'A spiritu dominatus…' They raised their voices in the

Litany, their harmonies echoing back at them, chiming from the rock. The acoustics were flawless, and Augusta felt a chill go down her back.

The darkest of places…

This was Caro, the smallest moon of the planet Lena Beta, orbiting its blue-white star. And upon its bleak, rocky surface, there stood a miracle.

Forgotten for a thousand years, encased and defended by this carved, rock-walled gorge, it was a great, dark edifice, its bell towers and arches soaring over their heads. That much was imposing enough.

But the cathedral was also black.

Made from pure, black glass it was shadow, a cut-out, a great silhouette that took towering bites from the planet's perfect curve. It was flat pane after flat pane, every one held in place by thin struts of dark flexsteel, every one glittering with myriad crystalline reflections. Warrior statues stood guard at its doorway, their strong faces bearing familiar fleur-de-lys tattoos, their carved armour bearing the mark of the Bloody Rose.

From the very first days of their order: their Sisters.

Augusta wondered if they judged her, her newness and inexperience.

Between the stone Sisters, the cathedral's huge front doors stood open, and the squad could see that the building's insides were also dark, lit only by the flickering, ruddy gleam of electro-sconces. Despite the gloom, however, the congregation already waited within.

'We beseech Thee, destroy them.'

As the Litany came to an end, Veradis' voice sounded in their vox-beads: 'Witness our Sisters, Farus and Neva. The Accords of the Rose tell us that they defended this moon once before, a thousand years ago. Upon the site of their victory, and in the Emperor's name, was this cathedral constructed. It is a true phenomenon, the only one of its kind.'

'Yes, Sister.' Augusta was still staring, transfixed by the wonder that awaited them, nervous of making any misstep.

'Stand ready,' Veradis said.

Ahead of them, the organ blasted the first notes of the hymn of greeting.

'And move!'

The squad formed up, double file, and stamped crisply up the steps.

Her boots ringing from the stone, the young Sister Augusta marched with her chin up, her gaze straight ahead. With a rustle, the congregation came to their feet, their dataslates in their hands and already flowing with the text of the hymn. The slates' pale light reflected from the people's faces and throats – dignitaries all, their robes and jewellery sparkling.

Expectation rose from them like smoke.

At the aisle's far end, the great Sol-facing window was as black as everything else, its images lost to opacity. The altar was a great block of dark stone, the organ-pipes all but unseen in the shadows of the steel-supported roof. Only the pulpit and the choirstalls retained any glimmer of light, and, as the Sisters approached, so the choir took up the words of the hymn, their harmonies shiveringly perfect.

The darkest of places.

Beautiful, incredible though this was, something about this great building made Augusta tense – it provoked a sense of anticipation, almost, a feeling of huge expectation. The squad were here as an honour guard, marking its reconsecration, but still...

In the pulpit, the deacon eyed her as if he could see her very thoughts. With a prayer for the unworthiness of the doubt, she lowered her gaze and remembered her humility.

Nodding sternly, the deacon joined the hymn. Broadcast out through the vox-coder, his bass boom rose to the black glassaic roof, its power making Augusta's arms prickle. It seemed almost as if the hymn would shatter the building asunder, bring it down in a tumble of glittering and sharp-edged fragments...

Her tension grew sharper, whetted like a good blade.

Levis est mihi!

Show me the Light!

They came to the altar rail, and spread out to kneel. Augusta's blonde hair fell over her face, but even as it did so...

'By the Throne!'

The soft exclamation came from Veradis – startling from the severe and disciplined Sister Superior.

Before them, the very tip of the Sol window was touched with Lena's rising light.

Augusta stared, rapt.

Slowly, the light spread down through the glassaic. And not only through the window; it pooled out through the walls, and across the great arched curve of the roof. It chased the darkness away, turning panes of shadow into panes of pure, blue-white light. Rainbows danced in the vaults of the ceiling; the ruddy gleam of the sconces paled as the pillars rippled with dazzling illumination.

They had known to expect this – as this tiny moon curved about its planet, as the planet curved about its star, so this, its singular conjunction, came again. It was the only time in a thousand years that the light touched the bottom of this valley, the site of the previous battle, and the glassaic of the building it now contained.

But still, the wonder of it...!

Augusta knew she should lower her head, but she could not look away.

Illumination flowed down through the great window, revealing Him in all His glory, His armour gleaming, His flaming blade upheld. The singing rose to a crescendo, a crashing celebration of His presence, and of the great victory that had taken place here. It carried a strong contralto line that picked up the thread of the Sisters' own Litany.

Again, she shivered.

She could not avert her gaze, she was transfixed – the light continued to spread, making the polished brass of the organ pipes shine. It made rainbow patterns slide down the aisle; it brought a gleam to the circling cherubim, their metal eyelids clicking as they surveyed the scene below.

Overcome and breathless, bereft of the words of hymn and Litany both, Augusta could only watch.

The splintering of the roof took the Sisters completely by surprise.

And the screams rang like music.

'This will be a straightforward reconnaissance mission,' Veradis had told them, in the back of the shuttle. 'We are to attend the reconsecration of the great crystal cathedral, upon the mining moon Caro. The building is a true marvel, commemorating the victory of Sister Superior Farus against the xenos contagion that had infected Caro's tunnels.' She surveyed her squad, her expression stern. 'You have studied your texts, I hope?'

The Arvus juddered as it hit the upper atmosphere.

Sister Leona answered, 'Most certainly. Caro has an odd, elliptical orbit about its planet, pulled back once every thousand years before being flung out into the void once more. Its resources, however, are considerable, and, after the Great Crusade, the planetary governor deemed it enough of a blessing to be mined for its gemstones. It has brought its planet great wealth.'

'Just so,' Veradis said.

The Arvus continued to shudder. Augusta, her helm between her knees, held onto her straps and prayed – this was never her favourite part of a mission.

Sister Pia, the squad's second, chimed in, reciting the text verbatim: *'But lo! From the unsanctified places of the Emperor's tunnels there came forth darkness unendurable, heresy manifest in claw and tooth, in hunger given form. And, though the humble servants of the Emperor's mines gave battle with great bravery, the beasts were a seethe of cruelty beyond their ken, and thus, they were slain.'*

Veradis nodded, approving. The pict screen in the back of the shuttle was showing the moon's long orbit.

'They survived long enough to call for help,' Veradis said. 'And Sister Superior Farus, may she rest in His grace, brought her squad to eliminate the menace. The crystal cathedral marks the site of our Sisters' triumph, and the point at which the xenos infection was finally purged.' Veradis paused, watching the pict screen and the slowly tumbling moon. 'Caro's atmosphere has been fully restored, and the mines will commence their formal reopening once the service has taken place. We are to attend this service, and then undertake our reconnaissance mission. Needless to say, my Sisters, extreme vigilance must be maintained at all times.'

'Yes, Sister Superior.'

She gave Augusta a long look, 'And no mistakes this time, Sister.'

Augusta looked at her red boots, shamed by the loss of her bolter on their previous mission. 'I will make no errors.'

'Good.' Veradis' tone was grim. 'His eyes will be upon you. As will mine.'

The shuttle's juddering smoothed as the vehicle settled to a level flight path. On the screen, the orbit-image had given way to a close-up of the moon itself, riddled with a familiar pattern of mines, chimneys and manufactoria. Across the bottom of the screen flowed the necessary data – hours of daylight, atmospheric components, pollutant levels, air temperature.

Next to Augusta, Sister Lucienne shot her a sideways look. Across their tight-beam vox-link she muttered, 'Why do I bear a shadow in my heart, Sister? It is unworthy. And yet, there is something about this…'

Augusta glanced at her friend, but did not reply. The same shadow had crossed her also.

The crash was tremendous.

Glass splintered and tumbled, its edges glittering. A thousand dancing reflections spun across the shattered roof. People came to their feet, shocked, backing up…

As a huge, dark shape crunched to the floor amid a smash of fallen shards.

Instantly, reflexively, Augusta went for her bolter, but her gauntlet came back empty. Her heart pounding, she was on her feet, turning, drawing the small fleur-de-lys punch-dagger from the front of her armour.

Around her, her sisters were doing the same, each woman dropping to a guarded crouch.

In the centre of the nave, a colossal, savage monster bared huge teeth at the fleeing congregation.

The people were shrieking, now, gathering their robes and their families and scrambling out of the way. Panicking and shoving, they tumbled from its impact like ripples.

By the Light! Augusta stared at it, her hand tightening on her blade. *What is that?*

It was huge, pure savagery, and far bigger than the Sisters; its carapace was a glitter of spine-spiked darkness in the now brilliant rainbow light. It crouched, its tail lashing, whipping its head this way and that as it watched the fleeing, shrieking people.

The hymn had tumbled from the air like a broken thing. In the pulpit, the deacon raged, leaning down to rant like fanatic. *'This is the house of the Emperor! There will be no defilement here!'*

He rounded on the Sisters, blazing zeal and fury, but Veradis was already moving.

'Squad,' she snapped into the vox. 'With me, by twos, watch each other's backs. Leona, get to the vestibule and secure the heavy bolter.' Aloud, she roared, *'Get out of the way!'*

The people, already scrabbling, had no need to be told. As the Sisters closed ranks and began to move, the crowd was stumbling over the seating, tripping and crunching over the fallen glassaic. The braver amongst them had been trying to build some sort of hasty barricade, but it was a pitiful attempt – the thing's claws were as long as a Sister's forearm and they lashed a lethal left-right, sending pews and bodies flying.

Snarling and screaming echoed loudly, the noises carrying as perfectly as the words of the hymn had done.

'Sisters!' Veradis barked the order aloud. *'On the double!'*

They broke into a run, their metal feet clanging a challenge. Each woman had her punch-dagger in her grip; in the lead, Veradis was using her free hand to pull the slower or less wary people clean out of her way.

The Litany came from her like pure, cold outrage.

From the lightning and the tempest!

The creature did not care. It was a boil of motion, a cyclone of violence. Its speed was terrifying. It was a harbinger of death, its tail like a whip, its claws ripping through flesh and stone alike. In a blur of speed, its huge maw bit at a fleeing dignitary. The man's headless body ran another full step before it fell forwards, its ringed hands outstretched. Blood pooled from the neck.

The creature pounced again, picking up a robed woman and tearing her clean in half.

Shocked, horrified, her gorge rising with a toxic alloy of fury and nausea, Augusta almost skidded; she had to force herself to keep running, to maintain the Litany's defiant song. The people were almost all out of the way now, but the creature was already flanked by piles of flung bodies, some of them only injured, desperate and struggling. Ignoring them, focused now on the Sisters, it slashed through the nearest heap and jumped on a fallen pew, all spine and spike and tail, a knot of shoulders and claws. Its shining head turned towards Veradis and it extended a long tongue, tasting the air.

For a split second, Augusta wondered if it was grinning at them.

But this was no time for such whimsical nonsense.

Our Emperor, deliver us!

The floor was slick with scarlet; it steamed in the bright, crystal light, and wreathed the monster like an aura.

'Xenos.' Veradis' snarl didn't even sound surprised. 'We do not fear you, creature.'

The thing tilted its head at her, almost as if it understood.

From the pulpit, the deacon was still roaring: 'Defiler! Slay it, Sister Superior, in the Emperor's name!'

The creature leapt. Barehanded, bereft of both bolter and chainsword, Veradis did not hesitate. Fearless, she met it head-on, catching it as it leapt, and throwing it over and past her. It landed on its back, kicked frantically for a moment, and then righted itself.

It spun snarling, lowering its head at them.

'Go, get out!' Behind Augusta, Sister Lucienne was ushering the last of the people, pushing them towards the two side doors that led back out to the cloisters, and to the high, tight walls of the valley. Horrified, their faces etched in terror and sickness, streaked by blood and tears, they followed her directions, pulling each other away.

One of them, a young man barely older than Lucienne herself, clutched at her and said, 'Why? What did we do to merit such punishment?'

'This is not punishment,' she told him, her tone livid with suppressed outrage. 'This is an abomination. And it will be purged!'

He nodded, though his eyes were as much glass as the great building itself.

'Run!' she told him.

But Augusta had reached the fight.

The thing was upright, all four arms mantled over its head; it was leering down at Veradis, its horrific teeth still bared.

Augusta looked up at it, gauging its weapons, its weak points, its potential attacks. Images lashed at her, memories of the schola's lessons – but she could never have guessed that such a beast would be this cold, this utterly pure and focused.

And so *fast!*

Snarling, it lunged at Veradis with each set of massive claws, left and right, one after the other. They tore through her armour as if it were only grox-leather, ripping huge parallel dents in her breastplate and pauldrons; but the Sister Superior was indomitable, she did not falter or fall back. Still singing, rage and battle and defiance, she slashed with the dagger, a sideways lunge aimed at the joints in the beast's armoured belly.

But it moved like a blur, too swift to see.

Another set of claws slammed down on Veradis' shoulder, sending her spinning to the floor.

From plague, temptation and war!

Over the vox, Sister Pia barked, 'Spread out!'

The Sisters separated to surround the beast, coming at it from all sides. Its head twitched to and fro as it followed them, its tail lashed at their boots.

Our Emperor, deliver us!

The thing hissed at them.

And then, almost faster than they could see, it exploded into motion.

It was like fighting a tornado.

Too strong, too many arms, too fast to follow. Glassaic crunched beneath their boots, the rainbow light still spreading over their heads – but they had no time to look up.

One savage tail-lash took Lucienne off her feet, dropping her with a thunderous crash. A slash of claws sent Pia reeling, her armour sliced like cloth. The thing's strength was enormous, its ferocity brutal. The Sisters came at it from every direction, but their daggers seemed to skitter off its carapace; it slashed and stuck at them, and their armour rent and buckled under blows too fast to follow. Pia lunged at its back, but it whipped around, lashing out with one huge arm to send her staggering back, slamming into the nearest pillar. As it did so, Augusta struck at its side but the thing's hard chitin turned the point of her small dagger. The blow skidded, doing no harm.

She swore under her breath, and kept singing.

From the scourge of the Kraken!

From the corner of her eye, she could see that Veradis was back on her feet, though the Sister Superior had not closed back into the melee. Instead, she had discarded her dagger and held her position, watching the monster, her eyes narrow.

But Augusta could not stop to consider this – the thing whirled again, its tail knocking Lucienne flying for a second time. Its gleaming, foot-long teeth snapped at Augusta's arm; its claws lashed hard at her cheek. She yanked her head backwards and it missed her, but only just. She felt the whack of wind as they passed within a whisper of her nose.

If those claws caught her, they would take her face clean off.

It followed the attack and leapt at her – one slash, and another, and another, each one slamming into her and making her reel. She raised her arms to defend herself; her ears rang with song and fury. The Sisters followed it, pressing in close, stopping the thing moving, preventing it getting away. Blades struck at it from all sides, but its arms were fast, knocking them aside, sending the squad skidding backwards, their boots screeching on the stone. Without their bolters they had nothing that could touch it, and it was almost as if it knew. Amid its chilling focus, it seemed to be mocking them.

The deacon was still shouting from the pulpit, almost frothing at the mouth. Augusta lunged again, hard enough to stick her dagger point first into the beast's chest, but she lost her grip on the weapon as the monster whipped around. It turned too fast, taking the blade with it.

It snapped its teeth downwards at Pia's shoulder. For an instant, they crunched on ceramite, then Pia dropped to one knee and they slammed shut on air.

An instant later, Pia was back on her feet, her song twisting into a vicious, stubborn curse.

How could they stop this thing?

Panic was beginning to swell in Augusta's chest, though she would not succumb to it. How was this accursed thing even here?

Our Emperor, deliver us!

Beside her, Sister Pia raised the Litany once more. Clenching her gauntleted fists, Augusta closed again – but the beast barely even noticed. She might as well have been hitting the rock wall.

Then she saw her dagger, sticking from the thing's carapace. She made a grab for it, catching it and pulling it free.

Snarling, the beast whirled again. It hurled itself straight at her, its teeth bared, all four sets of claws coming for her chest. She threw up her arms in a cross block, felt the force of its impact through her elbows and shoulders, but she could not stand in its path, it was just too big. It smashed her to the floor, hurled itself past her and spun, turning back to the squad.

Another claw strike, a reaching left-right, and Sister Lucienne was falling, dark fluid staining the rips in her armour.

In His name! You will not do this!

Sister Emlyn leaned down and pulled Lucienne out of the way. Augusta kept striking, slashing, singing, distracting its attention.

How was it here? Had it always been here, surviving a thousand years from the previous battle? Had it been waiting, hiding somewhere outside this valley, just waiting for the…

Waiting for the light.

By the Throne!

The realisation struck her like a claw. Of course. It had been here all along, dormant, curled about itself in patient stillness, and the very conjunction that had brought life and light back to the cathedral – it had touched this thing, and roused it from its stasis.

Had brought it, leaping, and tearing, and hungry, into their midst.

Furious at its sacrilege, at its presence, at the memory of their Sisters that it had now despoiled, she threw herself at it. The squad moved with her, all of them closing once more about its flanks.

Over the vox, Veradis barked, 'Pia! *Now!*'

'Aye.' Her movements absolutely precise, Sister Pia grabbed the thing's extended tongue in one red-gauntleted hand. With a single, deft twist, she wrapped it around her wrist and brought its head down into her raised knee. There was a sharp crack, and its teeth closed on its own flesh.

Gore and squeals spurted from its mouth.

The Sister Superior roared, *'Leona! Fire!'*

From the far side of the now empty nave came the unmistakeable metallic cocking of the heavy bolter.

Veradis bawled, *'Down!'*

Augusta was moving, even as the Sister Superior wrapped an arm over her shoulders.

They crashed to the floor together.

The thunder was tremendous.

A full directed burst roared across the air. It cut though the pews, through the glassaic, and though the chitinous hide of the monster. The heavy bolter boomed its song of death, the noise immense. White-light panes shattered as rounds blew them outwards.

On the floor, face down on the glass-pebbled stone and half-crushed by Veradis' weight, Augusta couldn't see – but she could hear the creature scream in pain and fury, hear it thrashing as the rounds bit home. She heard its claws as it turned and ran, hurling itself bodily across the nave and towards Leona.

But Leona was still firing, steady and unintimidated. Her voice over the vox sang defiance.

Bring them only death!

Veradis shifted, was back on her feet. Augusta, too, started to stand up. From out of the corner of her eye she saw Lucienne, bloodied and battered and rolling back to her knees; saw Sister Emlyn, shaking herself, but moving.

Saw Sister Pia, lying curled on her side, blood sliding from her mouth, her armour smoking from multiple holes.

What?

Only one weapon made scars like those.

In the vestibule, the heavy bolter was still firing, its muzzle tracking the incoming beast. Leona had stepped back, given herself the full range and rate of fire; the monster was spraying thick, dark blood, shuddering under the onslaught, but it was still coming, climbing over the pews as if nothing could bring it down...

But Sister Pia lay still.

Facing the monster, Leona was still singing, her voice rising as the thing closed on her; she was back to the wall, now, had nowhere else to go. The deacon was still in his pulpit, still bellowing orders...

But Sister Pia lay still.

Stunned, Augusta watched as the heavy bolter started to cough. Leona swore, knowing she was down to her last few rounds, but she still kept firing as the monster skidded the last pews out of its way...

But Sister Pia lay still.

'By the Throne.' Over the vox, Leona cursed aloud. 'You'll go down if I have to beat you to death myself!' With a final rumble, the heavy bolter clacked loudly, and stopped.

The silence was suddenly tremendous, echoing in Augusta's ears.

But – finally – the monster was down. Barely two feet from where Leona was standing, it had crashed to the floor, its chitin cracked, its arms splayed, its body coated in its own fluids.

Its rear claws kicked once, and were still.

The deacon cried, 'Yes! Thank the Emperor!' but they did not look up at him.

Because Sister Pia lay still.

Calmly, Veradis said, 'Be sure, Leona.' Her voice was full – victory, sacrifice, sadness.

'Aye.' Boots sounded as Leona walked over to the thing, her heavy bolter still in her hands. The single shot to its skull rang out like the last line of a hymn.

'One round left in the chamber,' she said, quietly. Like the presence of their small, hidden daggers, no one needed to ask her why it was there.

But Sister Pia had not moved.

'Her death was not your doing,' Veradis said, one hand on Sister Leona's shoulder. 'It was a risk, and Sister Pia understood. We fight as the Emperor decrees.'

Leona's lean, lined face was stone hard, her chin lifted, as if she kept any emotions to herself.

At their feet, Sister Pia lay crumpled upon a bed of shattered glassaic, her black hair spread out, her expression frozen in the bared-teeth determination of pure combat. All down one side of her armour there were the telltale holes made by the heavy bolter.

Her courage had enabled them to injure the beast, and had forced it to react to the weapon, rather than killing the rest of the squad.

They – and the people – owed Pia their lives.

Augusta knew that sacrifice was the greatest honour to which a Sister could aspire, but she had never before seen it in the field, and she stayed silent, looking down at Pia's fallen form.

She seemed so small.

Veradis, however, was glaring at the deacon.

'You declared this location secure.' It was not a question.

The deacon had not lost his pompousness. He was a small, round man, and he puffed himself up before answering: 'How was I to know that your long-lost Sisters had not purged this moon completely? The failure is yours, Sororitas, not mine.'

Veradis eyed him as if she would break him in half, but said nothing. Instead, she said to the squad, 'Retrieve your weapons. I want every doorway guarded. There will be no service here until we deploy fully through the tunnels and ensure that there are no further,' she eyed the deacon, 'surprises.'

'Aye.' The Sisters did as they were ordered, but Augusta paused, Lucienne beside her.

'Sister Superior, a question, if I may?'

'Of course.'

'This is the house of the Emperor. We do not bear weapons–'

'You're asking why He did not defend us, Sister?' Veradis' tone held a certain wry amusement, perhaps at Augusta's inexperience. 'As the Scriptures would have us believe?'

Feeling the gazes of both deacon and Sister Superior, Augusta looked down at Pia's fallen body and nodded. 'Is that so foolish a question? How could such a creature be permitted…'

The deacon glowered at her. 'He does not come when you call, Sister…'

Veradis held up a hand, and he quietened, tapping his foot.

The Sister Superior said, 'The xenos knows no respect. And what are we but His defence? What are we but His weapons? Twice now, you have faced foes without your bolter, and twice, you have triumphed. This is a test of our faith and mettle, like any other, wherever it may take place.'

Augusta stole a look at the now shining window, remembering the stone Sisters that stood at the doorway. 'Our Sisters did not fail?'

'That is not for us to judge.' Veradis shot the deacon a sideways glare. 'We only do as we are bid, by His presence. You may grieve for Sister Pia, in the proper time, but you must first follow your orders.'

'Yes, Sister.'

'Have no fear,' Veradis said, her face softening to a rare smile. 'Sister Pia stands before the Throne, and she does so in honour, her life given in battle.' She glanced at the fallen creature, drawing Augusta's attention and making the point. 'We can only pray that, one day, we will be so blessed.'

YOUR
NEXT READ

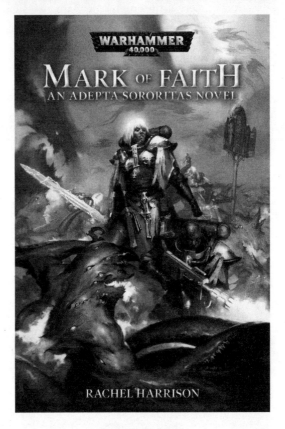

MARK OF FAITH
by Rachel Harrison

In the wake of the war for Ophelia VII, Battle-Sister Evangeline
of the Order of Our Martyred Lady embarks on a crusade into the darkness
that lies beyond the Great Rift, seeking vengeance and revelation, but surviving
the journey will only be the first and most simple test of her faith.

YOUR
NEXT READ

CELESTINE: THE LIVING SAINT
by Andy Clark

Saint Celestine is one of the greatest heroes of the Dark Imperium,
an immortal warrior who returns time and again, even when struck
down by a foe, like the Emperor's avenging angel. But what happens when
she dies and comes back? Prepare to find out.

TO SPEAK AS ONE

GUY HALEY

The **Adeptus Mechanicus** are the mysterious and
insular tech-savants of the Imperium of Man.
Obsessed with the sanctity and preservation of the
machine, theirs is a dogma of stagnation. But there
is one among them who still pursues innovation:
Archmagos Dominus Belisarius Cawl.

In *To Speak as One*, Cawl sends his most trusted
acolytes to an Inquisitorial fortress to acquire a xenos
specimen. But when the Inquisition refuse to hand
over their prisoner, the agents of Cawl are forced to
take drastic action.

'What is this?' Inquisitor Cehen-qui unrolled the message scrip and pulled it through his hands. Paper rasped on his soft gloves. As he read the message again, his expression grew more incredulous. His fine brows narrowed. His glossy black topknot fell from his shoulder and laid itself across his shining white tunic.

Four of Cehen-qui's most important staff attended the inquisitor. The first was a small, bald figure of non-specific gender. Callow had no title. Factotum was the closest word for what Callow did. Callow fetched, Callow carried, Callow smoothed away the irritations of the day. Cehen-qui expected little more than that, so it was Callow's great misfortune that they'd been given the message to deliver.

Callow blinked nervously. 'It is an astropathic message, my lord, from the Archmagos Dominus Belisarius Cawl.'

'I can see that, you fool,' Cehen-qui snapped. 'And stop cringing.' He reread the message for the third time before screwing it up and throwing it down onto the deck of the station command centre. The paper rolled in and out of shadow as it passed under broken lumens, then fell down a hole left by a missing plate. 'Who by the Sacred Throne of Terra does he think he is?' He straightened his very white gloves.

'My lord?' said Callow, in some distress.

The second attendant, a tall man of late middle years, at least in appearance, shifted the heavy book he carried and laid a calming hand on Callow's arm. He shook his head. Don't say anything else, he meant to convey. Callow didn't notice.

'Who does he think he is to demand our prisoner?' Cehen-qui continued. 'Who does he think he is that he can command the Emperor's Inquisition, the *Inquisition*,' he growled, 'to do his bidding like that?' He clapped his hands together. His gloves muffled the sound. The gold braid on his jacket swung violently. Callow flinched.

'What do you think of him, Gamma?' Cehen-qui asked his third attendant.

Gamma was an adept of the Machine Cult. He wore black robes fringed with golden cog teeth. His augmetics, most obvious of which were a pair of heavy industrial claws poised over his shoulders, were plated gold to match. His armour was a very deep red, with the smallest accents of cream. His forge world was so obscure that few would have recognised the colours. He liked it that way.

His full name was Frenk Gamma-87-Nu-3-Psi. Cehen-qui never used it.

'He is a heretic and a blasphemer,' said Gamma firmly. 'He pollutes the Omnissiah's work with his meddling. He makes free use of xenos technology, and,' his voice thickened with disgust, 'he conducts original research. We cannot give him the aeldari. Who knows what perfidious use he will put it to.'

The second servant, whose name was Valeneez, sucked in a breath between unevenly spaced teeth. He had been in Cehen-qui's service longer than any of the others.

'I disagree, Frenk, and respectively with you, my lord. His communique bears the seal of Lord Regent Roboute Guilliman himself. Technically, there is a case to be made for the legitimacy of the archmagos dominus' request.'

'Cawl is a puppet of the usurper,' said Gamma. His bloodshot eyes glared above his respirator mask. His augmetics made an angry clicking.

'Gamma has a point,' Cehen-qui said. 'While I believe the returned primarch to be true to the cause of human survival, Lord Guilliman has no more right to command the Inquisition than Cawl has. To whom is the Inquisition answerable, Valeneez?'

'The Emperor Himself,' said Valeneez deferentially. 'But the Lord Guilliman is the Emperor's son, and His appointed deputy, ruling in His stead, so therefore it is reasonable to–'

'Appointed by whom?' said Cehen-qui loudly. The few crew on the command deck tried very hard not to listen in. 'We only have his word that the Emperor gave him this role. Of course,' he said, tugging his coat into place, 'his right to command the armies of the Imperium in defence and reconquest of the Emperor's domains is indisputable, but command the Inquisition, whose operations he has actively worked against? Never. The primarch's authority in this matter will not stand. The prisoner remains where he is, imprisoned, until the excrutiators from Cypra Largo arrive.'

'If we assume you are right…' began Valeneez.

'I am right!' Cehen-qui shouted. He tapped at the Inquis-itorial badge pinned to his sash. 'This says I am right.'

'Well then, my lord, given that you are right,' Valeneez said, 'we are not in a good position. This station has not been occupied for some time, most of its systems are offline, we've multiple blind spots, not enough storm troopers to patrol it, and a barely functioning weapons grid. If we stay here we are leaving ourselves open to attack. We should take the prisoner elsewhere.'

'Maybe,' said Cehen-qui, becoming thoughtful. He looked out of the long slit window overlooking the station's three prongs. The orange gas giant it orbited filled much of the view beyond. 'Cawl is a maverick. If we do not give him what he wants, then the danger is that he will attempt to take it from us. However, we cannot change the rendezvous. None of our messages to Inquisitor-Castellan DelGrani have got through the warp storms. We must assume that the ship is still coming, and will be here within the week. The prisoner cannot get free. He must be presented to excrutia-tors with the appropriate abilities as soon as is possible. His own kind will be looking for him. We must be ready to stop Cawl. I will not have the prisoner's knowledge fall into the hands of the Adeptus Mechanicus. We might be exposed, but we are not without our own weapons now, are we, ShoShonai?'

He turned to his fourth servant. She stayed off the few spots where the deck was properly illuminated. She stood totally silent, face downcast.

'ShoShonai, I am speaking to you,' Cehen-qui said. 'Are you ready?'

She lifted her head. Her face was shadowed by her hood. Silvered eyes shone in the dark. 'My lord,' she said with a voice of inhuman quality. The cloth of her robe moved disturbingly, as if a nest of serpents writhed beneath. 'We are ready.'

'My lord!' one of Cehen-qui's minions called from the etheric monitoring station.

'What is it?' Cehen-qui said.

'I have a warp signature on the edge of the system.'

'Any indication of provenance?'

'Datapulse signum identifier will not reach us for another four hours, my lord, but etheric waveform patterning suggests a vessel of middling gravitic draught.'

'Well then,' said Cehen-qui briskly. 'They're here. To action stations, everyone. They shall take our prize over my dead body. If that happens, I'll make sure the rest of you die first.'

Otranti was a gas giant of a vivid shade of orange, with a fuzzy atmospheric boundary. It reminded Primus of a rare fruit he'd tried thousands of years ago, the albaricoque. It had been velvety and sweet. He had liked it.

He tried to remember if that had been one of the last things that had moved him.

The station was a bright dot against the equator, and growing fast.

'Interesting,' said Qvo-87.

'Interesting?' said Alpha Primus. His purple lips were downturned. Only the slight raise to his voice's pitch indicated he was, in fact, interested in what Qvo had to say. Even so, he sounded like he was on the cusp of crippling ennui.

'This facility is very poorly defended,' Qvo went on. A small forest of pistons lifted his command cradle up so that he could peer into a set of displays hidden behind rubber viewing visors, forcing Primus out of the way. The command deck of the *0-101-0* was too tight for the Space Marine. Qvo's command crew were bulky creatures, high-level magi possessing many extra limbs. None looked remotely human any more, and although Primus could feel the flickering of humanity within their metal bodies, his eyes insisted they were not people, but ugly idols to the Machine-God. They were creatures with steel souls.

Primus was the first to acknowledge he was as artificial as them himself, everything about him having been rewritten down to the genetic level. The big difference between he and they was that they had chosen to be the way they were. He most definitely had not. Thinking about it made his scars itch, and as much of Primus' skin was scar tissue, the experience was unpleasant, so he stopped thinking about it. He cleared his mind as easily as switching off a lumen. Blankness took the place of irksome thought, until Qvo started gabbling again.

'Interesting, interesting, interesting,' said Qvo. It was impossible to tell where the magos ended and the ship began. Primus had known all the iterations of Qvo. He still wasn't sure if he was a machine or not.

'You will not provoke more interest in me by repeating the word interesting,' said Primus. His voice was low and miserable as a leaden bell. 'You are irritatingly predictable.'

'I am, aren't I?' said Qvo brightly. 'I do wish that the Archmagos Dominus Belisarius Cawl had seen fit to give me a broader range of self-determinative logic patterning.' He gave Primus a mock-serious look. 'But that would break the lore.'

'I care not at all that your red-robed brethren would find you an abomination,' said Primus.

'Lucky me, I am unique,' said Qvo. He spoke distractedly,

flitting on hissing pistons between screens and interface ports. He hummed a few bars of an ancient tune, and stopped. Primus lifted his heavy head. Qvo tapped away on a brass claviboard with four of his hands. Green logic code scrolled down a wafer-thin glass screen.

'Are you going to give me the appropriate data to accomplish my mission or not?' said Primus.

'I am hoping it will not come to that.'

'When our dear master is involved, it always comes to *that*,' said Primus. 'We are here. I shall be fighting. It is never any other way. Why this place? We are asking for trouble.'

'Ahem.' Qvo cleared his throat preparatory to speaking. The noise was entirely synthetic; only his head appeared to be organic, therefore he probably had no throat. If Primus was honest, he was mildly curious about what parts of Qvo were flesh and what were not, but asking the infuriating pseudo-magos would have felt like a defeat, so he never did. That, like so much else, annoyed him.

'Because this station has the exact combination of circumstances that will allow us to secure what we need without anybody finding out about it, that's why,' said Qvo. 'It is a genius plan on the part of the archmagos.'

Qvo pulled a number of levers. A high-detail hololith in far-spectrum colours sprang up in the middle of the bridge. Primus ducked a hissing pipe to get a better view, coming to stand to the front of Qvo.

Primus' eyes possessed the spectral spread to see the hololith. Qvo knew that, Primus knew Qvo knew; presenting the diagram in such exotic shades was his way of making some kind of point. Qvo always seemed to be making a point. Primus was often at a loss as to why, or indeed what the point was.

The station had an unusual configuration: a tall cylinder

topped with a wide disc with three long, boxy limbs point-ing towards the gas giant, the spread of which was contained within forty-five degrees. It looked like a primitive wheel with all but three of the spokes broken off. The rear of the hub had a bulge fringed by the piers of a modest dock. A single ship was berthed there: swift, deadly and highly tech-nologically advanced, with a superstructure surmounted by a gilded Inquisitorial 'I' surrounded by lightning bolts.

'The station is an ex-void dungeon,' Qvo said. 'Run by the Ordo Xenos to imprison and interrogate xenos captives. The number of different types of containment unit it boasts is quite fascinating, with facilities to hold life forms of extreme sorts – high-pressure beings, high-G, non-water-based life, non-carbon-based life, gaseous entities, beings both trans-dimensional and temporally unstable, warp sensitive and warp native, even–'

Primus' fist clenched involuntarily. 'It's a prison for aliens. I understand. Please continue.'

'It *was* a prison for aliens,' corrected Qvo. 'It has not been in use for several hundred years.' The hololith zoomed out until it incorporated a tri-D light model of Otranti. Qvo depressed a button with an unnecessary flourish. A decay-ing orbital track was projected onto the image. 'Behold! A decaying orbital track,' he said, also unnecessarily, as Pri-mus could clearly see it for what it was. 'It looks to me like this moon here...' More images flickered on. A small moon was outlined in a shade only visible to creatures with infra-red sensitive vision. '...was hit by an asteroid – you see the debris about it?'

Primus did see. It was blindingly obvious. Qvo was begin-ning to give him a headache.

'The moon's orbit is not where it should be. Its gravitic

interference has perturbed the facility's orbit. Cosmic billiards, if you will.'

'What's billiards?'

'Never mind,' said Qvo.

'It must not have been very important, or the Ordo Xenos would have corrected the fault,' said Primus.

'Or,' said Qvo smugly, 'it is very, very important. Bringing out the kind of vessel required to pull the station back into a stable anchor, or a construction barge to fit it with engines to allow it to do the task itself, would require the requisition of a great deal of men and materials. Even were the workforce liquidated in its entirety, the news would get out. The station's secrecy would be compromised. Did you not think of that?'

'Politicking and secrecy are the methods of cowards,' said Primus. 'They are not my way.'

'You're more of a direct mass strike sort of man, aren't you?' said Qvo. 'I wonder what they were doing there? I wonder why they have come here now?'

'The prisoner,' said Primus.

'Yes, but if they wanted only to interrogate it, then why not take it to another facility? Why this one? Because if there is one thing more secret than a top-secret facility, it's an abandoned top-secret facility. Something's afoot here. How exciting!'

'You are like a child.'

'A child's curiosity and enthusiasm gives the energy of a star to any inquiry,' said Qvo. 'You must learn to enjoy your work.'

'I enjoy nothing,' said Primus.

'That's not true. I know you like killing people.'

'Like is too strong,' said Primus. 'Combat alleviates boredom. That is all.'

The station in the oculus proper had grown in size from a glint to a round of light. Primus stiffened, and took a few steps forward towards the armourglass.

'What is it?' asked Qvo.

'There's a psyker on the station, a powerful one,' said Primus.

'You can handle that,' said Qvo. 'The archmagos made you powerful too.'

'This one feels different,' said Primus.

'How?'

'There is more than one voice to the mind.'

Qvo disengaged himself from some of the cables. Not many, only enough to allow him to be carried forward on tentacles of banded steel until he was beside Primus; otherwise he remained joined to the ship as thoroughly as if he were a component. He adjusted his elevation so his face was level with Primus'.

'Can you be more specific?' asked Qvo.

'No.' Primus felt the smallest twitch at the corner of his mouth.

'Are you smiling? Are you well?' said Qvo, with genuine concern.

Primus wasn't listening. The being on the station knew he was coming. A brightness in his witch-sight flashed, then went dark. He was being actively blocked.

'This could almost be interesting,' Primus said.

'We are being hailed by the approaching vessel,' reported one of Cehen-qui's followers. The inquisitor did not have anything as specialised as a vox-master. All his troops were expected to be flexible and well versed in multiple arts. All but his four principal servants – Callow, Valeneez, Gamma and ShoShonai – were dressed in identical uniforms, as fuliginous as Cehen-qui's robes were white.

'Make them wait,' said Cehen-qui.

'As you command, inquisitor.'

'Gamma, give me a deep augur scan, if you would.'

Gamma's industrial claws reached down and ripped out a dusty chair so he could get close to the augury. His supplemental limbs jabbed at buttons and levers, his mechadendrites plugged into multiple input jacks, so that he was working three stations simultaneously.

'The ship is that of Cawl's principal lackey, Qvo-87,' Gamma said. 'He styles himself a magos, but he is nothing of the kind.'

'Meaning?' said Cehen-qui.

'Cawl has many blasphemous creations in his service. Things that think and act like men, but are not. He has only avoided censure because his followers are so many, and Cawl is cunning, always sure to make his things so they almost adhere to the principles of the lore. Qvo-87 is a clone, in a way. As such, it could be argued that he falls within the lore laid out in the Warnings. But there are others that say he is not a clone, not even within a very wide margin of error.'

'You are one of those.'

'I am. They call Cawl the Prime Conduit of the Omnissiah. I call him blasphemer.'

'That's all fascinating, Gamma,' said Cehen-qui dismissively. He stretched out his back. It cracked. 'Do they have their weapons powered?'

'Not yet. All weapons are retracted and inactive, all defensive and offensive subsystems unengaged, but they could be hiding their intentions.'

'Are they?'

'They have allowed a full augur sweep. No interference on the macro or micro levels.' Gamma sounded disappointed.

'In that case, we shall keep this cordial, for the time being. Be alert to any attempt to infiltrate the base while we are communicating.'

'I am receiving another hail from the ship, lord inquisitor.'

'They can wait a little longer,' said Cehen-qui. 'They will not consider leaving empty-handed. If Cawl is true to his reputation he will take the aeldari witch. Xenic guard to battle stations. Prime defensive weapons batteries. Activate internal defences.'

Cehen-qui pointed at the comms station. 'Prepare to open channels in three minutes. Let them see the weaponry of this station awake, then we shall find out how brave they are.'

'Only a fraction of it is operable,' warned Valeneez.

'It will be enough,' said Cehen-qui.

Primus paced the short distance between the *0-101-0*'s principal hololith pit and Qvo's command cradle.

'They are stalling for time.'

'They are,' said Qvo, busy with some esoteric task.

'They are not answering our requests for contact,' said Primus.

'They are not.' Qvo moved from one bank of instruments to another.

'They will be powering their weaponry,' said Primus.

'They are powering their weaponry,' said Qvo distractedly.

'Then what are we waiting for?' said Primus.

'Really, Primus,' said Qvo. 'You may prefer frontal assault, but sometimes it pays to be cunning.' He blurted a jarring stream of binaric at one of his followers. The priest, a box with a fringe of flailing metal extrusions, responded in kind. 'Of course they are stalling for time. Of course they are making a show of strength. We shall show ourselves to be unconcerned. Meanwhile, I am making use of the time to infiltrate their cogitator systems with subversion code script that will make your task a great deal easier.' Qvo's voice rose in exasperation. 'So if you please, allow me to concentrate. Thank you.'

'I should be going,' said Primus.

'Yes.' Qvo peered at a screen. He frowned. 'That's looking about right.' He pushed a plunger down with his humanoid hand while a dozen other stick-thin metal limbs jabbed at the keys of an input device. 'Very good. You can go. They will not see you. I have made sure of that.'

'I have been alive for millennia,' said Primus. 'I am tormented by such boredom and despair, I sometimes cannot think, but I do not wish to end my time by being obliterated in the void because of one of your mistakes.'

'There shall be none,' said Qvo.

'Good,' said Primus. 'Because if there is, I shall find a way to exact revenge upon you.'

The big Space Marine struggled around the data-posts and draping cables of the command sphere, and exited.

Qvo rolled his eyes and continued with his work.

'Magos Qvo.' Adept-Dialogus Kurubik addressed his lord from his bronze speaking trumpet. 'The Inquisitorial facility has indicated that they are ready to begin communications.'

'Aha!' said Qvo. 'Excellent. Let's have him then, this inquisitor who likes to keep the servant of the Prime Conduit waiting.'

The hololith blinked. A figure appeared in full over the pit. The hololith was presented solely in shades of orange, but Qvo's internal mechanisms provided life-true colours to the projection. The inquisitor wore a startling white jacket and gloves, blue trousers piped with grey, high boots, a lot of brocade and many metal badges. His hair was meticulously arranged. He was handsome, with a single scar on his cheek that Qvo suspected had been deliberately left in place for effect.

'Greetings!' Qvo said loudly. 'I am Qvo-87, servant and confidant of the Archmagos Dominus Belisarius Cawl, Prime Conduit of the Omnissiah and foremost practitioner of the Machine-God's mysteries. I believe you have something that my lord desires.'

The inquisitor gave no name. *'He shall not have it. The prisoner you desire is in the custody of the Ordo Xenos.'*

'Then we find ourselves at odds,' said Qvo.

Primus passed across the gap between the *0-101-0* and the dungeon. His armour spirit broadcast anti-augur obfuscation noise. He had his reactor and systems down at the lowest possible settings. Qvo's infiltration codes kept the station's augurs from picking up this fleck of man-shaped metal, so Primus was to all intents invisible to machine senses, and so small and insignificant against the great emptiness of the void it was unlikely any human eye would see him either.

With Primus' radiation vents shut to keep his thermal profile low, there was nowhere for his reactor's energy to go but inward. An internal thermometer rose steadily in his retinal display. His altered physiology had a broader thermal tolerance than a standard human's, but he was not immune. A chronograph ticked down above the gauge. Fifteen minutes, eleven seconds until internal temperature became dangerous. He was already perspiring profusely. Sweat stung his eyes and pooled around the soft seal collar of his undersuit.

He couldn't let that distract him. The psyker on board the ship was looking for him. He felt its attention sweep across the stars like a searchlight. He must maintain a perfect psychic cloak at all times, for even when the psyker's inner eye was looking elsewhere, his unshielded soul would burn bright, drawing them inevitably to him.

The psyker was looking everywhere for him. The inquisition were not stupid. They suspected infiltration.

'But so it must play out,' Primus said to himself.

The station loomed ahead. Primus had shoved himself off with his feet. His aim had to be perfect. He could not risk a burst from his stabiliser jets to correct his course. If that became necessary, he would have to choose between discovery or overshooting the station completely.

He was near enough now to see automated guns tracking back and forth. Their single red targeting eyes passed over him, not seeing him. He breathed shallowly nonetheless, although the idea of them hearing him was ludicrous.

He had no idea why he was so tense. Qvo was irritating him more than usual. Being with Qvo was not overly different to being with the magos himself. There seemed to be no escape from Cawl.

He lost sight of the shape of the station. It became a huge metal cliff adorned with blindfolded angels and windowless arches. The speed of his approach appeared to increase the closer he got, now he had a reference point for his progress. He lifted his feet and activated his maglocks. His feet hit the hull hard. He was thrown forward, and had to swing back his arms violently to counteract his momentum.

Primus checked his equipment was still attached to his belt, then stepped around.

The hull there was two hundred feet tall. Dozens of decks were contained inside. He had a long search ahead of him. He called up the station's cartolith. The nearest airlock was thirty yards above.

Feet locking jerkily to the plasteel hull, Primus made his way upwards.

'You must give up the prisoner,' said Qvo, for the sixteenth time. He had tried every modulation of the human voice he could. None had worked. Nor had logic, or emotive pleas. Inquisitor Cehen-qui remained immovable.

'*The prisoner is a high-ranking xenos of a power in active opposition to the Imperium of Man,*' said Cehen-qui. '*It falls within the purview of our ordo to interrogate him and decide upon the correct usage of any information that might be yielded from that interrogation. You cannot have the alien, not under any circumstances.*'

'I will not leave until you have given it up,' said Qvo.

'*If you do not, we will be forced to regard your trespass in our orbit as an aggressive act. We will open fire upon your ship.*'

'That would constitute a direct act of war against the Adeptus Mechanicus,' countered Qvo. 'There will be severe repercussions.'

'*If anyone ever gets to hear about it,*' said Cehen-qui. '*And you will be dead whether they do or not.*'

'I wouldn't be so sure about either of those things,' said Qvo. 'I am the servant of the Prime Conduit of the Omn–'

'*By the Emperor, the lord of all the galaxy, you are a tedious creature,*' said Cehen-qui.

'Perhaps we should resolve this face-to-face?' said

Qvo. 'It may go more quickly. If I could but present the lord primarch's documents to you so you may see their authenticity...'

'You must think I was born outside the Emperor's Light if you think I'll fall for that trick. Of course I will not agree to meeting you. Either on your ship or on mine. You are going to leave, immediately. You have two minutes to power your drives and move off, or we will open fire.'

The hololith blinked out.

Qvo sighed. 'Tricky, tricky, tricky.'

'You can't have thought it would be easy, magos,' said Loseol-Azeriph, the *0-101-0*'s arch-belligerus.

'No, no, I didn't,' said Qvo. 'It would be quite dull if it were.'

'Then your orders?'

'Bring the shields up. Ignite our main drive, take us out from the station. We'll make them think we're on our way.'

'Then we can open fire?' said Loseol-Azeriph with relish.

'Then we can open fire. Power our weapons as soon as the void shields are active. Secure targeting locks on all their active weapons batteries. Come about, and attack.'

Primus crept as well as an eight foot tall warrior in power armour could through the station. His suit was of the Intercessor type, tooled for direct confrontation rather than stealth, yet he moved quietly enough. The sigh of his motors and muffled tread did little to penetrate the dungeon's sepulchral silence. It was a quiet that went beyond the material realm. A heavy weight of suffering smothered all sensation. The pain and sorrow of the creatures once incarcerated there steeped the fabric of the place. Primus passed along many corridors, each one lined with dozens of cells. He peered into a few through the viewing slots. A significant proportion contained age-yellowed bones. The variety of beings was astonishing. But though the creatures were different, their lingering imprints were the same; each and every cell shared the same psychic taint of despair. These last occupants had been left to their fate when the dungeon was abandoned. Primus was so old his emotions were worn away to stubs, but the atmosphere of the place got to him even so.

The tremor of a weapons strike on shields made him pause. Qvo had begun his attack. Further strikes followed. He was going to have to be quick.

He dropped his psychic mask a moment to let out his mind, searching for the greatest concentration of souls. He found two, one up in the hub, the other not far distant. At the second he felt the strange psyker's presence, and it felt him.

Throwing off stealth, Primus hurried towards his target.

Loseol-Azeriph's mechadendrites clicked in and out of interface sockets all over his vast, cathedral-organ operations station. Lines of data text were reflected in each of his six eyes.

'I regret to inform you, Magos Qvo, that although their void shields have collapsed, the Ordo Xenos dungeon will withstand our weapons for several days.'

The *0-101-0* trembled under return fire. Void discharge lit up the command sphere in violent purples and greens.

'Now now, we don't want to blow it up,' said Qvo. 'You're too eager for destruction.'

'Forgive me, my lord,' said Loseol-Azeriph. 'One loses oneself in one's specialisation.'

'Praise the Machine-God that it is so,' said Qvo. 'Current status of enemy weapons, if you please, Loseol.'

'Eighty per cent reduction in destructive capability. Their guns outnumber ours, but they are very much outmatched by our targeting speed and prioritisation protocols. I have taken the liberty of removing their voidward weaponry first. They are toothless.'

'You are enjoying yourself.'

'I shall answer affirmatively to that,' said Loseol-Azeriph gladly.

'Then might we approach?' asked Qvo.

'In complete safety.'

'Engage main engines, quarter speed. Bring us back towards the dungeon, and prepare to launch boarding craft.'

<Polite interrogative (request insolence amelioration): Why?> canted the box of wires and nerves in fluid Qvo called Sixer.

'I concur with the magos-transmechanic. Quarter speed is insufficient for a ramming run,' said Loseol-Azeriph. 'The tonnage of the station is in excess of ours by a factor of three hundred. We shall die, broken against their higher mass.'

'We're not going to ram it, Loseol,' said Qvo with a gleeful grin. 'We're just going to give it a little *push*. The dungeon is falling into the world it orbits anyway. Let's help it along. That will keep their eyes off the ball, as I believe people used to say a very long time ago.'

The station was under heavy attack, and so Primus approached his target openly. Light bursts from hotshot lasguns blasted at him down the narrow approach way. Their overpowered beams punched smoking craters into his grey ceramite, but failed to penetrate. He replied with his bolter, cutting down three men in a single burst. He walked into the crossroads they were covering, and came into view of a tripod-mounted heavy bolter sheltered behind a barricade of rusted boxes to his right. His battleplate and his psychic senses warned him before it opened up, and he stepped back as a swarm of large-calibre bolts screamed down the corridor.

He would save his psychic strength. Mundane methods of death were called for. He pulled out a frag grenade from his bandolier, flicked out the pin and tossed it around the corner, angling it perfectly so that it bounced from the wall and came down behind the barricade. As soon as it exploded, he strode forward. Shouts came from his left. Half a dozen men in heavy carapace were coming at him. Bolts from his gun drove them into cover. The magazine ran dry and he ejected it one-handed, raising the other hand to call upon the warp.

A barrier of purple fire roared across the corridor. The foremost troopers were caught and screamed as the uncanny flames ate into their bodies. The rest were driven back.

The station shook to a direct hit. Then another, then several more. Primus recognised the shock patterns of Mechanicus assault boats boring through the hull.

Qvo had sent in his tech-thralls.

Primus pressed on.

'I can't believe they're doing this! Bring the damn thing down!' shouted Cehen-qui apoplectically.

'The men are trying, my lord inquisitor,' said Valeneez calmly. 'We cannot penetrate their shields. The full weapons grid of the station is non-functional due to neglect. What might we had, we have now lost.'

'My lord, we have reports of hostile forces upon multiple decks,' said one of Cehen-qui's technicians.

'How many are close to the prisoner?' asked Cehen-qui.

'Some fifty or more, my lord. More assault boats are coming. The main vessel is not slowing.'

'Then shoot it! Shoot them all.'

'By the Emperor, they're going to ram us!' shouted Valeneez.

A heavy impact rocked the station, sending Cehen-qui staggering. He stared with disbelieving fury at the Adeptus Mechanicus ship. The vessel's flat prow nosed against the hub, the tail swinging from side to side as it adjusted its position to stop itself from slipping free. The hub vibrated as the ship pushed against it. Metal creaked as, slowly, the station began to move towards its host planet.

The vessel sparkled under a constant rain of fire from the station, but none of the weapons were powerful enough to break the void shields.

'Oh, my lord!' Callow squeaked.

'How long do we have?' asked Cehen-qui.

'Time to planetary impact is deceptively short,' said Gamma. 'Once Otranti has us in its grasp, we shall accelerate rapidly. I calculate not longer than three hours.'

'What about our ship?'

'Undamaged,' reported one of his men.

'They are giving us a way out,' said Valeneez. 'Clever.'

'Will you stop praising them!' Cehen-qui swore. 'Prepare to evacuate. Get the prisoner ready. They'll never chase down an Inquisitorial cutter.'

Primus came within a hundred yards of a raging battle waged between demi-men and Inquisitorial shock troops. He passed them by, his powerful mind clouding their perceptions. The sounds of shouts and the crack of las-beams receded, and he reached a T-junction. To his left, towards the hub of the station, was the greatest concentration of troops. They clustered around their sleeping prisoner, waiting for their enemy, their minds filled with fear and thoughts of duty.

Primus brought up a cartolith. A red dot pulsed half a mile away in the opposite direction. Quietly, he stepped into the corridor, and turned right.

Cehen-qui blasted a cyborg warrior at point-blank range. There was so little human left it was practically a servitor. Whoever this Qvo-87 was, he had no skitarii troops to call on, only the dregs of the Adeptus Mechanicus military. The machine-man died in a spray of oil and brain matter. The storm troopers pushed on ahead, shooting more of the clumsy foe with characteristic efficiency. Gamma marched with them, remorselessly gunning down the servants of his own cult.

Cehen-qui reached the cell of the prisoner. The fighting moved away, and he whistled impatiently up the corridor.

'You can come out now!' he shouted.

Valeneez emerged from a side door. Callow cowered in his shadow.

Cehen-qui holstered his bolt pistol and looked at the door to the cell. Active psychic wards gleamed on the metal. 'Open it.'

Valeneez came down the corridor, taking out a bunch of data wands as he came. He employed the keys in a strict sequence to deactivate the door's defensive measures, and it opened with a warning fanfare. Chilled nitrogen billowed out, clearing to reveal a small room with a clear methanol suspension tube at its centre. Within was the spindly form of a naked male aeldari. His hands and feet were bound in all-encompassing manacles. His head was locked into a psychic cradle.

'Amateurs,' growled Cehen-qui. 'The Adeptus Mechanicus do not have the wit for this kind of work.' He spoke into a vox-bead mounted on his collar. 'Get the prisoner onto the ship.'

Men and servitors moved up, and began locking chains to the tube's transit points.

He looked around. 'Where by the Throne is ShoShonai?'

The further Primus got from the hub, the more dilapidated the dungeon became. Holes in the metal were crudely patched. Readings from his cogitator warned of chambers open to the void behind closed doors. The gravity plating was inconstant in effect, and many lumens were out.

Finally, he reached his destination. A locked door closed so long ago it had rusted shut.

Primus rested his hand on the door and closed his eyes. He attempted to scry the room, but his clairvoyance showed him only blankness. Absence in this case was evidence of presence.

His eyes snapped open. The psyker was close by. Perhaps even in the room. He extended his senses. The blank spot extended in all directions.

Battle was coming. He checked his bolt pistol and loosened his chainsword before dealing with the door. Other psykers preferred force weapons, but Primus did not care for them. He was physically strong enough to put the chainsword through a bulkhead, if need be.

He checked the devices in pouches on his belt: a platinum signum projector, and three locking blackstone rings.

He placed a melta bomb on the door, twisted the activation handle, and stepped back.

Metal flashed with white heat as the fusion reaction bit. The melta bomb evaporated with a roar, taking the door and part of the wall with it.

Primus drew his sword, and stepped over cooling slag.

A stasis coffin was clamped to the far wall, fed by a series of conduits that glowed with green energies. They, like the coffin, were not of human origin.

Primus looked around. He saw nothing, not with his second sight nor with his auto-senses. The psyker was not in the room.

He moved towards his target. Through a window of clear mineral, he saw the occupant of the coffin uplit by more of the soft green energy – a metal skull for a face on a body as tall as Primus. It had a lidless, cyclopean eye of glassy stone. Its head was crowned with a crest of precious metals.

'You were right, Cawl,' said Primus. 'It's here.'

Primus opened the coffin with the wand. Ancient locks lifted. Cylinders of alien steels spun from the side, and the coffin lid rose up.

A necron lay in funereal splendour within. Primus tossed out priceless grave goods, locked the blackstone rings about his neck and wrists, and clamped a teleport locator to the spidery design on its chest.

He sent a coded datapulse.

'I have it, Qvo,' he said. 'Let's go.'

Cehen-qui slaughtered his way to the dock. Qvo's troops did what they could to block the way to the *Ruptor Xenorum*, but they were no match for him. He and his party gained the quayside, bloody and exhausted, but mostly alive.

His master of cargoes was waiting. A small tractor dragged the prisoner on a grav-sled onto the ship through a loading umbilical. Cehen-qui strode aboard.

He waited a few minutes for his remaining servants to retreat to the ship, but the station's internal augurs showed a large force of Qvo's cyborg troops making for the berth, and he decided to leave the rest of his men to their fate.

'Cast off,' he said. 'Ignite engines. Forty-five degrees down, full speed. We'll go under the dungeon and be away.'

The psyker decided to show itself. Primus turned. A woman stood in the doorway, emanating a dangerous power.

'That is not yours to take,' she said. Her voice was doubled, two speaking as one.

Primus gunned his sword. Witch-fire burst into life around his head.

'Then you'll have to stop me taking it,' he said.

Pale warp light lit the room. The woman raised a hand. Primus flew against the wall with a booming clang. She held him there. With a twitch of her head, she slammed his hand against the wall until his chainsword clattered to the ground.

Her triumphant grin faltered. She blinked, confused.

'I… I don't want to hurt you,' she said.

Primus snarled. A sphere of energy burst from his heart, blasting away her psychic bonds.

'Then don't,' he said. He threw aside his bolt pistol, and punched out. A ball of telekinetic force hit her in the chest, throwing her out of the room into the corridor. He pulled, and she hurtled into the room towards him. He lifted his hands and she rose up, her arms and legs stretching behind her.

'Please,' she said. 'Stop. I have blocked it, for now. Please listen.' Her robes writhed. Primus narrowed his eyes. He felt two souls, not one.

He pinched his fingers and ripped away the psyker's outer garment. Underneath, the woman wore a tight-fitting body-suit with no seams. She was emaciated. The flesh clung tightly to the bones of her skull, making her eyes appear shockingly huge.

Another organism was clasped about her head. Squid-like in appearance, its soft body draped down her back, tentacles wrapped about her throat and gripping her face. Their hooks were embedded so deep that the woman's skin had grown over them. Eyes of marbled yellow with cruciform pupils stared at Primus from either side of the woman's face.

He faltered at the sight of this abomination.

'He put it on me,' she said. 'It enslaved me.' The doubled nature of her voice wavered. 'Please, help me. When I sensed you, I knew you were strong enough to break it. Kill it. Kill me. I am impure.'

He sensed the woman fighting the creature. She was a psyker, but so was it. Its xenos mind mingled with hers. He had never seen anything like it before.

'Quickly! I can't hold it back any longer!' The twinned nature of her voice came back with redoubled strength. Primus pushed his own powers harder, keeping it restrained. He strode towards the woman, and gripped the boneless parasite in his right hand.

A rush of images bled from its soul. Its world devastated, its kind driven to the edge of extinction, the last of them exploited and enslaved. The focus of its hatred wore many faces, but all were human.

His grip loosened.

'Please,' said the xenos. 'Kill me.'

'You are the xenos, you are talking to me,' he said. He looked into the woman's eyes. She stared at him angrily, but she could not speak.

'Yes. I, not it,' the xenos said. 'Kill me. Free me from this rigid creature. End my suffering.'

Primus obliged. His hand clenched. The creature was leathery and tough, but he was strong. It gave a thin bubbling scream as its organs were pulped. Primus ripped it free, the hooked tentacles flaying the woman's skin from her face.

He stamped the last of the life from the alien and released his telekinetic hold on the host.

The woman fell down.

She lifted her ruined head. 'Why did you do that? Why are you fighting against us? We are both servants of the Emperor.'

Primus went to retrieve his bolt pistol, batting away her feeble psychic assault as he picked it up from the corner.

The gun felt good in his hand.

'Those words ceased to mean anything to me centuries ago,' he said.

He obliterated her head and torso with three shots.

'Qvo, Qvo, this is Alpha Primus. I have our target. Bring me back.'

Corposant wisped up from the ground. Lightning crackled from his armour and the skin of the necron. The familiar, horrible sensation of imminent teleportation crawled through his bones.

Primus closed his eyes.

With a thunderclap of air rushing to fill a void, Primus and the necron were gone.

* * *

The *Ruptor Xenorum* sped around the curve of Otranti, leaving the slower Mechanicus ship far behind.

Cehen-qui watched it vanish in the hololith and smiled triumphantly.

'So fail all who would oppose the Emperor's Inquisition,' he said.

'Wait.' Gamma stepped forward, his human arms folded, his mechanical claws twitching and snapping as he thought. 'Scan for etheric disturbance.'

A moment passed.

'There's an echo – single or double teleport from the outer reaches of the dungeon,' reported an ensign.

'What was kept there?' asked Gamma.

'Unknown. Records missing,' another crewman said.

Cehen-qui leaned forward in his chair. 'Why are you asking?'

'Do you not think that was a little easy?' said Gamma.

'Are you suggesting they let us go?'

'Have you considered, my lord,' said Gamma, 'that the false priest Qvo might not have been there for our farseer after all?'

Cehen-qui's face hardened.

'Bring us about. Lock on to that ship. Begin pursuit.'

Nervous faces peered into blank scopes.

'My lord,' said the man at the prime augury. 'The Mechanicus ship has vanished.'

Cehen-qui slammed his fist hard into the armrest of his throne.

'Maybe not so amateurish after all,' said Valeneez drily.

YOUR
NEXT READ

BELISARIUS CAWL: THE GREAT WORK
by Guy Haley

In the wake of the Great Rift, Belisarius Cawl turns his attention to the abandoned world of Sotha. Once home to the Scythes of the Emperor, it also hides a long-buried secret… and an ancient evil.

YOUR NEXT READ

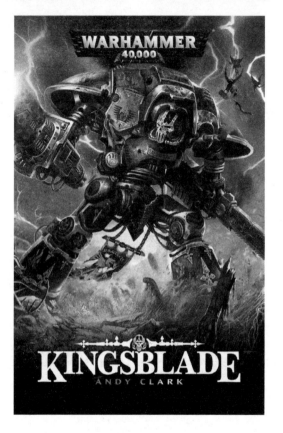

KINGSBLADE
by Andy Clark

When a tragedy occurs and an Imperial retribution force is shattered,
two young Imperial Knight pilots must work together and learn the ways
of war if they – or the world of Donatos – are to survive.

WHERE DERE'S DA WARP DERE'S A WAY

MIKE BROOKS

Countless bestial **ork** empires rise and fall amidst
the seething tides of war and bloodshed, destroying
themselves in their unending thirst for battle. But
when a leader emerges mighty enough to unify the
warring masses, the galaxy trembles…

In *Where Dere's Da Warp Dere's a Way*, Mike Brooks
brings insight to the ultra-violent. Ufthak Blackhawk
joins the mob storming a stalled ship laden with
treasures, intent on tearing the defenders apart to
claim the prize for his warboss.

''Ere we go, 'ere we go, 'ere we go!'

Ufthak Blackhawk, Bad Moon warrior and definite second-biggest in Badgit Snazzhammer's mob, no matter what that zoggin' idiot Mogrot thought, raised his voice in the rolling, rollicking war cry as they piled into the 'Ullbreaker. Outside in the cold vacuum of space, Da Meklord's warfleet was busy crumping the humie ships, but that wasn't Ufthak's fight. Blowing stuff up from a long way off was fine in its way, but he preferred getting up close and personal. Let the gunboyz have their fun: Ufthak was on his way to the *real* fight.

The last few boyz piled in, along with Dok Drozfang and various grots, and then came Da Boffin. A Bad Moon like Ufthak and Da Meklord himself, and one of the warboss' most trusted meks, Da Boffin had replaced his own legs with a single wheel, powered by a fuel made of concentrated squig dung. Ufthak had never worked out how Da

Boffin stayed upright on it, since even warbikes needed at least two wheels, plus either a kickstand or the rider's leg – or a kickstand made from someone else's leg – on the few occasions they were stationary. When Ufthak had asked, Da Boffin had just started talking about 'whirly bitz inside it', as though that made any sense.

The last hatch slammed shut and the flyboyz in the cockpit whooped, firing up the engines and vaporising anything immediately behind the shuttle. Ufthak had been on boarding missions before, so he knew what to do: grab on to one of the handholds roughly welded into the walls, and hang on like a grot on a warboar.

The flyboy kaptin stamped down on the lever which released the mag-clamp fastening them to the deck of *Da Meklord's Fury*, and they were away. Immediately, all the boyz who hadn't been in an 'Ullbreaker before went flying back to the rear of the ship, where they were crushed into a painful and indignant heap against the metal bulkhead. Ufthak laughed uproariously as they tumbled past him with expressions of confusion plastered across their faces.

'Ullbreakers got up to full speed quickly, and so it was only a few moments before the G-forces subsided enough for the newbies to untangle themselves from each other and start the important process of working out whose gun was whose. It only took a few moments more for fists to start to fly as they began bad-mouthing each other's shootas.

'If you gitz don't settle down den I'm turnin' dis fing around!'

Boss Snazzhammer stormed down the shuttle, spittle flying from his gob as he kicked boyz out of his way. He was a huge ork, head and shoulders taller than the rest of them, and bedecked in the most ostentatious finery that teef could buy – and, since he was a Bad Moon, he had a lot of teef.

There was barely a surface of his armour that wasn't dec-orated with loot, whether that was medals taken off the corpses of humie bosses, those little bits of wax and paper from the armour of dead beakies, or even some of the fancy gems the pointy-earz wore. In his right hand he carried the massive weapon that had given him his second name: a metal shaft the height of a humie with its legs still attached, with a hammer on one side of the head and a choppa blade on the other. The entire head could be engulfed in a crack-ling power field with one flick of Snazzhammer's clawed thumb, and Ufthak had seen the boss smash right through a humie tank with it.

The boyz ducked their heads, grabbed their own shootas and tried to avoid the boss' eye. No one wanted to end up like that tank.

'Dat's betta,' Snazzhammer growled. He turned on the spot, addressing the entire 'Ullbreaker. 'Right, we ain't da only 'Ullbreaker wot's flyin' today…'

Boos and jeers.

'…but we got da most important job!' Snazzhammer con-tinued. 'Da Meklord 'imself told me wot we gots ta do, so you all best listen.'

The mob quietened down, as much as they ever would. If Da Meklord had told them what to do, they'd probably bet-ter do it. Da Meklord was no ordinary warboss, if there was such a thing: he was Da Biggest Big Mek, and his gear was legendary. He'd gone toe to toe with rival warboss Oldfang Krumpthunda, and after one hit with Da Meklord's shokk-hamma no one had found any part of the Goff larger than a finger. Da Meklord's personal force field could shrug off hits from a humie Titan's cooka kannon. His supa-shoota could cut a Deff Dread in half before you could say 'Gork

413

and Mork'. He was what any Bad Moon wanted to be: massive, 'ard as nails and carrying enough weapons and armour to kit out a small warband in his own right.

'Now,' Snazzhammer declared. 'Humies don't got Gork 'n' Mork ta guide dem froo da warp, ta take dem to where da next fight is. Dey gotta use some fancy worky bitz wot dey keeps in da middle of dere ships. Wot we gots ta do is get Da Boffin dere, where he's gonna do some mek stuff. Got it?'

There was a general muttering and nodding of heads, and Snazzhammer beamed. 'Good. Now den. *Who are we?*'

'SNAZZHAMMER'S MOB!' the assembled mass of orks bellowed, Ufthak amongst them.

'Are we da biggest?'

'YES!'

'Are we da baddest!'

'YES!'

'Are we da shootiest?'

'YES!' the mob yelled, and everyone waved their shootas, which were almost all kustom jobs with extra dakka. No one pulled their trigger yet, though, which was good: Ufthak had once been in an 'Ullbreaker where some git with a kannon had managed to crack the flyboyz' seeing-window, and it turned out there was a reason why these things weren't open-topped.

'Dat's what I fort,' Snazzhammer said with grim satisfaction. He reached up and grabbed a handhold overhead. 'Now, everyone hold on to sumfing.'

Ufthak had known this was coming, and reached up with his other hand. 'Ullbreakers flew quick.

There was a shudder as the shuttle's short-range torpedoes all fired at once, concentrating on a small part of the enemy ship's hull to weaken it. Ufthak began counting down.

Five…
Four…
Free…
Two…
One…
He frowned.
Bit of one…

The 'Ullbreaker smashed into the humie ship, its specially reinforced nose cone taking the brunt of the impact and punching them clean through into the interior. The force of the sudden deceleration lifted Ufthak's boots from the floor and nearly wrenched his arms from their sockets, but he held firm. Some of the new ladz who hadn't minded the boss' words enough went flying the other way down the shuttle. One of them collided with a support strut hard enough to snap his back clean in two, much to the disdain of the other boyz who'd managed to remain upright.

'Leave 'im!' Snazzhammer bellowed as a few of them started putting the boot in. 'We got humies ta paste! Get out dere, and get clobberin'!' He aimed a kick at the downed ork's head as he acted on his own words, and his steel toecap hit hard enough to knock it right off. Dark blood sprayed out across the nearby members of the mob, while the flying head caught a lurking grot clean in the chest and knocked it backwards into the wall.

'WAAAAAAAAGGGGHHHHH!'

Ufthak drew his weapons and surged forwards with the mass of green around him. This was life; this was what it meant to be an ork. Enemies in front of him, ladz around him, ammo in his slugga and a good right arm to swing his choppa. What more could anyone ask for?

The fore hatches burst outwards and the boyz spilled out.

415

Ufthak shouldered his way forwards and forced his way through, looking for something to kill.

They'd busted through into a vast chamber of metal, the ceiling of which arched up overhead into gloomy shadow. The walls looked to consist largely of pipes, cables and contact points, some of which spat blue-white sparks, but Ufthak couldn't see much of them. That was partly because of the strange humie machines which loomed throughout the chamber – strange even to him, who'd fought a lot of different humies in a lot of different places – and partly because the humies that crewed this ship had decided they wanted to fight.

They were already swarming inwards, like buzzer squigs converging on an intruder into their nest. Ufthak saw the red-robes and the first flashes of gunfire and grunted in recognition: humie mekboyz! No wonder Da Meklord had his eyes on something fancy; humie tek could do some pretty wild stuff so long as you didn't hit it too hard.

The red-robes slowed, setting themselves to shoot, and Ufthak groaned. Why did humies never want to fight properly? Only beakies ever fancied a real rumble, and they didn't even taste good once you got them out of their armour. The rest of them got close enough for you to smell 'em, then hung back to shoot like Mork-damned Deathskulls.

They also always seemed to think that da boyz would just stand still.

'All right, ladz! 'Ave 'em!' Snazzhammer bellowed, and the mob surged forwards. Ufthak could feel Mork urging him on, and time slowed. His strides seemed to eat up the metal deck beneath him, and the figures in the humie gun line grew larger with each step. He saw an individual barrel track towards him, saw the humie's finger tighten on the trigger, but he took his next step at an angle and Mork smiled on him, because the bolt of spitting energy flew past his head instead of taking him full in the face. The next shot hit him in the shoulder, a white-cold shock that staggered him for a moment, but Ufthak had taken worse in the past, and the humie had gone for the kill instead of turning to run while it could. Not all of its fellows had done the same; some of them were already fleeing in the face of the unstoppable green tide bearing down on them.

Ufthak bared his fangs, bellowed his war cry and cannoned into the humie line with the rest of the mob.

The humie who'd shot him tried to parry his choppa with its rifle; Ufthak gave it respect for the effort but nothing for the execution, because his heavy blade smashed through the spindly weapon and split its torso from neck down to the middle of its chest. Like most humies, it died after one hit, sagging to the floor as he wrenched his choppa free and fired his shoota into what passed for the face of another, although this one was wearing a lot more metal there than most humies did. The metal didn't help it: Ufthak's slugga shots blew its head apart, metal face and all, and it dropped as well.

A humie lunged at him, wielding some sort of spear. The blade buried itself in Ufthak's chest and he bellowed in pain, then booted the wielder in its stomach. It flew backwards, disappearing with a despairing wail into the rolling maul of bodies around Boss Snazzhammer. Ufthak wrenched the spear out – it turned out to be one of the electro-guns with a knife stuck on the end – and threw it after its owner. There was a roar of anger, and Ufthak grinned as Mogrot Redtoof whirled around and clobbered a humie which had had nothing to do with the fact that there was now a knife in his back.

Next to Ufthak, Deffrow had lost his choppa – probably stuck in the ribcage of a dead humie somewhere – and so was using the next best thing: a stikkbomb. He battered one humie aside into the path of Dok Drozfang, who carved it apart with the power klaw he called Da Surjun, broke the skull of another, then wound up and took a swing at a third–

The world went white, very loud and extremely sharp.

Ufthak realised he was on the floor, along with everyone else within three yards of Deffrow. Deffrow himself was on his back, staring stupidly at the handle clutched in his somewhat shredded fist.

'Dey go bang, squigbrain!' Ufthak yelled at him as he got back to his feet. 'Dat's why we frow dem!' Deffrow's idiocy had left him with a bunch of shrapnel in his right-hand side, but it was nothing he couldn't deal with later. The humies, on the other hand, hadn't fared so well. The one Deffrow had hit most recently had taken the brunt of the impact and was now rather red and squishy, and even those further back weren't in a good way, rolling around, wailing and crying like a grot that had swallowed a fire squig.

'Seems like a design flaw t'me,' Deffrow muttered, pushing himself up. He winced and shook his mangled hand, and a finger that had only been attached by a shred of flesh pinwheeled off. 'Ow, dat smartz…'

'Now look what you did!' Ufthak complained at him. 'Dey're running away!' Sure enough, the remaining humies had clearly decided that enough was enough, as they were turning tail and fleeing from the slaughter. Or at least, they were trying to: those of Snazzhammer's mob who hadn't still been picking themselves up because their idiotic neighbour had blown everyone up were jumping on the humies from behind and sending them to see their

Emprah. Humies liked to yell about their Emprah a lot, but Ufthak had once heard a bunch of really tough beakies in spiky black armour shouting that the Emprah was dead. With worshippers like this, he could see why. He raised his slugga and shot one in the back, but his heart wasn't in it.

A high-pitched whine grabbed Ufthak's attention. For a moment he thought it was just the after-effects of Deffrow's stikkbomb going off, but then he saw a crackle of blue power, and one of the machines lurched into life. It was a big trukk of some sort, with wheels taller than an ork, and if the blue-crackling thing on the top of it wasn't some sort of gun then he, Ufthak Blackhawk, was a Blood Axe.

'Oh *zog*,' he muttered fervently. 'Boss! You got ya hammer?'

'Don't worry about dat,' Snazzhammer retorted confidently, spinning his hammer and casually decapitating a stray grot with the backswing. 'Dat humie stuff breaks if you look at it funny.'

Ufthak had his doubts. Humies might not be much good in a proper scrap, but their guns tended to be the business. The dirty little gitz also had a nasty habit of aiming, instead of pulling the trigger and letting Gork and Mork decide what would land where, as was right and proper.

The big trukk-gun fizzed noisily, and glowed brighter. Ufthak braced himself: he had a feeling this was going to hurt more than a carelessly detonated stikkbomb.

There was a tremendous sound of tortured, tearing metal from behind them, and a huge shape came sliding across the chamber's floor, careering off humie machines and leaving the wailing red-robes it struck as mere red smears. It collided with the gun trukk, which exploded in a ball of blue fire, and came to a halt. Hatches popped open and boyz emerged, bellowing in anticipation.

'Told you we wasn't da only 'Ullbreaker flyin' today!' Snazzhammer said with satisfaction. He raised his voice in a mocking shout. 'What 'appened to you gitz? Got lost?'

The other mob's boss responded with a rude hand gesture, and Snazzhammer laughed. 'Right, on wiv da job. Boffin! You know where we're goin'?'

Through a lot of doors, as it turned out.

'Beats me how dese humies ever get anywhere,' Mogrot commented, as Wazzock fired up his burna to cut through yet another sealed hatch.

'Dey know how to open 'em,' Ufthak snorted.

'We know how to open 'em!' Mogrot protested, pointing at where Wazzock was dragging a white-hot line down the hatch.

'Open 'em wivout burnas,' Ufthak said patiently. Mogrot was hot squig dung in a fight, no doubt about it, but he wasn't what you'd call a thinker. That was why Ufthak was second-in-command, even though they were more or less the same size. 'Dey're lockin' us out, right?'

'Don't seem too bovvered we're here, den,' Mogrot countered. 'We ain't 'ardly 'ad no one to fight since dat scrap when we got out da 'Ullbreaker!' He nudged a red-robed corpse with his boot, but the mob outnumbered this bunch of humies, and they'd barely been worth the effort.

'Dere's a whole buncha ladz on dis ship by now,' Snazzhammer put in. 'So da humies don't twig wot we're up to. Dey're what da humies call a "destruction".' He raised his weapon and activated the power field. 'All right, outta da way!'

The ladz parted, and the boss stepped forwards. He swung his hammer and, with a *krakka-boom!* like thunder, the burna-bisected door caved in as though it were made of sticks. It revealed a long corridor, wide enough for five orks abreast. A few yards down it were another bunch of red-robes, aiming their guns somewhat shakily at the gaping hole where their door had been.

Snazzhammer lunged forwards, swinging his weapon two-handed by the very base of its handle to maximise his reach. The powered head smashed through their squishy humie bodies and killed most of them with a single blow. The other two turned to flee: Snazzhammer let them get a few steps before hurling his hammer after them, decapitating them both, one after another. The mighty weapon skidded to a halt, slippery with red humie blood, and Snazzhammer turned to look at Da Boffin.

'Def'nitely dis way, right?'

Da Boffin held up a clicking gizmo, and revved the motor of his mono-wheel excitedly. 'Yup! We got supa-strong warp stuff down da uvver end. Dat's where we needs ta be.'

'You heard da ork!' Snazzhammer bellowed. 'Get to it!' He turned back towards his hammer and began to stride down the corridor. Ufthak was just taking his first step after the boss when the door at the other end of the corridor slid open, not thanks to the destructive activities of some other ladz but with the smooth action of a machine operated by someone who knew how to work it properly.

A huge shape stamped into view, blocking out much of the light behind it.

'Now *dat*,' Mogrot said from behind him, 'looks like a proper fight.'

It was on two legs, but it was no humie. It wasn't an ork, either. Ufthak reckoned it was twice his height at least, and nearly the same across. It sort of looked a bit like a humie Dread, the kind the beakies sometimes had, but not quite. It had two power klaws, the weird round humie ones instead of a proper pointy klaw like any self-respecting ork would have, and some sort of 'eavy shoota looming over its right shoulder.

'Tinboy!' Da Boffin exclaimed with what sounded like real excitement. 'Always wanted ta see one up-close!'

The 'eavy shoota opened up just as Badgit Snazzhammer broke into a roaring charge. He got three strides before his head exploded in a welter of gore and pulverised bone, and he dropped as dead as a swatted squig.

'Zoggin' 'eck!' Ufthak yelled. 'Back round da corner, ladz, sharpish!' The tinboy was tracking its shots towards them, and in the confines of the corridor there was nowhere to take cover. He shouldered Deffrow aside and scrambled back out of the line of fire, and a moment later the rest of the mob joined him, hunkering down on either side of the doorway. More thuds of shoota fire sent gouts of blood spraying across the corridor's floor and over the threshold of the ruined door, as a couple of stragglers got well and truly crumped. As soon as there were no more orks in view, the tinboy's gun fell silent.

'Why'd you run for?!' Mogrot demanded from the other side of the gap. Ufthak found faces turning towards him, red eyes focusing on him. He'd given a command, and the boyz had followed him. The only problem was, he'd told them all to run away.

That wasn't going to wash for long, if he wanted to stake his claim as boss. He had to prove himself once and for all as the bigger ork.

'Dat wasn't runnin',' he declared firmly. 'Dat was a... strateejik wivdrawal.'

'If it looks like a squiggoth, an' it smells like a squiggoth...'

Mogrot began menacingly. He drew himself up, fingering the activation switch on his chain-choppa. 'I don't fink you'z proper boss material, Ufthak. Don't fink you should be givin' orders.'

'Yeah?' Ufthak shot back, making a rude hand gesture. 'Why don't you walk over 'ere an' say dat?'

Mogrot growled, deep in his chest, and took one step…

…then paused, frowning distrustfully at the gap between them. Ufthak tried not to look at the same bit of floor, but it was no good. Even Mogrot's brain had remembered why they were hiding in the first place.

'Gimme a grot,' Mogrot grunted, reaching out behind him. One of the mob's hangers-on was seized and passed forwards with a squeak of protest, and Mogrot tossed it into the corridor.

The tinboy's shoota opened up immediately, and the sad, mangled remains of the grot thudded to the floor.

Ufthak cursed inwardly. That would have been *hilarious*, as well as useful. Nothing for it, then.

'We need to kill da tinboy,' he declared, as though Mogrot had never challenged him. 'An' we ain't doin' dat from here, an' we can't get to it ta kill it easy, coz it knows we'z orks, right?'

The ladz nodded. All of that seemed logical.

'Wot you finkin'?' Da Boffin asked, scratching one ear and looking at him thoughtfully as he rocked back and forth on his monowheel.

Ufthak beamed.

'All right, ladz, I'z 'ad a great idea…'

''Ello, I'm a humie!'

Humie spaceships, it turned out, had a lot of decent metal

sheeting lying around if you had access to a burna to cut it
off the walls, so Wazzock had been put to work. Before too
long, the mob had several large chunks, to which they'd
strapped the more intact of the red-robe corpses they'd
made on the way to the door.

'We'z just humies, walkin' down dis corridor!'

Ufthak's plan was proper cunning if he said so himself,
which he did, so that was okay. The tinboy must be able
to tell humies from orks, or the humies would never let
it walk around their spaceship. Therefore, it stood to reason that if it saw humies in front of it, it wouldn't shoot.

Into the corridor they went, a few boyz behind each metal
plate, with dead humies on the front to confuse the tinboy.
Simple, but genius.

'Wot if it don't work?' Deffrow hissed.

'S'gotta work,' Ufthak argued. 'I'm talkin' in humie, ain't
I? An' makin' my voice squeaky an'–'

The shoota opened up again. The three boyz behind the
foremost plate leaned into the impacts on what had suddenly become a makeshift shield, but the metal sheeting
wasn't designed to stand up to firepower of that magnitude.
One of them came apart as a shell punched right through,
and Ufthak suddenly had guts over his steel toecaps.

'Zog it!' he shouted. 'Next plan!'

The boyz hadn't got far down the corridor before the tinboy had rumbled them, but they'd reached Snazzhammer's
body. They dropped their apparently useless humie-shields
and opened up, pouring fire into their enemy.

Which stopped short of reaching it, swallowed up and
destroyed by some sort of force field.

'I've 'ad enuff of dis,' Ufthak growled as another ork was
blown apart. He reached behind his back and pulled out

what he'd decided he'd call a bombstikk. It was basically half the mob's stikkbombs all taped together courtesy of Da Boffin's toolbox, and by 'basically' he meant 'exactly'. He took a quick two-step run-up and hurled it overarm.

When *that* hit the tinboy's force field it was like Gork himself had stamped on them all.

Ufthak's vision cleared a moment or so before his ears stopped ringing, and he picked himself up and peered down the corridor.

The Mork-damned thing was only still standing, wasn't it?

'Dat woz s'posed ta blow its bloody arms off!' Mogrot yelled.

'Nevamind!' Ufthak shouted. 'It's stunned, innit? Scrag da zoggin' fing!'

He ran forwards, snatching up the Snazzhammer as he passed it. Sure enough, the tinboy was standing wonky, and making confused buzzing noises. Shots began to fly past him from behind, and this time one or two of them raised sparks as they struck home: the force field had been overloaded.

Lenses in the tinboy's face whirred as the machine suddenly seemed to recover itself, and the 'eavy shoota lowered to target him.

Ufthak threw himself into a slide as the big weapon began kicking out shots again, and he felt the shiver of impacts as they chewed up the floor behind him. The tinboy's power klaws crackled into life as whatever tek powered it realised that he was getting close, but it was a shade too slow: it lunged for him, looking to crush him, but he was already sliding between its legs and lashing out with the Snazzhammer.

Which bounced clean off with barely a scratch caused, since he hadn't activated the power field.

'Mork's teef!'

The tinboy lurched around to follow him, alarmingly fast for such a big thing. The 'eavy shoota remained steady somehow, pouring shots into the boyz that'd been following him, but the two power klaws were all for Ufthak. It swung at him again, and he barely dodged back from it, then ducked under the counterswing from the other arm. When the tinboy tried to clobber him on the backswing, he set his feet and swung the Snazzhammer to meet it.

He'd activated the power field this time, and it took the tinboy's arm off at the elbow.

Laughter erupted out of him as the huge thing staggered, its balance thrown off by the sudden lack of weight on one side. The sound of its detached power klaw skittering away across the deck was the sound of his triumph.

Then it punched him in the chest with the other one.

Ufthak had never known such pain, and he'd taken shots from a beakie gun before that had left half his insides hanging out, until Dok Drozfang had stuck them back in and stitched him up once the fighting had calmed down a bit. It was like someone had let buzzer squigs the size of grots loose on his chest, and that was before he flew backwards and hit the wall behind him hard enough to dent it.

He lay there for a moment, vision foggy, as the tinboy turned its attention back to the rest of the boyz. They'd now reached it and were hacking away at it with choppas, blasting it point-blank with their shootas, and were surely going to bring it down any moment now. They didn't need him to help, he could catch his breath.

Any moment now.

'Zog it,' Ufthak muttered, as another boy got pulped by the tinboy's remaining power klaw. 'If you want somefing dun right...' He levered himself back to his feet, ignoring the sensation and indeed the smell of scorched flesh coming from his front, and took up the Snazzhammer again.

'Oi! I ain't finished wiv you yet!'

The tinboy didn't turn around, which was its second mistake, the first having been to not make sure he was properly dead. He ran at its back, crackling Snazzhammer held high, and smashed the axe side into its armour plating.

KRAKKA-BOOM!

The tinboy spasmed and fell forwards, circuits overloading and sparks shooting in all directions. Ufthak forced his own battered body to climb atop it, then raised the Snazzhammer for the killing blow, laughing as he did so. Let Mogrot try to lead the mob after *this*!

He saw Da Boffin raising one hand in apparent warning just as he brought the weapon down for the final time.

Everything went red.

He was on his back when his brain was actually working well enough again to figure out what was going on. He stared up at the ceiling, which looked to be blackened and scorched as though a massive explosion had washed across it. He could hear the sound of ork boots tramping past him, but no one seemed to be stopping to congratulate him on his kill.

A face appeared in his line of sight. It was Dok Drozfang, who was wearing what Ufthak thought of as his considerin' face, which was never a sight an ork wanted to see.

'Dok,' Ufthak managed, although it was surprisingly hard to speak. 'I can't feel me legs.'

'Well, dere's a reason for dat,' the dok shrugged. 'Look down.'

Ufthak managed to do as Drozfang suggested. For a

moment, he couldn't work out what he was seeing. Then he realised that it was what he *wasn't* seeing that was the issue.

'Where's me legs?'

'One's over dere,' Drozfang said, pointing out of Ufthak's view. 'Not too sure about da uvver one. Or yer arms, ta be honest.'

'Dat'd explain why dey ain't hurtin',' Ufthak muttered. He frowned. 'Wot about da hammer?'

'Mogrot's got it,' Drozfang replied. 'Said 'e's da boss now, an' no one argued wiv 'im.'

'Ungrateful grots,' Ufthak managed. Air was definitely becoming a problem, which was only to be expected when you looked to be missing the bottom part of your lungs. 'Well, see us off den, dok. No point waitin' – may'z we'll get back ta Gork 'n' Mork so dey can put me in anuvver body an' I can get back ta fightin' again.'

Drozfang frowned. 'Yeah, about dat… Wot if I'z got a better idea?'

Ufthak tried not to let his trepidation show. Painboyz were useful to have about if you needed stapling back up, or a new arm sewing on, but some of them could get a bit 'creative' at times, especially when the patient wasn't in a condition to have much say in the matter.

'Nah, yer all right, dok,' he said, managing a grin. 'Nuffin' ta worry about, is it?'

'Yeah, well, I ain't finkin' Mogrot is da best boss da mob could 'ave,' Drozfang replied, lowering his voice. 'I reckon dey could do wiv da sort of ork wot has da smartz ta plan for a tinboy, an' da gutz ta bring it down. An' if I could fix dat ork up, he might remember da painboy wot fixed 'im, coz I reckon dat ork might be goin' places. Know wot I mean?'

'Wotever you'z finkin', yer gonna 'ave to do it quick,'

Ufthak told him flatly, as darkness began to encroach on his vision.

'Fankfully, da raw materials are at 'and,' Drozfang grinned, and pursed his leathery lips to emit a piercing whistle. High-pitched grunts and swearing heralded the arrival of the dok's grot 'disorderlies', apparently towing something heavy. They stopped next to Ufthak, and he turned his head to look at it.

It was Badgit Snazzhammer's body. Huge, battle-scarred and untouched apart from the small point of completely lacking a head, thanks to the tinboy.

'Now,' Drozfang said, producing an intimidatingly large cleaver and placing it at the base of Ufthak's neck. 'Dis may 'urt a bit...'

Ufthak hadn't really registered the blow given that, percentage-wise, he wasn't losing much more than he had already. The staples that the dok used to fix his head onto Snazzhammer's neck – which had been 'tidied up' with the same cleaver – only registered as minor pricks of discomfort.

What *really* hurt was the injection.

'You'd be lookin' at a day or so before you'd be up an' about, normally,' Drozfang told him matter-of-factly, as burning agony began to spread downwards from what remained of his neck into what had until recently been Snazzhammer's. The dok tucked his syringe back into his belt. 'But fanks to Dok Drozfang's Healin' Juice, da nerve endin's will connect right up an' you'll 'ave full control in a matter of minutes. Course, dere's always da side effects,' he added.

Ufthak tried to swear at him, but he was too busy convulsing.

* * *

The tinboy looked to have been the humies' last real line of defence of their 'fancy worky bitz', as Snazzhammer had called them. There were a few bodies scattered here and there on the route to the massive double doors from which an eldritch glow was emerging, but little sign of an organised resistance. The alarms going off suggested that perhaps Da Meklord's 'destruction' techniques had been extremely effective. All Ufthak knew was that they weren't helping his headache much.

"Ere we are, boss,' Drozfang said with a grin, gesturing at the one open door. 'Da rest of da ladz should be in dere. Time ta make yer grand entrance.'

Ufthak bared his fangs, squared his – or possibly Snazzhammer's – shoulders, and strode in as though his neck weren't still leaking a bit, and his left leg weren't dragging slightly.

It was a vast space, as big as one of the humies' buildings which they seemed to put up simply to sit in and have a proper good think about their Emprah. However, whereas those had lots of empty space in, perhaps in order for the thoughts to fly around properly, this one was jam-packed full of… stuff, was the only term Ufthak could come up with. Huge metal pillars which gave off a glow that only partially obscured the runes carved into them. Enormous pistons, crackling with energy. Giant wheels larger than his outstretched arms. And yet, despite how impressive it all looked, there was the distinct impression that this place wasn't fulfilling its function. It was heavy with potential, an almost palpable heaviness in the air. It was as though the room itself were yearning for something.

Which probably wasn't Da Boffin and Mogrot Redtoof having a scuffle, but that was what it currently had.

'Gerroff it!'

'I'm da boss, I get ta push da button!'

'Yooz gonna break it, you stoopid–'

'Gonna break yer face in a minute–'

Mogrot, facing away from Ufthak, reared back with the Snazzhammer in his grip, ready to knock Da Boffin's lights out with it.

Ufthak grabbed it just under the head and yanked it out of his grip. Mogrot whirled around, fumbling at his belt for his chain-choppa, but pulled up short when he came face-to-chest with Ufthak. His brow creased in uncommon cogitation.

'Wot da zog…?'

'Sumfin' like dat,' Ufthak agreed, and nutted him.

Mogrot went down. Ufthak winced, and reflected that possibly hadn't been the smartest thing to do with a stapled-up neck, but what was done was done. He brandished the Snazzhammer over his head.

'Anyone else wanna be boss?'

There was a distinct lack of volunteers, as the rest of the ladz took a sudden interest in their boots. They weren't sure if Badgit had got a new head or Ufthak had got a new body, but they weren't planning to argue with either eventuality.

'Dat's settled, den,' Ufthak said with satisfaction. He could almost feel Dok Drozfang grinning behind him, but that was fine. Fair was fair, and he'd see that the dok got his due. A few extra teef passed his way, the occasional 'volunteer' for surjury, that sort of thing.

'You done ya mek fing yet?' he asked Da Boffin, who shook his head.

'Mogrot wanted ta press da button.'

'Well, get on wiv it,' Ufthak commanded him. He wasn't interested in pressing buttons: that sounded like a mek job.

Da Boffin's device was surprisingly small, and was clamped to what looked like some sort of humie control panel. It had three buttons on it: 'STOP', 'GO' and 'MEGA-GO'.

'Wot is dat, anyway?' Ufthak asked.

'Dis,' Da Boffin said gleefully, 'is da Warp Dekapitator. You know how humies choose where dey're gonna fly through da warp?'

'Yeah?' said Ufthak, who didn't.

'Well, dey leave tracks behind in da warp. Sorta like squig trails, only nuffin' like dat,' Da Boffin explained. 'Dese are humie mekboyz, so dey prob'ly came from a humie mekboy planet, where dere's loadsa shiny tek Da Meklord can nab.'

'Right,' Ufthak nodded. Shiny tek sounded good. Da Meklord would get the best, obviously, but that didn't mean there wouldn't be some left over.

'So when I turn dis on, it uses da energy of dese warp engines to cause a katastroffic warp implosion!'

Ufthak frowned. 'Is dat good?'

'Course it's good!' Da Boffin scoffed. 'S'got a lot of fingies, syllables, innit? Like, "grot" is bad, but "Wazbom Blasta-jet" is good.'

Ufthak nodded. It was a powerful argument.

'Dis ship gets sucked into da warp, right back to da startin' point of da last warp jump it made, and den pops back out again,' Da Boffin continued. 'An' it sucks all da rest of da ships around in wiv it too, includin' Da Meklord's fleet. Job's a good'un!'

He reached out, and pressed the button labelled 'MEGA-GO'.

The control panel sparked. More alarms started sounding,

but these weren't the high-pitched whiny klaxons that denoted a relatively minor problem like rampaging, murderous orks aboard the ship. These were bone-deep and throbbing, and bore an inherent sense of panic. If a star could have screamed a warning, it would have sounded like that.

All around Ufthak and his mob, the glowing, crackling parts of the room began to move: slowly at first, then faster and faster. Ufthak frowned. He could have sworn that something apparently solid just passed through something else equally apparently solid.

'Is dat s'posed to 'ap–'

There was a stomach-churning, resonant *bloorp!* and everything turned inside out.

It took Ufthak a few moments to check that his arms weren't now five miles long, or that his stomach hadn't swelled to the size of a planet, both of which felt like they could be viable options. He definitely had an annoying tic in his left eye, but that was less unusual, and he glowered at Da Boffin with it.

'If dat's your definition of "good"…'

Da Boffin held his hand up for quiet. Ufthak was about to clobber him for disrespect when he heard it too.

It was the screaming of tortured metal. And that, Ufthak realised, was not fancy words. It was the voice of actual metal, and it was actually screaming, and the whole thing was overlaid with a bubbling, wet giggle. From outside in the corridor came the slithering thump of something malformed dragging its huge bulk along with nothing more than brute strength and an endless malice directed at all living things.

'Course,' Da Boffin commented, 'dere's always da side effects.'

'All right, ladz!' Ufthak barked, laying about him. The boyz hadn't coped well with the katakrumpic warm diffusion, or whatever it was Da Boffin had said, and most of them were still on their backs or counting their fingers to see if they still had the same amount – which was causing some problems in Deffrow's case, as he couldn't now remember how many he'd started with. A few knocks with the haft end of the hammer got them back into it, however. 'Da entertainment's comin'! Up ya get!'

The other massive door slammed back, and something made of blood and steel and endless hunger squirmed in, all sharp teeth and barbed tongues, and glistening black talons that reached out hungrily for flesh.

Ufthak grinned at it. Time to see what his new body could do.

'On me, ladz! One, two, free...'

'WAAAAAAAAGGGGHHHHHHH!'

YOUR
NEXT READ

BRUTAL KUNNIN
by Mike Brooks

When Ufthak and his orks attack the forge world of Hephaesto, the last thing they want
is to share the spoils with the notorious Kaptin Badrukk. But with armies to defeat and
loot to seize, Ufthak's boyz might just need Badrukk's help – though they doesn't mean
they can trust him…

YOUR
NEXT READ

WARHAMMER
40,000

BLOOD OF IAX

ROBBIE MacNIVEN

BLOOD OF IAX
by Robbie MacNiven

When Ultramarines Primaris Chaplain Kastor and Apothecary Polixis
are separated in the fight against a fearsome ork warlord, they must battle
to survive and be reunited.

REDEMPTION ON DAL'YTH
PHIL KELLY

The **t'au** are a technologically advanced xenos race
whose rapidly expanding empire and lethal battlesuit
tech threatens the Imperium. Divided into four
castes and guided by the enigmatic ethereals, the t'au
work tirelessly in furtherance of their all-consuming
philosophy: the Greater Good.

On Dal'yth, a pair of living statues stand in stasis.
Commander Sha'kanthas, renowned battlesuit pilot,
is locked in a duel with his opponent, a Space Marine
Chapter Master who attempted to conquer the planet
centuries earlier. Were the stasis field to suddenly
falter, the two warriors could wreak untold havoc
upon the t'au's peaceful training facility...

CORE ASSEMBLY HOUSE, GEL'BRYN
DAL'YTH (T'AU SEPT WORLD)

'These are no mere statues, dear cadets, but rival lords of war.'

Magister Por'klai made the gesture of the unveiling hand, his slender fingers stretched towards the spherical force field the Dal'ythans called the Clash of Empires. Its duelling inhabitants, a fire caste hero in a vintage XV8 battlesuit and a monstrous Imperial Space Marine with his crackling broadsword raised high, stood frozen in the act of killing one another.

The dynamism of the t'au battlesuit's posture, twinned with the roaring, hideous visage of the human grotesque, spoke volumes. The two warriors stood upon a thin section of tunnel, its underpiping exposed by the faint shimmering sphere delineating the tableau.

'These adversaries live on, held in stasis, immortal and

unchanging. They have inspired generations of the fire caste for over three hundred tau'cyr. A living monument to our victory over the Imperium here upon Dal'yth, they show the Hero's Mantle in action, and the bravery of those who wear it.'

Por'klai's audience, a tight knot of fire caste cadets no more than twelve short tau'cyr of age, stared up at the piece with rapt attention. It would be the high point of their day, a fitting reward for their excellent results in training and a thrill they would remember for the rest of their short lives.

'The monument does not merely commemorate the sacrifice of Sha'kanthas, one of the Second Sphere's most lauded heroes. It *contains* him. It *is* him, in fact.'

This time, there was a murmur of appreciation; Por'klai considered it sufficient enough to continue. His legs were already aching, and he had given the same speech hundreds of times to bright new cadet classes over the span of several tau'cyr. He would give the raconteur's craft his all, of course; he always did. But already the air shimmered with intense heat – a record year, if the earth caste were to be believed. He would be glad to move further into the mushroom-like domes of the muster complex and take his rest in the refreshment zone that overlapped its southern edge. His usual vice, an ice-cool *dzincta*, would be more than welcome.

'Is it true that Monat Sha'kanthas once served the Traitor?' asked Kha'lithra, making the cupped hands of the inquiring student. A fierce young cadet, since entering the muster complex she had let her war face gradually be replaced by wide-eyed awe.

'He did indeed,' said Por'klai, his expression darkening. 'Sha'kanthas was Farsight's first tutor, and during the Battle of Gel'bryn City, it was the Traitor that gave him his war name. Yet the rot spread not from his teachings. Before Dal'yth, Tutor Sha'kanthas went on record many times as to the rebel's true nature. His servitude was an artefact of its time. It does not diminish his sacrifice as a *Monat* assassin, nor his victory in stopping the so-called "Scar Lords" in their subterranean strike on Shas'ar'tol High Command.'

'The Imperial war leader uses blade and shield,' said Cadet Tsh'varian, mystified by the anachronism. 'With such a primitive mindset, how can they hope to deny us?'

'A good question, young Tsh'varian. The humans are great in number, and they have a callous disrespect for their own lives. That can sometimes make them dangerous.'

'Can the warriors hear us?' said Kha'lithra.

Por'klai chuckled. 'No, cautious one, they cannot. They are caught in a single moment that they cannot escape.'

'Oh,' she said, biting her lip. 'Is it human war-tech that holds them so still?'

'As the glacier holds the ancient skeleton in its wintery grip, this *gue'la* force field holds both hero and villain in place,' said Por'klai. 'The stasis field is a fluke of technology, a brute's little-understood weapon triggered as a last resort. By seeking safe haven in timelessness, the Imperial savage has unwittingly left us with a work of art.'

'But how do we know they cannot hear us, honoured por?' asked Kha'lithra, the olfactory chasm running down the front of her face puckering in consternation. 'The class before us said there was a flicker in–'

Por'klai scowled, making the cutting hand. 'The earth caste have assured us of the field's integrity, ever since the day they scooped these warriors from their mutual tomb and elevated them to the glory you see before you. The

Imperial stasis field has held unchanging for eight generations. Do you doubt the expertise of the earth caste?'

Casting her gaze downwards, the cadet made the
closing-book gesture of the matter settled. 'No, magister.'

'Perhaps you question the vigilance of the water caste?'

'I… I offer contrition, magister.'

'Excellent. Then let us make our way inside.'

Por'klai ushered the cadets onwards; they went in good
order, as ever. A few of them nodded their thanks to him,
eyes still shining and eager. The magister felt a subtle
warmth within his chest. Maybe he could stand a few more
tau'cyr of instruction duty after all.

Behind him, the force field atop the monument pillar
flickered and spat.

There was a blur of light. Tutor Sha'kanthas gave a wordless
cry as he triggered a kill shot. His battlesuit's plasma rifle
was inches from the gue'ron'sha war leader's face. Nothing
happened. The Imperial brute brought his sword down, cutting the rifle's cylindrical barrel in half. Sha'kanthas raised
his fusion blaster, eye-stabbing its crosshairs. It blipped in
alarm. Readouts scrolled red text.

••• DATA DISCONTINUATION ••• TRANSMISSION
UPDATE DENIED •••

Sha'kanthas felt a solid impact as the brute's shield slammed
into him. There was a moment of weightlessness as his suit
fell away from some manner of ledge. For a moment he saw
the violet-and-white sky of Dal'yth. Then the XV8 righted
itself, putting distance between him and his assailant.

Where were the tunnels? How was he suddenly outside?

He opened a priority channel to the command cadrenet.
'Commander Farsight,' he said, 'close strike abort. Primary

target used teleport device. Still engaged, but weapons scrambled.'

There was no reply. The cadrenet was dead.

Sha'kanthas cast a glance at his battlefield disposition suite. His surroundings were some manner of urban inzone. Civilians scrambled away in all directions. His gaze darted back to the Space Marine king, who was gaining the edge of the high podium they had occupied moments before.

He tried his rifle again. Still unresponsive.

The Imperial brute landed with an audible crunch, the plaza cracking beneath the boots of its bulky powered armour. Raising his fist, the gue'ron'sha took a shot with the barrel-shaped weapon system on the back of his gauntlet. A pair of tiny self-detonating rockets hurtled out. Sha'kanthas turned his shoulder, and a shell gouged a crater from the multilayered alloy of his suit. The gue'ron'sha barked something unintelligible, then broke into a run.

Sha'kanthas called up more crosshairs, this time settling on the beast's unhelmeted face. Why the Imperials were so ready to expose their most vulnerable locations, he would never know. To them, bravery and foolhardiness were one and the same. The monster had already been horrifically disfigured by some old wound, half of his chin missing to expose a row of yellow teeth jutting from a ropy bed of muscle and sinew. A flick of the eye, and the whole gnarled head would be no more than vapour.

He took the shot–

Nothing.

••• TRANSMISSION UPDATE DENIED ••• SYSTEM LOG UNTENABLE •••

'T'au'va's grace,' cursed Sha'kanthas. 'This is unacceptable! Commander Farsight, please reply!'

••• SIGNAL LINK DEFUNCT •••

The beast was nearly upon him. He leapt backward as its longblade came scything round, a killing diagonal swipe that would have opened his battlesuit a split second before. There was a clatter from behind as he collided with a cluster of hover-platforms. Civilians screamed as they hurried to clear the immediate surroundings. He boosted upwards out of reach, gaining a moment with which to catch his breath.

A knot of fire caste warriors, dipping into food cylinders a moment before, pulled their tables into a rough barricade. They hastily formed a two-tier gun line. Pulling pulse pistols from side holsters, they levelled a fusillade at the rampaging human warrior.

The monster raised his shield and charged towards them. Plasma shots that would have seared straight through an ork's torso splashed from the ornate shield in a cascade of clashing energies. The gue'ron'sha's stamping run gathered momentum to smash through the barricade, bowling over the warriors behind it.

One, two, three swings of that oversized broadsword. The first of the fire warriors lost a hand at the wrist, then half of his cranium an eye-blink later. Grey matter oozed out from a skull seeping blood. The second had his throat cut so deep his head hinged away from his chest like an open casket. The third, shouldered so hard he was taken from his feet, was cut bodily in half even as he flailed through the air. Blood arced, jetted, sprayed thick.

Sha'kanthas was already boosting in. In the space of time it took him to close the distance, three more t'au lives met a brutal end. One t'au warrior fired point-blank at the invader, but it passed straight through his heavy cloak to glance from the bulky power unit behind. The fire warrior caught a heavy elbow to the throat in return. The follow-up blow from the pommel of the human's sword caved in his skull. The blade swept around in a three-quarter spin. Two more t'au went to their deaths, their mangled corpses falling amongst the ruin of their team.

His battlesuit's jets roaring, Sha'kanthas smashed bodily into his heavily armoured foe. The human did not sprawl, as he had hoped, but instead staggered to one knee. Sha'kanthas kicked out, but the gue'ron'sha deflected the blow with his shield, righting himself with a deep growl of anger.

The last two fire warriors ran, disengaging as fast as possible. The human shot one of them in the back with his wrist-mounted gun. The shell pierced the fire warrior's lumbar armour and detonated a moment later to end the poor infantryman's life in an explosion of viscera, blood and fragments of spine.

The beast grinned, its ruined lip gaping. Sha'kanthas lined up a shot once more, but the weapon system yielded nothing.

'– – YOUR GUNS – –' spooled Sha'kanthas' autotrans as it made sense of the creature's guttural growls. '– – THEY DESERT YOU – – ALLOW ME TO DIVEST YOU OF THEM – –'

The broadsword came around hard. Sha'kanthas parried it with what was left of his plasma rifle, and the barrel was sheared through to the point it was nothing more than a smoking stub.

'Die in flames, savage.' Sha'kanthas jabbed forward with his fusion blaster, intending to physically smash the hulking thing's face into the back of its skull. The human beast was fast despite its size. It turned, the blow glancing from the curvature of its massive shoulder pad. That lethal sword came around once more in a blur of ice blue, hacking a thick wedge from the midsection of the XV8 and crazing the left-hand screens of his control suite.

Pulse rifle fire shot in from above, slamming into the giant warrior as a group of student marksmen fired from a commanding position on the balcony. Their shots spun the brutish warrior away from Sha'kanthas to put a spear's length between them. He boosted backwards, hastening for the building's core structure where the comms antennae would be directly accessible. His suit was glitching badly – perhaps due to some scrambling element of the Imperial warrior's teleport field – but he had to get word to his fellow commanders. If the gue'ron'sha war leader got loose amongst the civilians of the muster point, it would be a massacre.

Sha'kanthas saw the Imperial warrior turn his shield towards the marksmen on the balcony, covering his massive bulk with a canopy of inches-thick metal. Beyond the fire caste students, a loose group of earth caste civilians were hastening to get through the iris portal to the complex's interior. The brute raised his gun-gauntlet over his shield and sent two shells winging towards them. One detonated amongst the fire warriors as another burst an earth caste civilian apart like a sack of wet offal. Two more, this time aimed at the balcony itself. They tore great chunks from the supporting structure, and with an ominous crack the entire platform gave way, sending the marksmen toppling down to break amongst a cascade of rubble on the floor below.

'No!' shouted Sha'kanthas, flick-sliding his autotrans to broadcast in Imperial Gothic. 'Your fight is with me! Or have you no honour?'

At this, the brute turned.

'– – THERE IS NO HONOUR IN CRUSHING AN INSECT – –'

The monstrosity came on, despite his words, to finish the job. Sha'kanthas fell back down an arterial corridor, leading the giant after him towards the comms hub. If he could keep its attention, keep that perfect distance between predator and prey, he could protect those around him without firing a single shot.

Just as well, given that his XV8 was a suit of armour without a blade.

The complex's core was close, now. Sha'kanthas could see the tall pillar that manually interfaced with its antennae and satellite arrays visible at the heart of a raised torus. It glittered faintly with readout displays and holo-mite images waiting to be enlarged, understated in appearance, yet powerful enough to send a broadcast across the star system and beyond.

Sha'kanthas burned the last of his thrust fuel to reach the communion console, then flicked his suit to direct interface and placed its antenna in broadcast uplink mode. The timing of his message would be critical if it were to reach the high commander. As one of shas'o rank, his ident should see the data conveyed far and wide.

'Commander Farsight! Request reinforcement. Rogue gue'ron'sha war leader at Gel'bryn muster complex. Garrison assets insufficient!'

Holo displays winked, his ident failing to process. He could still hear the thumping footsteps of the Imperial giant in the middle distance. The sharp crack-boom of its solid-shot weapons and screams of garrison personnel hinted at a panorama of destruction.

Primitive weapons, those gue'ron'sha guns. Yet they

worked, and with horrible efficiency, each rocket-propelled shell making a hideous mess of those they hit. It was more than he could say for the systems of his Hero's Mantle, scrambled entirely by whatever strange tech the Imperial had used to translocate them. Here, the very complexity of the battlesuit's systems was working against it, and he had no idea how to remedy the situation.

Still no reply from the cadrenet.

'T'au'va shine a light,' swore Sha'kanthas. 'Please reinforce. Anybody! A Monat cannot fight without his gun!'

A solid shot hit him from behind, detonating on the thrust pack of his XV8 to send him veering away from the console. He turned, eye-flicking a crosshair on reflex over the grimacing monstrosity advancing upon him, but his weapon readouts were still stubbornly red. Those of his jetpack flared crimson alongside them.

••• THRUST VECTOR SUITE CRITICALLY DAMAGED •••

Feeling desperation well up in his throat, Sha'kanthas forced his XV8 into a loping run away from the advancing Space Marine. He moved around the balcony and fled into the atrium-like hub behind. If the complex was anything like its equivalent on Vior'la, it would have armed escort units at its heart for those times the ethereal caste made their diplomatic forays.

Another shell struck him, this time at the waist. One of the gimbals was fouled in his hip; he could see the tiny holo of the XV8 on his damage control suite flaring red to show it was badly compromised. The Crisis battlesuit, which had wrought such havoc in the battle under the city, limped out of the comms room as best it could.

If he was to stand any chance of victory, he would soon have to leave it behind altogether.

Magister Por'klai could not help but dart a glance down the corridor they had fled down, despite the fact he knew he risked catching a stray shot. There was the Imperial monstrosity, in the comms hub, stamping its way towards the atrium in which they were taking shelter. Ahead of it came an XV8 battlesuit, its weapon systems buckled and shorn away as it fled the battle.

'Sacred T'au'va,' whispered Por'klai. 'It's unstoppable.'

'The statues live,' said Kha'lithra, her teammates around her echoing her words as if they were a mantra. 'The statues live!'

'But how is the intruder still active?' said Tsh'varian. 'Should he not have been slain?'

'Hush,' replied Por'klai. 'You should not be here, child. Move back to the exclusion zone.'

'We are fire warrior cadets,' said Kha'lithra, sticking her chin out. Her diminutive fellows nodded in support, desperate to be seen as a capable asset against the Imperial revenant stalking towards them. 'We can make the difference.'

'I doubt a team of sub-*la* will fare better than an XV8.'

'Do you have the access codes to the weapons display cache in the secondary muster hall, honoured por?' said Tsh'varian.

'Of course not,' he replied, making the sign of the pinched-out flame.

'I do,' grinned the boy, his eyes alight.

'More Farsight than Shadowsun, this one,' muttered Por'klai.

In the corridor ahead, the XV8 limped out into the atrium, lurching left as it entered the wide, flora-fringed entranceway. There was a harsh detonation upon its shoulder. The battlesuit staggered into a pillar, smashing down an array of light sculptures in a spray of glass and shrapnel.

The XV8 righted itself, and then – as another detonation tore its sensor head from its shoulders – sagged downwards as if suddenly exhausted. Its plexus hatch burst open, and a tall, wild-eyed battlesuit pilot burst out.

Drones, coming in low from the upper dome of the atrium, swooped past him to open fire at the Imperial monster lumbering down the corridor. One was shot out of the air, the other bisected by a lunge of the invader's power sword.

'Move!' shouted the battlesuit pilot, his face streaked with sweat and blood. 'Get away!'

'Is that… is that Sha'kanthas?' said Kha'lithra.

'It cannot be,' said Por'klai. 'No. It cannot be.'

'But look, magister,' said Kha'lithra. 'It is.'

Sha'kanthas stumbled away from his battlesuit, gasping with a mixture of raw adrenaline and fear. The Imperial beast was less than a hundred yards behind him. One clear shot, and a solid shell would detonate between his shoulder blades, killing him in a spectacular eruption of gore. He could feel the very possibility burning into his psyche, hovering like a knot of hot potential in the middle of his spine. Yet he had to lead the warrior away from the civilian areas, even if he was to be little more than a declawed lynx to the invader's raging, frenzied bear. He could not let fear overtake him, despite it closing its cold claws around his windpipe and stopping him from swallowing down the rising tide of panic. A moment of such weakness, and his people would pay the cost in blood.

In the plaza ahead, a tall water caste magister in strange, unfamiliar garb stood amongst a knot of fire caste cadets. They were looking intently at him, as if he were a ghost.

'Move!' he shouted at them. 'Get away!'

They did not move. In fact, one of the youngsters beckoned him in close.

'Tutor Sha'kanthas!' she shouted. 'You must come with us. There is a weapons display beyond us!'

He was about to refuse on principle, but then turned in his flight, making the gesture of swift furtherance so the young cadets moved off. A shell blurred past him, perhaps a hand's breadth from his shoulder. Thank the T'au'va, it detonated not amongst the cadets, but on a tall florasynth tree at the centre of the atrium. Wood splinters pricked the side of his face as he hurdled the low beam of an abstract sculpture. A moment later, he heard a deafening boom from the other side of the atrium, and a series of screams. He glanced over to see an illustration façade shot to pieces, exposing a knot of cowering air caste students. They cried out in fear as the Imperial brute growled in animalistic rage in their direction.

Desperate to keep the beast pursuing him, Sha'kanthas snatched a winking notation disc from the water caste magister as he caught up with the knot of cadets. He veered left away from them once more and hurled it hard at the brute's head. The disc flew most of the way there, then smoothly reversed its direction, swooping back to emit a bright, chiming tone.

'You appear to have hurled me, master user,' it said. 'May I return myself to your service?'

Sha'kanthas blinked in disbelief, casting about himself for something he could use as a weapon. His eyes alit on the stones of an elemental garden; snatching up a jagged, roughly triangular rock, he threw it as hard as he could at the side of the brute's head. It struck home hard on his temple, laying open a flap of flesh and causing blood to ooze down his cheek.

The Imperial scooped up a slew of gravel from a flora-synth bed and rubbed it into the open wound, grunting out something in his guttural tongue.

'He thanks you for the scar,' said the water caste magister, his tone querulous, 'and says his Emperor will be pleased.'

'These humans are animals,' said Sha'kanthas. 'Now move!'

Pushing the magister before him, the battlesuit pilot hustled down the narrow corridor across the atrium, the fire caste cadets arranging themselves as an escort detail around them. The sound of explosions in the atrium faded, replaced by the rhythmic stomping of the Imperial warrior at full advance.

'Get to the museum,' said Sha'kanthas. 'Full spread, burning rain configuration.'

The cadets exchanged puzzled glances, but did not react.

'Burning rain, I said!'

'Forgive them, shas'o,' said the water caste operative. 'Your military cant is some three hundred tau'cyr old.'

Sha'kanthas had no idea what he was talking about. His mind was entirely occupied by acts of survival, firing corridors and ballistics angles. Should the brute start firing down the corridor after them, the cadets would be gunned down in short order. They would give their lives quite happily in the name of the T'au'va. But their blood would be on his hands.

'Just get behind that vestibule wall!' he shouted, pushing two of the cadets towards it.

'We cannot!' shouted the fierce-looking girl amongst them. 'The exhibits are this way. There is an original XV8 there!'

'It is a relic,' hissed her companion, Tsh'varian. 'Its hardware will be incompatible.'

'And what do you think he is?' she replied.

'Very well,' said Sha'kanthas, changing direction after the girl. 'If there is an intact battlesuit in the complex, guide me to it. It could save many lives.'

As they ran onward, he caught snatches of their conversation.

'They have guns there, Kha'lithra, near the Traitor's Denouncement,' said Tsh'varian. 'And my data stream maintains we are the only fire caste on-site.'

'None of us are above *la* rank,' said the girl.

'We have the Hero to draw his ire. Together, we will prevail.'

'Here he comes!' shouted the water caste magister, his voice shrill with fear. 'Heads down–'

There was a loud purr of repulsor engines as a Piranha arced down through the air above them. Small enough to pass through the arterial corridors, the T-shaped craft had scrambled through the complex and flown right over their heads. The craft's gunner opened fire with the drones on its wingtips.

Sha'kanthas felt a measure of hope. The Piranha's pulse carbines would struggle against Imperial power armour, but if they kept the monster pinned in place, the fusion blaster at the craft's tip could finish the job. The craft's wing drones detached as it came in close, flying wide to baffle the intruder's target priority.

The Space Marine ignored them. He leapt up onto the lip of a communion table and sprung right for the craft, sword blurring. The tip of the blade took the nose of the craft clean away. Twisting mid-leap, the gue'ron'sha shot the

Piranha in the wing before landing in a skidding crouch. The craft veered, wobbled, and went out of control to smash headlong into the wall beyond, smoke gouting from its wreckage.

Sha'kanthas ran onwards, privately glad of the distraction even if it had cost two more t'au lives. Only a warrior clad in the Hero's Mantle could truly hope to match the invader, but the Piranha had bought them time. Though there would inevitably be some XV8 reinforcements inbound by this point, the intruder would likely have slain another score of t'au by the time they arrived.

Ahead was a large hall, faceted like a gemstone but with all the hard edges smoothed into perfect contours. In its heart was a wide variety of exhibits covering the glory of the fire caste. Sha'kanthas passed a holo schematic; the hall was one of four such places, each focused on one caste and intended for the edification of the others. They all adjoined one another around a central ethereal garden that lay just beyond the hall, a place for quiet contemplation on the sovereignty of the celestial caste.

This day, quiet contemplation was not a likely outcome.

The fire caste's hall had been built around the evolution of t'au military achievement. Holo strats of famous t'au battles ringed the outside, intended to be seen in sequence and each supported by artefacts from that time. The pinnacle of the spiralling exhibit was occupied by the most advanced battlesuit Sha'kanthas had ever seen. It was taller and more anatomically advanced than the standard XV8 – one of which stood at its waist by way of contrast – and was labelled under the banner of the Third Sphere Expansion.

But there had been no Third Sphere Expansion. Not yet.

Sha'kanthas put it from his mind. Thank the Greater

Good, both battlesuits had their plexus hatches open, the better to show their inner workings to those t'au cadets who would seek a surface understanding of their glory. He ran up the spiralling ramp, past the time-sequential exhibits, towards them.

In doing so, he saw the truth.

Two-thirds of the way along the ramp, he passed the display pertaining to the Damocles War, and the Battle of Gel'bryn City. History had marched on without him. He had not been translocated by the Imperial's field, but stilled completely. Frozen in time, and only now released, three hundred tau'cyr later. But that was not the worst of it.

Beyond the display, he saw exhibits on the Farsight Expedition, each more damning and hurtful than the last. They were titled the Great Treason.

His eyes widened, heart hammering in his chest. His thoughts of pursuit from the monster still screamed from his hindbrain, but for a moment, they had been put aside.

Farsight the Rebel. Farsight the Traitor. It was all there, plain as day.

Had he known it all along? Had his first instincts back in Mont'yr Battle Dome been correct? The one to whom he had offered his sword during the Dal'yth war, who had given him the honour name Sha'ko'vash – Fire's Worthy Cause – was himself unworthy. Had he been a false prophet of the T'au'va?

Grimacing, his mind reeling at the barrage of truths, Sha'kanthas vaulted the rail and climbed up to the battlesuit exhibits. He made his way not to the huge, multi-vaned masterpiece at the hall's centre, but the smaller, standard XV8. *The wise warrior fights with the blade with which he has trained.* It was something Farsight himself had taught him, when the student had become the master, so long ago. Be it from the lips of a traitor or no, the maxim held true.

Sha'kanthas stretched, put a foot on the battlesuit's knee, and leapt smoothly into the control cocoon. Kicking away the elegant scaffold that projected informational holos around the machine, he slid into the pilot's recess and closed the plexus hatch. Taking a deep breath, he used the command cadre's activation protocol.

Thank the T'au'va, the machine leapt into life.

The suit had been kept as a working example, a classic XV8 like those he had trained with on Vior'la, to show how far weapons tech had come. To Sha'kanthas, it was like putting on an old glove; it would have enough power to make at least one killing shot. It was a testament to the singular communality of the t'au that such a powerful weapon of war could be left on standby without reservation. Only one with the right to wear the Hero's Mantle would dare step inside, and even then only in extremis. That was something the selfish barbarians of the Imperium would never understand.

'Sha'ko'vash.'

The voice came across the command-and-control link as he initiated the XV8's war systems and tore the battlesuit free from its moorings in the exhibit. Its deep, authoritative tones echoed from across the span of history, piercing his mind.

'Honoured Sha'ko'vash. Have we communion?'

It was the voice of the Traitor, unmistakeable despite the timbre of age. Whether it came from a recording, some remote link, or perhaps even from beyond the grave, was not clear.

'O'Shovah,' he whispered back. 'You cannot be here. You were found to be a rebel, and denounced.'

'You called for me on a wavelength I have not used since the Dal'ythan campaign. So do I respond. Listen well, for I am not as far away as you might think. Events on Prefectia came to a head. Thanks to O'Vesa, I can reach you on a tight-beam relay via the muster complex itself.'

'You and your commanders forsook the Greater Good,' he said, a measure of his old bitterness spilling into his tone. 'I knew you would.'

'I forsook the sept worlds, old friend. Not the T'au'va. And if there is blame to be had, it belongs at my door.'

'The Dal'ythan campaign still burns.'

'Then the earth caste found a way to free you?'

'No. But I am free nonetheless. As is the target you sent me to kill.'

'Durian? The Chapter Master of the Scar Lords?'

'He has escaped the prison of his making, and is raging as we speak.'

'Then put him down! He is the last of his kind. A ghost.'

'It is not so easy,' replied Sha'kanthas through gritted teeth. He punched in the ident codes for the command suite as its autoset software scanned his eyes for retinal link. 'He is too resilient. All engagements have proven fatal.'

'Have you at least identified a weakness? Is there a distraction you could use? These are things you taught me to look for, long ago.'

'There is another battlesuit here, on display,' he said. 'An XV86, whatever that might be. It looks flight capable. Yet there are none here who could pilot it.'

There was a booming crash as the gue'ron'sha war leader smashed his way through the inner cordon. With a double boom his gauntlet spat out two shells. They ignited and shot out towards the two cadets hunkered down to his right as they tried to prise open a weapons display. A split dec, and they would all be dead.

Sha'kanthas lunged. With a squeal of metal, the vintage battlesuit lurched from the displays and extended its arm to echo the movement. The twin shells detonated on the battlesuit's forearm, flinging it out wide. Other than bathing the youngsters in a backwash of heat it did not harm them.

'Enough!' shouted Sha'kanthas, his voice booming from the XV8's speaker grilles as he stamped down onto the spiral ramp. The gue'ron'sha war leader barked an unintelligible war cry, a fierce joy in his tone as he pounded his way up the slope towards him.

Sha'kanthas drew a bead with the suit's plasma rifle, held his breath as the crosshairs slid into place, and fired.

The Space Marine raised his shield at the last moment. The energy bolt splashed over its rim to burn away a good inch of his skull.

He came on nonetheless.

'Buy time,' said Farsight. *'Distract. And trust to your fellow t'au.'*

The giant stormed forward once more, shield in front and massive blade raised. Sha'kanthas leapt forward to meet him, putting himself in between the cadets and the brutish invader. He saw one of them run past him and clamber into the XV86, another persisting with the weapons cache.

The gue'ron'sha war leader swept his sword down hard, cutting the knee from Sha'kanthas' battlesuit. He leapt forward, injured leg raised to slam the shield and send the brute skidding backwards. The impact jarred him even in the control cocoon; it was like charging a rockcrete bunker.

'Surrender or die,' said Sha'kanthas, eye-swiping the

translation suite so it broadcast the message in Imperial Gothic. 'Put down your weapons. You are alone on an alien planet, three hundred cycles past your time, and your warrior brotherhood is dead.'

'– – THEN I CHOOSE DEATH – –' spooled the autotrans as the gue'ron'sha recovered his footing. '– – YOUR SPECIES PROFESSES TO WANT PEACE, BUT YOU WOULD SLAUGHTER US AS BEASTS IF YOU COULD – –'

The brute lunged, covering the distance between them with shocking ease. He cut the XV8's arm from its torso as if it were no more than rotten wood. Sha'kanthas made a clumsy punch with the XV8's outsize arm, but the warrior ducked the blow, laughing darkly, and slid past him.

A cry came from behind. 'I can't get it to work!' said Tsh'varian.

'Keep trying!' came Kha'lithra's reply.

'Sha'ko'vash,' came Farsight's voice once more. It was old, and heavy with the wisdom of years. *'Get your adversary to shield against your feint. Allow those he sees as lesser threats to seize their moment.'*

'No,' said Sha'kanthas, turning. 'Why should I disgrace myself by listening to you? I shall give my life to buy time.'

'Tutor, please. Allow yourself to survive.'

Sha'kanthas saw the Space Marine raise his double-barrelled gauntlet once more. He kicked out to spoil his aim, but he was too late. The gue'ron'sha blasted a shell straight into the cockpit of the XV86. It detonated, the blood of its would-be pilot spilling from within to paint angular white limbs red.

'Tsh'varian!' shouted Kha'lithra.

'Distract the foe! Raise the shield!' came Farsight's voice.

Sha'kanthas took the leap. He jumped high, the XV8's powerful limbs propelling him upwards; though its long-dormant jets did not catch, the gue'ron'sha lifted his shield on instinct to ward away the blow from above.

There was a blaze of light from near the weapons cache. The human war leader fell back, dropping his sword to clutch one-handed at the ruined wreckage of his neck. The female cadet, Kha'lithra, advanced with a pulse carbine blazing at his chest, sending the war leader stumbling backwards blindly.

'You cannot prevail, human!' Her voice was taut, high, but utterly sure of its righteousness. 'Our destiny is to inherit the stars!'

Sha'kanthas raised his arms high. His XV8 mimicked him as he stepped forward. He brought its heavy metal fists down hard, and smashed the reeling Space Marine's head like an egg. The giant toppled back, slid down the ramp, and was still.

When he was sure his enemy was dead, Sha'kanthas slid the communion link with Farsight to full priority, intending to isolate his broadcast location.

It was already cold.

*** *Two kai'rotaa later* ***

Sha'kanthas looked up at the vintage XV8, inert once more and back in its informational scaffold in the shadow of the XV86. The cutting-edge Coldstar suit had been cleared of the unfortunate cadet's remains and reinstalled, along with a holo of commemoration dealing the entire post-stasis incident. Sha'kanthas had not reported Farsight's involvement in it, nor made further investigation as to the source of the broadcast, though he was still not quite sure as to why.

The water caste were calling the incident the Coda of

Immutable Truths. A lyrical name for a messy business, thought Sha'kanthas. How very like the por to mask such a dire mistake with poetry. Of late he had heard it implied amongst certain members of the fire caste, albeit in terms that could be easily disavowed, that the culture of the Farsight Enclaves had no need for half-truths. One day, he would find out for himself.

Still. In unity, in hegemony, there was strength. This had been proven on Dal'yth three hundred tau'cyr ago, and just recently it had been proven again.

Sha'kanthas looked up at the new exhibit at the centre of the hall. The dismembered, half-dissected corpse of the Space Marine Chapter Master stared back, an exploded diagram of defunct power armour and plasticised, autopsied human flesh that had been annotated by extensive holo-informationals. A ghoulish spectacle, perhaps, but educational. In knowledge there was power; this Sha'kanthas knew.

Twinned with belief in the T'au'va, it was unstoppable.

YOUR
NEXT READ

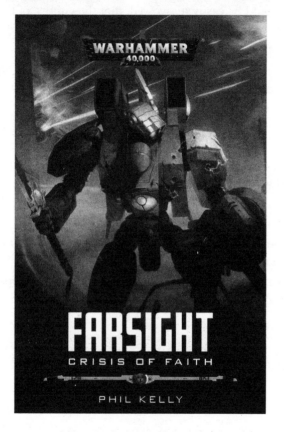

FARSIGHT: CRISIS OF FAITH
by Phil Kelly

Fresh from his victory on Arkunasha, the young Commander Farsight
leads a crusade to reclaim colonies lost to mankind's Imperium. But stiff
resistance will test him to his limits, and beyond.

YOUR
NEXT READ

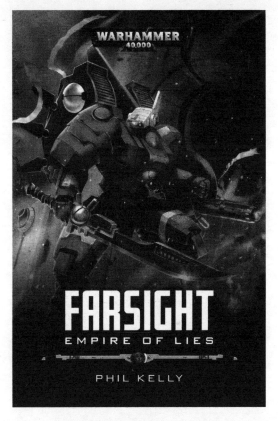

FARSIGHT: EMPIRE OF LIES
by Phil Kelly

The T'au Empire has long been plagued by the brutal orks –
and Commander Farsight will see them destroyed. As his obsessive
war against the greenskins escalates, other forces are at work, driving Farsight
to an encounter that will change his view of the universe,
the T'au Empire… and himself.

VOID CROSSED
J C STEARNS

Once rulers of the galaxy, the **aeldari** have fallen
far, and their remnants have split. The venomous
drukhari launch raids from their webway-trapped
city of Commorragh in hedonistic attempts to salve
their fading souls, while the craftworlders sail across
the black void of space, chasing survival
and a chance to rebuild.

In *Void Crossed*, J C Stearns shows what happens when
these two opposing forces collide. A craftworlder
and a drukhari bring the might of their respective
militaries to bear, with the full weight of their
personal history behind them.

Archon Melandyr strode across the battlefield, kicking a severed arm from his path. There were many among the drukhari who disdained setting foot on the ground. Xevrik Tayne, the haemonculus who had been paid to accompany him, went into battle borne aloft by microthrusters, hovering an arm's length above the ground like a malevolent spectre. He was far from the only one; Melandyr had frequently collaborated with the hekatarii of the Scarring Barb, who waged war almost exclusively from jetbikes and skyboards. Even the Harlequins he occasionally worked with belonged to the Soaring Spite, who took pride in leaping through the battlefield in an endless series of acrobatics, feet rarely touching the ground.

Not so for Archon Melandyr, lord of the Emerald Talon. For him, grinding his boots into the dirt of yet another world was a mark of pride. What was another spatter of blood or gore across his armour compared to the very flesh of a planet itself? Each boot print was a scar upon another celestial body, marking his conquests, his mud-streaked greaves a testament to the injuries he'd brought upon the very earth.

The world of Dunwiddian already had its share of scars, of course. The few aeldari outcasts who had lived there guarding the ancient Dunwiddian Gate had been no match for the mon-keigh colonists who had come to wrest it from them. The departing rangers had felt no need to warn the Imperium of the ork raids in the sector, however, and the humans had spent centuries combatting the greenskin pirates. When the humans were finally overrun, the orks had stripped their colonies for whatever they could scavenge, then turned to warring with themselves. Finally they had departed, leaving the planet alone. With the Dunwiddian Gate unguarded for the first time in years, the aeldari had come to reclaim their prize.

Across the expanse of the Plains of Isha'nne, knots of craftworld Guardians exchanged volleys of fire with kabalite warriors. Grav-tanks and Raiders zoomed across the battlefield, perilously low to the ground, as graceful fighter craft dominated the skies, trading missiles and lances of energy with one another.

Once again, Dunwiddian had become a warzone. Melandyr's interests largely lay in other sectors, and he'd initially had no interest in the webway gate, but when he had heard that the craftworld of Tir-Val had dispatched forces to claim it, he had seized the right to lead the drukhari in opposition.

Archon Melandyr spied a group of kabalites in the glossy black of the Emerald Talon, their armour edged in fluorescent green, routed from their position and fleeing from a huge wraith construct. The wraithlord swung its sword, cleaving a dracon in twain, and unleashed a gout of flame from a wrist-mount. The long limbs of the deadwalker were the same purple hue as the armour of the Guardians, the dark purple of a livid bruise, trimmed in golden yellow. The banner that hung from its back proclaimed the spirit within as Venzaynthe of House Cruiran.

Pausing for a moment, the archon lifted his hand, signalling to the trio of Ravagers that drifted above him. The incubi who dogged his footsteps flanked him as Melandyr indicated the rampaging wraithlord. The Ravagers, crewed by bloodthirsty gunners he had selected personally, were the second portion of Melandyr's personal guard. Their dark lances allowed him to extend his reach across entire battlefields, and they protected him from above as his incubi protected him from threats below.

There was a colossal whine as the Ravagers fired in unison. Nine beams of concentrated dark matter particles lanced across the battlefield, transfixing the awesome form of Venzaynthe. The undead scion of House Cruiran vanished, his wraithbone shell blown apart in an instant, vaporised by the potent celestial forces employed against him.

Archon Melandyr howled in laughter as the drukhari rallied, charging over the smoking remnants where Venzaynthe had stood. He took off again, racing deeper into the fray. There had been battle lines when the bloodshed had begun, but they had long since dissolved. For the aeldari, they meant very little anyway. When their forces could redeploy at an instant in gravity-defying Wave Serpents and nimble Raiders, or soar over enemy entrenchments on wings wrought of psychoplastic or haemonculus fleshcraft, deployments soon became hopelessly enmeshed.

The grass had been trampled, the gentle slopes reduced to fields of muddy gore. Hundreds had been slain in the hours since the first shot had been fired, and hundreds more would die before one side yielded. Archon Melandyr had waited patiently for his quarry to appear, but he could wait no longer. He ran across the killing fields, seeking his victim. The Dark City might wish to see the gate reclaimed for their use, and his allies might have been enticed into battle by the promise of valuable craftworld playthings, but Melandyr had crossed the stars with an entire army at his side to kill but a single person.

Ciorstah was here. He just needed to find her.

The deck of the freighter was covered in scorch marks, the rounded beige walls marred by low-yield plasma rounds and studded with errant shuriken. The few remaining t'au cowered in terror, waiting for their captors to shackle them and take them away. Their defenders had been slain to the last, leaving the crew at the mercy of the Corsairs that had boarded. The aeldari pirates moved through the hold, inspecting the cargo and roughly handling their new prisoners.

Melandyr spied the woman he was looking for, and weaved his way around his fellow Corsairs, bearing down on her with the stealthy grace of a jungle predator. Springing from behind, he grabbed her by the waist and spun her in a giddy circle. Her helmet removed after the crew had surrendered, Ciorstah's long black braids fanned out around her in a raven halo, and she laughed with him.

'What's the final tally, levressa?' *Melandyr asked, releasing her. Like him, she was clad in the orange armour of Prince Eidear's Nova Blades. Like all the Corsairs in the hold of the t'au freightship, they each bore the red slashes across their shoulders,*

resembling feline claw marks, that marked them as part of the coterie of Jolanial the Twice-bladed.

Ciorstah wrapped one arm around Melandyr's waist, drawing him close. She still smelled of baked earth and alkali salts: the scent of t'au blood. He still bore the tang of ionised air about him, from the engineering compartment he had cleared, battling the t'au crew hand to hand rather than risking weapons fire in the volatile environment.

'We have yet to finish, my shoathé,*' she said, drawing close to his ear, 'but we count two full keels of refined solinium. Wezdarciel also found over twenty trusses of gossamine stalk.' He thrilled at the feel of her breath on his neck, but almost as thrilling was the value of their capture: rare commodities and valuable narcotics that could be traded at any port that would receive them.*

'How does it feel to have been so thoroughly vindicated?' he asked. Lenfionne and Ardren had argued against attacking the t'au shipping lanes, but Ciorstah, with Melandyr's aid, had persuaded, bullied and intimidated the barons into accepting Jolanial's proposition, a plan their baron and prince both knew had originated with the two lovers.

'It feels justified,' Ciorstah said. Closing her eyes, she spread her arms and walked past him with the slow, stately stride of a regent on procession. 'It feels like fate crowning us with the glory we're due.'

'Speaking of the crowning that we're due,' Melandyr said. 'Jolanial's coterie may have succeeded wildly, but Ardren's people had a much harder time of it.'

'Oh?' Ciorstah turned her face to her lover, arching one delicate eyebrow quizzically.

'Indeed,' he said. 'They were ambushed from behind and routed from the medical bay. They were put to such flight that Prince Eidear himself had to take the bay. Imagine his surprise when

he found that an entire coterie had been sent running by nothing but a lone engineer and a flight of those drones the t'au are so fond of.'

'Executed?' Ciorstah's eyes glittered with avarice. They had still not lost the translucent cerulean hue common in young aeldari adults. They would deepen to violet as she aged, but Melandyr loved them as they were, a living, moving reminder that the two of them had not yet been ground down as their elders had. His rounded cheeks, not yet hollowed to the sharpness of full adulthood, were a similar point of fascination for her.

Melandyr nodded. 'Oh, immediately,' he laughed. 'And our dear prince has proclaimed he will give command of their coterie to another, so complete was their failure.' He caught her hand and drew her closer, until their chests were touching and he was looking down into her eyes. 'And who do you think he will give them to?'

'We shall share them, of course.' She put her palm to his cheek, her hand shaking with excitement. 'What marking shall we have them bear to signify our leadership?'

Melandyr grinned. 'What about the rune of the open hand, placed upon their chest?'

'To show the heart you have taken from me?' she whispered, pulling his face down to hers.

'And you from me,' he replied.

The Dire Avengers leapt from behind a wrecked Falcon, their shuriken catapults setting up a razor storm to impede his progress. Melandyr merely laughed. His incubi charged, covering the short distance to the Aspect Warriors before they could retreat.

The Shrine of the Severed Spine was one of his greatest achievements. Left leaderless and scattered after the humiliating defeat of Archon Xarat, the incubi shrine had been on the verge of extinction when Melandyr had offered them his patronage. With his wealth, he had brought them back from the brink of ruin, and now they served him above all others, their loyalty purchased in perpetuity. Haughty leaders that wouldn't have spat upon the Severed Spine three decades ago now offered priceless treasures or holds full of slaves for the service of a single incubus.

In gunmetal-grey warsuits accented with blood red, the incubi were masters of their craft. Each of them wielded their two-handed klaives as deftly as though the broad-bladed weapons weighed less than a wych knife. The impact-ablating armour of the Dire Avengers, capable of shrugging off lasers or even explosive bolter shells, offered no more protection than a sheet of parchment. The incubi's klaivex, the leader of their shrine, was a potent warrior named Throvein, whose bladed trophy vanes were festooned with silver service studs prised from the skulls of Adeptus Astartes officers, shattered spirit-stones and the tips of broken honour blades.

The Dire Avengers' exarch commanded the warriors from the centre of their ranks, and it was he that Throvein was making his way towards. The two commanders met, power sabre to klaive, as the Dire Avengers found themselves unable to give ground fast enough to prevent the murderous attack of the incubi. The exarch was the master of a hundred battlefields, his life given in dedication to the close-range assault warfare his shrine exalted. His fixation allowed him a level of skill most living beings could scarcely conceive, much less aspire to. His very soul was blended with all those who had worn his armour before him, their skills and knowledge melded into the exarch's own considerable repertoire. Throvein killed him in the space of six heartbeats. He deflected the exarch's power-blade, hooked his klaive behind the Dire Avenger's knees, and yanked him forward. Against a fellow incubus, or a heavily armoured Space Marine, the manoeuvre might have toppled the enemy to their back. Against this foe, the blade severed the exarch's legs at the knee. His swing unarrested, Melandyr saw Throvein continue his stroke, arcing his blade up and over, chopping the craftworlder in half at the waist before his body had even hit the ground.

Not every engagement was proving as decisive.

'Onzeisch reports heavy losses,' a voice crackled in Melandyr's ear. The energy discharges in the atmosphere were so intense that they were beginning to cause interference, even in the advanced aeldari communication systems.

'This was anticipated,' Melandyr replied. 'The archite knew what she was getting herself into.' He had great respect for the venerated Onzeisch, champion of the arenas and one-third of the *ynnitach* rulers of the Scarring Barb. The hellion gangs that followed her to war were an invaluable asset, but at the end of the day they were still little better than street scum. Onzeisch's only forces of any real value were her personal attendants, a flight of Reavers who flew to war trailing immense garlands of heads taken from enemy commanders, and the archite would not fritter their lives away on petty targets.

'She's threatening to withdraw if she isn't supported, lord.'

Melandyr considered for the briefest of moments. Onzeisch was a valuable ally, but she was deployed at the edge of the Plains of Isha'nne, where the Corennan River ran fat and slow, clogged with human and ork pollutants. That was far from the main knot of the battle, where the

Tir-Val leadership had been spotted. He began looking for a Raider to signal. It appeared he would have to find Ciorstah another time.

Then he saw it: a flash of blue and violet amid a flood of palest green. He knew who it was, even without confirmation. His command runes showed a squad of kabalites near her position, and they winked out as he watched. He imagined he could hear the mournful wail even over the slicing of razor discs.

'I will send my Ravagers to reinforce, but I myself cannot relocate,' he said. He gestured for the Severed Spine to follow and set off at a sprint. 'If the archite cannot fulfil her commitments, then she's welcome to return to the Dark City.'

'We cannot stay,' Melandyr muttered peevishly.

'Of course we cannot stay,' Ciorstah snapped. Both of them knew it. Prince Eidear had grown cold and paranoid. He'd ceased to be a true Corsair ages ago. They hadn't raided in months, had taken no prisoners, seized no treasures. Increasingly, he had made the Nova Blades into nothing but a large mercenary force for the asuryani. He'd even gone so far as to take to battle allied with their hated rivals, the Insolent Kin under Prince Isbeil. 'But you cannot seriously think we would go to Commorragh?'

'We've sold scores of prisoners in their slave markets!' Melandyr said. 'Our reputations as slave-takers are more than sufficient to secure a position for ourselves.'

The baron's quarters that they shared, so large and spacious in comparison with the coterie racks, had grown small and cramped. Melandyr could barely turn around without bumping into some trinket his partner had tucked away, some memento of rebellion she clung to as though it were a child's toy.

'To do what?' Ciorstah asked. 'Bathe in gore? Liquify our minds with narcotic cocktails? Fight in the streets like animals?' She turned away, as though unable to stomach looking at him.

'As opposed to what?' he yelled.

'Tir-Val offers respite,' she snapped. 'Will you live as a child your whole life? Do you not feel a call to some form of responsibility, to build something with your existence?'

Melandyr rolled his eyes and threw his hands aloft.

'Back to the craftworlds?' he shouted. 'You would have us run like whipped beasts, to cower at the heels of our elders? Do you even hear yourself? Your cowardice?' He pointed an accusing finger at her. 'I have spent too long, done too much, to throw my name away for the grand and illustrious life of a common labourer or a hand-wringing artist!'

She took a step towards him, face contorted in patronising contempt.

'You need not abandon your calling,' she said. 'There are dozens of paths that honour Khaine, if you truly feel your life's work amounts to nothing more than bloodshed.'

He stalked towards her, glaring into her eyes, the eyes that had darkened to violet.

'Do you not see?' he asked. 'Bloodshed is what we do. Would you so carelessly throw away the thrill of the hunt, the electric song of the kill? The glory of laying hands on your prize? In Tir-Val, we could be useful,' he spat, as if the very word offended him, 'but in Commorragh we would be glorious.'

She sneered, staring at him as though he were a stranger.

'You disgust me,' she snarled. They stood chest-to-chest. He could feel the tension in that moment. Their pride would never allow either to walk their words back now, but he knew that even a single insult more might bring them to violence.

The alarm chimes blazed through the Corsair ship. They both

snapped their heads around. The chimes sounded once, twice, and a third long tone. Orks. They scrambled for their armaments. This argument, like all the others, would have to keep until another time.

The Storm Guardians tried to stand before him, but Archon Melandyr was in no mood for delays. He didn't even take time to savour the kills, merely ducked and weaved his way through the melee. Shuriken pistols hissed, the shots pinging from his ghostplate armour. The Moebian Edge, the arcane power sword that he had taken from the steaming corpse of Archon Kholanthe, battered the feeble blades of his aggressors aside. The gauntlet on his hand wove delicate wires from his blade down to the pentauric crystalline matrix he wore beneath his plate. With each life his blade reaped, the soul trap fed more and more vitality into his body. It would fade over the course of hours, but he had taken dozens of victims already. The soul trap was a rush when used on lesser life forms, but nothing compared to the thrill of taking other aeldari. Even the self-denying craftworlders lived longer and more intensely than the oldest of the weaker races, and Melandyr was able to taste the entirety of that experience in but an instant, their every triumph and joy feeding not only his body, but his monstrous ego as well.

He was a master swordsman, but the Storm Guardians required no great skill to dispatch. His hacking chops were swift and brutal, relying on his augmented strength to pound through his enemies' defences, sending sprays of blood up in his wake. The Severed Spine draughted behind him, their own blades cleaving through the asuryani as scythes felling crops. Arms and legs and heads rained down on the ground, the craftworlders dead before their severed limbs had even begun to bleed.

Melandyr could see her escort ahead of him. Just as he had been stalled at the last minute by the knot of Storm Guardians, Ciorstah had been ambushed at the last by a flock of scourges. Her personal retinue, the Shrine of the Woeful Wail, had accompanied her across Dunwiddian, and stood their ground, firing their shuriken pistols at the bat-winged mercenaries that shrieked above them, raking the Aspect Warriors with splinterfire. The Howling Banshees refused to yield, their disciplined shots tracking their enemy even as their spectral green armour was studded with shards of envenomed crystal.

He heard her piercing shriek, saw one of the scourges struck from the sky, and there she was. Her dark purple armour was a masterpiece of aeldari craftsmanship, but it was only the basest fragment of her raiment. Graceful wings, delicately sculpted to the likeness of a bird's, the feathers coloured in rows of vibrant purples and blues, stretched out from her shoulders. The pale green mask over her face, contorted into the visage of a shrieking woman, matched those of the Woeful Wail, right down to the coal-black hair that fanned out from the crown. At her side was a fusion pistol, chased in images of golden flames, and a slim chainsword with a beaded tassel dangling from the hilt; in her hands a spear tipped with a broad crystalline blade. Her weapons, her wings, her armour – even the bladed, force shield-projecting gauntlet she wore on her wrist – each boasted of another facet of warfare that she had mastered without falling victim to the hyper-obsession that would have locked her into her path forever. The crested helm, plumed with fibres of vivid pink, was her highest achievement, and proclaimed her Ciorstah of House Opalion, autarch of Tir-Val and commander of the Maidenblade Warhost.

He could hear reports from his subordinates ringing in his ears as he launched himself forward. The wyches and hellions of the Scarring Barb had withdrawn, after an ambush from a group of Dark Reapers had blown the bulk of their Reavers from the sky. Xevrik Tayne, his loyalty sorely tested by the extended battle, was demanding a withdrawal. His own dracons, however, reported the support elements that had accompanied the Tir-Val asuryani were fleeing as well. Melandyr didn't bother responding. Their forces were comparable in strength. So long as the hangers-on to the battle were fleeing in equal number, it was no matter. Tir-Val and the Emerald Talon could settle their war without help.

'Why do I care about the Dunwiddian Gate?' Archon Melandyr asked. Lady Stryxe merely smiled, gesturing for one of her slaves to refill her goblet. 'Why should I be the one to claim it?'

Her proposal was interesting, to be sure: with the ork withdrawal, the webway gate would surely profit someone greatly. The Emerald Talon already had access to webway portals, however, as well as safe passage through certain routes in the webway itself. The Dunwiddian Gate did not connect to any territory that Melandyr could consider friendly. It was a valuable resource, to be sure, but not to him.

'Have you not heard, Melandyr? Tir-Val has already proclaimed it as theirs. They have sent the Maidenblade to secure their claim.' His business ally reclined in her seat and waited for his jealous thoughts to work themselves out.

His supremacy had been centuries in the making. He'd served first as a lowly gunner on one of Kholanthe's Raider crews, rising slowly but surely through the ranks until he was one of the

Emerald Talon's most trusted dracons, a trust he had betrayed when he drove an envenomed dagger through Kholanthe's heart and seized the kabal for himself.

Melandyr had heard the news of his love's ascendancy as well. At first he had tried to destroy her by proxy, to show her how little she meant to him. He had sent the Soaring Spite to ambush her at the Fletchan Cluster. He had planted false information that had culminated in the Hammers of Dorn routing the Maidenblade on the ice world of Lhynn. Still she thrived. More than that, she had fought back. After he took the Emerald Talon, a quartet of rangers in her employ had spent months dogging his realspace raids, assassinating his dracons one by one. Acting on advice planted by Tir-Val agents, the t'au of Cha'nel had ambushed his forces on Sancta Rordan Secundus, turning a routine slave raid into a calamitous defeat.

Melandyr seethed. He'd rebuilt his forces. His kabal had never been stronger. His star had never been higher. Only one thorn remained in his side, a splinter in his psyche he had never been able to dislodge.

'I'd be delighted to lead the invasion,' he said, his demeanour the very picture of gracious good humour. It would not do to let Lady Stryxe see his fury, his obsession. 'I trust our allies have already begun preparation?'

His allies had fled. The archon paid it no mind. He could see Harlequins and Corsairs leaving the battlefield in the opposite direction. Ciorstah's forces were no stronger than his own.

She descended on him with a cry of incoherent rage. The Banshee mask she wore amplified her howls of fury, casting her screams into psychic waves. The Woeful Wail followed behind their mistress, their own shrieks adding to the chorus of doom.

The Splintered Spine were too experienced, too disciplined, to be felled completely by the tricks of their asuryani peers, but Ciorstah's wail was something else. Her hate, intense in the way only an aeldari's emotions could be, was too much even for the veteran incubi to bear. Their breath caught in their throats, their limbs suddenly too leaden to move. The Banshees were among them before they could counter-attack.

Melandyr caught Ciorstah's spear with the Moebian Edge. She wrenched his sword to the side. He let her, taking the moment to step in and drive his fist into her face. Her momentum was unarrestable. He felt a grinding web of pain shooting up his hand as several bones cracked, but Ciorstah fared far worse. Stunned, her dive became a plummet, and she smashed into the ground of Dunwiddian.

The Severed Spine, freed from the autarch's baleful influence, rallied at the last moment. Klaives came up to deflect power swords, and the shrieking gave way to the clash of blades. One of the Woeful Wail diverted towards Melandyr, foolishly believing she could strike down her mistress' foe before he realised she was upon him. He met her charge. His sword cast one of her blades to the side, the other he caught on his shoulder guard. With his free hand he grabbed her by her mane of ebony hair, and smashed her face against his knee.

Augmented by the soul trap, his strength was titanic. Her helm cracked and caved. Blood spurted through the maze of cracks, and the Banshee was thrown to the ground. Archon Melandyr moved to take her head, but before the stroke could fall, he saw the blur of colour as Ciorstah rose from the muck, and he was forced to turn and defend against her assault.

'Soul-drinking for power?' Autarch Ciorstah's voice was raspy and metallic through the mask. 'Pathetic.' The spear jabbed at him, forcing Melandyr to give ground before the asuryani. Her movements were practised and rapid, too swift to catch the blade and wrest it from her grasp.

'Your hypocrisy is thick enough to deflect gunfire,' laughed Melandyr. 'How many trinkets do you have doing your work for you? Still collecting toys, little levressa?' The use of his old pet name for her had the desired effect: she roared in rage and swung her spear in a brutal chop. Rather than move to meet her, he took the time as she swung to scramble back and clear some distance between them.

He dropped to one knee, pulled his pistol, and fired a hail of crystal splinters in her direction. The spinning spear deflected more than he would have thought possible, the rest pinging harmlessly from her masterful armour. That was fine; he had never intended to kill her with the pistol. The Severed Spine saw him take the knee, and they knew their signal. One of the incubi broke away from the Howling Banshee he was duelling with and lunged at Ciorstah from behind.

As swiftly as she had deflected his shots, Ciorstah spun on her heel, hearing the approach of the incubus before he had closed enough distance to strike her. Her spear thrust took him through the gut, and with a strength Melandyr had not known she possessed, she bore the drukhari foe aloft, bellowing in anger and triumph.

Melandyr was already lunging for the autarch. Realising her mistake, Ciorstah tried to pull her spear from the body of the incubus she had impaled, but he bowled into her. The spear fell from her hands as the two of them fell into the mud of Dunwiddian.

They rolled down the shallow slope they were fighting on, separating and struggling to their feet. The muck which stained their armour was as much blood as it was dirt and water; the battlefield had become a killing ground that Khaine himself would have been proud of. The dead numbered in the hundreds, perhaps even the thousands. Scores of fighter craft and personnel transports lay about the hillsides, twisted into ruins. With their allies fully fled, the troops of Tir-Val and the Emerald Talon were outnumbered by the corpses.

'Lord,' said the voice in his helmet, barely audible over the crackling interference, 'we have incoming... have a mix of... aeldari craft... look to be Corsairs.'

All around them their escorts continued to fight unabated. Throvein and the Howling Banshee exarch were locked in a duel, mirror swords flickering against klaive strokes in an unmatched test of skill. Even Melandyr and Ciorstah could not boast such prowess with their weapons. Melandyr's gaze snapped to Ciorstah, but his fury at her intervention turned to elation when he saw that her head was also cocked to the side, listening to a transmission.

'They aren't hers, either,' he growled. If the pirates had been her allies, she wouldn't have needed to stop and respond to the news. He raced towards her, determined to strike her down before she could return to the fray. As he passed, a Howling Banshee somersaulted over the shoulder of one of his incubi, plunging her power sword through the warrior's back. Melandyr lashed out with the Moebian Edge, severing her leg at the knee, but that was all the thought he could spare for her before he was upon Ciorstah.

'Calling pirates in at the last, my shoathé?' she howled as he approached. She'd seen him coming the moment he'd began moving, her scorpion chainsword drawn and ready. 'Your old friend Prince Eidear, no doubt. Your reward for years of continued service.'

The chainblade smashed into his helm. The curved ghostplate deflected the worst of the attack, but some part of his communication lattice failed, and the distortion turned to a high-pitched shriek. Melandyr tore the ruined helmet from his head before his former lover could capitalise on his distraction. In the middle of such a killing field, his visage was at the peak of vitality. His skin shone like alabaster. His ashen hair cascaded down the back of his armour. His eyes, once soulful and deep, were now the purest of black.

He managed to raise his power sword in time to ward off her renewed attack. She was laughing as she rained strikes down on him. The chainsword was a far less intimidating weapon, but she wielded it with greater precision than she had the pike.

'Your mind has been addled by your chanting and meditation,' he sneered. 'I left Eidear's service the very day that you did.' Their blades clashed together, their footwork forgotten. A competent swordsman could have slain either of them in their state, but they were both lost in the throes of their hatred.

'Too cowardly to ply the stars alone?' she said. Behind her, one of Melandyr's incubi had circled around the Howling Banshee exarch that Throvein was fighting. Throvein feinted and the exarch committed, and when she did the second incubus struck her head from her shoulders. His victory was short-lived: a shuriken round sliced straight through the incubus' warsuit, cleaving through his throat in a gout of blood. The asuryani whose face Melandyr had smashed earlier laughed, circling the melee with her pistol still outstretched.

'Ha!' Melandyr's blade slammed into the chainsword. She pulled her fusion pistol but he grabbed her by the wrist with his free hand, pinning her hand to her side. They ground their blades into one another, weapons locked. His stolen vitality was beginning to fail him, and he struggled to maintain his stance. 'I only stayed as long as I did to keep you alive,' he said. 'Once you left there was nothing to hold me back any longer.'

Melandyr couldn't keep the deadlock going forever. His strength nearly depleted, he snapped his head forward, bashing her mask with his forehead. She reeled, her fusion pistol flying from her hand, and he threw himself backwards, delivering a brutal kick to her chest.

He rolled back, pushing himself to his feet before she could set on him with the chainsword. To his relief, she was struggling to pull her own helm from her face. She cast it aside and shook her head. Blood flew from her nose. Time had hardened her features, ground away the soft edges and left her as unyielding as marble. A pair of brutal, winding scars ran in parallel from above her left eye to the bottom of her right jaw, where a clawed hand had clearly tried to tear her face off at some point. Her own hair had been shorn completely away. There was no part of her now which was devoted to anything but discipline and efficiency.

Ciorstah stared down at her chest in shock. The pale blue spirit-stone set into her armour had been shattered by his kick, exactly as Melandyr intended. It had taken the last iota of energy his soul trap had reaped during the course of the battle, but the look of horror on her face made it worth the cost.

'Have you forgotten what it meant to dance on the blade's edge?' Melandyr said, taunting her. 'How long has it been since you've been without your little spirit prison?'

Ciorstah spat on the ground. 'You think to cow me with your threats?' she hissed. 'You're as mortal as I, now.' She held one hand aloft. 'Your own kabal is fleeing. The Dark City has abandoned you. Slight chance of your haemonculus allies returning you to life now.'

Melandyr spared a glance to the side, where he could see Raiders and Venoms, glossy black and trimmed in green. His personal pennants were being discarded even as he watched, the treacherous Emerald Talon deserting their commander to his killing field. They were mixed with the bruise-purple craft of Tir-Val, however, which brought a smile to his face.

'Retreat with your ascetics,' he said, waving one hand towards her fleeing forces. Only the Woeful Wail and Severed Spine remained with them, although there were barely a handful of each. Throvein was down, a mirror sword jutting up from his shoulder, plunged down through his torso. Melandyr had not seen the deed, and couldn't say which Banshee had taken up the blade to avenge her leader. 'Run home to Tir-Val. I'll even be magnanimous enough to let you use my new webway gate.'

She lunged at him. Their swords clashed together again and they circled each other, striking high and low, seeking an entry. His power sword impaled her hip, but she caught his sword arm in a vicious uppercut. The entire limb went numb and limp.

'I would sooner bow down and kiss the withered feet of the mon-keigh corpse-god,' she gasped, 'than allow you to leave this world alive.' Her eyes were deep amethyst now. He wondered when she had made the decision to shave her hair. Somehow, impossibly, she was more beautiful now than she had ever been to him before. He closed with her, gripping his sword in his uninjured hand.

An impact nearly drove him to the ground. The contest between the shrines had been decided. The last incubus lay dead, and the sole surviving Howling Banshee had ploughed into him, her power sword slashing against his ghostplate with the weakened arm of a wearied fighter. Melandyr realised that against all odds the lone survivor was the same asuryani that he had struck at the opening of their engagement. Her blood still pumped from her ruined mask with each laboured exhalation. Regaining his breath, Melandyr braced himself and slammed the sword through her abdomen.

Loyal to the last, the Banshee twisted as she fell, tearing the Moebian Edge from his grasp. She slid away in the gore beneath their feet, and before he could go after her Melandyr felt a slashing sensation in his thigh. He turned back to see the chainsword chewing through his upper leg, Ciorstah grimly bearing down on it with every ounce of her weight.

He screamed wordlessly, dropping to his knees. He drew the blade from his boot and buried it in her chest, her shoulder, her bicep. They were both gone, now. They were on their side in the mud, and she kicked at him with her one working leg, driving her knee into his gut. They both lurched as upright as they could, their screams melding into a chorus of hate. They would each have plucked the beating heart from their own breast if it meant they could bludgeon the other to death with it. Finally, she slashed the chainsword across his torso, driving him away from her.

Melandyr rose to one knee, his breath coming in shallow

gasps. His face felt cold. His scalp was going numb. His limbs would barely respond; they couldn't even support his weight to make it to her.

'You never knew when to retreat, levressa,' he rasped. 'In your entire existence, the only thing you've ever managed to leave was me. Even for our kind, obsession is in your blood. It's a wonder you weren't lost upon every path you trod.'

Ciorstah slumped. Her face was unhealthily pale, her blood loss already bordering on fatal. The chainsword tumbled from her grasp. She leaned against the corpse of Throvein.

'It was... was you,' she said, her speech halted by her failing breath. 'Every time I... felt myself becoming lost... lost to a path... I would remember your face. I could never become a – ahh – become an exarch, because that would mean... mean letting go of everything I had been. And nothing could make me forget how much... I hate you.'

Even with his failing vision, Melandyr could see the approaching craft. Raiders and Wave Serpents soared closer. The flags and pennants were slashed and torn, as if they had been through many battles, but as they drew closer he could make them out. The Sable Sword. The Hegrian Banshees. The Jade Labyrinth. The pink-on-black of the Bladed Lotus.

'You want to complain about real soul drinkers?' Melandyr mumbled, his speech slurred by blood. 'You... about to get your chance.' He lifted one finger with the last of his strength. 'Not Corsairs... Ynnari.'

'Let them take me, shoathé,' she said, lifting her face in a haughty sneer. 'If it means I first see you devoured by She Who Thirsts.'

Melandyr hacked a half-cough, half-laugh, spitting a gout of blood down his chest.

'Let the Dark Prince have me,' he wheezed, 'if it means I live long enough to see your own spirit eaten by the Young God and his bloodthirsty followers.'

Their shoulders slumped, and they locked eyes. There were no more words to be had; every breath was a literal life-or-death struggle now. They had led armies, met blade to blade, and now their battle to end one another had been reduced to a contest of who could draw the next breath. Melandyr's head weaved back and forth, fighting to stay aloft, as Ciorstah did likewise. They fought to triumph over one another, knowing their battle would last to death and beyond. No matter if the Ynnari arrived in time to add their souls to the Young God's growing spiritual collective, or if their essence was torn from their frames and devoured by Slaanesh, they would die as they lived, with each fixated on nothing but the other. It didn't matter which god took them, for neither had a claim upon them: she was his, and he hers, forever.

YOUR
NEXT READ

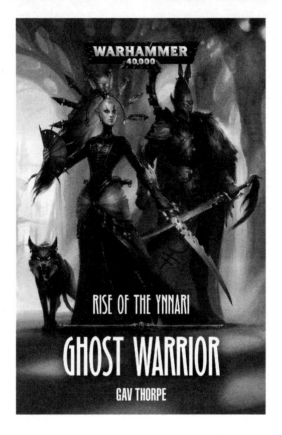

RISE OF THE YNNARI: GHOST WARRIOR
by Gav Thorpe

When the long-lost Craftworld Ziasuthra reappears, Iyanna Arienal and Yvraine of the Ynnari lead an expedition to it in hope of retrieving the last cronesword. But why has the craftworld returned now, and can its inhabitants be trusted?

YOUR NEXT READ

PATH OF THE ELDAR
by Gav Thorpe

Three friends – Korlandril, Thirianna and Aradryan – part company to walk
their chosen paths – Warrior, Seer and Outcast – little realising how the actions
of one will affect the others, and indeed their world.

LIGHT OF A CRYSTAL SUN

SUN
JOSH REYNOLDS

To be a **Heretic Astartes** is to be the most reviled of all humanity's foes. Once proud and majestic warriors, these Chaos Space Marines have turned from the Emperor's light. They are now foul champions to the Dark Gods, and would see the Imperium bathed in blood.

In *Light of a Crystal Sun*, Josh Reynolds tells a surprisingly human story of the infamous Fabius Bile. Desperate to stop his degeneration, the galaxy's most dangerous scientist seeks to discover the secrets of life and death.

The dead alien screamed.

An impossibility, the observer felt. The dead could not scream. And yet, somehow, it did. A long, ululating cry, brittle and sharp. It rose from the crystalline shape held within the flickering confines of a specially designed sensor array, and was echoed eerily by the enslaved witches who huddled in a circle about the device. The sound scratched at the edges of the observer's enhanced hearing, before spiralling upwards into inaudible ranges beyond comprehension.

'Cease.' Electro-chargers that marked the points of the sensor array fell silent, the echoes slithering through the chamber. The witches slumped, chests heaving, eyes and noses bleeding. They were all still alive – progress, in contrast to the earlier attempts. But some were not much more than that.

The observer stalked towards the circle, the ferrule of his skull-headed sceptre tapping against the rusty deck plates, the fading light of the electro-chargers playing across the worn amethyst of his battleplate and the stretched faces stitched into the folds of the flesh-coat he wore over it. The long, segmented limbs of an ancient medicae harness, tipped by a nightmarish collection of bone-saws, scalpels and syringes, loomed over his head and shoulders.

Armoured fingers caught the sweaty scalp of one of the witches and jerked the slack-jawed psyker backwards. Blank eyes stared.

'Damnation,' Fabius Bile growled. This was the third such failure in as many hours. Biological data gathered by his power armour's sensors spilled across the visual feed of his helmet. The unfortunate psyker had shallow respiration, a weak pulse and no signs of neurological activity. It was not dead yet, but it would be soon enough. Thus, it was no longer of any use, save that it could be processed into raw materials.

'This one is finished. Bring another. Quickly.' Fabius dragged the still-breathing husk upright and flung it aside, making room for its replacement. 'Hurry,' he reiterated, snapping his fingers. The mutants hastened to obey. They were twisted beasts, thick of muscle and brain. Many of them bore wounds – the marks of a ritual combat fought to decide who among their number would claim the honour of assisting *Pater Mutatis* in this experiment. The victors attended to him, while the losers contributed their bodies to his flesh-vats, there to be broken down into their component parts. Alive or dead, his creations had their uses.

Besides which, there were always more where they came from. The mouldering corridors of his Grand Apothecarium were home to more species than the average feral world. Some were of little use, except as chattel. But others had more specialised skills. The witches occupying the circle before him, for instance.

Introducing certain genetic flaws into a small percentage of the available abhuman population had shown commendable results. His servants harvested the resulting psykers with all due diligence, and quickly segregated them. Most were repurposed, their cerebral matter extracted and processed for scientific purposes. But others were trained, their given talents honed to precision.

Unfortunately, all the precision in the world could not make up for a lack of strength. Their minds, though powerful, rapidly broke against the barriers he had commanded that they hurl themselves at. Luckily, he had more.

As the grunting mutants stripped the rest of the brain-burnt psykers from the circle, Fabius stepped closer to the array and the crystalline fragments it contained. 'Even dead, you seek to pit your will against mine,' he murmured. 'Intriguing, if frustrating. Yet even the dead can be made to spill their secrets. If I wished, I could grind you into a fine powder, mix it with organic matter taken from the appropriate sources and grow a new you. I could draw you up from your essential salts, like some savage genomancer of Old Night, but there is no telling what might be lost in such a crude process.'

His hands played across the controls for the device, making alterations to the diagnostic alignment, even as the complex calculations necessary to do so flew through his mind. The array had been built to his specifications by a magos of his acquaintance, and for the fair price of a gunship's weight in wraithbone.

It was a bulbous apparatus, resembling a hunkered chelonian, save that its shell was splayed open like the blossom of a metallic flower. Suspended above the flower was a network of diagnostic scanners and sensor-lenses. Hololithic pict-captures floated in a slow dance around this network, each pinpointing and enlarging a facet of the crystalline shape.

The shards of crystal had congealed into one echinodermic mass, each facet grinding softly against another as they floated within a modified suspensor field. The facets contained a cacophony of colours, some utterly alien to his senses. Beneath that riot of shades was a milky opacity, within which was the hint of... something. Faces, perhaps. Movement, certainly.

'How many of you are in there, I wonder? How many minds, colliding like chunks of frozen rock in a debris field? Perhaps I should have made a more thorough study. Then, the moment was not conducive to such contemplation, was it?'

If the awareness within the shards heard him, they gave no sign. Whether due to stubborn refusal, or simple inability, he could not say. But he intended to find out.

The shards had come from an eldar craftworld called Lugganath. On the occasion of his visit, he'd had the opportunity to collect samples from the grove of crystal seers at the craftworld's heart – trees made from the crystallised forms of the farseers who had once guided their people, located in the wraithbone core. He'd come to learn of it through his studies, and learned as well of how the farseers' spirits were preserved in some fashion within the psych-reactive bio-circuitry that permeated such massive vessels.

The thought of it brought him a shiver of anticipation. Not immortality, but close. A perfect preservation of intellect, removing it from the vagaries of the physical. The key to his own research. The key to his salvation.

Fabius grunted and removed his helmet. The face reflected in the chrome surfaces of the sensor array was not that of a man, but a walking corpse. Of one steadily consumed from within by the fires of a blight beyond any other. A genetic cancer that reduced a healthy *corpus* to utter ruination in a scant few centuries.

He could feel it within him, a black weight, resting on his hearts and lungs. It gnawed at his vitals like a hungry beast. The chirurgeon attached to his back was busy pumping various opiates and chemical calmatives into his ravaged system. The medicae harness' efforts were a medicinal firebreak against the constant pain of his dissolution.

Fabius flexed a hand, feeling the old, familiar ache in his joints. Soon, it would be time to shed this withered flesh for a new sheath. One cloned from healthy cells, awaiting only the touch of his mind to activate it. But the process of such neural transference – of trading a faltering body for a healthy one – was not without an ever-increasing risk.

It was his hope that an answer to his problem might lie within the shards he'd sampled from Lugganath. A way of devising his own infinity circuit, and preserving his intellect across bodies, without risk of the neural patterns degrading, as they inevitably would. Once his mind was safe, he could turn his thoughts back to his great work. The only work that truly mattered: the preservation of humanity.

Not humanity as it was, obviously. But as it would be, thanks to his guidance. A new mankind, capable of weathering the gathering storm.

'But I cannot preserve them, without first preserving myself,' he said.

'Physician, heal thyself.'

Fabius turned. 'Exactly, Arrian. A simple truth, echoing

throughout the history of mankind. Those who have the most to offer must make every effort to preserve themselves for the good of all. As true today as it was a millennium ago.'

Arrian Zorzi was a hulking scion of what had once been the World Eaters Legion. But he had shed the blue-and-white heraldry for grey ceramite bare of any marking except the occasional blood stain, as he had shed his old loyalties for new ones. He served a new master now, and was as able an assistant as Fabius had ever had.

Like his new master, he had been an Apothecary in more innocent times. He still considered himself such, despite the collapse of his Legion's command structure, and wore the tools of his trade proudly, including a well-maintained narthecium. A plethora of skulls, bound by chains, hung from his chestplate, their torn cortical implants scraping softly against his armour.

'They refuse to speak, then?' he asked. As he spoke, he stroked the skulls, as if seeking to calm whatever spirits might reside within them.

'With the stubborn assurance of the inanimate,' Fabius said.

'What now?'

'We try again. I will have their secrets. It is only a matter of time.'

'Perhaps it is time to render them back onto this side of the veil, Chief Apothecary.' As always, Arrian spoke respectfully, even when pointing out what he felt was a flaw in his superior's methodology. 'We possess enough genetic matter to brew a stable clone. Why not put it to use?'

'I cannot take the risk of damaging or even erasing the very information I seek. I must have that information, and so I will, whatever the cost.' Fabius turned back to the sensor array. 'New methods are required.'

'A more potent breed of psyker, perhaps,' Arrian said, as the last of the brain-burnt witches was hauled away. New ones were herded into the experimentation chamber by snarling overseers a moment later. The overseers were tall, grey things, stretched and twisted into looming nightmares. Their skewed skulls bristled with psych-dampeners and other implants designed to protect them from the abilities of their charges. They prodded the nervous psykers forwards with shock-batons and guttural curses. One of the witches began to weep, as it was forced by an overseer to sit in a gap in the circle. 'They sense death on the air,' the World Eater murmured, watching.

'Something they must grow used to, if they wish to have any hope of survival in this grim age,' Fabius said, not looking up from his fine-tuning. 'Life is not for the weak.'

'A stronger mind might make the difference.'

Fabius turned. 'Elaborate.'

'One of Magnus' lot – this is a task for a true witch, not these pitiful slave-minds. Perhaps Ahriman, even. You have knowledge he seeks. Why not a trade?'

'Ahzek Ahriman is a deluded fool and, worse, a rapacious magpie of the first order. He would not trade. He would seek to take, whatever his promises. And I lack the stamina for such a distraction at this stage.' Fabius frowned. 'Besides, there is no way of telling whether he would even acknowledge such a proposal, especially from me. I doubt he has forgiven me for that misunderstanding on Aurelian's Folly.'

Arrian visibly winced. 'I had forgotten.'

'He hasn't. No, outside help is out of the question. Nonetheless, your proposal has merit. A stronger mind is required to breach the barriers of silicate intransigence. And that mind must be mine.' He gestured towards the back of the chamber, where an array of specialised servitors waited. One lurched into motion at his signal.

The chem-servitor trundled forwards on its mono-tread, single red eye glowing with muted excitement. It was a boxy thing, with a reinforced chassis, mounted atop a swivel-plinth. A plethora of oft-patched hoses and spliced cabling spilled from its back, to connect to the small generator unit attached to the foot-plate of the plinth. Streamers of cold fog leaked from within its bulky torso, where an ancient diagnostic analyser hummed. Fabius opened a panel set below the servitor's gilded skull, revealing rack upon rack of chemical concoctions, set into a wheel-shaped dispenser.

'Entheogenic compound X-7-D,' Fabius said. The servitor's eye flashed, and the dispenser rotated, until the selected concoction slid into the central aperture, for ease of extraction. Fabius took it. 'A potent mixture, shown to me by the savages who inhabit one of the lesser Crone Worlds. In the right doses, it can make the mind more receptive to a variety of neural stimuli.'

'And you intend to take it?' Arrian sounded concerned. Fabius smiled.

'I have done so before. Admittedly, the results were mixed, but today might conclusively prove its use as a tool of research.' Fabius glanced at the circle of psykers, and the fragments gleaming at the centre. It was almost taunting, that gleam. An invitation. Or a warning. He shook his head, annoyed by his own fancies. While it was conceivable that there might be some residual echo of personality within them, the crystals were now likely nothing more than repositories of stored information. Information he intended to acquire.

'Is this wise, Chief Apothecary?'

'No,' Fabius said simply. 'But it must be done, and my mind is the only one I trust to see to this task properly.' He beckoned and a mutant brought forward a brass-banded casket. Fabius deposited his sceptre into its silk-lined interior. The mutant closed the casket and scuttled backwards, bowing over its burden.

'The risk...' Arrian hesitated.

'It is within acceptable parameters, Arrian. And if it proves in excess, you will be on hand to separate me from the array.' Fabius held up the compound, noting the cloudy consistency with satisfaction. He lifted it, so that one of the chirurgeon's manipulator-claws could grasp it. The compound was set into place within one of the many chem-dispensers that lined the outer shell of the medicae harness.

'And how will I know when to do that?' Arrian asked, following Fabius to the edge of the circle.

'Use your best judgement,' Fabius said as he stepped into the circle, and sent a mental command to the chirurgeon. Ports set into the sides of the harness' chassis hissed open, extruding a tangle of dozens of wormlike bio-filaments.

The thin wires slithered outwards at his signal, seeking the specially prepared cerebral conduits implanted in the skull of each witch, creating a connective web within the circle. The witches groaned as one, as the bio-filaments slid into place with a series of distinctive clicks. When he was fully wired in, Fabius sent a second signal. The chirurgeon made a sound that might have been pleasure as it injected the entheogenic solution into Fabius' bloodstream. He extended a hand towards the sensor array, as the edges of his perception began to soften and melt away into whorls and spirals of liquid light.

'Now… Let us begin.'

The witches began to chant in guttural fashion, using the vocal techniques they'd been taught to focus their mental abilities. He'd found the strongest chains to be those of habit and ritual – psykers required both to function at peak productivity. The techniques themselves were a variant of those employed by the long-extinct warsingers of the Isstvan System. He had prowled the ancient choral conclaves in the days after Horus had ordered the purging of the Loyalists, and culled much of what he considered useful.

The chamber began to stretch and skew about him, its angles oscillating in a dissonant fashion. Flat planes became curves, and curves rolled up in on themselves, as the hues and textures of reality bled into one another. Fabius focused his expanding perceptions on the crystal fragments. He pressed his palms together and tried to clear his mind of all nonessential thought, using the Prosperine meditation techniques he had learned in better days, from absent friends.

The lights of the sensor array reflected from the fragments with kaleidoscopic ferocity, casting splinters of pale colour across his vision. His breathing fell into a rhythm as time slowed and the world corkscrewed into a maelstrom of flickering motes. The slight creak of his battleplate became an enduring whine, the whisper of the chirurgeon became a shriek, and his breath thundered through him as he exhaled one last time. He closed his eyes.

When he opened them, he was elsewhere.

The light was the first thing he noticed. Light, everywhere. It invaded his perceptions, and his mind reeled momentarily before his will reasserted itself. When he could see past the glare, he found himself in familiar surroundings. 'Lugganath,' he murmured. Or a reasonable facsimile thereof. A memory, carved from crystal. The swooping tiers and graceful towers, winding walkways and domed gardens of a craftworld were all as he remembered. A crystal world, from its skies to the wraithbone beneath his feet.

He stood on an immense causeway, before the towering portal that he knew led to the heart of the craftworld, and the grove of seers. The way before him was encrusted with shuddering mounds of crystal that resonated with the wailing of the wind. Above him was a false sun of vast fragments. The immensity moved against itself, filling the air with an omnipresent throb.

Beneath that itching pulse, he could hear the soft murmuring of the witches in the back of his head. Their voices rose and fell alongside the throbbing clamour of the crystal sun, somehow keeping its pulsations in check, as he'd hoped. The tatters of the eldar consciousnesses were likely not fully self-aware, but that made them no less dangerous. A flash of colour stretching across a nearby wall caught his eye. He turned swiftly and saw a familiar face.

He looked up at the wall of crystal rising before him and saw his reflection stretched across the facets. He wore no helmet. His face was fuller and unscarred. A thick mane of silvery hair was pulled back from his pointed features and bound tight in a single, coiling lock. His eyes were clear, and free of the all-too-familiar burst blood vessels and the yellowish tinge of unshakeable illness.

He was whole. Healthy.

Fabius looked down at himself. His mouldering flesh-coat and battered ceramite was gone, replaced by pearlescent white-and-amethyst battleplate, marked with the winged Cadacus. Instead of his grisly sceptre, he held a chainsword. He gazed down the length of the blade, recognising the delicate letters etched into the housing. He gave it an experimental sweep and felt the old familiar growl of its vibration. He had left it buried in the torso of one of the Khan's sons, in the final days of the Terran siege.

'A lie,' he murmured. 'Just like this place.' But it was his lie, rather than theirs. The way he had once been. 'The way I will be again, when I have what I need.'

His words echoed through the crystal world, and everything trembled slightly. He looked up and saw the enormous shards of the sun *flex*. Something had heard him. He looked towards the end of the causeway, where the grove of crystal seers waited. The answers he sought would no doubt be hidden there. Even as the thought occurred to him, the fluctuations of the crystal sun grew more evident. A sudden rush of noise, as of the shouting of many voices, buffeted him.

In the surface of crystal, he saw vague shapes take form. Memories, perhaps, or dreams. Fragments of life and death, dancing across the skewed walls and walkways like projected pict-feeds. Few of them made any sense, as if two or more separate events or recollections had been merged into one confusing tangle. Others were more recognisable – he saw scenes of hearth and home, as the eldar judged such things, and the distorted shapes of warriors of the Emperor's Children, as they laid waste to a world old before man had first sailed the stars.

And with every projected desecration, the shudders of the false sun above grew more pronounced. A phantom wind rose up from the depths of the artificial world, carrying with it a million voices. The wind tugged at him, as if ethereal claws sought to sink themselves in his armour. The murmur of his witches was growing strained and frantic. Their strength was faltering. And as their voices failed, those that rode the wind grew louder and more distinct.

They cast words at him like stones, cursing him and trying to distract him. Malign figures, dragged bodily from eldar myth and legend, formed in the crystal walls around him – gorgon-like shapes of impossible beauty, wielding blades of starlight, strove in vain to free themselves. Grinning faces, carved into support columns, cackled wildly and roared out jests in some unknowable dialect.

'If this is the best you can do, you may as well surrender now.'

At his words, the quaking mounds of crystal about him split, disgorging lean shapes. They resembled eldar warriors, save that they were crystal, rather than flesh. Colours swirled across their surface, darkening and then fading. The wind tore at him. He lifted his chainsword. 'Stand aside,' he said.

The wind ripped his words to shreds, and cast the echoes back at him. The sun seemed to draw closer to him, swelling to fill the sky. There were the hints of vast, twisted faces within its shifting planes. He heard a witch scream in agony, and a bright, white-hot pulse of sympathetic pain shot through him. He grimaced and shook his head to clear it. The strain was proving too much for his creations. Another flaw in need of correction.

'Fine, then. You will reveal to me your secrets, whatever barriers you throw up in my path.' Fabius revved the chainsword for emphasis. 'I wage a war of survival, old ghosts – and you are already dead. There is no contest.'

The crystal automatons sprang forwards, moving with

shimmering grace. Fabius spat a curse and lunged to meet them. He swept the chainsword out, and crystal shards pelted his battleplate. He bulled through their ranks, shielding his face with his free hand as best he could. More warrior-shapes ascended from the splintering ground and flung themselves at him, seeking to drag him down through sheer weight of numbers. He lashed out with hands and feet, smashing them aside, trampling some and simply flinging others from his path.

He reached the doors a moment later, and he crashed into them bodily. They slammed open and came apart with a sound like shattering glass. He staggered, momentarily off balance. Behind him, the broken doors flowed back into shape with a shrill clatter.

The chamber was as he had last seen it – a grove of crystal trees, stretching towards a domed roof. Immense columns of delicate design rose along the walls, like the ribcage of some great beast, and esoteric statuary occupied the recessed alcoves between them. The heads of the statues turned towards him, their unseeing eyes flashing with cold light.

Vast, vague shapes crouched within the walls, floor and ceiling of the chamber, glaring at him. They were at once images and reflections, not physical, but their presence was undeniable. They paced through the facets of the chamber, like shadows slipping from wall to wall, with the turning of the light.

Fabius met their glares with one of his own. 'I was wrong. You are still aware somehow, aren't you? Even broken and separate from the whole, your consciousnesses yet persist. As mine will persist, when you have been made to give up your secrets.'

Great mouths, stretched and wide, moved in soundless

demands. The weight of their minds pressed down on his from all sides. For a moment, he felt as ancient man must have felt with his back to a fire, facing the beasts beyond. Then, with a sneer, he spread his arms. 'Growl all you like. I will have what I wish from you, one way or another.'

He heard the crashing roar again, and felt a palpitation run through the crystal beneath his feet. Instinctively, his grip on his chainsword tightened. The weapon was not really there – it was but an extension of his idealisation – but it provided some small comfort. 'Have I angered you? Good. Maybe now you will listen. Show yourselves, and end this farce. You are dead, and I have bound you to my will. Acquiesce – or I shall tear this dream apart and take what I need, as I did before.' He advanced towards the trees, chainsword raised. The trees were the key, he thought. The knowledge was there, within them as it had been in the real world, and he would carve it out.

A bellow of rage shivered through the grove. Distorted, alien faces thrust towards him, as if seen through an alembic. He felt the weight of dozens of minds, all focusing on him with sudden clarity. His boast had cut through their madness. False trees twisted around, branches stretching to impossible lengths as if to throttle him. The walls bent inwards, bulging with monstrous growths.

An instant later, the chamber cracked open like an egg, and the walls fell away, revealing the false sun above. He was thrown at the shifting facets of the immensity. The craftworld grew wild around him. It was as if the whole edifice were in the process of being crumpled up. Tiers and balconies bent upwards and then fell towards him. Gaping cracks ran through the floor beneath his feet and the bowing walls, and jagged fangs of crystal surged through them.

Fabius staggered, his head in his hands, trying to block out the noise. It overwhelmed him, eating away at his certainties and senses. As he staggered, the floor began to splinter, and shards shot upwards to spin about him with ever-increasing speed.

The whirlwind enveloped him, piercing his flesh and armour with ease. He howled in pain, and he heard the witches howl with him. He wondered if they could feel his pain, as he felt theirs. Their shrieks seemed to indicate that such was the case. He felt the embedded pieces wriggle themselves deeper and the voices of the dead bellowed in his ears. Invisible claws plucked at his mind, stripping layers away to dig into the core of him. Memories were torn to shreds, as knowledge was wrung from him. He had come to prise secrets from the dead, not lose his own.

Desperate, he flung himself backwards, out of the whirlwind. He fell heavily, blood seeping from his ravaged face. The whirlwind contracted, taking on a roughly humanoid shape in the false light of the crystal sun that loomed above. He forced himself up and swung his chainsword at it. A glittering claw of shards caught the blade and stopped the blow. Its strength was immense, and as he strained against it, the chainsword lost its solidity, becoming crystal. It shattered in his grip and the disparate pieces joined the conglomerate mass.

Fabius reeled. He glanced up and saw that the sun had become an amalgamation of alien faces, twisted in expressions of rage and grief. They spoke in voices like thunder, and as the echoes swept over him, the crystal homunculus seemed to expand. It grew and spread, sprouting arms, legs, torsos, but remaining a singular entity. Many bodies, with one head of innumerable fragments, that shone like a bejewelled diadem. Many feet thudded down in a single step, as many hands reached for him. As the sun screamed alien curses, the construct it had conjured lumbered after him.

He avoided the construct's clutches, but only barely. Fingers grazed his armour, and where they touched, crystals sprouted and crumbled. He retreated, losing pieces of his battleplate the entire way. His head throbbed with the babble of dying witches, and as if from far away, he could hear the dim murmur of Arrian's voice. He pushed it aside, trying to focus. Spears of crystal thrust out at him from all directions, blocking his retreat.

He was hemmed in. Trapped. Perhaps that had always been their intent. They had drawn him in, just as their kin had on Lugganath. Then, too, he had been blinded by his desires. The construct lunged for him again. Crystal claws tore into the flesh of his face, gripping him. He howled in agony as striations of crystal slid through him. He punched at it, trying to break himself loose, as it pulled him closer. Images wavered across its many torsos and limbs. He ignored them, not wanting to see.

Fabius wrenched himself out of the construct's clutches and lurched back, sweeping crystals from his ruined armour. He felt blood filling his battleplate, and the old pain was lurking in the back of his mind. The witches' voices were fading. Not much time now. Never enough time. He had to break free of the trap, turn it back on them.

The construct screamed, many voices issuing through a single, too-wide mouth. As before, the voices crashed against him, threatening to cast him back, to impale him on the crystals that stretched hungrily about him. But he was ready this time. This was a place of the mind, and his mind was stronger than theirs. It had to be.

Fabius met their spite with his own. Their hate, with his hate. A millennium of cancerous rancour spilled from him, and congealed in his waiting hand. A familiar sceptre topped by a gleaming brass skull was suddenly in his hand. They had constructed this place for themselves, and he would take it away from them, piece by piece, shard by shard.

The construct lurched towards him, and he struck the groping paw. It exploded, and the crystal walls around him trembled. Another claw shattered. Then a leg. A torso. It retreated, wailing. He stalked after it, lashing out to smash away at the crystal cage around him. 'You think you are inviolate? Invincible, in the light of your crystal sun? Such arrogance is what cost your people a way of life. As it will cost you now.'

The air was filled with glittering debris. Walls emerged before Fabius, and he smashed them. The floor bucked, and he broke it apart. The world roiled about him, and he attacked without care. He tore himself a path, and saw the crystal-thing ahead, losing bits of itself as it stumbled along a projecting balcony.

It whirled, sweeping out dozens of arms. He broke them apart. The air stank of burning meat, and the light was fading. The crystal tiers and domes of Lugganath were gone, replaced by ruin, as far as the eye could see. Wherever he looked, a broken city rose or fell towards him. The construct grew taller, and its shimmering skull met the base of the sun, spearing into it, merging with it. The crystal sun blazed with cold fire, only it was no longer a sun, but the head of the construct itself. It spread its arms and drew the craftworld about itself like a cloak. Colours spilled out of the world and away, leaving only the absence of everything behind.

It was a giant, now, with a sun for a head, and a cloak made of millions of memories, at once the whole of the world and an extension of it. It crouched above him, looking down with millions of eyes, screaming at him with millions of mouths. It raised a glittering talon, as if to crush him. He hefted his sceptre. 'I will not be denied by such pale echoes as you. I have come too far, endured too much – I will not!'

The smell of burning meat was almost overwhelming now, and it ate away at everything else like acid. Cracks ran through every crystal, and the air was a solid throb of pain. Fabius felt as if he were moving in slow motion, as the sceptre snapped out, aimed at the centre of the vast claw that descended towards him.

And then, there was light.

Fabius staggered, his hearts thudding with an arrhythmic beat. His eyes were filled with blood, his ears ringing. The chirurgeon was shrieking in his head. He spat bile and wheeled about, hands flexing emptily. 'What–?' he croaked.

The witches were dead, consumed from within, as if by a fire. They slumped in their circle, a blackened ring of toadstools. The sensor array was weeping sparks and the suspensor field was shaking. Arrian stood nearby, blade drawn. It took Fabius a moment to realise that the World Eater had sliced through the filaments connecting him to the witches.

Fabius sagged, and Arrian caught him. 'What did you do?' Fabius hissed. Brief blooms of pain ran up and down inside him. His hands trembled like those of some withered ancient. He felt sick. Weak.

'I used my best judgement,' Arrian said. 'When the witches started burning, I took it as a sign that all was not well.'

Fabius blinked blood from his eyes and pushed away from his assistant. He forced himself to stand, and turned to look at the crystal fragments. They pulsed faintly, their light diminished. He was not the only one who had been weakened. He spat and wiped blood from his face. He glanced at Arrian. 'You did well.'

Arrian nodded. 'What now?'

Fabius turned back to the sensor array. 'We try again.'

Arrian hesitated. 'Are you sure?'

Fabius didn't look at him. 'Bring me more witches. We will try again. And again, and again, until I have what I need. I must.'

He coughed and tasted blood in his throat. His head ached, and he could feel phantom claws digging into his mind, tearing away memories and hard-won knowledge. Pain rose in him, and he forced it back. This body still had time. It would endure long enough.

It had to.

'We will try again,' he repeated.

Whatever the cost.

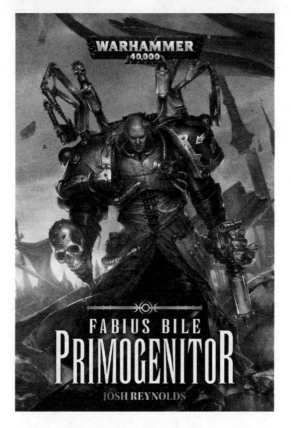

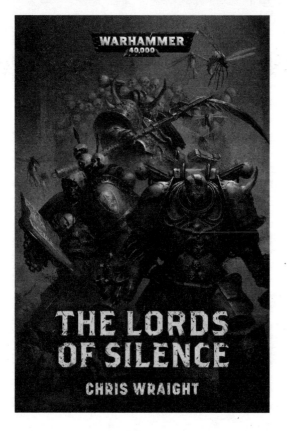

YOUR
NEXT READ

THE LORDS OF SILENCE
by Chris Wraight

The galaxy has changed. Armies of Chaos march across the Dark Imperium, among them the Death Guard, servants of the Plague God. But shadows of the past haunt these traitors…

WAR IN THE MUSEUM
ROBERT RATH

Dormant for millions of years and now reborn into
bodies of living metal, the **necrons** are among the
galaxy's most ancient races.

Of those necrons who have retained traces of their
former personalities, the most eccentric is Trazyn
the Infinite, overlord and master of the Solemnace
Galleries. He is a collector and historian, who has
gathered countless living artefacts of the galaxy's
history in his vast museum. In *War in the Museum*,
Trazyn must capture a deadly alien predator that has
escaped his collection.

VISHANI: *Phaeron, wise men say that common foes make common friends.*
NEPHRETH: *Wise advice – if one wishes to be common.*

– *War in Heaven*, Act V, Scene IX

Specimen rehydration at seventy-two per cent, lord archaeovist.

His arch-cryptek, Sannet, sent the thought as an interstitial message, preserving the silence.

Trazyn, Master of the Solemnace Galleries, Preserver of Histories, and He-Who-Is-Called-Infinite nodded and motioned with two metal fingers. The gesture opened Sannet's thoughts so that the glowing glyphs unfurled above his metal skull like a scroll. Trazyn liked what he saw there – they were getting close.

The organism's clawed hooves levitated a finger-width above the floor, held aloft by repulsor fields so gravity could not ravage its dripping corpse. Scalloped plates of chitin shielded the desiccated flesh of its limbs. A rock-ribbed exoskeleton encased shrivelled organs. Arms held wide, head erect, the hive tyrant dwarfed the metal giants that stood before it. A rehydration array elevated up and down its bulk, hissing as it sprayed the creature with anti-necrotic revivicants.

This was, Trazyn reflected, likely the most dangerous restoration he'd ever attempted. Tyranid synapse creatures were known to reanimate from even the most extreme wounds, so there was no sense taking chances. Indeed, the reason the specimen was in such poor shape owed something to the tortured nature of its acquisition.

It had been quite a puzzle, acquiring an undamaged tyranid splinter fleet. Baiting it to the tundra world of Vuros had been simple enough; the real difficulty had been identifying and intercepting the tyrant's atmospheric entry pod on its way to the surface. With their synaptic overlord freeze-drying in the cold of space, the disoriented splinter fleet had been easy to lure into the tesseract fields. The downside, of course, was that the tyrant had needed nearly a century of rehydration until it was fit for display.

Trazyn had earmarked it as the centrepiece of his Tyrannic Wars exhibit.

Outside in the main gallery stood a full splinter of Hive Fleet Kronos, frozen in the moment of landing, a wave of blue-tinted claws and crimson armour about to crash down on an Imperial outpost. Undulating waves of rippers. Termagant packs. Genestealers emerging from tunnels in the loamy earth. Gargoyles circling overhead.

And if the plumping bulge of the tyrant's flesh was any indication, it would soon join them.

Trazyn's cowardly kin had warned him against it, of course. In fact, when Hive Fleet Behemoth bore down on Solemnace, Trazyn's aeon-long rival Orikan the Diviner had even prophesied that the Great Devourer would destroy both Trazyn and his galleries. The mystic fool had been so disappointed when

Trazyn simply triggered deep-space lures so the swarm parted around Solemnace, like a river around a stone.

They were correct about one thing, however – this restoration demanded extra security. He'd banished all but a pair of crypteks and four lychguard to minimise the chance of mishap. A full legion waited outside the galleries, along with a new surrogate body in case Trazyn needed to evacuate his consciousness quickly. In the event of a containment break, secure doors would seal this small band in, sacrificial offerings to be atomised by the spider-leg banks of gauss flayers pointed at the limp tyrant.

After all – if it awoke, who knew what might happen to the exhibits outside?

But it should not come to that. A century ago, Trazyn had personally supervised the crypteks as they'd drilled into the tyrant's armoured skullcap and implanted six mindshackle scarabs into its shrunken brain. Trazyn's metal fingers danced across the haft of his empathic obliterator, beating a delighted tattoo on the weapon. Was this perilous? Certainly. But eternity got dull without a hint of peril. And for an immortal necron, boredom was more dangerous than even the largest alien horror.

An alert sketched across his vision, overlaying the thoughts of Arch-Cryptek Sannet. Behind him, the lychguards' metal necks shifted in their ball mounts.

Movement in the central gallery.

'My lord,' warned the lych-captain.

'Yes, yes, I see it,' said Trazyn. 'Continue to guard the specimen, I'll investigate.'

'Allow me to accompany you, lord,' the lych-captain answered, the balefire in his oculars flaring with concern. 'Safeguard protocols state–'

'Don't fuss, captain.' Trazyn picked up his empathic obliterator. 'What's going to hurt me in my own gallery?'

Trazyn turned and walked into the dark, holding the glowing headpiece of the staff before him like a torch.

Normally, Trazyn would have lit the central gallery – but power was better spent on the restoration. He walked into the back line of the invasion, weaving between carnifexes that rose like hills in the shadowed darkness. Warriors, their limbs fused into deadly bio-weapons, posed in the act of firing clouds of flesh-boring organisms.

Trazyn skirted around a tyrannocyte drop spore half-buried in the tundra floor. Hormagaunts emerged from it, clambering over each other to join the living carpet of organisms that made up the bulk of the invasion force.

Trazyn was well used to wandering the galleries alone, but he was not yet accustomed to this exhibit. Its scale was almost hard to comprehend – so much so that when arranging it he'd navigated the scene by floating overhead in a Catacomb command barge. Now, inside the ravening horde, he felt a novel tingle of fear. The soft glow of his obliterator reflected on long talons and venom spraying in arcs from baggy throat sacs. His heavy footfalls echoed back at him.

'Probably a wraith,' he muttered. 'Receivers go down and they default to their last task.'

He was being foolish, of course. These organisms were preserved in hard-light, encased like insects in amber. Touch a claw and it would cut you, but they could no more move than a wax figure could.

Unless there had been an earthquake. Unless a nexus fault opened a tesseract labyrinth. Unless...

The weight hit him from behind without warning, sending him toppling forward, pinning him to the simulated earth. Sensors wailed in agony as a scythe-talon as long as a gauss flayer punched through his shoulder with a shriek of bone on metal. Clawed feet dug into his scaled cloak.

Trazyn gripped the empathic obliterator, firing up the headpiece.

'Don't touch me,' he said, and struck blindly over his shoulder.

A clawed hand closed over his head and twisted.

Vertebrae servos whined and popped with strain, living metal groaning as it bent to its limit. Talons dug into his ocular sockets and green sparks burst in his vision.

Then with a crack, the tension broke and he could feel his head tear free from his shoulders, spine grating on shoulder guards as it slithered free. Phosphorescent reactor fluid spouted. Cables stretched like ligaments as the hand pulled his head upward and turned it to face the killer.

Trazyn got a glimpse of the creature – made kaleidoscope-mad by his shattered oculars – before the alien crushed his metal skull.

To be honest, Trazyn did not particularly like being murdered. The rush of transferring his consciousness from one body to another felt like free-falling through a planet's atmosphere.

The lychguard he'd possessed arched its back, limbs extending and metal skin bubbling as Trazyn's essence suppressed the host's personality-programs, rearranged the antique armour and refashioned the guard's warscythe into his own empathic obliterator.

'My lord. What happened?'

It took a moment for Trazyn to orient himself to who was speaking. The lychguard captain.

'A complication,' said Trazyn, rotating one wrist to test how it responded. 'It's the lictor. Flesh-Stealer. Vicious little creature. Hunted the tundric nomads for two years after the initial acquisition. At least only one hard-light field failed, and that bio-form was the only thing in–'

'Seal the door, arch-cryptek,' the lych-captain ordered, his safeguard protocols overriding normal chains of command. 'My lord, call in the legion.'

'And let ten thousand warriors loose in my collection with gauss flayers?' snorted Trazyn. 'I think not. *Perhaps* the deathmarks.'

'My lord,' said Sannet, furiously making notes with his stylus. The great sleep had damaged his engrammatic matrices, and he could no longer remember information unless he wrote it. 'I have diagnosed a nexus fault. The legion did not make its last check-in cycle. I'm not sure we *can* call the deathmarks.'

'I'm going up.' Trazyn let his consciousness flow into the nexus network, racing through cables and channels as if carried through an underground stream.

Then his spirit-algorithm stopped dead. He felt the data of his mind bunching up, boxed in, memories of past and present overlapping. He reversed himself before the code of his consciousness scrambled.

He opened his oculars. 'We are locked in. Sannet, have you detected seismic activity?'

'No, lord.'

Trazyn rubbed his chin, the alloy of his finger scraping his age-pitted death mask. He summoned a phos-glyph panel and scanned diagnostics. Normal, except he could not call data for anything past this floor. The shadow-clock was also two minutes behind planetary time. Clearly a fault had cascaded through the nexus, slowing the system.

Unless…

'Cease rehydrating,' said Trazyn. 'Scan for brainwaves.'

'None,' said Sannet.

'Could this creature cause a distortion?'

'Previous specimens have not.'

'We've never had a tyrant.'

'What is our protocol?' asked the lych-captain.

Trazyn thought for a moment. 'This beast is no match for an overlord and his lychguard, eh? Sannet, you stay. Seal the door behind us so the thing cannot reach its master.' He paused. 'And how many mindshackle scarabs can you spare? Pity to waste a good specimen if it can be avoided.'

So it would be a hunt, like in the days of flesh. An overlord and his retainers, going forth to capture a great beast with naught but their might and their wits.

Pity, Trazyn thought, *that we do not have a chariot.*

Blackstone doors ground shut behind them, the cyclopean blocks meeting with a tone that reverberated through the chamber. They moved in a miniature phalanx, two lychguard up front with their shields and hyperphase swords. Trazyn on one flank with his obliterator, the under-cryptek with his staff on the other. The lych-captain guarded their backs, his warscythe held high in a guard.

Slow and cautious. Scrying for bio-signatures.

But there were bio-signatures *everywhere.* Each hard-light hologram encased real, living flesh. The hunting party flicked through visual filters. Heat. Radiation. Empyric field.

Trazyn ran an ocular scry over the mid-sized creatures

arrayed in the back line. A brood of tyranid warriors stood, discharging foul ammunition. A lictor crouched, statue-still as if about to pounce. Tyrant guard circled protectively around the space where their master would soon reside.

Trazyn looked down the line, at the biovore battery with its fleshy spore-ammunition...

Wait.

That didn't make sense. Lictors were infiltration organisms. They didn't belong in the back line. How could he have made such a careless placement?

He hadn't, of course. When Trazyn turned back, the lictor was gone.

'On guard,' he warned, bracing for attack.

The thrown spore mine arced out of the darkness. Trazyn's ocular array analysed it in mid-air, noting the way its toxic sludge moved from chamber to chamber as it contracted. He saw its pulsing rapidly increase – like the heart of a panicked animal – as it neared the lych-captain.

Who raised his warscythe.

'No!'

The lych-captain intercepted it with a perfect vertical slice. Had it been a grenade or shell, he might have scythed through the detonation cap. Instead the spore opened, rotten and steaming. Ropy splashes of bio-acid descended on the phalanx. The lych-captain took the worst of it, tarry ichor covering his chest and face. His metal body screamed as it warped and deformed, the armour plates of his front expanding so quickly it bent him over backward and snapped his spine. The cryptek to Trazyn's left dashed away, one arm a melting ruin.

And as soon as they broke formation, Flesh-Stealer was on them.

It came for him, and Trazyn gathered power in his obliterator, bringing it to the floor like a hammer. The layer of tundra parted before him, a billowing shock wave of jade energy throwing immobilised termagants away from the furrow.

The lictor dodged aside, the blast bubbling its chitin and mangling one leg. That did not stop it. Tendrils of flesh, each tipped with a hooked curve of bone, lashed out like amphibian tongues. They snared his arm and dragged him close.

Trazyn screamed a curse in Old Necrontyr.

A sickle talon stabbed down through his open mouth and burst the base of his skull.

Trazyn activated the cryptek's oculars and saw his old surrogate – now reverting back to a lychguard – sink to the floor. The remaining two lychguards were boxing Flesh-Stealer in with their shields, getting between Trazyn and the marvellous specimen.

Flesh-Stealer howled as a blade bit its rubbery muscle. It smashed down at one of the guards and he raised his shield to take the blow. The lictor vaulted off it, using the hulking guard as a springboard in its leap towards Trazyn.

Trazyn raised the cryptek's staff of light, unleashing a white-hot beam at the horror falling towards him. Lightning speared through the chamber, strobing on frozen tyranid bodies. One of the lictor's grasping arms spun away, severed.

Flesh-Stealer still came down right on top of him, bone scythes burying deep in the space between his shoulder plates and ribcage. Then it heaved and opened his chest like a cabinet.

* * *

Before Trazyn activated his new oculars, he urged the hijacked body to run.

Scatter. He sent the communication as an interstitial command package, the new plan arriving in the remaining lychguard's mind instantly and fully formed. *It can only chase one of us. Head for the Imperial outpost display.*

Trazyn needed reinforcements.

He reshaped his legs for speed, not daring to look back. The lychguard was far to his left, heavy feet pounding the artificial ground. Trazyn weaved through packs of termagants, vaulted ripper swarms.

The settlement was close. Hab-blocks and bunkers emerged from the shadows. Trazyn pulled up a phos-glyph panel as he ran, keyed in an order. A bunker's plasteel double-doors drew open.

He could feel the beast behind him, gaining. Nearly there.

It caught his scaled cloak, dragged him down. This time he was smart enough to transfer *before* he died.

Trazyn did not even glance at the lictor savaging his former body. He leapt through the bunker's double-doors and keyed an order. They rolled shut with a reverberating clang.

'*Welcome to our special exhibit,* Imperial Heroes of the Tyrannic Wars,' said a voice. Trazyn's own voice, in fact. '*Please approach this gallery by starting on the left, and proceed in a shadow-clock fashion to see the greatest...*'

'Hush,' Trazyn said.

The voice cut off.

Trazyn didn't know why he'd installed the automated system. Dead Gods knew, no one came here without him as a guide. But a few millennia back he'd suffered an attack of conscience and began worrying whether anyone would understand his galleries if he were ever destroyed. So he'd taken on the responsible, if dull task of recording guides in every language known to the Necron Empire.

He passed warriors in blood-red ceramite and commissars leering under peaked caps. In one diorama, a group of snipers from the Catachan XVIII nestled in a shooting hide, their bio-signatures masked by the mound of termagant corpses piled atop the dugout roof.

Trazyn stopped in front of a case, summoned a phos-glyph panel.

'Assigned to study the aquatic wildlife of a remote world, Magos V–'

'I said hush,' Trazyn snapped. Then softer: 'Awaken, my friend.'

The magos biologis was hunched over the severed head of a tyranid warrior, his crab-like servo-arms paused in the act of trepanning open the cranium with a surgical laser. It was his rust-coloured robe that stirred first, falling slack as gravity took it – no longer buffeted by the sea winds of his maritime fortress.

<Trazyn,> the magos signalled, using Mechanicus binharic cant. The words came to Trazyn as if through a bad vox-speaker, nowhere near as clear or elegant as noemic glyphs.

<Magos,> he responded. <I have need of you.>

<I wish you would leave me conscious.>

<Standing unmoving for a century would drive you mad, my friend,> said Trazyn. <And a madman is no good to me.>

<Have you any idea what I could achieve in a century of silent cogitation, Trazyn? No, of course not. Immortality has made you a time-waster. Well, if you need more guidance on hormagaunt swarming patterns–>

'There's been a breakout,' Trazyn said, hoping auditory speech would break the thought-loop.

The magos paused. 'I advised you not to refurbish the tyrant.'

'It is not the tyrant. Though it may be… involved. There has been a nexus fault. We cannot signal the legion, I cannot transfer consciousness, and Flesh-Stealer has awoken.'

'Only the lictor?' The magos' eye-lenses rotated in suspicion.

'Keep staring at me like that, magos, and I'll stop sending your little research packages to the Mechanicus. Or should I keep sending them, but add a little gift of my own – a jokaero code-virus perhaps?'

'Lictors are precursor organisms,' the magos answered, dipping his head. 'Meant to operate at the limits of the hive mind. It is understandable that one might awaken from even a weak signal.'

'It still should not have broken out of its containment.'

'Tyranids project a psychic energy, Trazyn. A shadow in the warp. Especially Hive Fleet Kronos. You artificials can't feel it, but it disrupts more than psychic patterns. Technology, arcane devices, even languages can come under its effect. And what remains of my organics tell me that the shadow has fallen on Solemnace.'

'I need warriors,' said Trazyn. 'Those experienced in battling the swarm. My lychguard were… too single-minded. My kind are not flexible, as you know.'

'And poor in your understanding of organics,' added the magos. 'So you need a kill team.'

'Indeed. But no Deathwatch. In fact, no Astartes. I want to save the gallery, not burn it down.'

'Guardsmen, then?'

'Not enough firepower. I have only two mindshackle sca-rabs…' His gaze drifted. Settled.

'You will not convince them, Trazyn.'

'Their mind-training would help resist the shadow, they are resilient, manoeuvrable, and certainly have firepower.'

He stepped up to the case.

'*Clara and Setine Fontaine,*' said the automated guide. Tra-zyn let it play. '*Heroes of Okassis, nine years before the Great Awakening, Second Tyrannic War. Orphaned siblings raised in the schola progenium, they were recruited for the Adepta Sororitas in 968.M41 and fought two campaigns in the same Dominion squad. Last sighted on the walls of the cathedral-fortress, over-run and fighting against the hordes of Hive Fleet Kraken.*'

The Sisters stood back to back. Clara's storm bolter chopped fire into the reaching claws of a genestealer pack, its muzzle flash stabbing out so far that it blackened the creature's beetle-like armour. Setine loaded her final gas canister into her meltagun, her face tanned from its back-wash and a carnifex lying at her feet, torso melted into a bubbling crater by her final shot.

<They hate xenos,> signalled the magos.

'Exactly,' said Trazyn. 'And they have not heard of necrons.'

He released the scarabs. They skittered out of his palm and leapt, spidery legs finding purchase on the ornate power armour of the Sisters. They danced up embossed skulls and golden filigree until they nestled into the soft flesh of the humans' cranial base and embedded their legs, injecting their nano-scarab payload.

'Awaken,' ordered Trazyn.

Their eyes stirred first. Fluttering, blinking. Disoriented and in the grip of stasis-sickness.

'Hello, Sisters,' said Trazyn. 'I have a proposition for you.'

'Steel abomination,' growled Clara. She swung her storm bolter into Trazyn's face and pulled the trigger.

Or she tried to. Her finger would not tighten. Trazyn could see it locked tight, the muscles tensed so hard her leather glove creaked.

'I'm afraid that is not permitted,' said Trazyn.

'Perhaps a brief explanation, lord?' suggested the magos.

Trazyn looked the Sisters over. Clara tensed with every muscle in her frame, trying to burst his head with a bolt-round. Her sister Setine stood in shock, wide eyes searching the alien forms in the diorama around her.

'Very well,' grumbled Trazyn. 'You are correct, I am, to use your rather over-applied term, an "abomination". An artificial life form called a necron. I am overlord of this world and curator of the galaxy's greatest collection of historically and culturally significant objects – a collection of which you and your sister are a part. However, I have revived you because, much to my embarrassment, I need your assistance.'

'Where is my sister?' demanded Clara.

Trazyn gestured at the Battle Sister next to her, who seemed to be looking down the dead carnifex's throat.

'That is not my sister,' she said, shaking. 'What have you done with her?'

'Ah, I had forgotten,' Trazyn said. 'Your sister was sadly not recoverable, and I had to substitute a stand-in to complete the scene.' He gestured at the hormagaunts vaulting the dead carnifex. 'Specimen recovery can prove quite difficult when the specimen's opponent is so… voracious.'

'She… is dead and I am alive? We swore an oath we'd die together.' Clara's jaw tightened, pushing at the mindshackle scarabs.

'If it makes your grief easier to bear,' he said, 'your sister's corporeal form is not entirely gone. You have her right hand, for instance, plus one cornea and most of her organs.'

She dropped the storm bolter in shock, as if she could drop the hand that held it as well. 'You... you sewed pieces of us together?'

'It is a common enough practice. Even in human museums. If you have two incomplete carnodon skeletons, you combine them to make a full carnodon. The change is really only cosmetic.'

The false sister, meanwhile, seemed entranced by her own meltagun.

'Cosmetic? You have corrupted the sacred human form. The pinnacle of all organisms, made in the Emperor's image. A tainted species like yours could never understand such perfection.'

'Pardon me,' said Trazyn, 'But I would like to correct a few notions here. First, my kind are not a species. A species is naturally occurring. It has evolved. My kind are made, not born. Second, human perfection is, to be polite, debatable. Your kind are born defenceless and take an absurd amount of time to grow to adulthood, and even then, you spend a third of your lives unconscious. Everything you consume for energy eventually kills you, and your reproductive system is the same as your waste elimination system.'

'Dual-use systems are efficient,' the magos objected.

'But revolting,' Trazyn countered. 'Would you like to see the perfect organism?'

Trazyn waved in the air, calling forth a phos-glyph hologram. On it, his death memories of Flesh-Stealer played again and again, direct from his engrammatic matrices.

'This is the perfect organism. Humans are excellent

generalists, without doubt, but this organism changed tactics every time it faced me. Which is why I need you to help me entrap it.'

The false sister approached the hologram, peering at it. She swept a hand through the image in wonderment.

'Entrap it?' said the magos.

'Very well… kill it. I suppose. For the good of the collection.'

Clara sneered. 'I died to stop the tyranids on Okassis, and did so gladly. But I did that for the Emperor. I care not if the swarm eats your little world.'

'Stop?' said Trazyn. He suppressed a chuckle. 'You think you stopped them?' He waved a hand to call up another mem-hologram. This one was a cathedral city, seen from the air. Streams of men boarded troop ships – behind them, a curtain of murderous biomass drew across the burning chapel blocks and monastery towers. 'Oh, your Battle Sisters killed the tyrant organism and managed to evacuate the Ecclesiarchy, but the world was lost. The Imperium declared it a great victory, of course. Humans have such a talent for revisionism.'

As he spoke, one of the holographic troop ships panicked and lifted off with its rear hatch still open. It banked towards the sky, spilling tiny clawing forms onto the city below.

'Afterwards, the swarm carried on to devour three more worlds.' He closed his fist and the hologram snuffed out like a candle, its spectral remnant twisting upwards in a waft of green smoke. 'Once this lictor kills me, for the last time, it is likely it will target the containment systems. The swarm will be unleashed on more Imperial worlds.'

'Sister,' said the false sibling. She reached out and touched the shivering Clara. 'For I may not be your sister in blood, but we are Sisters in duty. These tyranids are unfamiliar to me. My service was spent fighting the Heretic Astartes. But I know my duty – to protect my lord's life, and defeat all enemies of the God-Emperor. I know not whether my lord lives or has fallen to the heretics, but I can see that the enemies of the Imperium are outside that door.' She nodded at the plasteel, then turned to Trazyn. 'You, xenos. If we do this service to you, will we be free to make our own destiny?'

'I will not return you to this exhibit,' said Trazyn. 'I swear on my honour. I can reunite you with your lord, if you wish it.'

'I wish it,' said the Sister, with a nod. 'My name is Magdelena, by the by. And now, Sister...' She grasped Clara by the shoulders and looked into her eyes. Bright fires glowed within, the light of holy faith. A righteous certainty that stilled the nerves of her rattled companion. 'Let us kill this alien, Sister. For the Emperor–'

'For the Emperor,' echoed Clara.

'...and Lord Vandire,' Magdelena finished.

The doors ground open and the quartet edged out. Close skirmish order, wide fields of fire. Trazyn stood behind, sighting along a plasma pistol he'd liberated from an arms display. Trazyn was not fool enough to engage Flesh-Stealer in close combat again, but he still felt a certain amount of embarrassment about the crude Imperial weapon.

I'll instruct Sannet to leave that part out of the official chronicle, I think. Trazyn made a mnemonic note to preserve the thought.

'Increase your scans,' said the magos. 'It will try to hit us where we are not looking.'

'There are so many of them,' said Clara. 'God-Emperor help us if they wake up.'

'Kill this lictor and they won't,' said Trazyn. 'Magos, is your scanner picking up anything?'

'False positives,' said the magos. 'Close the door behind us, I'm registering interference from the room.'

Trazyn banished his obliterator to its dimensional pocket and summoned up a control panel, his metal fingertip hovering over a glyph. Interference would make sense, of course. There were several dead lictors in the Imperial Heroes display. But there was a feeling he could not pin down.

So he looked up, above the open plasteel doors. To the fresh drops of ichor running down the rockcrete bunker face, to the shadowed form crouched at the top, breaking the bunker's roof outline like a gargoyle on an Imperial cathedral.

'Behind!' Trazyn shouted, mashing the plasma pistol's trigger.

He missed, unused to the warm-up before the fusion reactor unleashed its power. The beam chased the lictor as it sprinted down the steep glacis of the bunker, blackening rockcrete in its wake.

It leapt, camouflaged exoskeleton still the drab grey of the bunker – headed straight for Trazyn. Always Trazyn.

He ducked, rolled, came up behind the creature with his staff reforming in his hand – but it had already wheeled to face him, wobbling on the injured leg. Trazyn swiped the obliterator at its midsection, driving it back.

Into the encircling kill team.

A hail of bolter shells cracked into the creature from the side, blasting fist-sized chunks of armour plating off its thigh. Flesh-Stealer swung one grasping scythe backwards, catching Clara's breastplate and throwing her into a pack of frozen genestealers. Then it shrieked in pain.

A neon-red laser speared through its abdomen and struck the floor, kicking up a candle flame in the shallow dirt. Behind it, the magos advanced, chanting, directing more power into his dissection rig's surgical laser. His other servo-arm flicked through functions and settled on a circular saw. The sawtooth blade keened louder than the tyranid's howl.

The lictor went low, grabbing purchase on the dirt with its multiple limbs and leaping away.

Trazyn brought the empathic obliterator down two-handed on its bent spine. The charged head of the staff radiated so bright that it left an after-image in the air as it fell. Raw power, the power of a vanished race, hit the lictor's back like a lightning strike. A billow of cold emerald energy washed outward, stirring the magos' robes and blasting the floor of the chamber clean of dirt for a ten-foot radius.

The lictor broke, its midsection crushed as if a Leman Russ had rolled over it. Hooved feet kicked in spasm. Its top half, swirling as it searched for a camouflage pattern that might save it, tried to crawl away.

Magdelena stepped up, pressed her meltagun to its head, and pulled the trigger. She swept up and down, methodically rendering the bio-form down to a puddle of grease.

'Not so difficult,' she said. 'Our vow is complete.'

'Not quite,' Trazyn said. 'First we have to get to the Nexus Mundi.'

'The what?' said Magdelena, popping her hydrogen canister and fitting another.

'A control room, in crude vernacular,' said Trazyn. 'We can get there on my modified command barge. Once at the

Nexus Mundi I can contact the legions, get us out of this gallery and fulfil my end of the bargain. Which reminds me.' He reached out with his spirit-algorithm. *Sannet. Confirm the tyrant is secure.*

'Xenos,' said Clara.

'One moment,' he responded. *Arch-cryptek? Please confirm.*

'Trazyn,' said the magos.

'Yes, yes. What now?'

The magos pointed with a spindly, data-jack finger. Trazyn followed the path.

A lone termagant wandered towards them, through the no-man's-land between the front of the tyranid swarm and the Imperial settlement. It stumbled, weaving drunkenly, then halted and bent over, stiff tail pointing high as it rubbed its face in the dirt. Confused. Disoriented. Perhaps sick.

'The eyes,' said Magdelena. Trazyn could hear the tremor in her voice.

Trazyn looked at the breaking wave of tyranids and saw a starfield of red jewels. Every elongated hormagaunt skull was turned towards them. Every armoured warrior glared, teeth showing in a snarl. Even the great carnifexes, bodies immobile, looked straight at the little knot of humanoids.

In the eerie silence, twenty thousand eyes fixated on them.

A deep boom shook the cavernous gallery. Great tomb doors slid open, stone grating on stone. Long, sickle-like talons hooked the blackstone door frame, steadying the desiccated hive tyrant as it pulled itself into the chamber.

One clawed hoof slammed down, still dragging the impaled form of Arch-Cryptek Sannet.

Though it was more than half a mile away, the tyrant's

massive scale made Trazyn's central reactor cycle higher, preparing for a fight. The tyrant stood in the place he had set aside. And though he felt terror slip into the very code of his algorithmic soul, he could not help but feel pride in seeing his tableau complete. For a moment, at least.

'Its powers are weak,' he said. 'It's lost a great deal of fluid, with no way to regain it. We can contain it. The stasis fields are holding overall–'

A termagant weaved towards the tyrant, retching as if it had been poisoned. Others followed, staggering forward to hop at the feet of their synaptic overlord. Weak chirps and trills came from their throats.

The tyrant darted its head downward, snatching the broodlings two and three at a time in its dagger-fanged mouth. A termagant's head burst between its jaws, ichor running down its barbed chin. The tyrant sucked at the still-wiggling body and ducked back down into the chirping mob. The termagants made no attempt to run.

'Cannibalistic rehydration,' said the magos. 'Fascinating.'

'They're moving' said Clara, her voice a harsh whisper. 'They're all moving.'

They ran, followed by the sound of thousands of chitinous hooves clattering on blackstone.

This is not an accident, Trazyn thought as he ran through the Imperial settlement. *This is sabotage.*

A ravener lunged at him out of an alley. It dragged its spasming coils behind it, clawing its way along the floor with sabre-like talons. Stasis-sick. Hungover from decades severed from the hive mind.

Trazyn shot a bolt of plasma through it, leaving an ashen tunnel in its chest that crumbled in on itself.

Another fine specimen, ruined. That's what bothered him the most. Accidents happened. Seismic events. Raids. The occasional specimen insurrection. Dear Inquisitor Valeria, wandering in with her force – though in retrospect, he almost viewed her as a guest.

But this was a deliberate attack. The lictor, the perfect organism to tie him down while undermining the system. One that would emerge ready to fight, and could hide among the horde. Timing the rising during the one time when the tyrant could reanimate. And the door. No one but Trazyn and the crypteks could open the blackstone slab-doors that sealed off the refurbishment room. Certainly, the tyrant couldn't.

And only the tyranids were awakening, flesh-and-blood bodies breaking free of their hard-light prisons. So far, apart from his thralls, the Imperials were still living statues.

A general tesseract failure would not be so selective.

'Beware left,' said Clara, firing across his front, bolt-rounds chopping into a knot of genestealers emerging from an outflow pipe. 'Reloading,' she shouted, as those behind tried to clamber past the bodies of their kin.

Magdelena moved in and cooked the thick metal pipe with her melta. When it glowed, she kicked the lip with a power-armoured boot, crimping the softened metal inward to cut off the passage. 'They've become swifter.'

'The hive mind is reasserting control,' said the magos, toasting a lazily drifting spore mine with his dissection laser. 'How far to the barge?'

Trazyn was searching his command protocols as he ran. Identified the barge. Connected. 'There,' he said, and pointed.

A scorpion-shaped craft rose above the settlement's

outskirts, rotated towards them, and shot forward. Light danced in pulses across the lines of its panels and bathed the roofs of the low hab-blocks emerald as it skimmed past.

Trazyn shoulder-rammed through a hab door and took the stairs two at a time. Within seconds he'd gained the roof, three storeys up.

Only then did he look behind. For a moment, he thought of the deserts during rain season, when flash floods swept the dry canyons. Tyranids coursed through the gaps between buildings, swarming so thick on the streets that he could not see the cracked pavement below the writhing tide of muscle and chitin.

Magdelena was last up the stairs. She slammed the plasteel door and welded it shut behind her. Below them, Trazyn heard the crunch of hooked talons biting into brickwork.

'Climbers,' said Clara, firing straight down, before swinging the storm bolter up to throw rounds at an incoming gargoyle. 'Flyers.'

The building shook once, twice. Trazyn looked down to see a carnifex scaling the outer corner. Its bulbous wrecking claws punched holes in the building as it ascended, dusting its face with rockcrete powder.

A shadow passed over them. Trazyn ran to meet it.

'Forgive me,' he said, clambering up onto the command deck, and pointing at the empty wing-cradles. 'I neglected to mention that there are only three seats.'

The magos hunched, leapt onto the command deck with surprising agility, and maglocked himself to the scorpion tail. His surgical beam bisected a group of hormagaunts that tried to follow him. <Altitude, Trazyn,> he signalled. <Altitude. Altitude. Altitude.>

The Sisters were only half in their cradles when the

carnifex cleared the building top. It swiped for them with a boulder-like claw. Foul breath, like rotting sea life, washed over the craft.

Trazyn adjusted their attitude, nursed the repulsor field higher, careful that he did not slip off the roof's footprint too early and spill them all sideways. With his other hand, he aimed the plasma pistol straight for the carnifex. It cocked its head to look at them sideways like a bird, one jewel-red eye calculating distance for the next swing.

Trazyn held the trigger, cooking the shot. He felt the reactor grow hot and the grip vibrate in his hand as he sighted on the eye.

He let go of the trigger.

Blue-white light radiated from the coils, the vibration turned to a shake.

The magos snatched the pistol from Trazyn's hand with a servo-arm and flung it away.

<Up!> he urged.

Trazyn shot them upward as the pistol's reactor detonated like a small sun. It caught the carnifex under the chin, snapping its mammoth head backward like an uppercut so that it collapsed on the street, crushing the lesser creatures below.

Proximity alarm. Trazyn banked and a bone harpoon sailed past. A gargoyle dived onto the superstructure, latched on to a wing, and unleashed a blast of fleshborers that pattered harmlessly off Trazyn's metal body.

His fingers danced on the command orb, throttling up their speed so the gargoyle lost its grip, rolled along the hull and disappeared. He summoned a phos-glyph panel, keyed an entry code.

Before them, a wall half a mile high drew open as smooth as a curtain.

'Next gallery,' said Trazyn, as they swept past the doors.

Sparks danced in the darkness – and Trazyn heard the telltale whizz of bolter rounds passing.

The Solemnace galleries were awakening.

Trazyn kept them moving, skimming only slightly ahead of the tide that pursued them, heading towards the cylindrical bastion at the end of the gallery.

He didn't want the humans to see what was in this space, didn't even want them to think about it more than necessary. It appeared to be no less than a giant's library, with rows of shelves rising from the central plaza of fountains and sculptural gardens. Yet each shelf was the size of a starship hangar, and its contents varied from jungle to snowy plain.

Usually Trazyn cherished the quiet in this gallery – yet it was quiet no more. Battle raged in each diorama. Bolt shells and rockets sailed past the command barge less with intention to down the craft, and more because everyone was shooting everything.

In one hangar, an antique Dreadnought staggered as orks clung to its surface, beating it with pipes and wrenches. In the next, a group of Dusk Raiders, trudging through snow, had broken through to the adjoining display and engaged a troupe of Harlequins performing in a wraithbone palace. The next cubicle was a riot of motion blur. A pack of hounds leapt and snarled, slipping in and out of existence with each jump. One had blinked through the divider and was tearing at a t'au diplomat the water caste had unwisely dispatched to Solemnace.

The tyranid flood tide surged in after them, blanketing the floor of the plaza, covering the fountains, ornamental gardens and the plinths so recently vacated by their living statues.

From one of the side galleries, a torrent of bolter fire tore into the swarm's flank. Space Marines in blue power armour stormed out, driving a wedge into the tyranid advance. Trazyn took them lower and they saw strange plasma discharges – sun-bright bolts dancing across the spectrum of colours, matching the vertical stripes on the Space Marines' helms. A captain raised a crystalline power sword that shimmered with the iridescence of an oil slick.

Trazyn throttled forward, unable to watch his precious collection maul itself. Loss reports, triage priorities and restoration protocols filled his vision. He banished them with a thought.

Reach the Nexus Mundi, he thought. Stop the bleeding. Then, the restoration could begin.

Fighting raged outside the Nexus Mundi. Gunfire and artillery detonations rolled in from multiple floors. Imperial Navy interceptors and t'au strike fighters chased each other in the distant heights of the vault.

But all these battles were piecemeal compared to the tyranids. They alone drove straight for the Nexus Mundi, as if sensing its importance.

Trazyn stood at the control cartouche, pulling up system reports. Scanning for damage. A grinding sound reverberated in his throat.

'Can you fix it?' asked Clara, firing out a window slit.

'Not responding,' said Trazyn.

'Perchance at least close the front door?' asked Magdelena. She spun around a column and discharged her meltagun into a charging termagant brood, then limped back into cover. Fleshborers had made a mess of her leg. The magos, for his part, had gained control of the defensive gauss flayer battery, keeping the stairway clear even with two spike rifle rounds buried in his back.

'I have to enter the Nexus,' said Trazyn. 'Hold them. And do not try to move me.'

Trazyn doused the light in his oculars. Focused, rendering his essence down to code. Packaging his spirit-algorithm into the proper data format for the system.

He felt himself folded down, reformed, projected like one of his holograms. It was, in a strange way, not so different.

The chamber was all rough-hewn polygons in white and grey. A miniature of the galleries stood around him, rendered in data, small enough he could walk across one of the great chambers in a few strides and browse the displays as if they were terrariums.

Soft red warning lights were pulsing in two dozen displays – a sterile representation of the carnage occurring in the physical world. Only pure information existed here.

He drew his empathic obliterator.

'Do not make me flush you out,' called Trazyn. 'There has been enough unpleasantness.'

A figure stepped out from behind a databank, vertebrae tail twitching. The staff he carried against his shoulder was known, and feared, on a dozen dozen tomb worlds. Its starburst pattern and jewel lodestone were the symbols of a master chronomancer.

'Orikan,' said Trazyn. 'If I had known you wanted to visit, I would have invited you.'

'You are not supposed to be here, Trazyn,' Orikan answered. His voice scratched in his throat like the scrape of old pages turning. 'I have cast zodiac calculations upon the stars, and they told me you and your archives would fall to the Great Devourer. Visions from the sands of the great hourglass revealed it in detail. Your doom has been written in both atoms and gas giants, I have read it in the very whorl of the cosmos.' His metal teeth clicked in irritation. 'And yet here you stand.'

'Orikan, will you ever recover from that false prediction?'

'Your fall was foretold.'

'Foretold by Orikan,' sneered Trazyn. 'And Orikan is never wrong. For if Orikan is fallible, perhaps the stormlord should not gamble the fate of his dynasty on his visions. Perhaps all the tomb lords, the phaerons and phalanx captains that so hate and fear Orikan will realise that he does not see every assassin's phase-knife before it comes. Or perhaps the being who cannot handle Orikan being fallible is... Orikan.'

'I am not so petty.'

'You are exactly that petty,' said Trazyn, chuckling. 'So am I. That's why we loathe each other so. But we agreed Solemnace is sacrosanct – this is beneath you, Diviner.'

Orikan bristled, his golden headdress flaring upward like the hood on a particularly venomous snake. 'And this juvenile collection – these insects you so love – should be beneath you. It damages our view of the future. All these things out of time, past their moment, they form a knot in the timeline. An obstruction to every astromancer. Solemnace is a cataract on the eye of the galaxy, Trazyn, a cloudy film that prevents us from charting a course into the future.'

'And so you will force the future,' Trazyn said, calling up a phos-glyph panel. 'The gallery is now seven minutes behind planetary time. I dismissed that as a fault, but it's a temporal bubble, isn't it? Each time you failed to murder me, you went back, tried again. It's why the lictor was so effective against my lychguards, but not against those from another time.' He paused, looked at Orikan. 'But why now? Why not alter the timeline and destroy this place when Hive Fleet Behemoth arrived? Why not...'

He paused, chuckled.

'Oh, Orikan,' he said. 'You found out she was here.'

'She knows so much. I can perfect the transformation. Transition us all out of these steel prisons and into beings of light. She knows the secret. I can commune with her.'

'You can't,' snapped Trazyn. He recognised the balefire in Orikan's oculars. The obsession that Trazyn knew all too well. 'There is no life there. Her engrammatic matrices are of historical import, which is why she's here. But she's broken. No good to any–'

Orikan came at him without warning, a streak of light, bright as dawn on still water. The Diviner shone with golden radiance, a being of pure energy. The future Orikan wished for all necrons, the form he could only take when the stars were right. The astromancy he had used, Trazyn realised, to project himself to Solemnace.

Trazyn raised a tesseract labyrinth.

The light-being that was Orikan stopped, shimmering. 'Those do not work here.'

'My nexus,' said Trazyn. 'My rules. This is my second mind, Orikan, you didn't think I'd leave it defenceless, did you?'

Orikan fled, streaming around the corner, pouring himself into a red-lit shelf in the gallery.

Trazyn followed, two spirit-algorithms chasing each other through circuitry and programs. Switching protocols. Slamming electro-gates behind them, worming through exploitations.

One moment they raced through a coolant system in a snow display, the next, a stasis protocol for a large green beast. Orikan switched the stasis field off, delaying his pursuer a microsecond as Trazyn reasserted it and charged on. He could feel Orikan cursing him in the wires. But that was no concern of his – he was focused on composing his security measures. He had the Diviner's scent now, knew the signature of his code. Could close avenues and herd him.

He caught up, saw Orikan hesitate, cornered, then plunge into the only avenue open to him.

The mindshackle scarabs.

Trazyn took a different path.

He opened his eyes. It was strange to have flesh-and-blood eyes again, stranger still to get them when a genestealer was snapping at his throat.

Trazyn shoved the storm bolter under the genestealer's chin and blasted its brains onto the ceiling. It was not just the eyes. There were thoughts, so many thoughts in Clara's mind. Chief among them was *survive*, no surprise there, but just below that was *then kill the necron*.

Interesting.

He turned and saw Magdelena limping towards his helpless metal body with the meltagun.

'Orikan!' he yelled, surprised and delighted by the novelty of his new accent. He pointed the storm bolter and let loose a warning fusillade over the mind-slaved Bride of the Emperor.

Orikan turned, fumbled the meltagun, and Trazyn barrelled into him. Orikan hit Trazyn's borrowed body with a rib shot that slammed the breath out of him – breath, that was new too – and Trazyn launched Clara's thought-filled head into Magdelena's chin, close enough to execute a mind-jump to the other woman's mindshackle scarabs.

Two necron consciousnesses in one human mind, and all Trazyn felt was... peace. Magdelena's sense of self was a glassy lake. A lake on Ophelia VII, that lay protected in the hills near the monastery. A lake untroubled by the bodies that floated face up beneath the surface. All the men, women and children she had killed during the Reign of Blood. The Imperial Fists and Black Templars she'd gunned down on Terra with the word 'heretic' on her lips. None of it troubled her at all, for she had done so for the Emperor – and Lord Vandire.

And as Trazyn burrowed deeper, he could read Orikan's thoughts, as well...

Orikan fled screaming, terrified of what might be revealed. He tried to puppet the magos, but his techno-wards were too strong, and he instead jumped to Clara.

Clara got off her knees, her back to Trazyn and storm bolter dangling from one hand. She looked up.

The tyrant was in the doorway, long-limbed and rehydrated. Skull crackling with synaptic power that jumped in sparks from the mindshackle scarabs still implanted in its brain tissue.

Its four long, scything talons drew back for a blow.

Orikan turned Clara's head towards Trazyn and smiled, a grin with all the spite of an ancient mind turned to malice. Clara dropped, a puppet with its strings cut, and Trazyn saw a blur of grasping light shoot upward and suffuse the four mindshackle scarabs embedded in the tyrant's brain.

The swarm stopped moving, sprinting termagants slowing to a lope and turning their heads towards the tyrant. It hacked acid. Bit twice at something invisible. Shuddered so hard, Trazyn thought it might break its own neck. Then it threw its head back and screamed.

A lightform clawed out of the brain case, howling in pain and shock. Trazyn did not want to know what Orikan had seen in there. The endless galactic abyss? Hunger beyond satiating? Perhaps he glimpsed the hive mind – perhaps it spoke to him.

Whatever he saw, it was a vision he did not desire.

His light-ghost was already shooting out through the ceiling when Trazyn poured back into his own body and activated the stasis fields.

The tyrant was, as Trazyn knew it would be, a fine centrepiece. Majestic and powerful, a true representative of its species.

And he had outdone himself on the poses. Clara stood before it, the spent shells of her storm bolter frozen as they arced through the air. The magos, conscious this time as requested, leaned over the controls of his gauss flayer turrets, two spike rifle rounds in his back. Trazyn would remove them when the magos was needed again.

His own double, a surrogate, stood at the control cartouche. And Magdelena covered the back entrance with her meltagun. That back entrance hadn't existed in the real Nexus Mundi, but he wanted to position her so that she could see the tableau directly across: *The Beheading of Goge Vandire*.

He had, after all, promised that he would not return them to their exhibit – and this new feature, titled *War in the Museum*, was indeed not their original exhibit. So they stood with updated identification plaques, preserved for eternity.

There was only one missing touch.

Trazyn dragged a finger across the air, creating a glyph-plaque. With a flick, he sent it to rest just above the tyrant's cranium, where it would wait in empty space until Trazyn could complete the display.

It read: ORIKAN THE DIVINER.

YOUR
NEXT READ

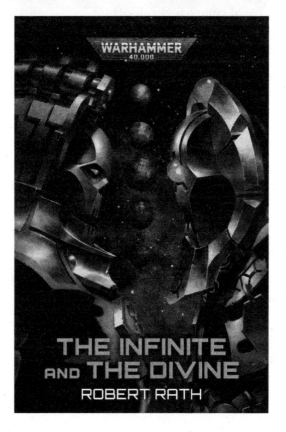

THE INFINITE AND THE DIVINE
by Robert Rath

Trazyn the Infinite and Orikan the Diviner are opposites. Each is obsessed
with their own speciality, and their rivalry spans millennia. Yet together,
they may hold the secret to saving the necron race…

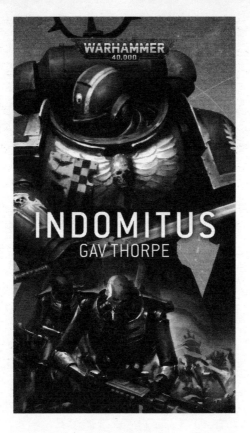

HEADHUNTED
STEVE PARKER

The Adeptus Astartes of the **Deathwatch** stand firm
against the terrifying xenos swarms. Compiled of
elite, veteran battle-brothers from myriad Chapters,
it is their duty to investigate, analyse and destroy
the most dangerous alien threats to the sanctity of
mankind's realms.

In *Headhunted*, a squad of Deathwatch Space Marines
must infiltrate an ork space craft to investigate and
eradicate a new threat. But they soon learn that
the rabid greenskins are not the true danger;
something all the more dangerous lurks,
threatening to destroy them all.

Something vast, dark and brutish moved across the pin-pricked curtain of space, blotting out the diamond lights of the constellations behind it as if swallowing them whole. It was the size of a city block, and its bulbous eyes, like those of a great blind fish, glowed with a green and baleful light.

It was a terrible thing to behold, this leviathan – a harbinger of doom – and its passage had brought agony and destruction to countless victims in the centuries it had swum among the stars. It travelled, now, through the Charybdis Subsector on trails of angry red plasma, cutting across the inky darkness with a purpose.

That purpose was close at hand, and a change began to take place on its bestial features. New lights flickered to life on its muzzle, shining far brighter and sharper than its eyes, illuminating myriad shapes, large and small, that danced and spun in high orbit above the glowing orange sphere of Arronax II. With a slow, deliberate motion, the leviathan unhinged its massive lower jaw, and opened its mouth to feed.

At first, the glimmering pieces of debris it swallowed were mere fragments, nothing much larger than a man. But soon, heavier, bulkier pieces drifted into that gaping maw, passing between its bladelike teeth and down into its black throat.

For hours, the monster gorged itself on space-borne scrap, devouring everything it could fit into its mouth. The pickings were good. There had been heavy fighting here in ages past. Scoured worlds and lifeless wrecks were all that remained now, locked in a slow elliptical dance around the local star. But the wrecks, at least, had a future. Once salvaged, they would be forged anew, recast in forms that would bring death and suffering down upon countless others. For, of course, this beast, this hungry monster of the void, was no beast at all.

It was an ork ship. And the massive glyphs daubed sloppily on its hull marked it as a vessel of the Deathskull clan.

Re-pressurisation began the moment the ship's vast metal jaws clanged shut. The process took around twenty minutes, pumps flooding the salvage bay with breathable, if foul-smelling, air. The orks crowding the corridor beyond the bay's airlock doors roared their impatience and hammered their fists against the thick metal bulkheads. They shoved and jostled for position. Then, just when it seemed murderous violence was sure to erupt, sirens sounded and the heavy doors split apart. The orks surged forward, pushing and scrambling, racing towards the mountains of scrap, each utterly focused on claiming the choicest pieces for himself.

Fights broke out between the biggest and darkest skinned.

They roared and wrestled with each other, and snapped at each other with tusk-filled jaws. They lashed out with the tools and weapons that bristled on their augmented limbs. They might have killed each other but for the massive suits of cybernetic armour they wore. These were no mere green-skin foot soldiers. They were orks of a unique genus, the engineers of their race, each born with an inherent under-standing of machines. It was hard-coded into their marrow in the same way as violence and torture.

As was true of every caste, however, some among them were cleverer than others. While the mightiest bellowed and beat their metal-plated chests, one ork, marginally shorter and leaner than the rest, slid around them and into the shadows, intent on getting first pickings.

This ork was called Gorgrot in the rough speech of his race, and, despite the sheer density of salvage the ship had swallowed, it didn't take him long to find something truly valuable. At the very back of the junk-filled bay, closest to the ship's great metal teeth, he found the ruined, severed prow of a mid-sized human craft. As he studied it, he noticed weapon barrels protruding from the front end. His alien heart quickened.

Functional or not, he could do great things with salvaged weapon systems. He would make himself more dangerous, an ork to be reckoned with.

After a furtive look over his shoulder to make sure none of the bigger orks had noticed him, he moved straight across to the wrecked prow, reached out a gnarled hand and touched the hull. Its armour-plating was in bad shape, pocked and cratered by plasma fire and torpedo impacts. To the rear, the metal was twisted and black where it had sheared away from the rest of the craft. It looked like an explosion had torn the ship apart. To Gorgrot, however, the nature of the ship's destruction mattered not at all.

What mattered was its potential. Already, visions of murderous creativity were flashing through his tiny mind in rapid succession, so many at once, in fact, that he forgot to breathe until his lungs sent him a painful reminder. These visions were a gift from Gork and Mork, the bloodthirsty greenskin gods, and he had received their like many times before. All greenskin engineers received them, and nothing, save the rending of an enemy's flesh, felt so utterly right.

Even so, it was something small and insignificant that pulled him out of his rapture.

A light had begun to flash on the lower left side of the ruined prow, winking at him from beneath a tangle of beams and cables and dented armour plates, igniting his simple-minded curiosity, drawing him towards it. It was small and green, and it looked like it might be a button of some kind. Gorgrot began clearing debris from the area around it. Soon, he was grunting and growling with the effort, sweating despite the assistance of his armour's strength-boosting hydraulics.

Within minutes, he had removed all obstructions between himself and the blinking light, and discovered that it was indeed a kind of button.

Gorgrot was extending his finger out to press it when something suddenly wrenched him backwards with irresistible force. He was hurled to the ground and landed hard on his back with a snarl. Immediately, he tried to scramble up again, but a huge metal boot stamped down on him, denting his belly-armour and pushing him deep into the carpet of sharp scrap.

Gorgrot looked up into the blazing red eyes of the biggest, heaviest ork in the salvage bay.

This was Zazog, personal engineer to the mighty Warboss Balthazog Bludwrekk, and few orks on the ship were foolish enough to challenge any of his salvage claims. It was the reason he always arrived in the salvage bay last of all; his tardiness was the supreme symbol of his dominance among the scavengers.

Zazog staked his claim now, turning from Gorgrot and stomping over to the wrecked prow. There, he hunkered down to examine the winking button. He knew well enough what it meant. There had to be a working power source onboard, something far more valuable than most scrap. He flicked out a blowtorch attachment from the middle knuckle of his mechanised left claw and burned a rough likeness of his personal glyph into the side of the wrecked prow. Then he rose and bellowed a challenge to those around him.

Scores of gretchin, puniest members of the orkoid race, skittered away in panic, disappearing into the protection of the shadows. The other orks stepped back, growling at Zazog, snarling in anger. But none dared challenge him.

Zazog glared at each in turn, forcing them, one by one, to drop their gazes or die by his hand. Then, satisfied at their deference, he turned and pressed a thick finger to the winking green button.

For a brief moment, nothing happened. Zazog growled and pressed it again. Still nothing. He was about to begin pounding it with his mighty fist when he heard a noise.

It was the sound of atmospheric seals unlocking.

The door shuddered, and began sliding up into the hull.

Zazog's craggy, scar-covered face twisted into a hideous

grin. Yes, there *was* a power source on board. The door's
motion proved it. He, like Gorgrot, began to experience
flashes of divine inspiration, visions of weaponry so grand
and deadly that his limited brain could hardly cope. No
matter; the gods would work through him once he got
started. His hands would automatically fashion what his
brain could barely comprehend. It was always the way.

The sliding door retracted fully now, revealing an entrance
just large enough for Zazog's armoured bulk to squeeze
through. He shifted forward with that very intention, but
the moment never came.

From the shadows inside the doorway, there was a soft
coughing sound.

Zazog's skull disintegrated in a haze of blood and bone
chips. His headless corpse crashed backwards onto the carpet of junk.

The other orks gaped in slack-jawed wonder. They looked
down at Zazog's body, trying to make sense of the dim
warnings that rolled through their minds. Ignoring the
obvious threat, the biggest orks quickly began roaring fresh
claims and shoving the others aside, little realising that their
own deaths were imminent.

But imminent they were.

A great black shadow appeared, bursting from the door
Zazog had opened. It was humanoid, not quite as large as
the orks surrounding it, but bulky nonetheless, though it
moved with a speed and confidence no ork could ever have
matched. Its long adamantium talons sparked and crackled
with deadly energy as it slashed and stabbed in all directions, a whirlwind of lethal motion. Great fountains of
thick red blood arced through the air as it killed again and
again. Greenskins fell like sacks of meat.

More shadows emerged from the wreck now. Four of them. Like the first, all were dressed in heavy black ceramite armour. All bore an intricate skull and 'I' design on their massive left pauldrons. The icons on their right pauldrons, however, were each unique.

'Clear the room,' barked one over his comm-link as he gunned down a greenskin in front of him, spitting death from the barrel of his silenced bolter. 'Quick and quiet. Kill the rest before they raise the alarm.' Switching comm channels, he said, 'Sigma, this is Talon Alpha. Phase one complete. Kill-team is aboard. Securing entry point now.'

'*Understood, Alpha,*' replied the toneless voice at the other end of the link. '*Proceed on mission. Extract within the hour, as instructed. Captain Redthorne has orders to pull out if you miss your pick-up, so keep your team on a tight leash. This is not a purge operation. Is that clear?*'

'I'm well aware of that, Sigma,' the kill-team leader replied brusquely.

'*You had better be,*' replied the voice. '*Sigma, out.*'

It took Talon squad less than sixty seconds to clear the salvage bay. Brother Rauth of the Exorcists Chapter gunned down the last of the fleeing gretchin as it dashed for the exit. The creature stumbled as a single silenced bolt punched into its back. Half a second later, a flesh-muffled detonation ripped it apart.

It was the last of twenty-six bodies to fall among the litter of salvaged scrap. 'Target down, Karras,' reported Rauth. 'Area clear.'

'Confirmed,' replied Karras. He turned to face a Space Marine with a heavy flamer. 'Omni, you know what to do. The rest of you, cover the entrance.'

With the exception of Omni, the team immediately

moved to positions covering the mouth of the corridor through which the orks had come. Omni, otherwise known as Maximmion Voss of the Imperial Fists, moved to the side walls, first the left, then the right, working quickly at a number of thick hydraulic pistons and power cables there.

'That was messy, Karras,' said Brother Solarion, 'letting them see us as we came out. I told you we should have used smoke. If one had escaped and raised the alarm…'

Karras ignored the comment. It was just Solarion being Solarion.

'Give it a rest, Prophet,' said Brother Zeed, opting to use Solarion's nickname. Zeed had coined it himself, and knew precisely how much it irritated the proud Ultramarine. 'The room is clear. No runners. No alarms. Scholar knows what he's doing.'

Scholar. That was what they called Karras, or at least Brothers Voss and Zeed did. Rauth and Solarion insisted on calling him by his second name. Sigma always called him Alpha. And his battle-brothers back on Occludus, home-world of the Death Spectres Chapter, simply called him by his first name, Lyandro, or sometimes simply Codicier – his rank in the Librarius.

Karras didn't much care what anyone called him so long as they all did their jobs. The honour of serving in the Deathwatch had been offered to him, and he had taken it, knowing the great glory it would bring both himself and his Chapter. But he wouldn't be sorry when his obligation to the Emperor's Holy Inquisition was over. Astartes life seemed far less complicated among one's own Chapter-brothers.

When would he return to the fold? He didn't know. There was no fixed term for Deathwatch service. The Inquisition made high demands of all it called upon. Karras might not see the darkly beautiful crypt-cities of his home world again for decades... if he lived that long.

'Done, Scholar,' reported Voss as he rejoined the rest of the team.

Karras nodded and pointed towards a shattered pict screen and rune-board that protruded from the wall, close to the bay's only exit. 'Think you can get anything from that?' he asked.

'Nothing from the screen,' said Voss, 'but I could try wiring the data-feed directly into my visor.'

'Do it,' said Karras, 'but be quick.' To the others, he said, 'Proceed with phase two. Solarion, take point.'

The Ultramarine nodded curtly, rose from his position among the scrap and stalked forward into the shadowy corridor, bolter raised and ready. He moved with smooth, near-silent steps despite the massive weight of his armour. Torias Telion, famed Ultramarine Scout Master and Solarion's former mentor, would have been proud of his prize student.

One by one, with the exception of Voss, the rest of the kill-team followed in his wake.

The filthy, rusting corridors of the ork ship were lit, but the electric lamps the greenskins had strung up along pipes and ducts were old and in poor repair. Barely half of them seemed to be working at all. Even these buzzed and flickered in a constant battle to throw out their weak illumination. Still, the little light they did give was enough to bother the kill-team leader. The inquisitor, known to the members of Talon only by his call-sign, Sigma, had estimated the ork population of the ship at somewhere over twenty thousand. Against odds like these, Karras knew only too well that darkness and stealth were among his best weapons.

'I want the lights taken out,' he growled. 'The longer we stay hidden, the better our chances of making it off this damned heap.'

'We could shoot them out as we go,' offered Solarion, 'but I'd rather not waste my ammunition on something that doesn't bleed.'

Just then, Karras heard Voss on the comm-link. 'I've finished with the terminal, Scholar. I managed to pull some old cargo manifests from the ship's memory core. Not much else, though. Apparently, this ship used to be a civilian heavy-transport, Magellan-class, built on Stygies. It was called *The Pegasus*.'

'No schematics?'

'Most of the memory core is heavily corrupted. It's thousands of years old. We were lucky to get that much.'

'Sigma, this is Alpha,' said Karras. 'The ork ship is built around an Imperial transport called *The Pegasus*. Requesting schematics, priority one.'

'*I heard*,' said Sigma. '*You'll have them as soon as I do.*'

'Voss, where are you now?' Karras asked.

'Close to your position,' said the Imperial Fist.

'Do you have any idea which cable provides power to the lights?'

'Look up,' said Voss. 'See those cables running along the ceiling? The thick one, third from the left. I'd wager my knife on it.'

Karras didn't have to issue the order. The moment Zeed heard Voss' words, his right arm flashed upwards. There was a crackle of blue energy as the Raven Guard's claws sliced through the cable, and the corridor went utterly dark.

To the Space Marines, however, everything remained clear as day. Their MkVII helmets, like everything else in their arsenal, had been heavily modified by the Inquisition's finest artificers. They boasted a composite low-light/thermal vision mode that was superior to anything else Karras had ever used. In the three years he had been leading Talon, it had tipped the balance in his favour more times than he cared to count. He hoped it would do so many more times in the years to come, but that would all depend on their survival here, and he knew all too well that the odds were against them from the start. It wasn't just the numbers they were up against, or the tight deadline.

There was something here the likes of which few Death-watch kill-teams had ever faced before.

Karras could already feel its presence somewhere on the upper levels of the ship. 'Keep moving,' he told the others.

Three minutes after Zeed had killed the lights, Solarion hissed for them all to stop. 'Karras,' he rasped, 'I have multiple xenos up ahead. Suggest you move up and take a look.'

Karras ordered the others to hold and went forward, careful not to bang or scrape his broad pauldrons against the clutter of twisting pipes that lined both walls. Crouching beside Solarion, he realised he needn't have worried about a little noise. In front of him, over a hundred orks had crowded into a high-ceilinged, octagonal chamber. They were hooting and laughing and wrestling with each other to get nearer the centre of the room.

Neither Karras nor Solarion could see beyond the wall of broad green backs, but there was clearly something in the middle that was holding their attention.

'What are they doing?' whispered Solarion.

Karras decided there was only one way to find out. He centred his awareness down in the pit of his stomach, and began reciting the *Litany of the Sight Beyond Sight* that his former master, Chief Librarian Athio Cordatus, had taught him during his earliest years in the Librarius. Beneath his helmet, hidden from Solarion's view, Karras' eyes, normally deep red in colour, began to glow with an ethereal white flame. On his forehead, a wound appeared. A single drop of blood rolled over his brow and down to the bridge of his narrow, angular nose. Slowly, as he opened his soul fractionally more to the dangerous power within him, the wound widened, revealing the physical manifestation of his psychic inner eye.

Karras felt his awareness lift out of his body now. He willed it deeper into the chamber, rising above the backs of the orks, looking down on them from above.

He saw a great pit sunk into the centre of the metal floor. It was filled with hideous ovoid creatures of every possible colour, their tiny red eyes set above oversized mouths crammed with razor-edged teeth.

'It's a mess hall,' Karras told his team over the link. 'There's a squig pit in the centre.'

As his projected consciousness watched, the greenskins at the rim of the pit stabbed downwards with cruelly barbed poles, hooking their prey through soft flesh. Then they lifted the squigs, bleeding and screaming, into the air before reaching for them, tearing them from the hooks, and feasting on them.

'They're busy,' said Karras, 'but we'll need to find another way through.'

'Send me in, Scholar,' said Voss from the rear. 'I'll turn them all into cooked meat before they even realise they're under attack. Ghost can back me up.'

'On your order, Scholar,' said Zeed eagerly.

Ghost. That was Siefer Zeed. With his helmet off, it was

easy to see how he'd come by the name. Like Karras, and like all brothers of their respective Chapters, Zeed was the victim of a failed melanochromic implant, a slight mutation in his ancient and otherwise worthy gene-seed. The skin of both he and the kill-team leader was as white as porcelain. But, whereas Karras bore the blood-red eyes and chalk-white hair of the true albino, Zeed's eyes were black as coals, and his hair no less dark.

'Negative,' said Karras. 'We'll find another way through.'

He pushed his astral-self further into the chamber, desperate to find a means that didn't involve alerting the foe, but there seemed little choice. Only when he turned his awareness upwards did he see what he was looking for.

'There's a walkway near the ceiling,' he reported. 'It looks frail, rusting badly, but if we cross it one at a time, it should hold.'

A sharp, icy voice on the comm-link interrupted him. *'Talon Alpha, get ready to receive those schematics. Transmitting now.'*

Karras willed his consciousness back into his body, and his glowing third eye sealed itself, leaving only the barest trace of a scar. Using conventional sight, he consulted his helmet's heads-up display and watched the last few percent of the schematics file being downloaded. When it was finished, he called it up with a thought, and the helmet projected it as a shimmering green image cast directly onto his left retina.

The others, he knew, were seeing the same thing.

'According to these plans,' he told them, 'there's an access ladder set into the wall near the second junction we passed. We'll backtrack to it. The corridor above this one will give us access to the walkway.'

'If it's still there,' said Solarion. 'The orks may have removed it.'

'And backtracking will cost us time,' grumbled Voss.

'Less time than a firefight would cost us,' countered Rauth. His hard, gravelly tones were made even harder by the slight distortion on the comm-link. 'There's a time and place for that kind of killing, but it isn't now.'

'Watcher's right,' said Zeed reluctantly. It was rare for he and Rauth to agree.

'I've told you before,' warned Rauth. 'Don't call me that.'

'Right or wrong,' said Karras, 'I'm not taking votes. I've made my call. Let's move.'

Karras was the last to cross the gantry above the ork feeding pit. The shadows up here were dense and, so far, the orks had noticed nothing, though there had been a few moments when it looked as if the aging iron were about to collapse, particularly beneath the tremendous weight of Voss with his heavy flamer, high explosives, and back-mounted promethium supply.

Such was the weight of the Imperial Fist and his kit that Karras had decided to send him over first. Voss had made it across, but it was nothing short of a miracle that the orks below hadn't noticed the rain of red flakes showering down on them.

Lucky we didn't bring old Chyron after all, thought Karras.

The sixth member of Talon wouldn't have made it out of the salvage bay. The corridors on this ship were too narrow for such a mighty Space Marine. Instead, Sigma had ordered the redoubtable Dreadnought, formerly of the Lamenters Chapter but now permanently attached to Talon, to remain behind on Redthorne's ship, the *Saint*

Nevarre. That had caused a few tense moments. Chyron had a vile temper.

Karras made his way, centimetre by centimetre, along the creaking metal grille, his silenced bolter fixed securely to the magnetic couplings on his right thigh plate, his force sword sheathed on his left hip. Over one massive shoulder was slung the cryo-case that Sigma had insisted he carry. Karras cursed it, but there was no way he could leave it behind. It added twenty kilogrammes to his already significant weight, but the case was absolutely critical to the mission. He had no choice.

Up ahead, he could see Rauth watching him, as ever, from the end of the gangway.

What was the Exorcist thinking? Karras had no clue. He had never been able to read the mysterious Astartes. Rauth seemed to have no warp signature whatsoever. He simply didn't register at all. Even his armour, even his bolter for Throne's sake, resonated more than he did. And it was an anomaly that Rauth was singularly unwilling to discuss.

There was no love lost between them, Karras knew, and, for his part, he regretted that.

He had made gestures, occasional overtures, but for whatever reason, they had been rebuffed every time. The Exorcist was unreachable, distant, remote, and it seemed he planned to stay that way.

As Karras took his next step, the cryo-case suddenly swung forward on its strap, shifting his centre of gravity and threatening to unbalance him. He compensated swiftly, but the effort caused the gangway to creak and a piece of rusted metal snapped off, spinning away under him.

He froze, praying that the orks wouldn't notice. But one did.

It was at the edge of the pit, poking a fat squig with its barbed pole, when the metal fragment struck its head. The ork immediately stopped what it was doing and scanned the shadows above it, squinting suspiciously up towards the unlit recesses of the high ceiling.

Karras stared back, willing it to turn away. Reading minds and controlling minds, however, were two very different things. The latter was a power beyond his gifts.

Ultimately, it wasn't Karras' will that turned the ork from its scrutiny. It was the nature of the greenskin species.

The other orks around it, impatient to feed, began grabbing at the barbed pole. One managed to snatch it, and the gazing ork suddenly found himself robbed of his chance to feed. He launched himself into a violent frenzy, lashing out at the pole-thief and those nearby. That was when the orks behind him surged forward, and pushed him into the squig pit.

Karras saw the squigs swarm on the hapless ork, sinking their long teeth into its flesh and tearing away great, bloody mouthfuls. The food chain had been turned on its head. The orks around the pit laughed and capered and struck at their dying fellow with their poles.

Karras didn't stop to watch. He moved on carefully, cursing the black case that was now pressed tight to his side with one arm. He rejoined his team in the mouth of a tunnel on the far side of the gantry, and they moved off, pressing deeper into the ship.

Solarion moved up front with Zeed. Voss stayed in the middle. Rauth and Karras brought up the rear.

'They need to do some damned maintenance around here,' Karras told Rauth in a wry tone.

The Exorcist said nothing.

By comparing Sigma's schematics of *The Pegasus* with the features he saw as he moved through it, it soon became clear to Karras that the orks had done very little to alter the interior of the ship beyond covering its walls in badly rendered glyphs, defecating wherever they pleased, leaving dead bodies to rot where they fell, and generally making the place unfit for habitation by anything save their own wretched kind. Masses of quivering fungi had sprouted from broken water pipes. Frayed electrical cables sparked and hissed at anyone who walked by. And there were so many bones strewn about that some sections almost looked like mass graves.

The Deathwatch members made a number of kills, or rather Solarion did, as they proceeded deeper into the ship's belly. Most of these were gretchin sent out on some errand or other by their slavemasters. The Ultramarine silently executed them wherever he found them and stuffed the small corpses under pipes or in dark alcoves. Only twice did the kill-team encounter parties of ork warriors, and both times, the greenskins announced themselves well in advance with their loud grunting and jabbering. Karras could tell that Voss and Zeed were both itching to engage, but stealth was still paramount. Instead, he, Rauth and Solarion eliminated the foe, loading powerful hellfire rounds into their silenced bolters to ensure quick, quiet one-shot kills.

'I've reached Waypoint Adrius,' Solarion soon reported from up ahead. 'No xenos contacts.'

'Okay, move in and secure,' Karras ordered. 'Check your corners and exits.'

The kill-team hurried forward, emerging from the blackness of the corridor into a towering square shaft. It was hundreds of metres high, its metal walls stained with age and rust and all kinds of spillage. Thick pipes ran across the walls at all angles, many of them venting steam or dripping icy coolant. There were broken staircases and rusting gantries at regular intervals, each of which led to gaping doorways. And, in the middle of the left-side wall, an open elevator shaft ran almost to the top.

It was here that Talon would be forced to split up. From this chamber, they could access any level in the ship. Voss and Zeed would go down via a metal stairway, the others would go up.

'Good luck using that,' said Voss, nodding towards the elevator cage. It was clearly of ork construction, a mishmash of metal bits bolted together. It had a blood-stained steel floor, a folding, lattice-work gate and a large lever which could be pushed forward for up, or pulled backwards for down.

There was no sign of what had happened to the original elevator.

Karras scowled under his helmet as he looked at it and cross-referenced what he saw against his schematics. 'We'll have to take it as high as it will go,' he told Rauth and Solarion. He pointed up towards the far ceiling. 'That landing at the top – that is where we are going. From there we can access the corridor to the bridge. Ghost, Omni, you have your own objectives.' He checked the mission chrono in the corner of his visor. 'Forty-three minutes,' he told them. 'Avoid confrontation if you can. And stay in contact.'

'Understood, Scholar,' said Voss.

Karras frowned. He could sense the Imperial Fist's hunger for battle. It had been there since the moment they'd set foot on this mechanical abomination. Like most Imperial Fists, once Voss was in a fight, he tended to stay there until the foe was dead. He could be stubborn to the point of idiocy, but there was no denying his versatility. Weapons, vehicles, demolitions… Voss could do it all.

'Ghost,' said Karras. 'Make sure he gets back here on schedule.'

'If I have to knock him out and drag him back myself,' said Zeed.

'You can try,' Voss snorted, grinning under his helmet. He and the Raven Guard had enjoyed a good rapport since the moment they had met. Karras occasionally envied them that.

'Go,' he told them, and they moved off, disappearing down a stairwell on the right, their footsteps vibrating the grille under Karras' feet.

'Then there were three,' said Solarion.

'With the Emperor's blessing,' said Karras, 'that's all we'll need.' He strode over to the elevator, pulled the lattice-work gate aside, and got in. As the others joined him, he added, 'If either of you know a Mechanicus prayer, now would be a good time. Rauth, take us up.'

The Exorcist pushed the control lever forward, and it gave a harsh, metallic screech. A winch high above them began turning. Slowly at first, then with increasing speed, the lower levels dropped away beneath them. Pipes and landings flashed by, then the counterweight whistled past. The floor of the cage creaked and groaned under their feet as it carried them higher and higher. Disconcerting sounds issued from the cable and the assembly at the top, but the ride was short, lasting barely a minute, for which Karras thanked the Emperor.

When they were almost at the top of the shaft, Rauth eased the control lever backwards and the elevator slowed, issuing the same high-pitched complaint with which it had started.

Karras heard Solarion cursing. 'Problem, brother?' he asked.

'We'll be lucky if the whole damned ship doesn't know we're here by now,' spat the Ultramarine. 'Accursed piece of ork junk.'

The elevator ground to a halt at the level of the topmost landing, and Solarion almost tore the lattice-work gate from its fixings as he wrenched it aside. Stepping out, he took point again automatically.

The rickety steel landing led off in two directions. To the left, it led to a trio of dimly lit corridor entrances. To the right, it led towards a steep metal staircase in a severe state of disrepair.

Karras consulted his schematics. 'Now for the bad news,' he said. The others eyed the stair grimly.

'It won't hold us,' said Rauth. 'Not together.'

Some of the metal steps had rusted away completely leaving gaps of up to a metre.

Others were bent and twisted, torn halfway free of their bolts as if something heavy had landed hard on them.

'So we spread out,' said Karras. 'Stay close to the wall. Put as little pressure on each step as we can. We don't have time to debate it.'

They moved off, Solarion in front, Karras in the middle, Rauth at the rear. Karras watched his point-man carefully, noting exactly where he placed each foot. The Ultramarine moved with a certainty and fluidity that few could match. Had he registered more of a warp signature than he did, Karras might even have suspected some kind of extra-sensory perception, but, in fact, it was simply the superior training of the Master Scout, Telion.

Halfway up the stair, however, Solarion suddenly held up his hand and hissed, 'Hold!'

Rauth and Karras froze at once. The stairway creaked gently under them. 'Xenos, direct front. Twenty metres. Three big ones.'

Neither Karras nor Rauth could see them. The steep angle of the stair prevented it. 'Can you deal with them?' asked Karras.

'Not alone,' said Solarion. 'One is standing in a doorway. I don't have clear line of fire on him. It could go either way. If he charges, fine. But he may raise the alarm as soon as I drop the others. Better the three of us take them out at once, if you think you can move up quietly.'

The challenge in Solarion's words, not to mention his tone, could hardly be missed. Karras lifted a foot and placed it gently on the next step up. Slowly, he put his weight on it. There was a harsh grating sound.

'I said *quietly*,' hissed Solarion.

'I heard you, damn it,' Karras snapped back. Silently, he cursed the cryo-case strapped over his shoulder. Its extra weight and shifting centre of gravity was hampering him, as it had on the gantry above the squig pit, but what could he do?

'Rauth,' he said. 'Move past me. Don't touch this step. Place yourself on Solarion's left. Try to get an angle on the ork in the doorway. Solarion, open fire on Rauth's mark. You'll have to handle the other two yourself.'

'Confirmed,' rumbled Rauth. Slowly, carefully, the Exorcist moved out from behind Karras and continued climbing as quietly as he could. Flakes of rust fell from the underside of the stair like red snow.

Rauth was just ahead of Karras, barely a metre out in front, when, as he put the weight down on his right foot, the step under it gave way with a sharp snap. Rauth plunged into open space, nothing below him but two hundred metres of freefall and a lethally hard landing.

Karras moved on instinct with a speed that bordered on supernatural. His gauntleted fist shot out, catching Rauth just in time, closing around the Exorcist's left wrist with almost crushing force.

The orks turned their heads towards the sudden noise and stomped towards the top of the stairs, massive stubbers raised in front of them.

'By Guilliman's blood!' raged Solarion. He opened fire.

The first of the orks collapsed with its brainpan blown out.

Karras was struggling to haul Rauth back onto the stairway, but the metal under his own feet, forced to support the weight of both Astartes, began to scrape clear of its fixings.

'Quickly, psyker,' gasped Rauth, 'or we'll both die.'

'Not a damned chance,' Karras growled. With a monumental effort of strength, he heaved Rauth high enough that the Exorcist could grab the staircase and scramble back onto it.

As Rauth got to his feet, he breathed, 'Thank you, Karras… but you may live to regret saving me.'

Karras was scowling furiously under his helmet. 'You may not think of me as your brother, but, at the very least, you are a member of my team. However, the next time you call me psyker with such disdain, you will be the one to regret it. Is that understood?'

Rauth glared at him for a second, then nodded once. 'Fair words.'

Karras moved past him, stepping over the broad gap then stopping at Solarion's side.

On the landing ahead, he saw two ork bodies leaking copious amounts of fluid from severe head wounds.

As he looked at them, wailing alarms began to sound throughout the ship.

Solarion turned to face him. 'I told Sigma he should have put me in charge,' he hissed. 'Damn it, Karras.'

'Save it,' Karras barked. His eyes flicked to the countdown on his heads-up display. 'Thirty-three minutes left. They know we're here. The killing starts in earnest now, but we can't let them hold us up. Both of you follow me. Let's move!'

Without another word, the three Astartes pounded across the upper landing and into the mouth of the corridor down which the third ork had vanished, desperate to reach their primary objective before the whole damned horde descended on them.

'So much for keeping a low profile, eh, brother?' said Zeed as he guarded Voss' back.

A deafening, ululating wail had filled the air. Red lights began to rotate in their wall fixtures.

Voss grunted by way of response. He was concentrating hard on the task at hand. He crouched by the coolant valves of the ship's massive plasma reactor, power source for the vessel's gigantic main thrusters.

The noise in the reactor room was deafening even without the ork alarms, and none of the busy gretchin work crews had noticed the two Deathwatch members until it was too late. Zeed had hacked them limb from limb before they'd had a chance to scatter. Now that the alarm had been sounded, though, orks would be arming themselves and filling the corridors outside, each filthy alien desperate to claim a kill.

'We're done here,' said Voss, rising from his crouch. He

hefted his heavy flamer from the floor and turned. 'The rest is up to Scholar and the others.'

Voss couldn't check in with them. Not from here. Such close proximity to a reactor, particularly one with so much leakage, filled the kill-team's primary comm-channels with nothing but static.

Zeed moved to the thick steel door of the reactor room, opened it a crack, and peered outside.

'It's getting busy out there,' he reported. 'Lots of mean-looking bastards, but they can hardly see with all the lights knocked out. What do you say, brother? Are you ready to paint the walls with the blood of the foe?'

Under his helmet, Voss grinned. He thumbed his heavy-flamer's igniter switch and a hot blue flame burst to life just in front of the weapon's promethium nozzle. 'Always,' he said, coming abreast of the Raven Guard.

Together, the two comrades charged into the corridor, howling the names of their primarchs as battle cries.

'We're pinned,' hissed Rauth as ork stubber and pistol fire smacked into the metal wall beside him. Pipes shattered. Iron flakes showered the ground. Karras, Rauth and Solarion had pushed as far and as fast as they could once the alarms had been tripped. But now they found themselves penned-in at a junction, a confluence of three broad corridors, and mobs of howling, jabbering orks were pouring towards them from all sides.

With his knife, Solarion had already severed the cable that powered the lights, along with a score of others that did Throne-knew-what. A number of the orks, however, were equipped with goggles, not to mention weapons and armour far above typical greenskin standards. Karras had fought such fiends before. They were the greenskin equivalent of commando squads, far more cunning and deadly than the usual muscle-minded oafs.

Their red night-vision lenses glowed like daemons' eyes as they pressed closer and closer, keeping to cover as much as possible.

Karras and his Deathwatch Marines were outnumbered at least twenty to one, and that ratio would quickly change for the worse if they didn't break through soon.

'Orders, Karras,' growled Solarion as his right pauldron absorbed a direct hit. The ork shell left an ugly scrape on the blue and white Chapter insignia there. 'We're taking too much fire. The cover here is pitiful.'

Karras thought fast. A smokescreen would be useless. If the ork goggles were operating on thermal signatures, they would see right through it. Incendiaries or frags would kill a good score of them and dissuade the others from closing, but that wouldn't solve the problem of being pinned.

'Novas,' he told them. 'On my signal, one down each corridor. Short throws. Remember to cover your visors. The moment they detonate, we make a push. I'm taking point. Clear?'

'On your mark, Karras,' said Solarion with a nod.

'Give the word,' said Rauth.

Karras tugged a nova grenade from the webbing around his armoured waist. The others did the same. He pulled the pin, swung his arm back and called out, 'Now!'

Three small black cylinders flew through the darkness to clatter against the metal floor. Swept up in the excitement of the firefight, the orks didn't notice them.

'Eyes!' shouted Karras and threw an arm up over his visor.

Three deafening bangs sounded in quick succession,

louder even than the bark of the orks' guns. Howls of agony immediately followed, filling the close, damp air of the corridors. Karras looked up to see the orks reeling around in the dark with their great, thick-fingered hands pressed to their faces. They were crashing into the walls, weapons forgotten, thrown to the floor in their agony and confusion.

Nova grenades were typically employed for room clearance, but they worked well in any dark, enclosed space. They were far from standard-issue Astartes hardware, but the Deathwatch were the elite, the best of the best, and they had access to the kind of resources that few others could boast. The intense, phosphor-bright flash that the grenades produced overloaded optical receptors, both mechanical and biological. The blindness was temporary in most cases, but Karras was betting that the orks' goggles would magnify the glare.

Their retinas would be permanently burned out.

'With me,' he barked, and charged out from his corner. He moved in a blur, fixing his silenced bolter to the maglocks on his thigh plate and drawing his faithful force sword, Arquemann, from its scabbard as he raced towards the foe.

Rauth and Solarion came behind, but not so close as to gamble with their lives. The bite of Arquemann was certain death whenever it glowed with otherworldly energy, and it had begun to glow now, throwing out a chill, unnatural light.

Karras threw himself in among the greenskin commandos, turning great powerful arcs with his blade, despatching more xenos filth with every limb-severing stroke. Steaming corpses soon littered the floor. The orks in the corridors behind continued to flail blindly, attacking each other now, in their sightless desperation.

'The way is clear,' Karras gasped. 'We run.' He sheathed Arquemann and led the way, feet pounding on the metal deck. The cryo-case swung wildly behind him as he moved, but he paid it no mind. Beneath his helmet, his third eye was closing again. The dangerous energies that gave him his powers were retreating at his command, suppressed by the mantras that kept him strong, kept him safe.

The inquisitor's voice intruded on the comm-link. *'Alpha, this is Sigma. Respond.'*

'I hear you, Sigma,' said Karras as he ran.

'Where are you now?'

'Closing on Waypoint Barrius. We're about one minute out.'

'You're falling behind, Alpha. Perhaps I should begin preparing death certificates to your respective Chapters.'

'Damn you, inquisitor. We'll make it. Now if that's all you wanted…'

'Solarion is to leave you at Barrius. I have another task for him.'

'No,' said Karras flatly. 'We're already facing heavy resistance here. I need him with me.'

'I don't make requests, Deathwatch. According to naval intelligence reports, there is a large fighter bay on the ship's starboard side. Significant fuel dumps. Give Solarion your explosives. I want him to knock out that fighter bay while you and Rauth proceed to the bridge. If all goes well, the diversion may help clear your escape route. If not, you had better start praying for a miracle.'

'Rauth will blow the fuel dumps,' said Karras, opting to test a hunch.

'No,' said Sigma. *'Solarion is better acquainted with operating alone.'*

Karras wondered about Sigma's insistence that Solarion

go. Rauth hardly ever let Karras out of his sight. It had been that way ever since they'd met. Little wonder, then, that Zeed had settled on the nickname *'Watcher'*. Was Sigma behind it all? Karras couldn't be sure. The inquisitor had a point about Solarion's solo skills, and he knew it.

'Fine, I'll give Solarion the new orders.'

'No,' said Sigma. *'I'll do it directly. You and Rauth must hurry to the command bridge. Expect to lose comms once you get closer to the target. I'm sure you've sensed the creature's incredible power already. I want that thing eliminated, Alpha. Do not fail me.'*

'When have I ever?' Karras retorted, but Sigma had already cut the link. Judging by Solarion's body language as he ran, the inquisitor was already giving him his new orders.

At the next junction, Waypoint Barrius, the trio encountered another ork mob. But the speed at which Karras and his men were moving caught the orks by surprise. Karras didn't even have time to charge his blade with psychic energy before he was in among them, hacking and thrusting. Arquemann was lethally sharp even without the power of the immaterium running through it, and orks fell in a great tide of blood. Silenced bolters coughed on either side of him, Solarion and Rauth giving fire support, and soon the junction was heaped with twitching green meat.

Karras turned to Rauth. 'Give Solarion your frags and incendiaries,' he said, pulling his own from his webbing. 'But keep two breaching charges. We'll need them.'

Solarion accepted the grenades, quickly fixing them to his belt, then he said, 'Good hunting, brothers.'

Karras nodded. 'We'll rendezvous back at the elevator shaft. Whoever gets there first holds it until the others arrive. Keep the comm-link open. If it goes dead for more than ten minutes at our end, don't waste any time. Rendezvous with Voss and Zeed and get to the salvage bay.'

Solarion banged a fist on his breastplate in salute and turned.

Karras nodded to Rauth. 'Let's go,' he said, and together, they ran on towards the fore section of the ship while Solarion merged with the shadows in the other direction.

'Die!' spat Zeed as another massive greenskin slid to the floor, its body opened from gullet to groin. Then he was moving again. Instincts every bit as sharp as his lightning claws told him to sidestep just in time to avoid the stroke of a giant chainaxe that would have cleaved him in two. The ork wielding the axe roared in frustration as its whirring blade bit into the metal floor, sending up a shower of orange sparks. It made a grab for Zeed with its empty hand, but Zeed parried, slipped inside at the same instant, and thrust his right set of claws straight up under the creature's jutting jaw. The tips of the long slender blades punched through the top of its skull, and it stood there quivering, literally dead on its feet.

Zeed stepped back, wrenching his claws from the creature's throat, and watched its body drop beside the others.

He looked around hungrily, eager for another opponent to step forward, but there were none to be had. Voss and he stood surrounded by dead xenos. The Imperial Fist had already lowered his heavy flamer. He stood admiring his handiwork, a small hill of smoking black corpses. The two comrades had fought their way back to Waypoint Adrius. The air in the towering chamber was now thick with the stink of spilled blood and burnt flesh.

Zeed looked up at the landings overhead and said, 'No sign of the others.'

Voss moved up beside him. 'There's much less static on the comm-link here. Scholar, this is Omni. If you can hear me, respond.'

At first there was no answer. Voss was about to try again when the Death Spectre Librarian finally acknowledged. *'I hear you, Omni. This isn't the best time.'*

Karras sounded strained, as if fighting for his life.

'We are finished with the reactor,' Voss reported. 'Back at Waypoint Adrius, now. Do you need assistance?'

As he asked this, Voss automatically checked the mission countdown. Not good.

Twenty-seven minutes left.

'Hold that position,' Karras grunted. *'We need to keep that area secure for our escape. Rauth and I are–'*

His words were cut off in mid-sentence. For a brief instant, Voss and Zeed thought the kill-team leader had been hit, possibly even killed. But their fears were allayed when Karras heaved a sigh of relief and said, *'Damn, those bastards were strong. Ghost, you would have enjoyed that. Listen, brothers, Rauth and I are outside the ship's command bridge. Time is running out. If we don't make it back to Waypoint Adrius within the next twelve minutes, I want the rest of you to pull out. Do not miss the pick-up. Is that understood?'*

Voss scowled. The words *pull out* made him want to smash something. As far as his Chapter was concerned, they were curse words. But he knew Karras was right. There was little to be gained by dying here. 'Emperor's speed, Scholar,' he said.

'For Terra and the Throne,' Karras replied then signed off.

Zeed was scraping his claws together restlessly, a bad habit that manifested itself when he had excess adrenaline and no further outlet for it. 'Damn,' he said. 'I'm not standing around here while the others are fighting for their lives.' He pointed to the metal landing high above him where Karras and the others had got off the elevator. 'There has to be a way to call that piece of junk back down to this level. We can ride it up there and–'

He was interrupted by the clatter of heavy, iron-shod boots closing from multiple directions. The sounds echoed into the chamber from a dozen corridor mouths.

'I think we're about to be too busy for that, brother,' said Voss darkly.

Rauth stepped over the body of the massive ork guard he had just slain, flicked the beast's blood from the groove on his shortsword, and sheathed it at his side. There was a shallow crater in the ceramite of his right pauldron. Part of his Chapter icon was missing, cleaved off in the fight. The daemon-skull design now boasted only a single horn. The other pauldron, intricately detailed with the skull, bones and inquisitorial 'I' of the Deathwatch, was chipped and scraped, but had suffered no serious damage.

'That's the biggest I've slain in hand-to-hand,' the Exorcist muttered, mostly to himself.

The one Karras had just slain was no smaller, but the Death Spectre was focused on something else. He was standing with one hand pressed to a massive steel blast door covered in orkish glyphs. Tiny lambent arcs of unnatural energy flickered around him.

'There's a tremendous amount of psychic interference,' he said, 'but I sense at least thirty of them on this level. Our target is on the upper deck. And he knows we're here.'

Rauth nodded, but said nothing. *We?* No. Karras was wrong in that. Rauth knew well enough that the target couldn't have sensed him. Nothing psychic could. It was a side effect of the unspeakable horrors he had endured during his Chapter's selection and training programmes—programmes that had taught him to hate all psykers and the terrible daemons their powers sometimes loosed into the galaxy.

The frequency with which Lyandro Karras tapped the power of the immaterium disgusted Rauth. Did the Librarian not realise the great peril in which he placed his soul? Or was he simply a fool, spilling over with an arrogance that invited the ultimate calamity. Daemons of the warp rejoiced in the folly of such men.

Of course, that was why Rauth had been sequestered to Deathwatch in the first place.

The inquisitor had never said so explicitly, but it simply had to be the case. As enigmatic as Sigma was, he was clearly no fool. Who better than an Exorcist to watch over one such as Karras? Even the mighty Grey Knights, from whose seed Rauth's Chapter had been born, could hardly have been more suited to the task.

'Smoke,' said Karras. 'The moment we breach, I want smoke grenades in there. Don't spare them for later. Use what we have. We go in with bolters blazing. Remove your suppressor. There's no need for it now. Let them hear the bark of our guns. The minute the lower floor is cleared, we each take a side stair to the command deck. You go left. I'll take the right. We'll find the target at the top.'

'Bodyguards?' asked Rauth. Like Karras, he began unscrewing the sound suppressor from the barrel of his bolter.

'I can't tell. If there are, the psychic resonance is blotting them out. It's... incredible.'

The two Astartes stored their suppressors in pouches on their webbing, then Rauth fixed a rectangular breaching charge to the seam between the double doors. The Exorcist was about to step back when Karras said, 'No, brother. We'll need two. These doors are stronger than you think.'

Rauth fixed another charge just below the first, then he and Karras moved to either side of the doorway and pressed their backs to the wall.

Simultaneously, they checked the magazines in their bolters. Rauth slid in a fresh clip.

Karras tugged a smoke grenade from his webbing, and nodded. 'Now!'

Rauth pressed the tiny detonator in his hand, and the whole corridor shook with a deafening blast to rival the boom of any artillery piece. The heavy doors blew straight into the room causing immediate casualties among the orks closest to the explosion.

'Smoke!' ordered Karras as he threw his first grenade. Rauth discarded the detonator and did the same. Two, three, four small canisters bounced onto the ship's bridge, spread just enough to avoid redundancy. Within two seconds, the whole deck was covered in a dense grey cloud. The ork crew went into an uproar, barely able to see their hands in front of their faces. But to the Astartes, all was perfectly clear. They entered the room with bolters firing, each shot a vicious bark, and the greenskins fell where they stood.

Not a single bolt was wasted. Every last one found its target, every shot a headshot, an instant kill. In the time it took to draw three breaths, the lower floor of the bridge was cleared of threats.

'Move!' said Karras, making for the stair that jutted from the right-hand wall. The smoke had begun to billow upwards now, thinning as it did.

Rauth stormed the left-side stair.

Neither Space Marine, however, was entirely prepared for what he found at the top.

Solarion burst from the mouth of the corridor and sprinted along the metal landing in the direction of the elevator cage. He was breathing hard, and rivulets of red blood ran from grape-sized holes in the armour of his torso and left upper arm. If he could only stop, the wounds would quickly seal themselves, but there was no time for that. His normally dormant second heart was pumping in tandem with the first, flushing lactic acid from his muscles, helping him to keep going. Following barely a second behind him, a great mob of armoured orks with heavy pistols and blades surged out of the same corridor in hot pursuit. The platform trembled under their tremendous weight.

Solarion didn't stop to look behind. Just ahead of him, the upper section of the landing ended. Beyond it was the rusted stairway that had almost claimed Rauth's life. There was no time now to navigate those stairs.

He put on an extra burst of speed and leapt straight out over them.

It was an impressive jump. For a moment, he almost seemed to fly. Then he passed the apex of his jump and the ship's artificial gravity started to pull him downwards. He landed on the lower section of the landing with a loud clang. Sharp spears of pain shot up the nerves in his legs, but he ignored them and turned, bolter held ready at his shoulder.

The orks were following his example, leaping from the upper platform, hoping to land right beside him and cut him to pieces. Their lack of agility, however, betrayed them.

The first row crashed down onto the rickety stairs about

two thirds of the way down. The old iron steps couldn't take that kind of punishment. They crumbled and snapped, dropping the luckless orks into lethal freefall. The air filled with howls, but the others didn't catch on until it was too late. They, too, leapt from the platform's edge in their eagerness to make a kill. Step after step gave way with each heavy body that crashed down on it, and soon the stairway was reduced almost to nothing.

A broad chasm, some thirty metres across, now separated the metal platforms that had been joined by the stairs. The surviving orks saw that they couldn't follow the Space Marine across. Instead, they paced the edge of the upper platform, bellowing at Solarion in outrage and frustration and taking wild potshots at him with their clunky pistols.

'*It's raining greenskins,*' said a gruff voice on the link. '*What in Dorn's name is going on up there?*'

With one eye still on the pacing orks, Solarion moved to the edge of the platform. As he reached the twisted railing, he looked out over the edge and down towards the steel floor two-hundred metres below. Gouts of bright promethium flame illuminated a conflict there. Voss and Zeed were standing back to back, about five metres apart, fighting off an ork assault from all sides. The floor around them was heaped with dead aliens.

'This is Solarion,' the Ultramarine told them. 'Do you need aid, brothers?'

'*Prophet?*' said Zeed between lethal sweeps of his claws. '*Where are Scholar and Watcher?*'

'You've had no word?' asked Solarion.

'*They've been out of contact since they entered the command bridge. Sigma warned of that. But time is running out. Can you go to them?*'

'Impossible,' replied Solarion. 'The stairs are gone. I can't get back up there now.'

'Then pray for them,' said Voss.

Solarion checked his mission chrono. He remembered Karras' orders. Four more minutes. After that, he would have to assume they were dead. He would take the elevator down and, with the others, strike out for the salvage bay and their only hope of escape.

A shell from an ork pistol ricocheted from the platform and smacked against his breastplate. The shot wasn't powerful enough to penetrate ceramite, not like the heavy-stubber shells he had taken at close range, but it got his attention. He was about to return fire, to start clearing the upper platform in anticipation of Karras and Rauth's return, when a great boom shook the air and sent deep vibrations through the metal under his feet.

'That's not one of mine,' said Voss.

'It's mine,' said Solarion. 'I rigged the fuel dump in their fighter bay. If we're lucky, most of the greenskins will be drawn there, thinking that's where the conflict is. It might buy our brothers a little time.'

The mission chrono now read eighteen minutes and forty seconds. He watched it drop. Thirty-nine seconds. Thirty-eight. Thirty-seven.

Come on, Karras, he thought. What in Terra's name are you doing?

Karras barely had time to register the sheer size of Balthazog Bludwrekk's twin bodyguards, before their blistering assault began. They were easily the largest orks he had ever seen, even larger than the door guards he and Rauth had slain, and they wielded their massive two-handed warhammers

as if they weighed nothing at all. Under normal circumstances, orks of this size and strength would have become
mighty warbosses, but these two were nothing of the kind.
They were slaves to a far greater power than mere muscle
or aggression. They were mindless puppets held in servitude by a much deadlier force, and the puppeteer himself sat
some ten metres behind them, perched on a bizarre mechanical throne in the centre of the ship's command deck.

Bludwrekk!

Karras only needed an instant, a fraction of a second, to
take in the details of the fiend's appearance.

Even for an ork, the psychic warboss was hideous. Portions
of his head were vastly swollen, with great vein-marbled
bumps extending out in all directions from his crown. His
brow was ringed with large, blood-stained metal plugs sunk
deep into the bone of his skull. The beast's leering, lop-
sided face was twisted, like something seen in a curved
mirror, the features pathetically small on one side, gro-
tesquely overlarge on the other, and saliva dripped from
his slack jaw, great strands of it hanging from the spaces
between his tusks.

He wore a patchwork robe of cured human skins stitched
together with gut, and a trio of decaying heads hung
between his knees, fixed to his belt by long, braided hair.

Karras had the immediate impression that the heads had
been taken from murdered women, perhaps the wives of
some human lord or tribal leader that the beast had slain
during a raid. Orks had a known fondness for such grisly
trophies.

The beast's throne was just as strange; a mass of coils,
cogs and moving pistons without any apparent purpose whatsoever. Thick bundles of wire linked it to an

inexplicable clutter of vast, arcane machines that crackled and hummed with sickly green light. In the instant Karras took all this in, he felt his anger and hate break over him like a thunderstorm.

It was as if this creature, this blasted aberration, sat in sickening, blasphemous parody of the immortal Emperor Himself.

The two Space Marines opened fire at the same time, eager to drop the bodyguards and engage the real target quickly. Their bolters chattered, spitting their deadly hail, but somehow each round detonated harmlessly in the air.

'He's shielding them!' Karras called out. 'Draw your blade!'

He dropped the cryo-case from his shoulder, pulled Arquemann from its scabbard and let the power of the immaterium flow through him, focusing it into the ancient crystalline matrix that lay embedded in the blade.

'To me, xenos scum!' he roared at the hulking beast in front of him.

The bodyguard's massive hammer whistled up into the air, then changed direction with a speed that seemed impossible. Karras barely managed to step aside. Sparks flew as the weapon clipped his left pauldron, sending a painful shock along his arm. The thick steel floor fared worse. The hammer left a hole in it the size of a human head.

On his right, Karras heard Rauth loose a great battle cry as he clashed with his own opponent, barely ducking a lateral blow that would have taken his head clean off. The Exorcist's shortsword looked awfully small compared to his enemy's hammer.

Bludwrekk was laughing, revelling in the life and death struggle that was playing out before him, as if it were some kind of grand entertainment laid on just for him. The more he cackled, the more the green light seemed to shimmer and churn around him. Karras felt the resonance of that power disorienting him. The air was supercharged with it. He felt his own power surging up inside him, rising to meet it. Only so much could be channelled into his force sword. Already, the blade sang with deadly energy as it slashed through the air.

This surge is dangerous, he warned himself. I mustn't let it get out of control.

Automatically, he began reciting the mantras Master Cordatus had taught him, but the effort of wrestling to maintain his equilibrium cost him an opening in which he could have killed his foe with a stroke. The ork bodyguard, on the other hand, did not miss its chance. It caught Karras squarely on the right pauldron with the head of its hammer, shattering the Deathwatch insignia there, and knocking him sideways, straight off his feet.

The impact hurled Karras directly into Rauth's opponent, and the two tumbled to the metal floor. Karras' helmet was torn from his head, and rolled away. In the sudden tangle of thrashing Space Marine and ork bodies, Rauth saw an opening. He stepped straight in, plunging his shortsword up under the beast's sternum, shoving it deep, cleaving the ork's heart in two. Without hesitation, he then turned to face the remaining bodyguard while Karras kicked himself clear of the dead behemoth and got to his feet.

The last bodyguard was fast, and Rauth did well to stay clear of the whistling hammerhead, but the stabbing and slashing strokes of his shortsword were having little effect. It was only when Karras joined him, and the ork was faced with attacks from two directions at once, that the tables truly turned. Balthazog Bludwrekk had stopped laughing now. He gave a deafening roar of anger as Rauth and Karras thrust from opposite angles and, between them, pierced the greenskin's heart and lungs.

Blood bubbled from its wounds as it sank to the floor, dropping its mighty hammer with a crash.

Bludwrekk surged upwards from his throne. Arcs of green lightning lanced outwards from his fingers. Karras felt Waaagh! energy lick his armour, looking for chinks through which it might burn his flesh and corrode his soul. Together, blades raised, he and Rauth rounded on their foe.

The moment they stepped forward to engage, however, a great torrent of kinetic energy burst from the ork's outstretched hands and launched Rauth into the air. Karras ducked and rolled sideways, narrowly avoiding death, but he heard Rauth land with a heavy crash on the lower floor of the bridge.

'Rauth!' he shouted over the link. 'Answer!'

No answer was forthcoming. The comm-link was useless here. And perhaps Rauth was already dead.

Karras felt the ork's magnified power pressing in on him from all sides, and now he saw its source. Behind Bludwrekk's mechanical throne, beyond a filthy, blood-spattered window of thick glass, there were hundreds – no, thousands – of orks strapped to vertical slabs that looked like operating tables. The tops of their skulls had been removed, and cables and tubes ran from their exposed brains to the core of a vast power-siphoning system.

'By the Golden Throne,' gasped Karras. 'No wonder Sigma wants your ugly head.' How much time remained before the ship's reactors detonated? Without his helmet, he couldn't tell. Long enough to kill this monstrosity? Maybe. But, one on one, was he even a match for the thing?

Not without exploiting more of the dangerous power at his disposal. He had to trust in his master's teachings. The mantras would keep him safe. They had to. He opened himself up to the warp a little more, channelling it, focusing it with his mind.

Bludwrekk stepped forward to meet him, and the two powers clashed with apocalyptic fury.

Darrion Rauth was not dead. The searing impact of the ork warlord's psychic blast would have killed a lesser man on contact, ripping his soul from his body and leaving it a lifeless hunk of meat. But Rauth was no lesser man. The secret rites of his Chapter, and the suffering he had endured to earn his place in it, had proofed him against such a fate. Also, though a number of his bones were broken, his superhuman physiology was already about the business of re-knitting them, making them whole and strong again.

The internal bleeding would stop soon, too.

But there wasn't time to heal completely. Not if he wanted to make a difference.

With a grunt of pain, he rolled, pushed himself to one knee, and looked for his shortsword. He couldn't see it. His bolter, however, was still attached to his thigh plate. He tugged it free, slammed in a fresh magazine, cocked it, and struggled to his feet. He coughed wetly, tasting blood in his mouth. Looking up towards the place from which he had been thrown, he saw unnatural light blazing and strobing. There was a great deal of noise, too, almost like thunder, but not quite the same. It made the air tremble around him.

Karras must still be alive, he thought. He's still fighting.

Pushing aside the agony in his limbs, he ran to the stairs

on his right and, with an ancient litany of strength on his lips, charged up them to rejoin the battle.

Karras was failing. He could feel it. Balthazog Bludwrekk was drawing on an incredible reserve of power. The psychic Waaagh! energy he was tapping seemed boundless, pouring into the warlord from the brains of the tormented orks wired into his insane contraption.

Karras cursed as he struggled to turn aside another wave of roiling green fire. It buckled the deck plates all around him. Only those beneath his feet, those that fell inside the shimmering bubble he fought to maintain, remained undamaged.

His shield was holding, but only just, and the effort required to maintain it precluded him from launching attacks of his own. Worse yet, as the ork warlord pressed his advantage, Karras was forced to let the power of the warp flow through him more and more. A cacophony of voices had risen in his head, chittering and whispering in tongues he knew were blasphemous. This was the moment all Librarians feared, when the power they wielded threatened to consume them, when user became used, master became slave. The voices started to drown out his own. Much more of this and his soul would be lost for eternity, ripped from him and thrown into the maelstrom. Daemons would wrestle for command of his mortal flesh.

Was it right to slay this ork at the cost of his immortal soul? Should he not simply drop his shield and die so that something far worse than Bludwrekk would be denied entry into the material universe?

Karras could barely hear these questions in his head. So many other voices crowded them out.

Balthazog Bludwrekk seemed to sense the moment was his. He stepped nearer, still trailing thick cables from the metal plugs in his distorted skull.

Karras sank to one knee under the onslaught to both body and mind. His protective bubble was dissipating. Only seconds remained. One way or another, he realised, he was doomed.

Bludwrekk was almost on him now, still throwing green lightning from one hand, drawing a long, curved blade with the other. Glistening strands of drool shone in the fierce green light. His eyes were ablaze.

Karras sagged, barely able to hold himself upright, leaning heavily on the sword his mentor had given him.

I am Lyandro Karras, he tried to think. Librarian. Death Spectre. Space Marine. The Emperor will not let me fall.

But his inner voice was faint. Bludwrekk was barely two metres away. His psychic assault pierced Karras' shield. The Codicer felt the skin on his arms blazing and crisping. His nerves began to scream.

In his mind, one voice began to dominate the others. Was this the voice of the daemon that would claim him? It was so loud and clear that it seemed to issue from the very air around him. 'Get up, Karras!' it snarled. 'Fight!'

He realised it was speaking in High Gothic. He hadn't expected that.

His vision was darkening, despite the green fire that blazed all around, but, distantly, he caught a flicker of movement to his right. A hulking black figure appeared as if from nowhere, weapon raised before it. There was something familiar about it, an icon on the left shoulder; a skull with a single gleaming red eye.

Rauth!

The Exorcist's bolter spat a torrent of shells, forcing Balthazog Bludwrekk to spin and defend himself, concentrating all his psychic power on stopping the stream of deadly bolts.

Karras acted without pause for conscious thought. He moved on reflex, conditioned by decades of harsh daily training rituals. With Bludwrekk's merciless assault momentarily halted, he surged upwards, putting all his strength into a single horizontal swing of his force sword. The warp energy he had been trying to marshal crashed over him, flooding into the crystalline matrix of his blade as the razor-edged metal bit deep into the ork's thick green neck.

The monster didn't even have time to scream. Body and head fell in separate directions, the green light vanished, and the upper bridge was suddenly awash with steaming ork blood.

Karras fell to his knees, and screamed, dropping Arquemann at his side. His fight wasn't over. Not yet.

Now, he turned his attention to the battle for his soul.

Rauth saw all too clearly that his moment had come, as he had known it must, sooner or later, but he couldn't relish it. There was no joy to be had here. Psyker or not, Lyandro Karras was a Space Marine, a son of the Emperor just as he was himself, and he had saved Rauth's life.

But you must do it for him, Rauth told himself. You must do it to save his soul. Out of respect, Rauth took off his helmet so that he might bear witness to the Death

Spectre's final moments with his own naked eyes. Grimacing, he raised the barrel of his bolter to Karras' temple and began reciting the words of the *Mortis Morgatii Praetovo*. It was an ancient rite from long before the Great Crusade, forgotten by all save the Exorcists and the Grey Knights. If it worked, it would send Karras' spiritual essence beyond the reach of the warp's ravenous fiends, but it could not save his life.

It was not a long rite, and Rauth recited it perfectly.

As he came to the end of it, he prepared to squeeze the trigger.

War raged inside Lyandro Karras. Sickening entities filled with hate and hunger strove to overwhelm him. They were brutal and relentless, bombarding him with unholy visions that threatened to drown him in horror and disgust. He saw Imperial saints defiled and mutilated on altars of burning black rock. He saw the Golden Throne smashed and ruined, and the body of the Emperor trampled under the feet of vile capering beasts. He saw his Chapter house sundered, its walls covered in weeping sores as if the stones themselves had contracted a vile disease.

He cried out, railing against the visions, denying them. But still they came. He scrambled for something Cordatus had told him.

Cordatus!

The thought of that name alone gave him the strength to keep up the fight, if only for a moment. To avoid becoming lost in the empyrean, the old warrior had said, one must anchor oneself to the physical.

Karras reached for the physical now, for something real, a bastion against the visions.

He found it in a strange place, in a sensation he couldn't quite explain. Something hot and metallic was pressing hard against the skin of his temple.

The metal was scalding him, causing him physical pain.

Other pains joined it, accumulating so that the song of agony his nerves were singing became louder and louder. He felt again the pain of his burned hands, even while his gene-boosted body worked fast to heal them. He clutched at the pain, letting the sensation pull his mind back to the moment, to the here and now. He grasped it like a rock in a storm-tossed sea.

The voices of the vile multitude began to weaken. He heard his own inner voice again, and immediately resumed his mantras. Soon enough, the energy of the immaterium slowed to a trickle, then ceased completely. He felt the physical manifestation of his third eye closing. He felt the skin knitting on his brow once again.

What was it, he wondered, this hot metal pressed to his head, this thing that had saved him?

He opened his eyes and saw the craggy, battle-scarred features of Darrion Rauth. The Exorcist was standing very close, helmet at his side, muttering something that sounded like a prayer.

His bolter was pressed to Karras' head, and he was about to blow his brains out.

'What are you doing?' Karras asked quietly. Rauth looked surprised to hear his voice.

'I'm saving your soul, Death Spectre. Be at peace. Your honour will be spared. The daemons of the warp will not have you.'

'That is good to know,' said Karras. 'Now lower your weapon. My soul is exactly where it should be, and there it stays until my service to the Emperor is done.'

For a moment, neither Rauth nor Karras moved. The Exorcist did not seem convinced. 'Darrion Rauth,' said Karras.

'Are you so eager to spill my blood? Is this why you have shadowed my every movement for the last three years? Perhaps Solarion would thank you for killing me, but I don't think Sigma would.'

'That would depend,' Rauth replied. Hesitantly, however, he lowered his gun. 'You will submit to proper testing when we return to the *Saint Nevarre*. Sigma will insist on it, and so shall I.'

'As is your right, brother, but be assured that you will find no taint. Of course it won't matter either way unless we get off this ship alive. Quickly now, grab the monster's head. I will open the cryo-case.'

Rauth did as ordered, though he kept a wary eye on the kill-team leader. Lifting Bludwrekk's lifeless head, he offered it to Karras, saying, 'The machinery that boosted Bludwrekk's power should be analysed. If other ork psykers begin to employ such things...'

Karras took the ork's head from him, placed it inside the black case, and pressed a four-digit code into the keypad on the side. The lid fused itself shut with a hiss. Karras rose, slung it over his right shoulder, sheathed Arquemann, located his helmet, and fixed it back on his head. Rauth donned his own helmet, too.

'If Sigma wanted the machine,' said Karras as he led his comrade off the command bridge, 'he would have said so.'

Glancing at the mission chrono, he saw that barely seventeen minutes remained until the exfiltration deadline. He doubted it would be enough to escape the ship, but he wasn't about to give up without trying. Not after all they had been through here.

'Can you run?' he asked Rauth.

* * *

'Time is up,' said Solarion grimly. He stood in front of the open elevator cage. 'They're not going to make it. I'm coming down.'

'No,' said Voss. 'Give them another minute, Prophet.'

Voss and Zeed had finished slaughtering their attackers on the lower floor. It was just as well, too. Voss had used up the last of his promethium fuel in the fight. With great regret, he had slung the fuel pack off his back and relinquished the powerful weapon.

He drew his support weapon, a bolt pistol, from a holster on his webbing.

It felt pathetically small and light in his hand.

'Would you have us all die here, brother?' asked the Ultramarine. 'For no gain? Because that will be our lot if we don't get moving right now.'

'If only we had heard *something* on the link...' said Zeed. 'Omni, as much as I hate to say it, Prophet has a point.'

'Believe me,' said Solarion, 'I wish it were otherwise. As of this moment, however, it seems only prudent that I assume operational command. Sigma, if you are listening–'

A familiar voice cut him off.

'Wait until my boots have cooled before you step into them, Solarion!'

'Scholar!' exclaimed Zeed. 'And is Watcher with you?'

'How many times must I warn you, Raven Guard,' said the Exorcist. *'Don't call me that.'*

'At least another hundred,' replied Zeed.

'Karras,' said Voss, 'where in Dorn's name are you?'

'Almost at the platform now,' said Karras. *'We've got company. Ork commandos closing the distance from the rear.'*

'Keep your speed up,' said Solarion. 'The stairs are out. You'll have to jump. The gap is about thirty metres.'

'*Understood,*' said Karras. '*Coming out of the corridor now.*'

Solarion could hear the thunder of heavy feet pounding the upper metal platform from which he had so recently leaped. He watched from beside the elevator, and saw two bulky black figures soar out into the air.

Karras landed first, coming down hard. The cryo-case came free of his shoulder and skidded across the metal floor towards the edge. Solarion saw it and moved automatically, stopping it with one booted foot before it slid over the side.

Rauth landed a second later, slamming onto the platform in a heap. He gave a grunt of pain, pushed himself up and limped past Solarion into the elevator cage.

'Are you wounded, brother?' asked the Ultramarine.

'It is nothing,' growled Rauth.

Karras and Solarion joined him in the cage. The kill-team leader pulled the lever, starting them on their downward journey.

The cage started slowly at first, but soon gathered speed. Halfway down, the heavy counterweight again whooshed past them.

'Ghost, Omni,' said Karras over the link. 'Start clearing the route towards the salvage bay. We'll catch up with you as soon as we're at the bottom.'

'Loud and clear, Scholar,' said Zeed. He and Voss disappeared off into the darkness of the corridor through which the kill-team had originally come.

Suddenly, Rauth pointed upwards. 'Trouble,' he said. Karras and Solarion looked up.

Some of the ork commandos, those more resourceful than their kin, had used grapnels to cross the gap in the platforms. Now they were hacking at the elevator cables with their broad blades.

'Solarion,' said Karras.

He didn't need to say anything else. The Ultramarine raised his bolter, sighted along the barrel, and began firing up at the orks. Shots sparked from the metal around the greenskins' heads, but it was hard to fire accurately with the elevator shaking and shuddering throughout its descent.

Rauth stepped forward and ripped the lattice-work gate from its hinges. 'We should jump the last twenty metres,' he said.

Solarion stopped firing. 'Agreed.'

Karras looked down from the edge of the cage floor. 'Forty metres,' he said. 'Thirty- five. Thirty. Twenty-five. Go!'

Together, the three Astartes leapt clear of the elevator and landed on the metal floor below. Again, Rauth gave a pained grunt, but he was up just as fast as the others.

Behind them, the elevator cage slammed into the floor with a mighty clang. Karras turned just in time to see the heavy counterweight smash down on top of it. The orks had cut the cables after all. Had the three Space Marines stayed in the cage until it reached the bottom, they would have been crushed to a fleshy pulp.

'Ten minutes left,' said Karras, adjusting the cryo-case on his shoulder. 'In the Emperor's name, run!'

Karras, Rauth and Solarion soon caught up with Voss and Zeed. There wasn't time to move carefully now, but Karras dreaded getting caught up in another firefight. That would surely doom them. Perhaps the saints were smiling on him, though, because it seemed that most of the orks in the sections between the central shaft and the prow had responded to the earlier alarms and had already been slain by Zeed and Voss.

The corridors were comparatively empty, but the large mess room with its central squig pit was not.

The Space Marines charged straight in, this time on ground level, and opened fire with their bolters, cutting down the orks that were directly in their way. With his beloved blade, Karras hacked down all who stood before him, always maintaining his forward momentum, never stopping for a moment. In a matter of seconds, the kill-team crossed the mess hall and plunged into the shadowy corridor on the far side.

A great noise erupted behind them. Those orks that had not been killed or injured were taking up weapons and following close by. Their heavy, booted feet shook the grille-work floors of the corridor as they swarmed along it.

'Omni,' said Karras, feet hammering the metal floor, 'the moment we reach the bay, I want you to ready the shuttle. Do not stop to engage, is that clear?'

If Karras had been expecting some argument from the Imperial Fist, he was surprised. Voss acknowledged the order without dispute. The whole team had made it this far by the skin of their teeth, but he knew it would count for absolutely nothing if their shuttle didn't get clear of the ork ship in time.

Up ahead, just over Solarion's shoulder, Karras saw the light of the salvage bay.

Then, in another few seconds, they were out of the corridor and charging through the mountains of scrap towards the large piece of starship wreckage in which they had stolen aboard.

There was a crew of gretchin around it, working feverishly with wrenches and hammers that looked far too big for their sinewy little bodies. Some even had blowtorches and were cutting through sections of the outer plate.

Damn them, cursed Karras. If they've damaged any of our

critical systems… Bolters spat, and the gretchin dropped in a red mist.

'Omni, get those systems running,' Karras ordered. 'We'll hold them off.'

Voss tossed Karras his bolt pistol as he ran past, then disappeared into the doorway in the side of the ruined prow.

Karras saw Rauth and Solarion open fire as the first of the pursuing orks charged in.

At first, they came in twos and threes. Then they came in a great flood. Empty magazines fell to the scrap-covered floor, to be replaced by others that were quickly spent.

Karras drew his own bolt pistol from its holster and joined the firefight, wielding one in each hand. Orks fell before him with gaping exit wounds in their heads.

'I'm out!' yelled Solarion, drawing his shortsword.

'Dry,' called Rauth seconds later and did the same.

Frenzied orks continued to pour in, firing their guns and waving their oversized blades, despite the steadily growing number of their dead that they had to trample over.

'Blast it!' cursed Karras. 'Talk to me, Omni.'

'Forty seconds,' answered the Imperial Fist. 'Coils at sixty per cent.'

Karras' bolt pistols clicked empty within two rounds of each other. He holstered his own, fixed Voss' to a loop on his webbing, drew Arquemann and called to the others, 'Into the shuttle, now. We'll have to take our chances.'

And hope they don't cut through to our fuel lines, he thought sourly.

One member of the kill-team, however, didn't seem to like those odds much. 'They're mine!' Zeed roared, and he threw himself in among the orks, cutting and stabbing in a battle-fury, dropping the giant alien savages like flies. Karras felt a flash of anger, but he marvelled at the way the Raven Guard moved, as if every single flex of muscle and claw was part of a dance that sent xenos filth howling to their deaths.

Zeed's armour was soon drenched in blood, and still he fought, swiping this way and that, always moving in perpetual slaughter, as if he were a tireless engine of death.

'Plasma coils at eighty per cent,' Voss announced. 'What are we waiting on, Scholar?'

Solarion and Rauth had already broken from the orks they were fighting and had raced inside, but Karras hovered by the door.

Zeed was still fighting.

'Ghost,' shouted Karras. 'Fall back, damn you.'

Zeed didn't seem to hear him, and the seconds kept ticking away. Any moment now, Karras knew, the ork ship's reactor would explode. Voss had seen to that. Death would take all of them if they didn't leave right now.

'Raven Guard!' Karras roared. That did it.

Zeed plunged his lightning claws deep into the belly of one last ork, gutted him, then turned and raced towards Karras.

When they were through the door, Karras thumped the locking mechanism with the heel of his fist. 'You're worse than Omni,' he growled at the Raven Guard. Then, over the comm-link, he said, 'Blow the piston charges and get us out of here fast.'

He heard the sound of ork blades and hammers battering the hull as the orks tried to hack their way inside. The shuttle door would hold but, if Voss didn't get them out of the salvage bay soon, they would go up with the rest of the ship.

'Detonating charges now,' said the Imperial Fist.

In the salvage bay, the packages he had fixed to the big pistons and cables on either side of the bay at the start of the mission exploded, shearing straight through the metal. There was a great metallic screeching sound and the whole floor of the salvage bay began to shudder. Slowly, the ork ship's gigantic mouth fell open, and the cold void of space rushed in, stealing away the breathable atmosphere. Everything inside the salvage bay, both animate and inanimate, was blown out of the gigantic mouth, as if snatched up by a mighty hurricane. Anything that hit the great triangular teeth on the way out went into a wild spin. Karras' team was lucky. Their craft missed clipping the upper front teeth by less than a metre.

'Shedding the shell,' said Voss, 'in three... two... one...'

He hit a button on the pilot's console that fired a series of explosive bolts, and the wrecked prow façade fragmented and fell away, the pieces drifting off into space like metal blossoms on a breeze. The shuttle beneath was now revealed – a sleek, black wedge-shaped craft bearing the icons of both the Ordo Xenos and the Inquisition proper. All around it, metal debris and rapidly freezing ork bodies spun in zero gravity.

Inside the craft, Karras, Rauth, Solarion and Zeed fixed their weapons on storage racks, sat in their respective places, and locked themselves into impact frames.

'Hold on to something,' said Voss from the cockpit as he fired the ship's plasma thrusters.

The shuttle leapt forward, accelerating violently just as the stern of the massive ork ship exploded. There was a blinding flash of yellow light that outshone even the local star. Then a series of secondary explosions erupted, blowing each section of the vast metal monstrosity apart, from aft to fore, in a great chain of utter destruction. Twenty thousand ork lives were snuffed out in a matter of seconds, reduced to their component atoms in the plasma-charged blasts.

Aboard the shuttle, Zeed removed his helmet and shook out his long black hair. With a broad grin, he said, 'Damn, but I fought well today.'

Karras might have grinned at the Raven Guard's exaggerated arrogance, but not this time. His mood was dark, despite their survival. Sigma had asked a lot this time. He looked down at the black surface of the cryo-case between his booted feet.

Zeed followed his gaze. 'We got what we came for, right, Scholar?' he asked. Karras nodded.

'Going to let me see it?'

Zeed hated the ordo's need-to-know policies, hated not knowing exactly why Talon squad was put on the line, time after time. Karras could identify with that. Maybe they all could. But curiosity brought its own dangers.

In one sense, it didn't really matter *why* Sigma wanted Bludwrekk's head, or anything else, so long as each of the Space Marines honoured the obligations of their Chapters and lived to return to them.

One day, it would all be over.

One day, Karras would set foot on Occludus again, and return to the Librarius as a veteran of the Deathwatch.

He felt Rauth's eyes on him, watching as always, perhaps closer than ever now. There would be trouble later. Difficult questions. Tests. Karras didn't lie to himself. He knew how close he had come to losing his soul. He had never allowed so much of the power to flow through him before, and the results made him anxious never to do so again.

How readily would Rauth pull the trigger next time?

Focusing his attention back on Zeed, he shook his head and muttered, 'There's nothing to see, Ghost. Just an ugly green head with metal plugs in it.' He tapped the case. 'Besides, the moment I locked this thing, it fused itself shut. You could ask Sigma to let you see it, but we both know what he'll say.'

The mention of his name seemed to invoke the inquisitor. His voice sounded on the comm-link. *'That could have gone better, Alpha. I confess I'm disappointed.'*

'Don't be,' Karras replied coldly. 'We have what you wanted. How fine we cut it is beside the point.'

Sigma said nothing for a moment, then, *'Fly the shuttle to the extraction coordinates and prepare for pick-up. Redthorne is on her way. And rest while you can. Something else has come up, and I want Talon on it.'*

'What is it this time?' asked Karras.

'You'll know,' said the inquisitor, *'when you need to know. Sigma out.'*

Magos Altando, former member of both biologis and technicus arms of the glorious Adeptus Mechanicus, stared through the wide plex window at his current project.

Beyond the transparent barrier, a hundred captured orks lay strapped down to cold metal tables. Their skulls were trepanned, soft grey brains open to the air. Servo-arms dangling from the ceiling prodded each of them with short electrically-charged spikes, eliciting thunderous roars and howls of rage. The strange machine in the centre, wired directly to the greenskins' brains, siphoned off the psychic energy their collective anger and aggression was generating.

Altando's many eye-lenses watched his servitors

scuttle among the tables, taking the measurements he had demanded.

I must comprehend the manner of its function, he told himself. Who could have projected that the orks were capable of fabricating such a thing?

Frustratingly, much of the data surrounding the recovery of the ork machine was classified above Altando's clearance level. He knew that a Deathwatch kill-team, designation *Scimitar*, had uncovered it during a purge of mining tunnels on Delta IV Genova. The inquisitor had brought it to him, knowing Altando followed a school of thought which other tech-magi considered disconcertingly radical.

Of course, the machine would tell Altando very little without the last missing part of the puzzle.

A door slid open behind him, and he turned from his observations to greet a cloaked and hooded figure accompanied by a large, shambling servitor which carried a black case.

'Progress?' said the figure.

'Limited,' said Altando, 'and so it will remain, inquisitor, without the resources we need. Ah, but it appears you have solved that problem. Correct?'

The inquisitor muttered something and the blank-eyed servitor trudged forward. It stopped just in front of Altando and wordlessly passed him the black metal case.

Altando accepted it without thanks, his own heavily augmented body having no trouble with the weight. 'Let us go next door, inquisitor,' he said, 'to the primary laboratory.'

The hooded figure followed the magos into a chamber on the left, leaving the servitor where it stood, staring lifelessly into empty space.

The laboratory was large, but so packed with devices of

every conceivable scientific purpose that there was little room to move. Servo-skulls hovered in the air overhead, awaiting commands, their metallic components gleaming in the lamplight. Altando placed the black case on a table in the middle of the room, and unfurled a long mechanical arm from his back. It was tipped with a las-cutter.

'May I?' asked the magos.

'Proceed.'

The cutter sent bright red sparks out as it traced the circumference of the case. When it was done, the mechanical arm folded again behind the magos' back, and another unfurled over the opposite shoulder. This was tipped with a powerful metal manipulator, like an angular crab's claw but with three tapering digits instead of two. With it, the magos clutched the top of the case, lifted it, and set it aside. Then he dipped the manipulator into the box and lifted out the head of Balthazog Bludwrekk.

'Yes,' he grated through his vocaliser. 'This will be perfect.'

'It had better be,' said the inquisitor. 'These new orkoid machines represent a significant threat, and the Inquisition must have answers.'

The magos craned forward to examine the severed head. It was frozen solid, glittering with frost. The cut at its neck was incredibly clean, even at the highest magnification his eye-lenses would allow.

It must have been a fine weapon indeed that did this, Altando thought. No typical blade.

'Look at the distortion of the skull,' he said. 'Look at the features. Fascinating. A mutation, perhaps? Or a side effect of the channelling process? Give me time, inquisitor, and the august Ordo Xenos will have the answers it seeks.'

'Do not take *too* long, magos,' said the inquisitor as he turned to leave. 'And do not disappoint me. It took my best assets to acquire that abomination.'

The magos barely registered these words. Nor did he look up to watch the inquisitor and his servitor depart. He was already far too engrossed in his study of the monstrous head.

Now, at long last, he could begin to unravel the secrets of the strange ork machine.

YOUR NEXT READ

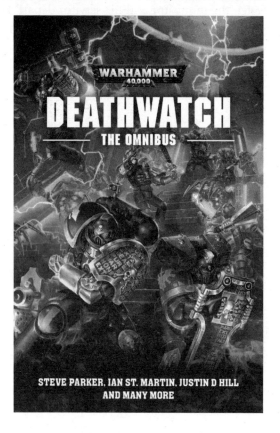

DEATHWATCH: THE OMNIBUS
by various authors

The elite alien-hunting Deathwatch spring into action in three novels
and a dozen short stories, collected together in a massive omnibus
full of xenos killing!

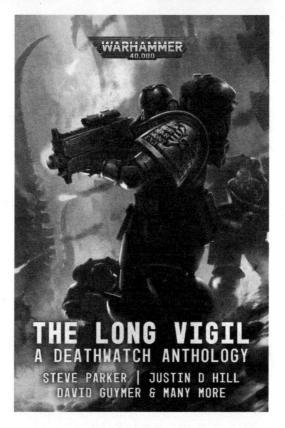

DUTY UNTO DEATH

MARC COLLINS

Of all the numerous brotherhoods of gene-crafted warriors serving the Imperium, none are as elite or as sacrosanct as the **Adeptus Custodes**, the watchers of the Imperial Palace on Terra. After centuries of vigilance on the walls of the Palace, these golden-armoured warriors now venture beyond the Sol System to ensure the Imperium is truly protected. In *Duty Unto Death*, a small group of Custodians travel to a feral world to guard a treasure beyond imagining. As the full wrath of a tyranid hive fleet descends, the warriors will prove that a single squad of the Adeptus Custodes is the equal of any army.

The flash of golden light blazed for one perfect moment upon the burning, broken surface of Loqe II; a fleeting blessing, a passing instant of grace. The warriors who strode from it did not look back, unbothered by their eldritch transit. Instead they formed a loose circle around the suspensor casket. Shield Captain Tamerlain laid one hand upon it, auramite against auramite.

'It is safe then?' Darnax asked. Tamerlain simply nodded.

'All survived transit intact. We–' He stopped and looked skyward. As one the warriors, brothers all, looked up. A new sun graced the heavens in a burst of atomic fire, as a primary drive detonated somewhere far above. A moment later, it was followed by a flurry of smaller explosions. Like a stellar cradle, failing. 'That was the *Terra Nostra* and her escorts,' Tamerlain said. 'The fleets will rally swiftly and then be upon us.'

'Then we shall hold them back,' Calith stated. 'You were

wise to abandon the vessel. While primordial, this world will provide a more nuanced battleground. One cannot fortify every last arterial in the body of a ship, but here we may sculpt the battlefield to our will. In His name.'

As the Palace is the Imperium, so the Imperium is the Palace. Tamerlain remembered the words that Trajann Valoris had imparted. *No matter where duty leads you, you are ever upon the walls. Unto death.*

'Unto death,' Tamerlain said. Each warrior raised their fist to their breastplate, and echoed him.

'Unto death.'

They advanced across the basalt plains of the death world, past the solidified lava flows of aeons past, and across the burning magma rivers of the present. It was a world in turmoil, wracked by its own inner tumult, even as war descended upon it – trailing burning biomatter through the heavens.

Few in number, they moved over the ashen drifts, the pyroclastic afterbirth clinging to their gleaming armour. They were only six, but there was no doubt that they would be more than a match for any number of alien foes. Each of them, Wardens all, had served mortal lifetimes in the Emperor's name. Together they had millennia of experience, fighting the most important war in human history – the battle to ensure His continuation. Tamerlain was the oldest of them, the most senior of their delegation, and so the one to bear the title of shield-captain. This was his prosecution to direct.

Above them lightning scored the sky, agitated by the volcanic eruptions and stirred by the atmospheric violation above. The wind picked up, casting dust and particulate stone about them. Their pace quickened as the world began to scream and convulse.

The clouds were disrupted, breaking apart with inconstant motion as the sudden deluge emerged from the fire and ash. Tendrils flailed in the atmosphere, pushing the mycetic spores onwards in a flurry of flagellating movement. They impacted the lowlands in a trickle at first, before becoming a tide. The lurid flare of bio-acid discharge cut through the gloom as the spores detonated, flaps of skin peeling free, and the newborn chorus of atrocity echoed from below.

The warriors of the Adeptus Custodes knew their foe was coming, knew that they were the focus of an enmity vaster than worlds, more immense than entire star systems. The psychic resonances of the hive mind would have detected their immaterial transit. Whether it understood what they were, what they represented, or the cargo they carried did not matter.

What mattered was that it hungered, and hated, and knew that they were there. The fleets above hurled their spite upon the barren sphere, swathing it in a mockery of life; a riot of hideous permutations that the natural world could never have birthed.

The Wardens did not speak as they turned axe and spear to the task before them. Powered blades hissed as they passed through the great black veins of basalt and obsidian, hewing them like the dead trees of a petrified forest. They hit the drifts with a muted thump, softer still beneath the birth screams and impact yowls of the enemy beasts. One by one the Wardens heaved the vast slabs of rock up, one atop the other.

'A fine bulwark,' Natreus said, nodding at the rising wall of stone. His voice was a terse vox-click, suddenly in Tamerlain's ear.

'It will suffice,' he answered. 'With time any fortress can be raised and defended.'

'Just as time tears them all down. All but one.' Calith spoke the words as he moved between his shield-brothers, lifting another spar of black rock effortlessly. 'They gather?' He dropped his burden upon the wall before him and gestured out across the plains.

'They gather,' Tamerlain said. 'They will swarm us with a living tide of blades, thinking none may outlast them. When the greater beasts come, they will expect to pick over our bones and take what we defend.' He shook his head, the crimson plume shifting in the rising, burning gale. 'As so many before them, they will be mistaken.'

They gathered amidst the sweltering heat of the world and the building howl of the foe – six warriors, each bearing their weapons with a surety that spoke not of arrogance or vainglory, but a professional aptitude in excess of other mortals. Spear point and axe blade crackled with power fields of near-perfect brilliance. They were personal relic-weapons, their mechanisms arcane wonders in this fallen age.

Shield-Captain Tamerlain stepped forward, gazing out beyond their modest ramparts. Behind him Calith and Natreus stood alongside Osran, Varamach and Darnax. Each was a warrior-savant in their own right. Their names were long, winding through their armour – as stolid and potent as their oaths to the Emperor. The firelight caught the edges of their auramite plate until every eagle seemed in flight, and every bolt of lightning seemed as vital as those teeming in the loaded thunderheads above.

Tamerlain lifted his axe and slammed its gilded ferrule against the stone. Behind him there was the barest whisper of powered plate as his comrades readied, stepping forward in perfect unison; guardian spears primed, under-slung bolters ready to fire.

'We are the wall. His wall,' Tamerlain said. There was a scream, inhuman and terrible, a single alien howl from a million throats.

The storm broke.

They came in a tide, like the rush of magma from the broken crust. Clawed feet barely touched the ground as they clattered and leapt, practically skimming the ash in great bounds. They screeched and chittered incessantly, a cacophony of the inhuman. Their talons skittered off the hot stone, kicking up clouds of debris as they bounded onwards with no regard for their own safety. The wave of bodies heaved up, and thousands of eyes saw their prey with a single all-consuming will.

The Custodians stood impassive, judging and assessing the horde as it did the same to them. They were few against multitudes, the finite against the infinite. They did not hesitate, did not cower in the face of mere odds. Each warrior raised their weapon, the gleaming points of spears lifting alongside Tamerlain's heavy axe blade. Their bolters waited. The warriors were patient. Their very beings were engineered for the long vigil, the endless defence of mankind's true master. To wait, to watch, to make ready, was nothing.

They waited for the precise moment in which to act, the optimal instant as the tyranids entered range. They knew it, intimately and innately. They opened fire in effortless precision. In perfect unity.

Their wrath was unleashed, the shots striking the first lines of onrushing attackers. The 'gaunts burst under the onslaught, detonating as mass-reactive shots ignited within their bodies. Heads exploded in clouds of ichor and chitin, and yet the enemy pushed on. Countless more aliens trampled their dead to paste beneath their hooves, throwing themselves into the arc of the guns. They burst asunder, but the remaining beasts leapt from the carrion heaps and clawed their way up and into the reach of the Custodians' spears.

Even as the tyranids bounded up and across the piles of their own dead, as their talons gouged at the walls the Custodians had erected, they were struck down. Alien bodies were hewn apart as they crossed into the storm of blades. The edges burned sun-bright, refracting off their auramite plate even as the blades' edges turned flesh to ash. Tamerlain bisected a screeching maw with his axe, firing as it cleaved the thing's curved skull apart.

We are the last wall, the final line between mankind and annihilation, he thought as he fired and slashed. He was a blur of economical motion, each strike directed with absolute purpose. *We are the bulwark of lightning and gold that has always stood between Him and those who would do Him harm. We heed His words, and guard His works. We carry hope to the stars, the promise of the future. We cannot allow it to be sullied, devoured or perverted.*

'In His name!' he cried. The words were taken up by his comrades, each locked in their own bubble of carnage. Blade strokes tore the xenos apart. Bolter shells ripped through beetle-backed exoskeletons and threw scything limbs from their joints. Tamerlain would have laughed, if not for his absolute focus. There was no room for joy in this killing, no time for the petty distractions of lesser men. There was only the moment – the complete immersion in killing.

The columns of stone and solidified magma, along with

the runnels of molten rock that still flowed, had helped to direct the beasts, to drive them in set directions and so succumb to the killing arcs of the warriors. Calith impaled a leaping warrior strain and pulled it to the ground. He drove his auramite boot into its carapace and shook it off, like the vermin it was. Varamach and Osran stood shoulder to shoulder, their shots still precise despite the overwhelming numbers.

Entire broods committed themselves to the lava, screeching as they died in droves. The first to die tested the edge of the pools, an entire generation sacrificed to the flames. The next hurled themselves forward, finding range as they sought to encircle the Custodians. Most hit the molten slag with a sizzle and a pop of burning carapace. Others were blasted from the air with exacting bolter rounds from the guardian spears. Slowly the rush of attackers ebbed, falling back like chastened curs. Behind the animal hunger of their eyes, there was greater scrutiny. Evaluation by a mind vaster than worlds.

Some might have thought such a consciousness a god, a new entrant into the galaxy's wracked and fitful pantheons. The warriors of the Adeptus Custodes gave such notions no credence.

Gods. Mortals. Intelligences. Vessels. All could die. All could be slain.

'They will come again,' Tamerlain said. The others simply nodded. 'We have the cover of the plumes for the moment, but they will adapt. When next they come it will be with might to match their numbers. Every death is an instruction for the mind which guides them. Each death is a lesson.'

'As we have fought, and died, and learned these millennia,'

Osran said. 'We stood on the rad-plains of Terra when they were yet unmastered. We walked in His shadow, as the galaxy was brought to heel. We saw the Traitors repelled, though at ruinous cost. We delivered His judgement as the Reign of Blood raged.' He paused, as though the memory itself were toxic. 'We kept our vigil and held the Palace against every threat conceivable. We prepared for every eventuality – be it xenos, oathbreaker or the horrors of Old Night come anew. Our order has always been there. As we are here now.'

'Neither of us lived through those times, Osran. Old though we are, we have only their legacy and their wisdom.'

'And that is enough, shield-captain,' Osran said. 'What we have been tasked with would have been impossible for others. Even before the ship was waylaid, it was daunting. We have marched forth into the darkness, bearing His light. We are exemplars. There is something to be said for such a duty.'

'For only in death does duty end,' Tamerlain said, speaking the First Maxim of their order. Since the days when the Ten Thousand had been the Legio Custodes, they had held to it. 'If we die here, then there is no better end. No greater service. The work we have carried from Sol will invigorate countless souls. It may be the key to turning the tide, even in this forsaken half of the Imperium.'

They gathered again, checking that arms and armour held true. None had yet fallen. There were not even any injuries. Tamerlain looked at his fellows critically, as though assessing where weakness might be found. He found nothing. These warriors were paragons of their craft, as he was. Examples of the most exacting and comprehensive genetic manipulation of which humanity was still capable.

'We must be ready,' Tamerlain said. 'They will not idle

long. We...' He paused. A low rumble built about them, the earth trembling with sudden palsy. The lava pits leapt and bubbled, agitated by geologic processes vaster than any of them. The mountains quaked and the skies blackened with roiling cloud. Static lightning danced amidst the rearing eruption, till the heavens were obscured by some ancient typhonic storm, like the imaginings of the hells of Old Earth.

On the plains, the cry went up again. The screaming of the alien did not sound like pain or defeat or frustration.

It sounded, somehow, like victory.

The next wave came in the dead of night, lit only by the inconstant fires of the volcanic eruptions.

As the hive fleet's bloated craft gathered in closer around Loqe II, so their gravity began to act upon the planet. The tremors had been ceaseless. The mountains behind them continued to spit fire, and rocks as large as battle tanks hammered into the slopes before them. Pyroclastic flows of superheated debris had rolled down the mountainsides, coating them and their surroundings in a pall of ash. The days had drawn out, and the sky had become so thick with smoke that the passage of time was marked only by fluctuations in the intensity of the darkness.

Each warrior stood still, a statue in the driving gale. They held their weapons tight, ready at a moment's notice for battle to once again be joined. They did not speak. There was nothing to be said. Only the waiting, the weathering of the onrushing storm – both of fire and of flesh.

The first of the beasts sought to undo them with lies.

It lunged through the smoke, suddenly visible and screeching. Chameleonic cells flared and died in a rush of chemical apoptosis. Pheromones bled from it in a torrent as its tendril-filled maw drooled acidic saliva. Osran turned, blocking the lictor's strike with the blade of his spear. Its spine-ridged limbs slammed against the powered edge, chitin smoking as it lashed out again. A claw skittered across the side of his helm, and Osran fell back, firing at it as the ash swirled about it.

He struck nothing but air.

Chittering rose from the shadows and the smog, as the darkness beyond changed and grew strange. Shapes that seemed to defy mortal logic resolved, spiteful and barbed in a way that the uncultured might think daemonic. Osran tightened his grip on his weapon, as lightning danced from the tormented skies and illuminated the host of abominations that the void had vomited forth like bile.

Warrior-forms hurled themselves forward as parasite-armaments spasmed and spat projectiles with whipping flagella, or fang-mawed beetles. They sent up puffs of ash and debris upon impact. One scraped across the auramite plate of his shoulder guard, but could not cling to it. Osran fell back, and the Custodians closed ranks. For a moment they were a barricade of gold and crimson before the horde. A final line between madness and civilisation.

They opened fire as one.

Bolt rounds found their mark easily, for there was no lack of targets. The alien warriors screamed and fired even as they were scythed down. Bone blades clattered against the hasty stone defences, either in ineffectual attack or to lever themselves up. Powerful haunches flexed and the attackers sprang, weapons raised and firing, slashing, spearing down towards them.

Tamerlain drew back, and his axe came round like a

threshing blade – reaping its tally of roaring alien bodies. Heads flew in a shower of bitter ichor, bodies came apart in a welter of hissing acidic blood. The powered blade smoked with burning flesh, star-hot from ceaseless use. At his side his fellow Wardens fought – each an army unto themselves. There had been days, dark days, where a single Custodian could have brought a city, a culture, a world, to heel. Those days were lost now, to time and the wrath of hateful gods.

Before a force such as this, none of this mattered. The xenos were soulless, mindless, unending. Tamerlain and the others were legends set against puppets. Even the greatest of blades could only cut the strings.

Lashes uncoiled, their fanged ends scraping over oath-carved armour. Tamerlain gritted his teeth, spinning his axe round and bisecting the whips. He squeezed the trigger, and the tyranid warrior was near atomised by the point-blank detonations. It staggered back, headless, before it dropped to the burning dunes.

The onslaught was relentless. Entire waves of the enemy fired even as they died, cut down only to be replaced with another phalanx of horror. They were like the gears of a vast machine, progressing through its set motions. Each one interchangeable, replaceable, expendable. Tamerlain had seen the milling pilgrim masses of Terra, and thought them a near infinite faceless multitude. Those numbers paled before the tyranids.

'Hold!' he called. They drew together at his word, side by side. A wall of thrust and parry. Talons and boneblades broke and cracked against their powered blades. Claws and whips tried to gain purchase on the staves of the spears, but the swift and efficient movements of the warriors broke their fleeting holds. They gave no ground, defending their narrow bulwark of stone and rubble as though it were the Eternity Gate itself.

You are ever upon the walls.

The thought came again, as sure as a physical blow. As certain as the enemy before them. He embraced it. He did not know doubt, or fear, and so he leant in to certainty. To the surety of duty.

A convergence of shots snapped across the maelstrom of battle, impacting against Darnax's armour. The projectiles burst, erupting into a mass of biting, barbed tendrils. Darnax tried to bring his spear to bear, but his arms were engulfed. He struggled, even as other alien bio-weaponry burst and sizzled against his plate. Ornate inscriptions were obliterated by maliciously directed fire. Eagles and lightning bolts were worn away, seared down. Plasma detonated in bright plumes of fire, and Darnax sank to his knees. He still struggled, breaking his bonds as he did, forcing himself back to his feet. Another lance of burning bio-plasma seared through his helm, and he tumbled back. Through a ruin of melting auramite, Tamerlain could see his lips still moving. His brothers turned in the same moment, cutting their way towards him – hacking through the suffocating vines.

Osran dragged Darnax back, breath ragged over their shared vox. The others stepped forward, Varamach and Calith firing into the throng. More bodies tumbled into the dust, precise holes in their carapaces, the backs of them blown out by percussive detonations. Trails of viscera stained the ground, already smouldering with chemical vitriol. Osran laid Darnax before the golden casket that formed the core of their defence, lifting him so his back lay against it. Gold against gold. He scooped up his spear and laid it reverently across the top of it. He looked to

Tamerlain and shook his head. It was a wound, as sure as any physical impact. Centuries upon centuries of experience and service, snuffed out by *beasts*. No warrior of the Adeptus Custodes should meet such an end, and yet it had come to this.

New thunder rose, and the earth shook. The darkness was filled with sudden and terrible light. The foe took on a hellish look, lit by chthonic fires. The golden-armoured warriors formed a knot about the casket, shielding their fallen brother as they fired into the tumult. The storm rushed down upon them, with flame and whipping winds. The enemy held for a moment, then faltered as they were driven back by the world's fury.

Above the planet's agony and the screaming winds, Tamerlain heard the click of bolters running empty. The last of their ammunition was finally spent.

There was a moment of respite; not enough time to truly mourn, but only to prepare for what was to come.

'He served, as all must. He passes, as all do.' Tamerlain bowed his head. 'There can be no greater duty.'

'He will be remembered,' Natreus said. 'He fought to the last. That is all any of us can ask. As so many fought in the war beyond the Throne, in the days before the Siege. As others fell as the Lion's Gate burned anew.' Natreus brought his fist against his breastplate with the ringing of auramite. 'Unto death.'

'Unto death,' they said as one.

'Make ready,' Tamerlain said. The others looked to him, away from the sombre end of Darnax. 'The beast has scented blood and it will redouble its efforts.' He raised his axe, its edge keen and undulled even as its ranged weaponry was silenced. 'We shall not fail in our duty. We shall not fail Him.'

The parade of days continued, reduced to a contest of arms and the charting of the dead.

Thousands, tens of thousands, fell. Just as one by one, the defenders succumbed.

The tide of enemies rattled on, breaking again and again against their defences and against the spite of the world. The closer they came, by ground and from orbit, the more the planet rebelled. Gravity and tectonics fought their relentless war, just as the glorious few did.

Axe and spear rose and fell in a perpetual motion. They blocked the strikes of claw and bone-wrought blade. They cut projectiles from the air, turning them aside with the gleaming edges of their weapons. Reality contracted, reduced to the long moment of the melee. The immediacy of battle.

Tamerlain swung his axe, feeling his weariness but enduring. He pushed through it, sheened with sweat within his armour. They each fought bound by unity of purpose, just as Unity had bound Terra. They were a reflection of that duty, the sacred oaths which underpinned the Imperium. They fought to uphold them, even as the world died around them in fire and madness.

The swarms of 'gaunts and the warrior broods had given way to greater horrors – carnifex beasts with slabs of armour plating and wrenching claws, or with hideously swollen bio-cannons. Errant shots brought rockslides and landslips down on them, burying lesser creatures in a self-created disaster. Rocks battered against the Custodians' armour, but it remained inviolate. Despite the scrapes and rents, they held firm.

Calith was the next to die. Great barbs of envenomed bone arced through the air. He carved one of them from the sky, and then another. The third and fourth found their mark. His voice was a low hiss of pain across the vox, as he reached down to snap one and then the other. They broke in his auramite grip as he staggered forward. His spear spun round again, carving apart the tyranid beasts as they sought to encircle him, as though injury was a weakness they could exploit. Alien blood fountained from their wounds as Calith fought. 'Commend me, shield-captain,' he slurred. 'You will hold.'

'We will hold,' Tamerlain said. 'Your name will be remembered. We shall carry it back to Him.' He pushed forward, ducking under swiping tendrils and driving claws. He moved to stand with Calith, bracing a hand against his armour. Taking his place in the line.

'*Hold!*' he bellowed, and each warrior's resolve tightened. Each thrust was more measured and determined. They gouged and stabbed and slashed at the enemy raising against their bulwark of glittering defiance. Tamerlain had stepped ahead of Calith as the injured Custodian fell to his knees, wounds weeping slowly. Tamerlain was lit by the hellish light of the mountain and the storm, and the gold of his armour seemed to burn with it. Lesser men, the mortals who cleaved to the Imperial Creed, might have thought him an angel – the Emperor's wrath made numinous, living. He was not this. None of them were. Even in the days before, great Valdor had not been as such. They were flesh – perhaps the most flawless flesh of which the Imperium was still capable of producing, but still flesh.

Tamerlain's muscles bunched within his armour as he fought, holding every inch of sullied ground. He did not retreat or step over his fallen comrade. He stood, pushed forward. His blade clattered against chitin, denting and breaking it as he swung again. The siege beast screamed its hate, showering him with hissing saliva as it fell. He drew back his axe and buried it in the thing's skull.

There was a crackle of pale lightning and Tamerlain turned too slowly to stop its approach. Corposant danced across the exposed lobes of a pulsing brain, swollen beyond reason. It hovered, suspended by its own psychic might. Spines flexed and bristled as it bobbed in the air, rocks around it levitating before being atomised by its wrath. Osran lashed out at it, cutting away jutting cerebral spines in a rush of foul ichor. Its chittering rose to a scream, and reality shuddered with its fury.

Pale, cold fire coiled itself down Osran's spear. He still slashed and hacked at it, gouging chasms into its quivering flesh and glistening armour while the flames consumed him. It spasmed and every portion of it seemed to clench. As it did, the fire danced across his armour. Osran did not cry out, not when the psychic conflagration burned at the auramite and gnawed at flesh. His precise strikes faltered and grew erratic, before he tumbled back – ashen, and broken. Varamach and Natreus wove in a moment later, catching the zoanthrope between their competing spears. It screamed, ringing with its own agony, before it detonated in an eruption of psychic fire. The earth shook and cracked beneath it, and all the beasts reared back at the sudden synaptic disruption.

Tamerlain grinned savagely within his helm as he watched. The lesser beasts broke, reduced to feral animals. They sniffed the air and keened, turning on their heels as though to flee. It stank of alien blood and sulphurous smoke and the ozone crackle of expended psykana. The three warriors advanced, cutting down the stragglers even as they brayed and chittered in confusion.

A single pod cut through the toxic fumes and the burning sky, hammering into the centre of the plain and the milling confusion of the alien horde. There was an instant realignment, like constellations suddenly clarified in the heavens. The army turned as one, unified by singular purpose once more. The thing which tore itself free from the spore-pod was immense, the pinnacle of genetic mastery and a paragon of inhuman might. The greatest bio-scholars of Terra could not decide whether it was a consciousness in its own right, or an immune response of the hive mind – brought into being when the tide was set against it.

The swarmlord raised its head and bellowed as it rushed forward to meet them.

It closed the distance in what seemed like moments. A blur, the storm given form. Blades scissored down against the Custodians. They blocked, even their movements too slow. Bio-electric fields warred with the power fields of their weapons in a whine of feedback and a shower of sparks. It forced Varamach to his knees, and the great cleaver blade descended, burying itself in the armour of his neck. There was a spasm and a gout of blood, and he had only a moment to drive his spear up and into its flesh before he fell. Another loss, too massive to countenance. Natreus ducked under its guard and slashed across its chest, but the swarmlord brought all four of its blades to bear. It pinned Natreus, blades barely containing him as he struggled, blood coating them in furious smears. The Custodian's spear fell from his grasp, and the swarmlord cast him to the dust.

Only Tamerlain remained. He broke into a run, swinging his axe as he advanced. The heavy castellan blade impacted against one of the boneswords, chipping it. There was no surprise in its dead eyes, only a snarl of alien hate.

'This is His domain,' Tamerlain said, not caring whether or not it could hear or understand. 'I am His servant, and you shall not end me with my duty yet undone.' He moved beneath its dance of blades, feeling them scrape against his armour – turned aside by angle, speed and the armour's inherent strength. It snarled, dripping venom as it stabbed down at him. He dropped to his knees, his hand finding Natreus' spear. 'Forgive me,' he whispered, and drove the unpowered blade up with such force that it cracked the monster's armoured sternum. It slammed one of its blade limbs into his side, and he brought his axe up again. An arm flew free in a gush of sour fluid, and it batted him aside with the flat of another blade.

They were evenly matched. Opposites. Mirrors. One the pinnacle of human genetic mastery, the other a crescendo of accelerated hyper-evolution. One was golden, the other base.

They fought down the burning slopes, even as the tyranid swarm wove around them in a tightening noose. By-blows obliterated swathes of brood organisms. The swarmlord did not care as it scythed through its own, as it drove Tamerlain back. He fought with every century of his experience behind him. He could feel the names carved into his armour, pressed against his flesh. Each carried a burden.

He moved as fast as he was able, raising his axe to block and parry or to cut and slash. Their melee devolved into a grinding brawl, drawn out and bitter. He tensed as he fought, feeling the dull ache of fatigue. He struck for its thorax, cleaving it open even as it brought two of its blades round.

It pincered him in place. He felt something break in his armour's systems, his gauntlet clenching in palsy. He closed his eyes and focused. It was more gruelling and more intense than any Blood Game he had run in the service of the Throne, more pressing than any battle of his long years. He felt his fingers close, finally, around the hilt of his misericordia dagger, and pulled it free. He pushed it up and drove it into the thing's snarling visage. Dissonator spirits engaged with a flare and the blade blazed golden for a glorious instant as it sank through flesh and chitin. The beasts screamed, every last one of them howling in animal agony.

Tamerlain kicked out his leg and drove the dying monster back. Behind him, the world roared again – in sympathetic victory.

As below, so above.

The fleet that swept into the system was a tired and tarnished yellow, not sacred gold. Battle-barges and strike cruisers unleashed their explosive payloads into the heart of the looming alien fleet, or excoriated their void-thickened hides with precise volleys of lance fire.

The hive-ships seemed sluggish, distracted as they turned in their ponderous arcs. Only a few weapon-symbiotes were able to hurl themselves into the void, to die in their final burst of biological imperative. They smeared against active void shields with only the faintest pulse of light and heat.

At the head of the relief fleet was the battle-barge *In Glorious Purpose*, its slab sides marked with old scars. It drew ahead of the rest of the ships, raking the tyranids with ferocious broadsides as it rolled into Loqe II's orbit.

Bombardment cannons fired, rending the fickle atmosphere and adding new scars to the world's harsh surface. A mountain detonated under their guns, in a mega-eruption which hurled debris into the void itself.

'Take us down,' Captain Ignus Vrul growled. 'Find the signal.'

The world was dying, terminally wounded by the collision of warring factions.

Vrul strode down the ramp and onto the ash plains, already buffeted by the pyroclastic winds. He spat, and watched the ashes sizzle, before casting his eyes up.

He beheld a fortress, wrought of victory.

The corpses of the tyranids had been utilised, not as grim totems of warning or fear, but as once-living brick and mortar. Spurs of bone and chitin held the walls in place, adding to the solid foundations of hewn basalt which they augmented. The flesh of the beasts was seared, blackened, and had run together in places – further annealing the materials together.

Before it knelt a lone warrior, so still and grey that he seemed another victim of the calamity – an ashen sculpture of ruin. He moved, then, and the Space Marines jerked their weapons up. Vrul did not bother, merely sneering with bemused disdain.

'Who goes there?' he asked. 'We answered a priority transmission, swathed in clearances fit for a Chapter Master, and all we find is you?'

'I am Tamerlain,' the survivor said. 'Shield-captain of the Adeptus Custodes.' He forced himself to his feet, and gestured. Behind him, the techno-arcane mechanism of the sarcophagus hovered like a relic of ancient Gyptus.

His brothers and their arms were lain upon the Primaris gene-cache, reverently. Like honoured kings.

'I bear word from Terra, and the promise of the future. I bring the means by which brotherhoods such as yours shall weather these nights of fire and blood.' He touched his fingers to the casket. 'And you shall help me to bring it where it is needed most. That is my duty, in His name.'

YOUR NEXT READ

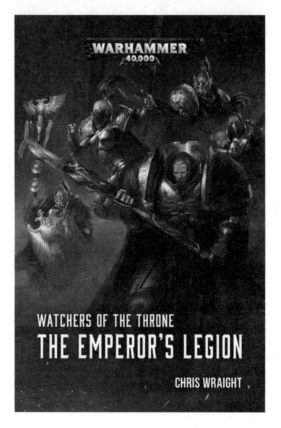

WATCHERS OF THE THRONE: THE EMPEROR'S LEGION
by Chris Wraight

The Adeptus Custodes are the Emperor's praetorian guard, the defenders of Terra and watchers over the Golden Throne. But when a threat arises, they and their Sisters of Silence allies may find themselves pressed almost beyond endurance…

YOUR
NEXT READ

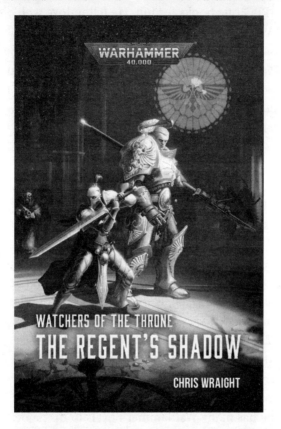

WATCHERS OF THE THRONE: THE REGENT'S SHADOW
by Chris Wraight

A new day has dawned for the Imperium, but not everyone sees the light.
The Custodian Guard and Sisters of Silence must battle not just Chaos,
but those who do not share Regent Guilliman's vision…

ABOUT THE AUTHORS

Thomas Parrott is the kind of person who reads RPG rule books for fun. He fell in love with Warhammer 40,000 when he was fifteen and read the short story 'Apothecary's Honour' in the *Dark Imperium* anthology, and has never looked back. 'Spiritus In Machina' was his first story for Black Library, and he has since written 'Salvage Rites', 'Fates and Fortunes' and the novellas *Nexus* and *Isha's Lament*.

Chris Wraight is the author of the Horus Heresy novels *Scars* and *The Path of Heaven*, the Primarchs novels *Leman Russ: The Great Wolf* and *Jaghatai Khan: Warhawk of Chogoris*, the novellas *Brotherhood of the Storm*, *Wolf King* and *Valdor: Birth of the Imperium*, and the audio drama *The Sigillite*. For Warhammer 40,000 he has written *The Lords of Silence, Vaults of Terra: The Carrion Throne, Vaults of Terra: The Hollow Mountain, Watchers of the Throne: The Emperor's Legion*, the Space Wolves novels *Blood of Asaheim* and *Stormcaller*, and many more. Additionally, he has many Warhammer novels to his name, including the Warhammer Chronicles novel *Master of Dragons*, which forms part of the War of Vengeance series. Chris lives and works in Bradford-on-Avon, in south-west England.

Guy Haley is the author of the Siege of Terra novel *The Lost and the Damned*, as well as the Horus Heresy novels *Titandeath*, *Wolfsbane* and *Pharos*, and the Primarchs novels *Konrad Curze: The Night Haunter*, *Corax: Lord of Shadows* and *Perturabo: The Hammer of Olympia*. He has also written many Warhammer 40,000 novels, including the first book in the Dawn of Fire series, *Avenging Son*, as well as *Belisarius Cawl: The Great Work*, *Dark Imperium*, *Dark Imperium: Plague War*, *The Devastation of Baal*, *Dante*, *Darkness in the Blood* and *Astorath: Angel of Mercy*. He has also written stories set in the Age of Sigmar, included in *War Storm*, *Ghal Maraz* and *Call of Archaon*. He lives in Yorkshire with his wife and son.

Rachel Harrison is the author of the Warhammer 40,000 novel *Honourbound*, featuring the character Commissar Severina Raine, as well as the accompanying short stories 'Execution', 'Trials', 'Fire and Thunder', 'A Company of Shadows', and 'The Darkling Hours', which won a 2019 Scribe Award in the Best Short Story category. Also for Warhammer 40,000 she has written the novel *Mark of Faith*, the novella *Blood Rite*, numerous short stories including 'The Third War' and 'Dishonoured', the short story 'Dirty Dealings' for Necromunda, and the Warhammer Horror audio drama *The Way Out*.

Peter McLean has written several short stories for Black Library, including 'Baphomet by Night', 'No Hero', 'Sand Lords' and 'Lightning Run' for Warhammer 40,000, and the Warhammer Horror tale 'Predations of the Eagle'. He grew up in Norwich, where he began story-writing, practising martial arts and practical magic, and lives there still with his wife.

Dan Abnett has written over fifty novels, including *Anarch*, the latest instalment in the acclaimed Gaunt's Ghosts series. He has also written the Ravenor and Eisenhorn books, the most recent of which is *The Magos*. For the Horus Heresy, he is the author of the Siege of Terra novel *Saturnine*, as well as *Horus Rising*, *Legion*, *The Unremembered Empire*, *Know No Fear* and *Prospero Burns*, the last two of which were both *New York Times* bestsellers. He also scripted *Macragge's Honour*, the first Horus Heresy graphic novel, as well as numerous Black Library audio dramas. Many of his short stories have been collected into the volume *Lord of the Dark Millennium*. He lives and works in Maidstone, Kent.

Danie Ware is the author of the novellas *The Bloodied Rose*, *Wreck and Ruin*, *The Rose in Anger* and the short story 'Mercy', all featuring the Sisters of Battle. She lives in Carshalton, south London, with her son and two cats and has long-held interests in role-playing, re-enactment, vinyl art toys and personal fitness.

Mike Brooks is a science fiction and fantasy author who lives in Nottingham, UK. His work for Black Library includes the Warhammer 40,000 novels *Rites of Passage* and *Brutal Kunnin*, the Necromunda novel *Road to Redemption* and the novella *Wanted: Dead*, and various short stories. When not writing, he plays guitar and sings in a punk band, and DJs wherever anyone will tolerate him.

Phil Kelly is the author of the Warhammer 40,000 novels *Farsight: Crisis of Faith* and *Farsight: Empire of Lies*, the Space Marine Conquests novel *War of Secrets*, the Space Marine Battles novel *Blades of Damocles* and the novellas *Farsight* and *Blood Oath*. For Warhammer he has written the titles *Sigmar's Blood* and *Dreadfleet*. He has also written 'The Woman in the Walls' for the Warhammer Horror portmanteau *The Wicked and the Damned*, and a number of short stories. He works as a background writer for Games Workshop, crafting the worlds of Warhammer and Warhammer 40,000. He lives in Nottingham.

J C Stearns is a writer who lives in a swamp in Illinois with his wife and son, as well as more animals than is reasonable. He started writing for Black Library in 2016 and is the author of Warhammer Horror novel *The Oubliette*. He has also written the the short stories 'Turn of the Adder' and 'Blackout' which have featured in various volumes of the anthology *Inferno!*, 'Wraithbound', and 'The Marauder Lives' in the Horror anthology *Maledictions*. He plays Salamanders, Dark Eldar, Sylvaneth, and as soon as he figures out how to paint lightning bolts, Night Lords.

Josh Reynolds' extensive Black Library back catalogue includes the Horus Heresy Primarchs novel *Fulgrim: The Palatine Phoenix*, and three Horus Heresy audio dramas featuring the Blackshields. His Warhammer 40,000 work includes the Space Marine Conquests novel *Apocalypse*, *Lukas the Trickster* and the Fabius Bile novels. He has written many stories set in the Age of Sigmar, including the novels *Shadespire: The Mirrored City*, *Soul Wars*, *Eight Lamentations: Spear of Shadows*, the Hallowed Knights novels *Plague Garden* and *Black Pyramid*, and *Nagash: The Undying King*. He has written the Warhammer Horror novel *Dark Harvest*, and novella *The Beast in the Trenches*, featured in the portmanteau novel *The Wicked and the Damned*. He has recently penned the Necromunda novel *Kal Jerico: Sinner's Bounty*. He lives and works in Sheffield.

Robert Rath is a freelance writer from Honolulu who is currently based in Hong Kong. Though mostly known for writing the YouTube series *Extra History*, his credits also include numerous articles and a book for the U.S. State Department. He is the author of the Black Library novel *The Infinite and the Divine*, and the short stories 'The Garden of Mortal Delights' and 'War in the Museum'.

Originally hailing from the rain-swept land of the Picts, **Steve Parker** currently resides in Tokyo, Japan, where he runs a specialist coaching business for men and writes genre fiction. His published works include the novels *Rebel Winter, Gunheads, Rynn's World, Deathwatch, Deathwatch: Shadowbreaker*, the novella *Survivor*, and several short stories featuring the Deathwatch kill-team Talon Squad, the Crimson Fists and various Astra Militarum regiments.

Marc Collins is a speculative fiction author living and working in Glasgow, Scotland. He is the writer of the Warhammer 40,000 short story 'Ghosts of Iron' and when not dreaming of the far future he works in Pathology with the NHS.

FURTHER READING

DARK ANGELS

Legacy of Caliban
Gav Thorpe

Knights of Caliban
Gav Thorpe

War of Secrets
Phil Kelly

BLOOD ANGELS

Dante
Guy Haley

Mephiston: Blood of Sanguinius
Darius Hinks

The Devastation of Baal
Guy Haley

Darkness in the Blood (out November 2020)
Guy Haley

CHAOS SPACE MARINES

Ahriman: The Omnibus
John French

Fabius Bile: Primogenitor
Josh Reynolds

Lucius: The Faultless Blade
Ian St Martin

Night Lords: The Omnibus
Aaron Dembski-Bowden

Talon of Horus
Aaron Dembski-Bowden

The Lords of Silence
Chris Wraight

ASTRA MILITARUM

Honourbound □
Rachel Harrison

Last Chancers: Armageddon Saint □
Gav Thorpe

Cadian Honour □
Justin D Hill

Baneblade □
Guy Haley

First and Only □
Dan Abnett

Ciaphas Cain: Hero of the Imperium □
Sandy Mitchell

Shield of the Emperor □
Steve Parker / Steve Lyons / Mitchel Scanlon

AERONAUTICA IMPERIALIS

Double Eagle □
Dan Abnett

On Wings of Blood □
Various

IMPERIAL AGENTS

Xenos □
Dan Abnett

Ravenor □
Dan Abnett

Watchers of the Throne: The Emperor's Legion □
Chris Wraight

The Horusian Wars: Resurrection □
John French

Vaults of Terra: The Carrion Throne
Chris Wraight

Rites of Passage
Mike Brooks

SISTERS OF BATTLE

Mark of Faith
Rachel Harrison

Celestine: The Living Saint
Andy Clark

Shroud of Night
Andy Clark

Sisters of Battle: The Omnibus
James Swallow

ADEPTUS MECHANICUS

Forges of Mars
David Guymer

Warlord: Fury of the God-Machine
David Annandale

Belisarius Cawl: The Great Work
Guy Haley

Kingsblade
Andy Clark

Imperator: Wrath of the Omnissiah
Gav Thorpe

AELDARI

Asurmen: Hand of Asuryan
Gav Thorpe

Jain Zar: The Storm of Silence
Gav Thorpe

Rise of the Ynnari: Ghost Warrior
Gav Thorpe

Path of the Eldar Omnibus
Gav Thorpe

Path of the Dark Eldar Omnibus
Andy Chambers

ORKS

Brutal Kunnin
Mike Brooks

The Beast Arises: I Am Slaughter
Dan Abnett

Blood of Iax
Robbie MacNiven

NECRONS

The Infinite and the Divine
Robert Rath

Severed
Nate Crowley

T'AU

Farsight: Crisis of Faith
Phil Kelly

THE HORUS HERESY

Horus Rising
Dan Abnett

False Gods
Graham McNeill

Galaxy in Flames
Ben Counter

The Primarchs: Lion El'Jonson – Lord of the First ☐
David Guymer

Valdor: Birth of the Imperium ☐
Chris Wraight

SIEGE OF TERRA

The Solar War ☐
John French

The Lost and the Damned ☐
Gav Thorpe

The First Wall ☐
Gav Thorpe

Saturnine ☐
Dan Abnett

AUDIO DRAMAS

Agent of the Throne: Blood and Lies ☐
John French

Corsair: The Face of the Void ☐
James Swallow

Titans' Bane ☐
Chris Dows

Agents of the Imperium ☐
Chris Wraight / David Annandale / Ben Counter

Prophets of Waaagh! ☐
Guy Haley

Our Martyred Lady ☐
Gav Thorpe

Saga of the Beast ☐
David Annandale